CW00450002

the spire

THE WALSH FAMILY

KATE CANTERBARY

VESPER PRESS

about the spire

Erin Walsh walked through fire and she lived to tell about it.

Not that the volcanologist is interested in telling anyone anything about her personal life. She ran away for a reason and she ran from everything—her home, her family, her secrets, their tragedies—and now that she's finally discovered a few shreds of peace, she's not about to destroy it by returning to the place that caused her so much pain.

But her brother is getting married and he's insisting she be there to celebrate with the whole family. Her plan is to white-knuckle and panic-sweat through the weekend. She never plans on falling for her brother's best friend.

Nick Acevedo woke up married.

He doesn't regret a single thing, not even marrying his best friend's sister behind his back, but Nick has no idea what happens next. His life—and the final years of his pediatric neurosurgery fellowship—are in Boston while his new wife has a research agenda packed with expeditions all over the globe.

There's no way they can make it work—but somehow they forge ahead with endless strings of emails, cozy video calls, getaways in far-away places. And secrets. So many secrets kept for so long.

Nick's willing to sacrifice everything to bring his wife home but it might not be enough.

CW: *History of emotional and sexual abuse by a parent (no on-page description); parent loss; estrangement from family; brief mention of a main character's parents' marital struggles; brief mention of a main character's sibling's experience with postpartum depression; reference to a main character losing patients as a surgeon*

Copyright

This is a work of fiction. Names, characters, places, and incidents are the product of the author's imagination or are used fictitiously, and any resemblance to actual persons, living or dead, business establishments, events, or locales is entirely coincidental.

Copyright © 2016 by Kate Canterbary
All rights reserved. No part of this book may be reproduced, stored in a retrieval system, or transmitted in any forms, or by any means, electronic, mechanical, photocopying, recording or otherwise, without prior written permission of the author.

Trademarked names appear throughout this book. Rather than use a trademark symbol with every occurrence of a trademarked name, names are used in an editorial fashion, with no intention of infringement of the respective owner's trademark(s).

Editing provided by Julia Ganis of JuliaEdits. www.juliaedits.com

Proofreading provided by Nicole Bailey of Proof Before You Publish. www.proofbeforeyoupublish.com

For the revolutionaries.

…and the entire cast of Grey's Anatomy.

prologue

ERIN

I THOUGHT about letting the call go to voicemail, but I'd done that to him too many times already. Two missed calls was reasonable. Three was avoidance. Four was the silent treatment.

At least as it pertained to *him*.

I pushed my glasses up to rest on my head and rubbed my eyes as I answered. "Hey," I said.

"Hey," he replied. He sounded surprised that I answered, and that was fair. I hadn't been terribly communicative recently. "How are you, Skip?"

Oh, but I'd missed him. I loved the weight of his voice, the heavy tumble of his words with just enough of that Texas accent to call up memories of *Dallas* and *Dynasty*. I streamed the old reruns of both—the ones that originally aired before I was born—when I needed a taste of home, and of him. I was well aware that the land of the oil-rich and heavily shoulder-padded wasn't *my* home, but after nine years away from mainland America, I didn't discriminate over regional variations. When I craved New England, I hit up Jessica Fletcher and *Murder, She Wrote*.

Glancing around my laboratory and the knee-high pile of sea level readouts in need of analysis, I said, "Not to end this conversation before it starts, but...I'm kinda busy."

"With?"

I glanced to the columns of data on my laptop screen. The details were irrelevant, and would only lead to more questions than answers. "Lab stuff."

He cleared his throat and paused, and I could almost see his head tilted to the side and his eyes staring into the distance as he thought. Probably dragging his thumb down his jaw, too.

"Shannon's having the baby tonight," he said. "Come home."

This was a request I'd long expected, and one I'd wrestled with since hearing that my sister was pregnant. Chewing my lower lip, I cut a glance at my notebook, and the detailed list of hand-drawn checkboxes with tasks beside them.

"Who's asking?" It was easier to default to defense mode than deal with the fact I hadn't spoken to my sister in nearly nine years, and coming home for the purpose of celebrating the arrival of her baby meant stopping the clock on our war of silence.

It also meant a tacit acknowledgement that this wasn't *our* war. No, it was all mine.

"Because I'm comfortable stating that I'm neither pivotal in the childbirth proceedings nor am I useful. I know all about things that explode, but not as it pertains to amniotic sacs, or vaginas," I continued. "Hell, me showing up would probably make the experience worse for her, and that would only add another crime to my tab. If anything, it will make this all about me and Shannon, and not Shannon and Will and Froggie. I don't want to force an awkward scene. Don't you think she has enough to worry about right now?"

"And I'm comfortable stating that vaginas do not explode during childbirth," he said.

"But if Patrick's asking," I continued, thinking of my checklist-loving older brother, "it's because he thinks he's going to reenact the Christmas Truce of 1914, and that is ludicrous—"

"I love when you force obscure bits of history to fit your arguments," he murmured. "Missed this so much."

"And this isn't the trenches of Saint-Yves," I said, ignoring his commentary. I missed him, and he missed me, and all of that was too big to get my arms around tonight. "If Matt's asking, please tell him that he's been formally relieved of his official role as Walsh Family Arbitrator."

"But he really likes it," he said. "Don't rob him of that joy."

"I know Sam isn't asking because he sent me an email two hours ago," I said, ticking off my siblings from oldest to youngest on my hand. "He and Tiel, they're having a boy, by the way."

He laughed. "Trust me, I've heard, and I believe he's buying the Green Monster at Fenway Park so he can have it painted with that news, too."

"It's not Riley. He texts me whenever he has something worth sharing," I said. "So, tell me. Who's asking?"

He sighed, and the noise started as a laugh but then twisted into a rough, snarling sound. The kind I loved. The kind I'd been aching for since walking away from him.

"Your husband," he said finally.

I looked down at the slim platinum band on my ring finger, the one I wasn't even sure why I was wearing.

"Your husband is asking because nine years is nine too many."

"Nick, you're—"

"I'm not having it, lovely. It's time for this to end, and it ends here."

PART ONE

Kilauea Lava Fields and King Tides

One

ERIN

TWO YEARS *ago*

I BLAMED it on the seven-year itch.

Or something like that.

That's what it was—seven angry, necessary, devastating, silent, healing, amazing, awful years.

Was it still considered home if you avoided it like plagues and pestilence?

I didn't know if Boston still qualified as *my* home—and by that logic, was anywhere my home?—but I was tucked into the only available seat on the midnight flight out of Rome and headed there now.

I'd waited until the last minute to make the call, book the flight, pack the bag. It was ridiculous, considering I never truly entertained the idea of missing Matt's wedding. I wouldn't miss *any* of my siblings' weddings, but Matt, he was a special one.

Between the six of us, there were always factions. The

oldests, the youngests, the boys, the girls, the good ones, the smart ones, the strange ones, the wild ones, the bad ones.

Or, as it often went down with our little tribe, the bad *one*.

That was me, but Matt didn't seem to mind. When my world condensed down to three little lines and there was nowhere for me to go, Matt put my pieces back together. He was the buffer between me and the rest of my family, and he helped me get away when I needed it the most.

So, yeah. I was going to his wedding even if I had to smile, nod, and panic-sweat my way through the entire fucking weekend.

It helped that my father had finally found his true calling. We could all breathe easier knowing he was now busy managing day-to-day operations in hell. Some would say it was wrong to disrespect the dead, but I'd say his inability to respect the living was the greater crime.

But it *was* easier to breathe with him gone. It was slow at first, no magical moonbeams of serenity here, and then it came down on me all at once. When I shook it off like a cloak I'd long since outgrown, I was left with a cold slap of reality.

I was completely fucking alone.

In my haste to run far and fast from Angus, I'd also shredded the threads that tied me and my siblings together. Little more than a trail of burnt bridges and breadcrumbs led the way to the only people I could call my own.

And in those seven angry, necessary, devastating, silent, healing, amazing, awful years, everything had changed. We'd grown up. We'd grown apart, or perhaps it was me who grew apart from them. *They'd* grown closer together; my siblings ran a third-generation sustainable preservation architecture firm in Boston. They worked together. They shared holidays, memories, milestones. They even ran the goddamn Boston Marathon every spring.

They were a unit, and I was the outlier.

This journey home was saddled with histories and high-water marks, and a quiet, bitter war with my sister. There was no minor disagreement keeping the ice cold between me and Shannon. Ours was a standoff, and while no one was fully on the side of right, many of the wrongs belonged to me.

The drumbeat of reconciliation had intensified since Angus's death, but it'd started long before that. Matt wanted to broker peace. Patrick was tired of my perennial position on his weekly to-do list. Sam was eager for anyone but him to be the source of our collective hand-wringing. Riley enjoyed reminding me that the only way to get the ball out of my court was to serve it back to Shannon.

No matter which way I cut it, my brothers were walking away from the watchtower. They weren't willing to abet this impasse any longer, and if I knew them at all, I knew they were jostling Shannon in the same way.

GETTING out of Terminal E at Logan International was a shitshow. The andesite in my bag raised suspicions in Customs, even when I explained it was a volcanic rock straight from the slopes of Mount Vesuvius. They stood down when I produced my badge from the last International Union of Geodesy and Geophysics conference, but they weren't thrilled when they came across my rock hammers and chisels.

Nothing shook the jet lag quite like the heavily armed attention of the U.S. Customs and Border Protection Agency.

The rest of my evening was similarly complicated.

While the car service that Matt had ordered was smart enough to send a driver uninterested in idle chatter, they failed to send adequate directions to the Cape Cod inn along with him. After driving in circles for forty-five minutes, Rocco and I stopped for frappés at one of those quaint ice cream stands that dotted New England roadsides every summer. We got directions, too.

I'd hoped to quietly arrive at the inn, sneak off to my room, and gird myself before diving into the deep end tomorrow morning. That would've worked if Patrick hadn't been pacing at the entrance while glancing at his watch, then checking his phone, and then scanning the parking lot. He'd claimed he was waiting for me, and I would've believed that if he hadn't continued on with that precise sequence of events. Always a secretive one, that Patrick.

He showed me to my suite and gave me a literal minute to change clothes before announcing we had "things to talk about with everyone else." A girl couldn't even wash the grime of air travel off her face before appearing in front of the family tribunal.

He led me outside to a sprawling patio area, and I had no idea I'd missed this side of the Atlantic until I felt the sea breeze on my skin. I didn't get much time to enjoy it, though. I was immediately slammed with six hundred percent more family than I knew how to swallow.

The upside to living the nomad's life—or downside, depending on your vantage point—was that I only consumed my family in bits and pieces. An email here, a video chat there, and then a month of silence and self-preservation. But that wasn't how this weekend was going to go.

Riley was a grown-ass man now, and a fucking enormous one at that. He hugged me tight enough to steal my breath and promised we'd get through this. I wasn't sure which "this" he had in mind, but I wasn't turning down the offer.

Sam belonged on the cover of *GQ*, and I told him as much. It took him all of three minutes to get me on board with a post-wedding camping trip to Vermont. He agreed to hike the Quechee Gorge—one of New England's oldest and oddest geological formations—and I was sold. Mesozoic mafic dikes and Vermont air were my soul food.

Matt was smitten. He was overflowing with so much love and happiness that I could've scooped some of it off him and smeared it all over myself. I didn't, of course. Love and happiness would've had me breaking out in hives.

His fiancée, Lauren, was the human equivalent of a birthday cake. She was sweet and cheerful, but more than that, she made people feel special. I wore the Really Fucking Jaded crown day in and day out, but five minutes with this lady and I was as smitten as Matt. Her family was the text-book definition of Good, Wholesome People complete with the bubbly mom, stern-but-supportive dad, and a set of Navy SEAL brothers. Her father even had a spanky nick-name for himself. The Commodore. How those nice people wound up with us was a question for the cosmos.

Matt's friend, Nick—the marathon buddy I'd been hearing about for *ages*—was tall, dark, and charming. Dr. Acevedo was southern—Texan, according to Matt's mentions of him—but he said my name with a flood of Spanish that had the *r* rolling for days. That my brother had systemically failed to inform me his Latin friend was hotter than the Kilauea lava field was troubling.

And my sister...She was still holding it all together with one hand and carrying the weight of the world in the other. As if I was Medusa, capable of turning anyone who met my monstrous gaze into stone, Shannon eluded me. She was careful to sit on the opposite end of the patio when Patrick gathered us together, and she never once glanced my way.

There was something complicated about sisters, and complicated didn't scratch the surface with me and Shannon. I wasn't ready to wade into that complication either. Not at all.

"Chill out," Riley murmured as he wedged in beside me on the wicker loveseat. "If this shit gets too heavy, just ask Patrick about his apprentice and I guarantee everyone will forget *all* about you and Shannon."

"You're wrong," I said under my breath. A waiter appeared, eager to take my drink order. I waved him off. "He wants to have this out. Right here, right now. It's like he won't sign off on Matt getting married until I lift the curse. He's got his 'let's get to the bottom of this' speech all ready. Just look at him."

Patrick was pacing, a small cardboard box tucked under his arm.

"Nope," Riley said. "That's not even on his top ten list right now."

"I don't know," I said, pinching my inner thigh. The pain pulled the stress of this moment out of focus, and it helped. Even if only for a minute.

"I do," Riley said. "Matt instituted a strict no-fly zone for the weekend, and those two"—he tipped his head back toward the bar with a pointed glance at Lauren's brothers, Will and Wes—"are responsible for enforcing it at all costs. The one with the beard is on Shannon duty, and the other one's on you. I believe they've been authorized to hog-tie you both if you so much as cough in the wrong direction."

"Oh, fantastic," I muttered. I'd be offended by the babysitting detail if it weren't so damned appropriate. My years

were few but my shameful moments of extraordinary care-
lessness were many.

"Shush," Riley admonished, jerking his chin toward
Patrick. "Optimus wants to talk now."

This time, Riley was right. Instead of calling an end to the
feud, Patrick opted to tell us about a haunted house. This
wasn't any old home, heavy with lingering souls. It was a
place that sucked the innocence from my skin and stripped
the optimism from my marrow. It was dark corners, steep
staircases, hidden passageways, and all of those things
reverberated with breath-stealing terror.

But for once, this old home wasn't handing down a
beating.

In his work to prepare our childhood home for sale,
Patrick and his apprentice Andy discovered a vault built
between the walls. All the things we thought Angus had
destroyed—my mother's clothes and journals, family photos
and handmade baby blankets—were lovingly preserved. For
nearly twenty-five years, we'd believed Angus's grief and
resentment drove him to obliterate every trace of my mother,
but now it seemed the old sap had built a shrine instead.

That was Angus's style: absolutely fucking demented,
with a side of melancholy.

So here I was, for once surrounded by remnants of my
mother. Her jewelry, her scrapbooks, her scarves. *Her*. She
was here, and she was real. My siblings knew her, in their
own ways, and the memories I had of her were borrowed
from them. For years, those ill-fitting hand-me-downs were
my best and only options.

But then Sam passed me a small cherrywood jewelry box,
and I found myself staring at a necklace that I'd seen only in
partially formed recollections that seemed more imagination
than reality. The small silver pendant warmed between my

fingers, and I stared directly at Shannon, willing her to meet my gaze.

It was Paris all over again.

Everything had memories, everything was charged with knowledge of that which had come before and before and before, but I didn't know that deep in my bones until I was poking around a Parisian drugstore two years ago. I was there for a conference but I also needed tampons, and when I walked through the doors, I was hit with a scent that unearthed a lifetime of memories. It was rosewater, delicate and fresh and overwhelming in an unexplainably-emotional-in-a-Parisian-drugstore kind of way.

In that moment, I *understood* something but I couldn't explain it. I bought a few bottles and spritzed it on daily, racking my brain for why it fucking mattered, but it took an entire year to realize it was my mother. Rosewater was the only thing that I remembered about her but with that one memory unlocked, I had *something*, and that was a fuck-ton more than the nothing I'd been operating with since she died. That something brought back the feel of her arms holding me tight, her voice in my ear, and her necklace—the one with the tiny compass pendant—between my fingers.

I'd cried—*really cried*—for the first time in years. We lost her when I was a toddler, but it took two decades for me to meet her, and then mourn her.

Now, with her necklace in my hands and rosewater in my lungs, and my sister's refusal to look at me and tell me that I was allowed to feel this much relief and loss at once, I was crumbling. It was overpowering—all of this was overpowering, everything—and I was desperate for some of the distance I'd clung to since leaving home all those years ago.

And I was taking this necklace with me.

Two

NICK

TWO THINGS WERE IMMEDIATELY apparent about Miss Erin Walsh.

First, she'd seen some shit. She shrouded herself in too much rough assertiveness to be a simple-hearted scientist. She'd lived through a time or two, and it showed.

And second, her eyes made me forget everything I'd ever known.

Green green green.

Green like sea witches and summer. Green like the holiest of pagan rituals. Green like the inside of a secret.

Right there, with Erin's name rolling off my tongue and her hand still shaking mine, I accepted that I'd be violating several articles of the Ex-Girlfriends and Sisters Code for Guys this weekend. I'd ask forgiveness from Matt—and Patrick, Sam, and Riley, too—at some point in the future because fuck asking permission. Even if she was their little sister, Erin was a grown woman, and she'd be the only Walsh granting permission here.

Meeting Erin tonight brought on the oddest sense of déjà vu, all hot and prickly on the back of my neck. Within a single breath, she looked everything like Shannon but nothing at all. Same autumn red hair. Same pale skin spattered with freckles. Same petite build. Same emerald eyes that could cut down grown men with little more than a glance. They were like identical twins, who—despite being genetically fucking identical—were so different in personality and nature that it appeared to alter their features.

I'd seen photos of her, plenty of them. Matt showed off her expeditions like the proud stand-in papa he was, but those images only told me that she was a pint-sized ginger with no concern about getting up close and personal with literal pits of fire.

Never once did those images flatten me with eyes that said *I know things you can't begin to comprehend*.

It wasn't as simple as attraction, not even close. Attraction boiled down to looking and liking, and I knew all about that. Looking and liking had been my preferred mode of operation for years, and it had never once grabbed me by the gut and said *Don't let that woman go*. Lust wasn't the culprit either. It was something else, something that resided past the bounds of language and fully in the land of intuition.

That left me staring at her while she examined long-lost family heirlooms with sad eyes that worked hard at blinking back tears. She watched Shannon's every move, but Shannon wasn't returning the favor. I wasn't ignorant of the issues, though. Anytime the Walsh boys congregated around an ample supply of liquor, the topic of Shannon and Erin's holy war was bound to come up. Something really fucking foul had gone down between them, and it was far from resolved.

Yeah, Erin had lived through a time.

Before I could ask her to get a drink with me, she was gone. Dragged back into the rattle and hum of Matt and Lauren's wedding weekend. She was passed around like the family Bible, everyone borrowing the chapter and verse that suited them best.

So I waited. This wasn't my ballgame. Not even my league. But I needed to see her. It was wild and illogical, and in the right light it was manic. I just didn't care.

It didn't help that my head was a fucking mess. This woman—*this week*—had a throb of confusion vibrating in my every breath and sent me on a long, aimless walk around the inn. I lacked both destination and plan, and knew only that if I kept moving, I'd find what I needed.

And what—*who*—I needed came bustling out of the inn's front door, a gray cardigan that looked too soft and thread-bare to be anything more than symbolically warm over her *Moby-Dick* t-shirt.

She was wearing different jeans now too, the traditional cut, not the stretchy, close-fitting kind from earlier in the evening. They looked good on her, as if she'd worn them long enough for the fabric to know her as well as she knew it. In place of her flip-flops were scuffed and scarred boots.

Nothing about her said *new*. Of course not. Her soul was centuries older than her skin.

"Hey. Nick?" She pushed her cat's-eye glasses up her nose —those were too fucking cute for life—and said, "Were you leaving? Can you get me out of here?"

"Sure thing, darlin'," I said. She remembered my name. I was taking that as a sign. "Where're we running to?"

"Just...anywhere," she said, looking into the wooded darkness behind me. "Away from here."

I brought my hand to her shoulder, and steered her toward my SUV. "Easy enough," I said. "What do you need?"

This was cool. It was friendly. I wasn't creeping on her personal space because I had an unbelievable need to touch her. Completely cool and friendly, and I wasn't thinking about stroking her hair. Not at all.

"Thanks for this," she said. "I could use a beer. Maybe some fresh air, too."

No sense mentioning our stone's-throw proximity to the Atlantic Ocean, or the availability of beer here either. The lady wanted to leave and thus I was fulfilling her orders.

Her eyebrow ring glinted in the moonlight as she settled into the passenger seat. It was a tiny piercing, just past the midline of her left brow. I leaned back in my seat, gripping the steering wheel harder than necessary to remind myself that climbing on top of her and exploring the feel of that ring against my tongue wasn't the polite way to start a conversation.

She drummed her fingers on the armrest, and I stared, completely caught in her spell. If this was the same curiosity that sent Odysseus sailing straight into the Sirens, then someone needed to tie me to the motherfucking mast because I was going in.

"I was thinking about getting a little farther away than the parking lot," she said. "What do you say?"

"Right, of course." I cleared my throat and turned over the ignition. "Are we drowning our sorrows tonight?"

She scraped her fingers through her hair, and that sent a gentle floral scent wafting toward me. "No. Just because alcohol is *a* solution doesn't mean it's *the* solution," she said.

I barked out a surprised laugh. "Was that a chemistry joke?"

"Atoms, man. They're in everything," she said, and my ribs were now aching from the force of my laughter. "But seriously, that's the extent of my small talk skill. I only know how to talk about the way lava is proof of reincarnation or that the amount of control wielded by tides is mind-boggling. That's it. That's me—no niceties, lots of oddly philosophical science. If you want to get drunk and debate the Pats' spread offense, I'm no good for you. I'm no good for anyone, but specifically in this context, I'm no good for you."

Well, *fuuuuuck*.

My first thought was of tasting that insouciant smile of hers, yes. But my second thought was of hearing the rest of that lava story. Maybe that was the most appropriate summary of my craving for Miss Walsh. Her beauty was the slap in the face, but her mind was the sucker punch.

"And you know what?" she continued. "Alcohol always tells me I can dance. I can*not*, and I shouldn't listen to alcohol. We're not friends anymore."

I glanced over at her. I was melting for her, just fucking melting, and she didn't even know it. "Are you sure you're a Walsh?"

"It's been debated," she murmured. "Head toward Provincetown. We'll find something on the way, but no chains and no tourist traps."

"Yes, ma'am," I said.

"I'm not old enough to be a *ma'am*," she replied, laughing. "Don't do that to me."

"What would you rather be?" I asked as I rolled to a stop near the main road. I bit my tongue—literally bit my tongue—to keep from offering a name more intimate. But *baby, sweetie, honey*, those wouldn't do. Not even *cariño* or *corazón* would work.

Mine. That was good. That would work.

"Call me Ishmael," she said, following my gaze to *Moby-Dick* scrawled across her chest. She was the kind of girl who wore a t-shirt well, and she didn't seem to mind me noticing. "Funny story, *Moby-Dick*. It's all about chasing down the thing that haunts you, but in that chase, losing everything else."

"Yeah, now that you mention it, I do see the humor," I said, failing to rip my eyes from her shirt. Yes, all right, it wasn't the *shirt* that had my attention. It was the woman wearing the shirt, and everything I could infer from the way she wore it. "Death at sea has always been hilarious."

"Well, no," she said, shaking a hand at me. "It's revered as this tale of good versus evil, man versus nature, blah, blah, blah. But it's really just a swan song for the good old days of Nantucket whaling. A sermon to the sea, and all of its machinations. Most people blame the rise of petroleum, the depleted stock of whales, and the seizure of northern ships by the Confederate Navy during the Civil War for the decline of the American whaling industry, specifically the decline here on the Cape, but it was actually the development of more efficient Norwegian ships. Instead of catching up to the Norwegians and furthering the decline of the entire species, American interests turned to railroads, mining, conquering the west."

I blinked at Erin while she studied the dark road before us. "Do you do that often?" I asked, scratching my chin. "Make odd observations about one thing and then drop a maritime history lesson like you had that information on the tip of your tongue?"

She shrugged. "Sometimes."

"Right, yeah. It was kind of amazing," I said, "and a little intimidating."

"I told you," she said. "I don't do small talk." Erin looked away, out her window, but then cut an up-and-down glance back at me. It was quick, but the smile that followed was more than enough to telegraph her interest. Okay. So it wasn't just me. "Take Route 6."

We rode along the far eastern arm of Cape Cod in amicable silence, and found a harborside tavern that screamed local-but-not-tourist. Not that I cared, but Erin knew what she wanted. As far as I was concerned, we could sit on a curb all night, so long as she kept talking and let me bury my face in her hair to find that scent again.

Once seated at the bar, I stole every opportunity to gaze at her. She didn't put much on display, but that didn't matter. When the Lord gave to Erin, he gave with two hands. She was small. Narrow, even. But that t-shirt showed off the curve of her waist in a manner that made my fingers itch. And her tits were a crime. They were that soup ladle shape that was too rare to be real, but there wasn't an ounce of artifice on this woman.

What you see is what you get.

Except it wasn't, not by a mile. I leaned back in my seat and draped my arm over the edge of hers. My fingers were drawn to her shoulder. No, that was bullshit. Complete bullshit. I was drawn to all of her, and touching her shoulder was an entry-level way of saying *I dig you, darlin'*.

She glanced at my fingers and then back to me, her eyebrow arching. I didn't respond to her unspoken question, instead staring at her pink lips. She'd be sweet there. Sweet but tart, too.

"What are you running away from tonight, lovely?"

She shook her head. "Nothing new," she said.

Her fingers tangled in the thin chains circling her neck, and she toyed with the small stone that sat in her jugular notch. "What is that?" I asked, pointing to the gem. "Onyx?"

"Carbonado. Black diamond. It's the toughest natural diamond form in existence. I found this one in Brazil."

"I've never heard of those," I said, my gaze drawn to her neck. I wanted to taste her there. I wanted her in nothing but that necklace. I wanted to wrap my fingers around that necklace and feel her pulse thrumming against my skin while I moved in her.

Oh, *shit*. Shit, shit, shit. I could *not* think about her naked. Not here. Not yet. And it wasn't about the touch-and-go nature of public erections. No, it was that I wanted to do this *right*.

"It's not quite clear how they came to exist," she continued, her voice taking on new authority. Her words were clear and efficient, and even her gestures rang with professional fascination that bordered on obsession. "They possess no mantle minerals, and that's fucking weird, but what's more strange is the lack of high-pressure minerals, like hexagonal carbon polymorph."

"No hexagonal carbon polymorph?" I asked. I had no idea what we were talking about. I mean, sure, I knew my share of chemistry, but this was beyond my share. "That's crazy."

"I know, right?" she said. "Fun fact—their isotopic values are low, which isn't how diamonds are supposed to behave. Some researchers have suggested that radiation was involved in their formation, given the presence of luminescence halos, but that calls into question a spontaneous fission of uranium and thorium."

"Right," I murmured, nodding in thanks as the bartender placed two beer bottles in front of us. "The luminescence halos. Of course."

She held up her index finger, pressing pause on the black diamond mystery while she sipped her beer. "Oh, sorry," she said, tapping her bottle to mine. "Here's to…surviving this weekend."

Here's to evading your big brothers. What they don't know won't hurt them. Right?

"To surviving the weekend," I said. I took a sip, but then returned the bottle to the bar top. Reaching over, I pulled her chair closer to mine. Fuck cool and friendly.

"Right, right," she said. She was looking down, inspecting the way I had us pressed together, and then back up at me. "What's this about?"

"You." I pressed my thumb right there, to the tender hollow where the stone sat. It was just a moment, a fleeting touch. A second longer and my hand would've moved up her neck and into her hair, and then we'd never hear the end of this wonky explanation because my mouth would be fused to hers. "You were telling me about this," I said, my eyes locked on her lips.

"Yeah…"

She eyed me for a wary beat, then pushed her glasses up her nose and leaned into me. *Leaned the fuck into me.* Her shoulder was on my chest and her head was tucked under my chin, and this, *this* was what I needed after the week from hell.

Patting my knee twice as if I was a well-behaved golden retriever, Erin blew out a soft breath. She relaxed in pieces, her shoulders sagging first, and it moved down her body. Back, hips, legs. I imagined her toes uncurling inside her boots. From this angle, I could see her lashes brushing against her cheeks, and I didn't even think about it when I pressed my lips to her temple. It was natural, for both of us. This was what she needed, too.

"So, carbonado," she said, patting my knee again. God, she was fucking cute. "The theory that keeps me up at night is this one—that it was formed deep inside an early genera-tion giant star, one that exploded forever ago into a super-nova. Which makes this"—she tapped the stone—"an artifact of forever ago. Of a time before words and thoughts and anything at all."

"That's...incredible," I whispered into her hair. Her voice did things to me. Really good things. And the nerdy science talk? Oh, shut the fuck up. I was done when I saw her, and I was well done now.

Her tongue darted out and ran along her top lip as her shoulder jerked. "Whenever the world is too much for me, I remember that this rock might have been thrown out of interstellar space when time began. Before the world was anything, this ball of carbon was flung into earth's atmosphere in one of the cosmos's greatest tantrums. I've had a lot of bad days, but never one as bad as this rock."

She really did know things I couldn't begin to comprehend. I hadn't expected it to involve black diamonds or supernovas but the means didn't matter. It was the method that had me entranced. And I wanted—no, *needed*—to know her.

"Is the world too much today?" I asked.

A quick nod. "A little bit, yeah."

She offered nothing more, and that was okay. The world was kicking my ass right now, too.

I tapped the tiny stone winking at me from her nose. "And what's this?"

"Diamond," she said. "The kimberlite variety. Nothing interstellar here."

"Boring," I murmured, and that earned me a hearty laugh. "Hawaii. Italy. Grad school. Volcanoes. Tell me everything. When do you finish?"

In other words, when can I keep you forever?

She wiggled her fingers as if she was counting on them. "Three...no, four months ago. I've been working on some random stuff since then. You know, testing stray theories and cleaning up messy data sets. I'm heading to Iceland soon," she added, and those wiggly fingers came to a rest on my thigh. My cock nearly strangled itself twitching toward her touch. "I'll be splitting my time between Iceland and England. Iceland for the field research. England for a new doctoral program. There's some innovative work being done at Oxford around environmental changes, climate, sea levels. Mostly planetary physics stuff. I don't know what I'm going to find, but it will be interesting."

"Does Matt know that?" I asked, already knowing the answer. He didn't. He was a sharer, and he would've shared that. Since meeting him five years ago in a Boston Marathon qualifying run, I'd been an unwitting recipient of his Erin updates. He probably hadn't anticipated that I'd call upon that information while his sister was edging her way into my lap.

She squinted at the liquor bottles shelved behind the bar. "I don't know. Maybe. I might've mentioned it." She held out her palms in surrender, and that came with the unfortunate consequence of separating her touch from my thigh. "Also, I might've forgotten."

I grabbed her hand and put it back. "You're on loan to an Icelandic research station from Oxford?"

"You say that like it's a big deal. Trust me, it's really *not* a big deal. It's how my little corner of the world works. Aren't you on loan from Harvard to some specialized pediatric neurosurgery program and have surgical privileges at every hospital in Boston?" she replied. "At least, that's what Matt told me."

Oh, I loved knowing that she had my info. It was better than having hers. "How old are you?" I asked. Demanded, really. I knew only that she was the youngest of the Walshes, and had filed that into the general category of *under thirty*.

"Twenty-six," she said. "How old are you?"

"Thirty-four," I said.

She shrugged, sloughing away this *thing* where she was twenty-fucking-six and working on her second doctorate and too magnificent for me to do anything but stare.

She started humming along with the song—"Stubborn Love" by The Lumineers—and her right hand was moving with the beat, rolling like the crest and crash of waves. Her hands were small. Dainty, even. If she ever grew tired of mining the planet for answers, those hands were perfect for heart surgery.

She smiled as she mouthed the words. Something about bringing me to my knees, and *come the fuck on, lovely*. I was already there.

"You're making it hard to think," I said.

"What?" she asked, glancing up at me with her beer frozen halfway to her mouth.

"Nothing," I murmured, and my fingers continued drawing circles along her arm.

"No," she said, her eyes dropping to my mouth. "Say that again. There can be no secrets among runaways."

I cleared my throat because if her eyes were on my mouth, her mind was there, too. "Your chromosomes have coupled quite remarkably. It's all I can think about right now."

I tipped my beer back for a long swallow and ran my hand from her shoulder to her elbow. It was dangerous touching her like this. Dangerous because it made me hungry for more. Really dangerous because she was edging closer and *giving* more.

"You have Doctor McDreamy hair," she said, dragging her nails over my scalp. I didn't think it was possible to orgasm from head scratching alone, but we were close to testing the theorem. "Speaking of McDreamy, I need you to tell me that *Grey's Anatomy* is a completely authentic depiction of hospital life."

"Can't comment," I said, shrugging. I couldn't think about the hospital right now. "Haven't seen it."

Erin sipped her beer and narrowed her eyes, not at all believing my response. "Do you have intensely deep relationships with your colleagues? Have you slept with the majority of them? Do you hear or deliver at least one self-righteous soliloquy per day? Do people show up in the emergency room impaled on unicorns?"

"Not quite," I said.

"That's disappointing," she murmured.

I tugged her closer, breathing in her scent while my lips brushed her ear. "Tell me how to fix it, lovely. I don't want you disappointed."

She waved away my words and looked around the bar. It was late, and the remaining patrons were focused on the flat screen television broadcasting the Red Sox game against the Orioles. It wasn't looking good for the home team.

"I slept on the red-eye from Rome, but I should've stayed up. Now I'm stuck on GMT. I'm…I'll be a mess tomorrow."

I was about to tell her that I knew several ways to tire her right out, but she shoved her sleeves to her elbows and reached for her beer. As I followed the movement, her wrist caught my attention. Most people probably noticed the compass tattoo, but it was what the fine lines of the tattoo hid that sent a bolt of adrenaline through my system.

Reaching out, I drew my thumb over the scars.

Three cuts, straight across, deep enough to be deadly.

"Were you trying to die?" I asked.

She stared at her beer bottle for a heavy moment.

Tell me it's not what I think. Tell me it was an accident. Tell me you're okay.

"I thought so," she said eventually, and my chest lurched at her admission. I didn't want that kind of despair for her. "At the time."

My arms went around her. It wasn't a choice. I had to hold her close. "But now?" I asked into her hair.

She shook her head. "No, not at all. But I think about life and death a lot, at least as it pertains"—she tapped her necklace—"to everything that's happened before me, and everything that will happen after. There's time and time and time, so much that I can barely wrap my head around it. Maybe that's the trick, right? You get these years, these completely inadequate years, and that's all the time you're granted to understand the secrets and the mysteries and the miracles. And it's crazy, you know, because there's so much time but there really isn't."

I dragged my hand up and down her spine, but the comfort probably served me more than her. Her words, they took me apart. In my mind, I saw Erin separating out my constituent parts, looking them over as she explained what they were, where they came from, why they mattered.

And just that quick, a drowsy bar on the Outer Cape was the wrong place for this. For us. For all the emotions that were rising up like a rogue wave. I slipped some bills under my beer bottle and waved to the bartender. "Come on, lovely," I said, my lips pressed to the crown of her head.

Her hand in mine, we walked along the sea wall as low tide lapped against the fishing boats moored in the harbor there. We stopped at the far end, and Erin turned her eyes to the sky. She glanced from constellation to planet to constellation, ticking them off as if she was taking attendance. I moved in behind her, wrapping my arms around her torso and pressing my lips to her neck because she was right. About there never being enough time, about all of it.

"I lost a patient yesterday," I said. "I used to be able to count the patients I'd lost on one hand. Now I can't."

Her head dropped back against my chest as she squeezed my wrist. "What happened?"

I shook my head with a sigh. "Came in with a concussion eight months ago. Seven years old. Fucking peewee football. MRI showed a brain stem tumor, and I went in, and I'd gotten it all. I *knew* I'd gotten it all. But it came back, and…I opened him up again. Thought I could get it. Thought I had it," I said. "He didn't survive the surgery."

Erin didn't offer any hollow words about me doing everything possible or how I shouldn't blame myself. Silence was better than bullshit, and she knew that.

"It's the worst thing in the world, Erin," I said. "Telling parents that I couldn't save their child, it makes me want to crawl out of my fucking skin and scream at the universe. I know the names of those six kids and their birthdays, and what they wanted to do after their surgeries, and I know exactly why they died and how I failed them. It makes me think I shouldn't hold a scalpel again, and right now, I really don't think I should."

She thought about that for a moment, her chin tipped up to the sky. "Okay," she said slowly. "Tell me about them."

I didn't understand how she knew exactly what I needed, but it was that. Right fucking that, stark and awful.

Just fuckin' take me, woman. Have me, flaws and failures and all.

We sat on the sea wall for hours while the tide crept in and the world slept around us, and we talked about everything. *Everything*. It started with the patients I'd lost, the cases that made me question my beliefs in modern medicine, the cases that restored it. Then it was my unlikely path into pediatric neurosurgery despite being squarely in the family practice camp at the start of med school, and Erin's equally unlikely path into geochemistry and volcanology. There was my contempt for managed care, and her frustrations with science and progress and politics, and a shared musing of whether anything we did mattered at all. We agreed it all mattered. It had to, because we couldn't do what we did without a thick streak of hope behind us.

She grew up in suburban Boston, me on a working horse ranch outside Dallas. Her siblings ran an architecture business, my sisters were beauty pageant veterans. There was her brother Sam's issues with anxiety, and my sister Maya's repeated bouts with postpartum depression. Her mother was from rural Ireland, mine was from old oil money and had the audacity to marry a ranch hand. My father loved horses and hated high society, and there were two straight years when he'd slept in the musty apartment above the stables because their marriage wasn't an easy one. It still wasn't easy. Erin's mother died too early and her father died too late, and nothing in between those events had been good for her. There was a high school teacher—one she thought she could handle, one who should've known better—who made things even worse, and her father's perversion and depravity, and a night when she didn't think she wanted to see morning.

"I'm happy you didn't succeed," I said. The quiet, hollow parts of night were behind us, and dawn was only a few hours away. "Let me say that again because I want you to believe it. I'm fucking thrilled that you're alive."

My palm was flat on the small of her back, under her sweater but over the t-shirt because it was the only way to keep this decent. We'd touched each other all night, but it wasn't suggestive, down-to-fuck flirting. This was affection like a Mazzy Star song, or The Smiths.

"You say that because you like my tits, and you'd have nothing to admire if I was dead," she said. That should *not* have been okay, but it was the kind of lightness one could only understand after some time alone in the dark.

"Of course I like your tits," I said, angling my head to speak directly to her chest. "I might've said that I lost my religion in med school but I'm ready to pray to the God who created those beauties. Lord, please take me back. I've seen the error of my ways, and I want to worship before your gifts. Specifically, these two."

"You're ridiculous," she said. "I didn't succeed, and that's good. I still do irresponsible things though."

"Yeah, I know all about that. I've seen the pictures of you next to lava flows," I countered. "Would you get in my lap, woman? Get over here, and tell me how irresponsible you want to be tonight."

"This night is almost over," Erin said as she rose up on her knees. She brought her hand to the back of my neck, and she tugged me down, closer. She was tentative at first, her lips brushing over mine and her fingers inching under my collar, but then she unleashed herself on me.

It was just like she'd said: she flew past the niceties and went straight for the rough stuff.

Wild, wild kisses. Hands all over, everywhere. Teeth and tongue in all the right places. Needy murmurs and hungry sighs.

In this kiss, she was confiding in me, speaking without the complication of words, and I was listening. I was answering.

My hands were locked on her waist, even if that was an exercise in willpower. I knew that if I took even an inch more, we'd need a level of privacy we didn't have handy at the moment.

"I dare you to steal a boat with me," she said against my jaw.

"Only if I can call you Skipper while we do it," I said.

She pressed her lips to my neck, and lightning struck far off on the horizon. I could smell it in the air, and I felt the jolt right in my nerves, as if the universe was saying *You've found her. Now keep her*.

Three

ERIN

"WHAT'S THE EXPAT LIFE LIKE?" Nick asked over the roar of the boat's engine.

That accent was working me over. Each drawled syllable was like an ax blow to a tree trunk. A few more good whacks, and we'd be yelling *timber*.

"Europe is great, and yes, I still vote and pay taxes," I said. It was my stock answer. I fielded this question with great frequency, but I wasn't trotting it out to give him the brush-off. God, *no*.

The reality was that he looked delicious with the ocean air rushing over him and the dark expanse of water at his back, and it was too damned distracting for me to form words. That, and I'd dropped my life story at his feet like the big bucket of shambles it was, and instead of sneering at it all, he offered up his own shambles.

We were headed north, toward Truro, and the best part was that I didn't even have to steal this boat. We'd found a lobsterman heading out on the water, and he'd looked us over with about as much suspicion as we deserved before accepting us as deckhands before the break of dawn.

Nick turned back toward me, his hands shoved into his pockets. "What's it really like? What do you love? What do you miss about the States?"

"That's hard to describe," I said. "I love discovering new places. It's one hundred percent true what they say about travel enriching your life. It's like…if you explore the world long enough, you'll stop trying to understand it, and then, suddenly, you will. It'll sneak up on you."

He nodded at that, bobbing his head as if I was preaching a sermon he'd already heard. "I have a buddy from med school who just left for a year-long rural medicine residency in New Zealand. He, and his wife and kids, are going to be rotating through villages and small towns, and that sounds fucking amazing," he said. "I'd love to do that some day. I've been thinking about applying to Doctors Without Borders."

I edged into Nick's space, my shoulder bumping his chest as if to say *why aren't you touching me right now?* And wasn't that a shocker? Of all the things I'd expected from this weekend, cozying up to a random guy wasn't one of them.

But I knew that Nick wasn't a *random guy,* and maybe that was because I'd steamrolled right past the pleasantries, told him most of my sad stories, and convinced him he wanted an adventure. But I didn't want to spend any time examining my attraction to him. For me, this was unusual, but it felt right and I wasn't about to kill that by putting it under a microscope.

"What's holding you back?" I asked. Nick glanced down at me, and my shameless nudges for his affection. It was a wonder he noticed at all. His chest was rock-solid.

He folded me into his arms and rested his chin on my head. "The fellowship I'm in now, it wraps up near the end of the year. I don't have much flexibility until then, and I haven't finalized what I'm doing after that point."

"You're waiting until you have the chessboard in order," I said.

I had one arm around his waist, but my free hand was flat on his tummy and lightly tracing the hard ridges of his abs. This right here? *This* was irresponsible.

"Yeah," he said, "pretty much. I don't have the next steps mapped out quite as well as you do, Skipper."

"Mapped out? No, I'm just an evergreen researcher," I said, shaking my head against his chest. "The only thing I have mapped out is which volcanoes I expect to blow next. Other than that, no plans."

"If it's working for you," he said. It almost sounded like a challenge, as if he doubted whether I truly preferred to tuck my life into a few trunks and never know anything but short-term homes. Or maybe I'd only interpreted it that way. "I'd sign on for Doctors Without Borders, or a rural medicine program, but I couldn't do that forever. I want to travel, but I need some permanence, too."

"What's next for you? After the fellowship?" I asked.

"Same stuff, different cities. Houston, Denver, Charlotte. And Boston," he added. "My mother is advocating hard for Houston. She seems to think I'd be dropping by for dinner, even though Houston is more than three hours away from Dallas."

"I think that's what mothers do," I said.

"You're probably right. My sister Dahlia and her husband are nearby, they're in Dallas, but my sister Maya and her husband moved farther out into the country last year. Yeah, Mom didn't handle that move too well. I'm the youngest, but Maya's the baby." He nodded, and his chin bobbed against my head. "Can I ask you something, Skipper?"

"Sure," I said. I'd tell him anything so long as those arms stayed locked around me.

"Why'd you bring me out here?" he asked.

"I'm opposed to moping of all manner," I said. I believed that too. It was okay to feel pain and burdens and regret, but it wasn't okay to let them take over. The line was fine, and it was hard to see it in the dark, but that didn't make it any less necessary.

The easier option was to take Nick back to the inn and climb him like a jungle gym. He looked like he was up to date on all the new developments in sex. Like he did a thoughtful, technical study of porn—the mass production shit but also the feminist films because he was an enlightened lover, and he damned well knew it didn't make him any less of a man. Which I appreciated.

But how often were we here, with a full moon sliding into the horizon and miles of open water ahead? Not nearly enough to pass this up. And that was the simple reason why I drank basement-distilled moonshine, snuck into Eastern Bloc countries, dragged my ass all the way up Machu Picchu, hitchhiked (sort of) to a sub-Antarctic Australian island to witness a rare eruption, and, once upon a time, recruited a high school baseball team to steal some cannonballs. These opportunities didn't come around with much frequency, and when you saw them, you had to seize them.

"That's it?" he asked. "I think there's more to it than that."

"More?" I asked. "Nothing more than *carpe noctem*."

"Seize the night?" he asked with a smirk.

I was deflecting, absolutely. Nick knew it, too. But I just didn't want to talk about heartbreaking things anymore.

"I was expecting another chapter from your theory of the universe, and how a night on a lobster boat would cure all that ailed me."

Before I could respond, the captain leaned away from the helm. "I hope you two know what you're in for," he said.

"I hope you do," Nick whispered into my hair, "because I don't."

The captain cut a wide arc around several buoys and came to a gentle stop between them. He had thick gloves in one hand, and long metal rods with hooks on the end in the other. He pointed to the buoy, and then a stack of plastic bins on the deck. "I'll haul 'em up, and then we'll sort 'em," he said. "Watch out for your fingers if you want to keep 'em."

When the lobster trap surfaced, the captain yanked it onto the deck. Thick whips of seaweed clung to the trap, and when he popped it open, dozens of lobsters spilled out into the sorting tray. He offered a quick lesson in maneuvers to get rubber bands over their claws, and a high-level overview of sorting them into two groups: canners and markets.

"You got all that?" he asked while simultaneously banding two claws and tossing them into bins without looking.

Nick scratched his chin. "No problem," he said. "It's like cutting the herd, but much smaller and"—he held up a hissing lobster—"meaner."

"All right, captain," I said, moving quick to keep my fingers away from the snapping grasp of these angry crustaceans. "What's your salty sea story? Where're you from and how many sharks have tried to eat your boat?"

"Maine," he murmured, shaking his head while he sorted. "And none."

"Okay, you have to work with me here. I'm trying to give the good doctor an experience he'll remember. Are there any mermaids in these parts? Oh, and have you noticed fuller high tides recently? The media keeps using the term 'king tide' but that's a lot like naming winter storms. Pointless."

"You went from *Jaws* to mermaids to high tides," Nick

murmured, his gaze focused on the lobsters. "There is no way I'll forget this."

"Toss that one over," the captain said, jerking his chin toward the lobster I was attempting to wrangle. It was wrapped in seaweed, and I couldn't get enough of a grip to slip a rubber band over its claws. "We don't keep the mamas."

"That might be the tagline for my entire life," I murmured. He grabbed the lobster, seaweed and all, and flung it right over my head.

"Wow," Nick said, laughing. "I hope you didn't strain yourself reaching for that one. I thought we weren't moping, Skip."

I snapped a rubber band at his head, but instead of connecting with his made-for-TV hair, it sailed straight over his shoulder. He followed its path and then looked back at me with an unimpressed smirk that vaporized my panties. *Poof.* They were done and gone.

"Don't ever castrate a bull with that aim, Skipper," he warned, his light hazel eyes trained on me.

I reached into my back pocket for my imaginary pencil and paper. "Let me make a note of that," I murmured. "Cancel the bull castration. Got it."

"She's a wise ass, this one," the captain muttered.

"Yeah, she is. But I'll keep her," Nick said, and then nodded toward the bin of market lobsters. I glanced between him and the captain, half amused, half affronted. "What's the going rate for these big guys?"

"Less than you'd expect," the captain said. "Much less."

"What about the high tides?" I asked. "Does that come up much, you know, among your fishermen friends?"

"The tides are higher," the captain said. "The water's been warmer, too."

"Yeah, that's not great," I said, humming to myself. "I want to know about the life of the lobsterman. Do you travel much? Sailing just for the enjoyment of it? Do you like Maine? Any special summer plans?"

The captain huffed out a breath, and Nick and I exchanged an amused glance. We were driving this poor guy fucking crazy.

"I know what you're thinking," Nick said to me. "And let me correct you, Skip. This was all your idea. *You're* the instigator."

"Stop it," I said, snapping another rubber band at Nick's head. Missed again. "We're giving the captain over here one hell of a story. We're the best things that could've happened to him today."

"I'm officiating a marriage tomorrow night," the captain said, and it sounded as though he was extraordinarily distressed by my questions.

"A seaman's life is never boring," I said. "So, I'm curious about the whole marriage at sea thing and—"

"Are you ever *not* curious?" Nick asked.

That gave me pause. My existence boiled down to one question after another, forever in search of explanations for…for everything, really.

"No," I admitted, "but there are far worse things to be."

"'Be curious, not judgmental,'" the captain said under his breath.

I looked up at him, smiling. "Whitman?"

"Yep," he replied, a slight grin turning up his lips. "It's not a marriage at sea. I got ordained a few years ago, for some friends. The internet, it's crazy. But it's good. A couple of my friends, they're not interested in church weddings, and they want people they trust, not the first officiant who comes up in a Google search. I've done a few weddings now. It feels right."

I sensed Nick's eyes first, and I took great care to band the lobster's claws before looking at him. It was a good thing, too, because I was struck the second our gazes locked. Astrologers liked to say that when the moon and sun and planets fell into a certain alignment, the energies present in the universe shifted. Currents flowed in different directions. Some were blocked, others unblocked. It all came down to gravity, and the unstable theory that the relative locations of the celestial bodies could impact behavior.

It was a small, contrived comfort of modern life. Look to the skies, and a wholly subjective reading of your future will unfold, right?

But over Nick's shoulder sat Jupiter, a pinpoint of brightness. I turned, finding Mars, the moon, Venus, and Saturn lined up across the sky like an arrow shot from a bow.

I pressed my hand to my breastbone and the unfamiliar shape of my mother's compass dug into my skin.

"Why'd you bring me out here, Skip?" he asked.

"We both know how short and completely unpredictable life can be."

"Really fucking short," he said. "Really fucking unpredictable."

"And time...it isn't something you should pass," I continued.

"Not even a minute."

"You should never sit around waiting for life to start because it's leaving you with every second," I said, and I was feeling it, too. There was an urgent throb in my chest, as if my heart was saying, *Yes! This is what I want from you!* "But you know, even after all of those seconds are up, we're never truly gone. We continue to exist. Instead of being people walking around, fighting with our families and trapping lobsters and doing brain surgery, we're energy, unbound and disorderly. And sometimes you need to get ten miles from shore in the middle of the night to remember that nothing is truly gone."

"I know what you're thinking," he said. "Say it, lovely. Say it, or I will."

"You should explore the world," I said, tears springing to my eyes for no rational reason. "Do dangerous things. Ignore the fuck out of conventional wisdom. Walk on fire. Treat everyone with kindness because people are the only things worth holding on to. Live without regrets because there is no time for that shit. Never forget the way home, and leave a trail of breadcrumbs if you have to. Love, and get your heart broken, and say fuck it, and love again and then again. And whatever you do, never pass up an opportunity to get married on a lobster boat under a full moon with Jupiter and Mars as your witnesses."

"All of it," he said, grabbing hold of my waist and pulling me to his chest. "I want all of it, and don't ever stop talking about time and diamonds and literally anything else that comes to your amazing fucking mind, and marry me before we lose another second."

"Right here?" I asked, breathless. "Right now?"

"Here. Now," he said, and I was grinning so hard that my cheeks hurt. "I dare you."

"You two are a real piece of work," the captain muttered.

Four

THE SUN WAS RISING over the inn when I pulled in, and it didn't feel like the same place we'd escaped only nine hours earlier. Erin felt it, too. She'd been giving me sidelong glances the entire drive back here, always with her lips curled up in a sinful smile.

I hopped out of the SUV after killing the engine and ordering Erin to stay put. Watching her as I rounded the hood, I saw a testy glint in her eyes. She didn't like taking orders, but her anger was so fucking cute that I had to laugh.

Once I had her door open, I leaned in and pinned her hands to the seat. There was too much unchecked emotion pumping through me, and if those fingers caressed my neck, I'd be taking her here in the parking lot.

I'd married her on a lobster boat, but I was still trying to do some of this right.

"I want everything," I whispered. I pressed my face to the hollow of her neck, and when I scraped my teeth over the delicate skin there, her body jerked against my hold. "Come to my room, lovely. Let me have you."

Erin nodded as I kissed my way up from her neck to her

mouth. "Umm," she murmured against my lips. "I think mine's closer."

I released her seatbelt but couldn't tear myself off her. Anything worth saying could be spoken straight to her skin. My hands, they had no greater purpose than touching her body. "Whatever you want, wife," I said.

That word was powerful. It was an aphrodisiac, the strongest known to man.

I scooped her up, her taut little backside in my palms and her legs around my waist. It would've been fine if she wasn't exactly as hot and soft and *everywhere* that I needed. I was kidding myself if I thought I'd get far in this position.

"Erin, darlin'," I started, groaning as I pressed her spine to the vehicle.

She raked her fingers through my hair as I rocked against her, and a mix of agony and relief that only left me wanting more speared through my body. "You're going to put me down now," she said, "and follow me inside like a normal boy, and not a strange one who likes carrying able-bodied women around like dolls."

I nodded, but didn't relinquish her. She'd be leaving me soon enough, and that was a fact never far from my mind.

"Nick," she said, her fingertips grazing my temples as they tangled in my hair. It was an affectionate warning, and after holding her tight against me for a few seconds, I set her on the ground.

She wobbled, and I laughed. I had to, even if it earned me an arched eyebrow and sharp glare. "Oh, darlin'," I said. "If you're unsteady now, you're not going to be able to walk tonight."

Her eyes stared off toward the shore. "I don't know what to say to that."

I kissed her slowly, wanting to bring back the woman

who—only a few hours ago—opened her darkest closets and secret hiding places to me, and then dared me to marry her. She was in there. "You don't have to say anything," I murmured against her jaw. "Just lead the way."

"You should know that I don't take a lot of guys home with me," she warned. "Or…any guys."

I tucked some stray wisps of hair over her ears. It was an effective diversion because I was still really fucking furious about the way *guys* had mistreated her in the past. Vengeance wasn't my style, but I wanted to have some words with that goddamn pedophile English teacher. If her father were alive, he'd be on my list, too.

"I'm not a *guy*," I said, aiming for an even tone. "I'm your husband. Big difference."

"This isn't real," she protested.

"It's as real as we want it to be."

"Don't delude yourself," she chided. "We had a beer together and shared some confessions, and then we sorted lobsters and you faux-proposed to me. We don't have to pretend this is anything even close to real."

It hadn't taken long for me to see that Erin was a runner. She ran because she'd been hurt in the past, and she ran to keep herself from getting hurt again. Now she was hunkering down in the starting blocks, ready to take off all over again.

"I know we didn't get a chance to talk through the specifics, but let me tell you this," I said, tapping a fingertip to her chest. "You and me? We're very much real."

"You're just saying that," she murmured. "You're good at the getting-laid sweet-talk."

"I should spank you for suggesting I'd use a line on you," I said lightly.

"Try it and I'll castrate you," she said. "Really, though.

There's a Swiss Army knife in my pocket that's just waiting to stab some sac."

I leaned back and met her eyes, nodding when I realized she was serious. She was a broken girl. *Was*. This woman was like roughly patched steel, rusty and thick with scars at the joints, but stronger for it.

And proficient in knife-wielding, apparently.

"Yeah, okay," I said. "Give me the rules, darlin'."

"It's nothing," she said, waving me away.

"It's something. I can't respect your limits if you don't define them for me." Erin folded her arms under her chest. I swallowed a groan because goddamn it, those tits were on a silver platter and she was having doubts and somehow —*some-fucking-how*—we were no closer to a bedroom. "Now you're taunting me," I said through a clenched jaw.

"Not intentional," she said, dropping her arms and reaching for me. "But no spanking, okay? None of that."

"That would've fit nicely in the vows, Skip," I said. "You know, the whole 'to have and to hold, until death—or spanking—do you part.'"

"We'll use that for our ten-year vow renewal, okay?"

"Fuck yes," I said. "But only if we can get that guy again. Bartlett. He's gotta be there."

"And the boat, too?" she asked. "Should we recreate the entire night?"

I scratched the back of my neck, considering. "If we can do it without the lobster sorting, yeah. I don't love the aroma of drying seaweed on me."

Erin nodded knowingly. "Yeah, I need to get these clothes off."

"Now we're talking," I cried. "Lead the way, wife."

Heading toward the inn's main entrance, she reached back and grabbed my hand, towing me along with her. It

was different, watching her now. Maybe it was the perspective or the morning sunlight, or the way she had her shoulder-length hair tied in a messy tail. Maybe it was that we got
married.

It was wild, and there was no arguing that, but it also
wasn't.

I wanted to kiss every inch of her, every last inch. I
wanted to know her thoughts, her journeys, her worries. I
wanted to understand Erin Walsh, and that *green green green*
told me it would take a lifetime.

"Umm," she said, and I tore my eyes off her ass to follow
her line of sight until it landed on the newest "umm" of the
hour.

I should've known I wasn't getting Erin in bed without
getting through one of her brothers first. They came with a
special brand of cockblocking radar, the sister edition.

Riley was seated on the inn's stone steps, his arms braced
on his knees and his head hanging low. A bottle of Don
Felipe Platinum tequila—a full bottle of the good shit—sat to
his left. He looked as if he'd been wrestling with himself all
night, his hair everywhere and his shirtsleeves wrenched up.
His Sperrys were untied. None of that was terribly
uncommon for Riley. He was the guy who always rolled into
happy hour with a mustard stain on his tie. But here, all
alone, he looked sad and conflicted.

"It's really fucking late," she said. "Or really fucking early.
What're you doing out here, kid?"

He brought his palms to his eyes with a miserable groan
before glaring at me.

"That's unacceptable. Make it stop," he said, pointing to
my hand on Erin's hip. "Didn't think I had to teach you
manners, Nick."

I shook my head at that. "All good here," I said.

"Oh, yeah. He's fine on the manners front," Erin said with a smirk. I gave her hip a meaningful squeeze. There were going to be zero manners when I got that girl naked. "I'm the offender here. I think you know I usually am."

She slipped her hand into my back pocket and pinched my ass. Fuck me, I'd met my match.

"Rogue, I really don't have the stomach for your catastrophes this weekend," he said, rubbing his eyes again. "Seriously. I can't do this with you. For one time in our lives, my problems are actually bigger than any stunt you can pull."

I tilted my head toward him as if that would turn down the accusation in his words, but nope, that didn't change it. I was still annoyed at the way he was speaking to my wife, like she was some bratty little girl who couldn't be trusted with anything. If I'd learned anything tonight, it was that these guys didn't know their sister at all.

"Seriously, no catastrophes, no stunts, nothing," she said, breaking away from me to nestle beside Riley on the steps. She offered me a small shrug, as if conceding that there might have been a stunt or two last night, but Riley didn't need those details right now. "What's your deal?"

His eyes drifted shut, and for a second, his chin quivered enough that I expected tears to fall next. "I've done everything in my power to stop it, E, I really have," he said, his head dropping to her shoulder. "I thought the dominatrix—"

"That was Josie? Or Mila?" Erin asked.

He nodded. "Mila. Josie's the yoga instructor from Tinder who wanted me to pee on her," he said, and we all winced at that. "So, I thought one of them would beat this out of my system, but it hasn't worked. I don't know what to do. I just know that I love her. She's the only one I want, the only one I think about, and I can't have her. I can't even *tell* her."

I met Erin's eyes, and she mouthed, "What the actual fuck is going on here?"

"I *love* Lauren," he continued, and we both struggled to contain our reactions to that one. "But Lauren loves *Matt*, and she's so happy. I don't want her to go through with it, but I don't want to ruin her wedding either."

"I'm sure you wouldn't ruin anything," I said. I reached a hand in his direction and helped him to his feet when he accepted it. "It's gonna be fine. You just need to sleep this off. You know, when we were kids and it was time for bed, my grandmother used to say we were going to Mrs. White's party. I haven't thought about that in years, and now that I say it, I'm not sure it translates cleanly. Regardless, you need to go to Mrs. White's party, dude."

Erin's closed fist was pressed against her mouth as she silently rocked with laughter. I shrugged like *what did you want me to say?*

"My grandmother, she was this little old Mexican lady who believed in magic and ghosts, and the chupacabra, and wacky shit like that, but she had a lot of wisdom, especially at the end. She claimed she was descended from a line of Mayan priestesses who'd conducted virgin sacrifices," I said. "She lived with us on the ranch, and listen, when she said it was time for Mrs. White's party, me and my sisters, we didn't fuck around. We got our asses into bed."

Riley was in his own world of misery and self-pity, and for his part, ignored everything I was saying. My wife, on the other hand, was slowly shaking her head as if she couldn't believe these things I said. Like it was a shtick we had, one where I was a walking non-sequitur and she was the honest-to-goodness woman who loved me.

Motherfuck. It was going to be hard letting her go. And *come on*. We all knew it was happening eventually.

Wanderers of the world didn't spontaneously abandon doctoral programs at Oxford to warm my bed and bear my children.

"I know some cultural anthropologists who'd love to run down the threads of that story," she said. "Especially that ritual bloodletting bit. That's fun."

"Bring it on," I said, reaching for her hand and pulling her up.

"Right, so we're all going to bed," Erin said, patting Riley's shoulder. "Separately. We're all going to bed, but we're going to separate beds."

"Of course," I said. "Lots of different beds."

Riley looked us over as if we were speaking around him in code. Which we were.

"I mean it, Rogue. *Swear.* Promise you won't let me ruin the wedding," Riley said, his bottom lip snared between his teeth and his arms folded over his chest. "Promise you'll punch me in the balls if I try to object because I can't hurt her like that."

Erin leaned over and collected the tequila from the steps. Her eyebrow lifted at the unbroken seal. Another thing we couldn't blame on alcohol right now.

"Happily," she replied. "Now where's your room, kid? Listen to the good doctor's bizarre stories. Sleep makes everything better."

He groaned. "I don't think I have one."

She gave him a hard shove, and it almost sent him stumbling to the ground. That was how bad this situation was: my little lovely could take down all two-hundred-odd pounds and six-and-a-half feet of Riley with one hand.

"How do you not have a room?" she asked. "Batman always has a room."

"That's because Alfred makes his reservations," he

murmured. "*This* Batman fucked up. That, and Shannon said I was supposed to be responsible for myself this weekend, and I forgot to do that. I have no Alfred. I have nothing, nothing at all."

"Shit happens, kid," she said. "We're not going to worry about any of it right now, we're just going to find you a place to crash." Erin glanced at me, her wide eyes asking what we were supposed to do now.

"Head over to my cottage," I said, digging through my wallet to find the keycard. I held it out to him, gesturing toward the beach, where a string of tiny, traditional gray Cape Cod homes stood near the dunes. The entire block of cottages was reserved for the wedding. "It's the one between Shannon and Sam."

Riley's bloodshot eyes swiveled between me and Erin. "This is still unacceptable," he said, snapping up the key. "But I didn't see anything and I'm not saying anything. Just don't let me stop the wedding."

He shuffled down the path toward the cottages, his shoulders slumped. My hand slipped under Erin's t-shirt to touch the small of her back. *Jesus.* She was soft, like a dollop of whipped cream, and that was just her back.

"Your room," I said, skimming the waist of her jeans. "Get me there now."

"In a rush?" she asked. There was a playful twinkle that popped into her eyes sometimes. It was sexy and adorable, and totally devious. I was hooked on that twinkle.

The interior of the inn was quiet, and I was careful to keep my voice low. The last thing we needed was to draw attention to ourselves and run into another Walsh. It was a matter of time until preparations for this evening's event got underway, and we were not getting conscripted into any of that. We were staying far out of sight, out of mind. "Only to get you behind closed doors and naked," I said.

She held up the bottle of Don Felipe when we reached her door. "Didn't think Riley needed to take this with him," she said. "Wait, am I reading the situation right? Is he saying he's in love with...*Lauren*? Lauren, Matt's fiancée?"

"That was my interpretation, yeah," I said, gesturing toward the door. "But I'm not interested in Riley right now."

"That's strange, since he's given us a lot of material this morning." She tapped her keycard against her chin. "I want to process this."

I shook my head slowly, drawing my knuckles down, over my jaw. The scruff scraped against my skin, yielding a rough, raspy sound. "And I want to lick that tequila off your tits, wife."

Snatching the keycard from her fingers, I slipped it into the reader and waited for the *whirl-whoosh* that would grant us some long-overdue privacy. I scooped her up, carry-the-bride-over-the-threshold-style, and kicked the door shut behind us.

My shoes were off, one abandoned right behind another, and three striding steps had us at the foot of the bed. I knew this wasn't a standard-issue marriage, and I knew she would leave and the spell she'd cast on me would go with her, but I smiled down at the woman in my arms. For this weekend, she was mine.

"Can I process while you lick?" she asked.

Her lips were on my neck, and that light pressure triggered a shiver down my spine. It was a hypothalamic response, a reaction tied to emotion and physiological arousal, but I couldn't tell which one was greater. I was feeling a whole hell of a lot, but I was also hotter than the sun for this woman.

"You know," I started, squeezing the back of her thigh, "I'm trying to have a moment here. We only get one wedding night, err—morning. I want to savor this. Then I'm gonna savor you, wife."

"You're a special one, husband," she said, and her words were followed by the fine trail of her tongue up my neck.

"Okay, all right," I muttered, setting her down. I plucked the tequila from her hands, and tossed it to the bed. "Go ahead and process. Let's see how long it takes me to turn your attention."

"Do you really think Riley's been hung up on Lauren *all* this time? I didn't think his attention span was that long, and I say that with love. He's a good kid—a good kid who dates a diverse cadre of women—just a bit flighty. How long *has* it been? Matt's been with Lauren since September," she said. I tugged her sweater down her arms, tossed it somewhere. "I remember because I was in the Azores, and then back in mainland Portugal, and I was recovering from my first hang-over in years—"

I yanked my shirt over my head, unbuckled my belt and left my jeans hanging open.

"Oh, I married well," she murmured, flattening her palm on my abs. "And you have the Hot Guy One-Handed Shirt Removal thing down *hard*."

I dragged her hand lower. I'd show her hard. "That wasn't even thirty seconds, Skip."

Her fingers slipped into my boxers, and she dropped her head to my chest as she circled me. She stroked me all the way down and back again, and her breath hitched as I growled into her hair.

"I guess it's true what they say about Texas," she murmured. She looked up at me with those eyes, her bottom lip pushed out in a pout. "Everything *is* bigger."

As far as my cock was concerned, Erin Walsh was the perfect woman and I'd chosen quite wisely last night. Choking on a laugh, I pressed my lips to her forehead. "I want this off," I said, my fingers edging up her t-shirt. "Yeah?"

Erin nodded, lifting her arms as I tugged her shirt up. It was off and flying, and there she was, creamy skin, simple black bra, silver necklace with a compass pendant hanging between her breasts, black diamond at her throat. There were flashes of ink, but those could wait. I'd explore them later.

"And this?" I asked, drawing my finger over the soft skin below her belly button. My thumb traced the button on her jeans, loosening it as she blew out a stilted breath.

"Yeah—but—fuck," she stammered, curling her hand around my wrist. "There are some scars. On my legs. I don't want to talk about it, okay?"

I nodded, and returned her hand to my boxers. "Whatever you want, darlin'. Whatever you want," I repeated. With her button fly popped, I shoved her jeans down. She stepped out of them, and I jerked my chin toward the headboard. "Lie back. Right there."

She stroked me for several glorious moments, and I was growling all over again. That was how she made me feel, like a snarling beast that wouldn't tolerate being caged. It'd never been like this before. I'd wanted women, sure, and even craved a few of them. But I'd never experienced this full-body wave of primal need.

My hand tangled in her hair, and when my lips found hers, I poured that beastly hunger into her. "Get up there, wife," I said, dragging her hand from my cock. "No more teasing."

I gave her a little shove, and she fell to the mattress. She aimed a meaningful glance at my jeans, and that was all the encouragement I needed to drop them to the ground. She crawled backward, and I followed her, stalking her every movement until we were flat against a bank of pillows.

"Hi," she said, running her hand up my flank and over my shoulder. She hooked her leg around my waist and pulled me flush against her. My cock was acutely aware that only my boxers and her panties separated us, and was alternately thrilled with that situation and impatient as hell. She smiled, a little shy. "I like the way you touch me."

"That's good because I really enjoy touching you," I said, bringing my lips to her neck and trailing them down between her breasts. "I didn't want to let you go when I met you last night. Wanted to keep you all to myself."

"Oh," she said, her eyebrow quirking as if this was an odd sentiment. "I don't think anyone's ever wanted to keep me before."

Fuck, she was too much. Just too much. Beautiful and rough around every edge yet vulnerable and secretly sensitive.

"I want to keep you," I said, sliding my fingers behind her back to unclasp her bra. "I'll keep you as long as you let me, lovely." Her arms went to her chest the minute her bra was sailing over my shoulder. "And I want to see you, too."

A groan was rumbling past my lips the second her arms went around my neck and she was bared to me. I thought her tits were a crime in that t-shirt, but I had no idea. They were full and pale, and delicious. I licked and sucked as if I was trying to consume her.

"Say something," she whispered, her fingers raking through my hair. "I want…I want to know what you're thinking."

I released her nipple with a satisfied groan, and then

dropped kisses on each of her breasts before meeting her eyes. "I'm thinking get me inside you right now."

Our lips met as my fingers inched her panties over her hips. I could take her just like this, face-to-face while I tasted her hungry hums, and I'd want for nothing.

"You probably thought I'd be crazy in bed," she said, her words muffled as she spoke against my neck. "Like, I don't know, adventurous and kinky. Like I keep nipple clamps in my back pocket and actually prefer wearing thongs, and I'm always down for anal. And it's my fault, really. This whole night has been pretty wild, and I kissed you like a maniac and then everything on the boat, and it wouldn't be wrong to think that tequila on my tits is an average Saturday morning but—"

"It only matters what you want," I said, tipping up her chin to find her eyes. "Don't worry about what I think, or what you think I'm thinking. Tell me what *you* think."

Erin's fingers clawed at my boxers, and together we got them over my hips and out of the way. Her panties were long gone and my cock was in love with the wet heat between her legs.

"Please don't make it hurt," she whispered.

I shook my head and dropped a kiss on her forehead. "Never."

I kissed down her belly and settled between her legs. I left a trail from hipbone to hipbone, and then down, over her mound.

"Stop," she said, sitting up when I turned my attention to her inner thighs.

The scars—there were more than some. Her skin was marked with one thin line after another. Dozens on each leg. They stopped a couple inches above her knees. It was like a rumble strip, the kind you found on the side of the highway to awaken sleepy drivers. The only bright side was that none of them were fresh.

"I've got you." Erin's breaths were rushing out in shallow heaves, her eyes panicked as if me seeing those scars would change something, even after everything we'd shared. "I've *got* you. Stay there. Watch."

My hands moved from her thighs to her ass, bringing her sweetness to my face. I thought about teasing her for a few minutes, letting her need build until she couldn't imagine a single reason to push me away, but then my tongue met her clit and I couldn't tease her if I tried. If there was anything to be learned from recent history it was that I *wanted* Erin too much to give her anything but exactly what she needed.

"Ohhh," she purred, her arms giving out and her torso dropping back to the bed as I traced her there. She released a sigh that rang with relief, but then layered her hands over her face, hiding from me.

"You're not watching," I said, gazing up the smooth expanse of her belly. Her lips were parted and her back was arching off the bed.

"Can't, too much," she said, her words breaking into a cry.

I flattened my tongue against her clit and sucked. Her legs were shaking around me, her fingers twisted around my hair, and there was a roar climbing up my throat as I watched her shatter. She wasn't loud, and she didn't thrash about, but that didn't make her orgasm any less seismic. Every inch of her was vibrating and flushed with a rosy glow.

I felt like a fucking conqueror.

"Shit, I'm sorry," she panted. "I didn't mean for that to happen."

"Why are you apologizing to me?" I asked, confused.

Uncertain seconds ticked by while I mentally walked through everything that had happened since hitting the bed. I didn't know where I'd gone wrong, and I couldn't take her hiding from me anymore. I needed to see her. I crawled up her body and pried her arms off her face.

"What's wrong?"

"That was like," she started, her eyes swiveling from side to side, "thirty seconds."

I dropped my weight between her legs. "Yeah, I'm pretty fucking pleased with myself, actually," I said, relieved. "Me and your clit? We're gonna be good friends. *Best* friends. I'm thinking we need those broken heart necklaces."

She turned her face to the pillow and said, "My body, it doesn't always know how it should react."

"Your body reacted like a champ, darlin'," I said. "You're perfect. So perfect that I'm kinda dying over here. There's a real possibility that I'm coming on your leg in the next minute. The only thing you're allowed to apologize for is waiting this long to marry me."

"I waited less than a day," she replied.

I shrugged as if she was making my point for me. "Exactly. It should've been 'Hi, I'm Erin, your future wife and owner of the clit to which you'll pray.'"

She burst out laughing beneath me. "You're insane," she said.

"You're *insane*," I retorted, tickling her sides. "You're the one apologizing because I proved that I'm the only one worthy of possessing your body."

"This isn't *The Sword in the Stone*," she said.

"I don't know, lovely," I said, rolling my hips against her. "I've got a sword right here for you."

"Condom," she said through a bark of laughter. "Get a condom."

Goddamn it. God*damn* it.

"Yeah, of course," I stammered, darting off the bed to find my jeans.

I tore through my wallet, but I hadn't kept protection in there since college, back when it was fashionable to show off one's sexual prowess by tucking a supersized rubber behind a student ID. It wasn't that I didn't believe in safe sex. *Of course* I did. But I was a man in my mid-thirties. I didn't have sex outside my apartment. Or hers, and that was all on the rare occasion that I found myself in the company of a willing woman. And I didn't even know the last time that'd happened.

Erin rolled to her belly and propped her chin on her hands, watching while I shuffled through every item in my wallet and came up empty.

Goddamn fucking condoms.

"Check the minibar," she said, nodding toward the cabinet tucked into the television console. "Or call the front desk. I'm sure they'd rustle some up for us."

Everything came out of the minibar. Tiny bottles of liquor and wine, chocolates and nuts, sunscreen and popcorn.

"Let's just drink the tequila," Erin said from behind me, "and then we can get really irresponsible. I'll beg you to let me suck your cock like a lollipop, and you'll convince me that you can pull out."

It was a wonder I didn't come right then.

"Bring me that mouth," I said, beckoning her to me.

She smiled, and pointed to the minibar I'd decimated. "Look again, dude. Top shelf."

Sure enough, I bent at the waist and found myself staring at a single box of condoms. "I *must* start going to church again. I need to thank the Lord for your tits and minibar condoms," I said while I shredded the thin packaging, suited up, and chucked the two spares to Erin. "Don't lose those, wife."

She made a show of carefully placing them in the bedside drawer, right next to the Bible. She was nestled into the pillows again, her legs stretched out in front of her and her arms covering her breasts, and those eyes shy like she didn't want to admit how much she wanted me right now. Like she could hide it.

I crawled to her, wild and hungry. I wasn't hiding it.

"Is this okay?" I asked, settling between her legs. I had one hand curled around her waist, the other flat on her back. My hips were rolling, my cock sliding over her slick skin.

"Yeah," she said. She nodded, her eyes wide as if she was surprised by this. "It's okay, it's good."

But I wasn't convinced, and I was willing to wait for a less tenuous response. I was getting this part right if it killed me.

"Where's that tequila?" I asked, looking around. It was marooned against a pillow on the other side of the bed, and I reached for it. The bulbous cork popped free, and I tossed it over my shoulder. "What do you say, lovely?"

Erin's teeth sank into her bottom lip as she hummed in agreement. I started to pour, a little at first, not wanting to douse the entire bed in alcohol. But goose bumps broke out over her chest, and her nipples were dark, shiny rubies demanding my attention, and then I poured *a lot*. Her shoulders shot up as a shiver moved through her body when the cool liquid splashed down her torso and pooled in her belly button.

"Now who's going to clean that up?" she asked, her lips pushed out in a small pout.

Kneeling between my wife's legs with my cock standing at high alert and a bottle of tequila dangling between my fingers, I knew this was right. This was *real*. Nothing else mattered, not her scars, not her brothers, not the distance between my life and hers, not the hours we'd known each other. Nothing but the moment when all of her vulnerabilities faded and the woman I knew on some raw, instinctual level was revealed.

I leaned down, bowing to her, and sipped tequila from her skin. I followed the paths the sticky liquid had traveled, licking her belly and breasts as I throbbed against her core. My tongue rolled over her nipple until her fingers found my hair and she arched back, moaning. I leaned up and kissed her, swallowing her sighs.

There was no multitasking this morning, no smooth moves. I was focused on searing these moments into memory because this was our last first time.

"I'm ready now," she whispered, wrapping her legs around my waist. "I need you."

I hummed against Erin's lips, my eyes closed and my forehead touching hers. Angling my hips, I thrust inside her and a flash of unbelievable pleasure shot up my spine. She was hot and tight and all the wonderful things that went along with good sex, but she was also *mine* and that changed everything.

"Oh, *fuck*, you're enormous," she panted out, her lips twisting in a grimace and her eyes squeezed shut.

"Are you okay? Do you need me to stop?" I asked, slowing my movements. I planted my hands on either side of her head and stared down at her. "Or are you trying to get me harder? You've succeeded, by the way."

"Don't stop, don't stop, don't stop," she whispered.

"Thank God," I said as she pulsed around me.

I pressed my lips to her neck and shoulders, licking and sucking while she gripped my hair and mumbled quiet words. There was a series of "Oh, oh, oh" and then "Please, and—oh fuck, *fuck*" and "Where did…how…Nick, oh yes…" while I stroked harder.

I hooked my arm under her leg, and that small adjustment had her eyes popping open. "You're the best husband in the world," she said. "I can't even believe that you're *mine*. That you're for *me*."

This woman, she always knew exactly what I needed to hear.

There were no more words, just the bedsprings, the slap of skin, and gasps and murmurs. We came within seconds of each other, one rough cry after another. Neither of us moved, instead panting and kissing and touching like we were teaching our bodies how to remember. She was probably sore and smothered under my weight, and I had to ditch this condom but none of that was urgent enough to tear us apart.

Erin yawned and I dropped a peck on the corner of her mouth. "Tired?" I asked.

She nodded, smiling up at me. "Stay with me," she said. "Stay *right here*."

Her hands were on my body, clutching me as if she was trying to tear off a pound of flesh to keep as her own and I wanted to give her that. Anything, I'd give it to her, and I didn't even try to understand that urge.

Five

ERIN

WARM WATER POUNDED down on my back as I dropped my head to my knees. I needed a timeout, a few minutes to breathe without Nick's—my *husband's*—gaze following my every move. We'd slept for a couple hours, but his embrace was too warm and I was too grimy from the flight, the boat, the sex, all of it.

Timeouts worked for me. Even saying that word over and over helped quiet my mind. *Timeout, timeout, timeout.*

That's what my therapist called it, a timeout from all the things I'd used to keep me numb.

And, yeah. Therapy. As much as I'd fought it, skipping out on therapy wasn't an option.

Not after a big, big bottle of sleeping pills. Not after a paring knife dug three ditches in my right wrist. Not after the pills turned my cheeks hot, and nothing, *nothing* at all hurt anymore, and then the blood pouring from my arm turned my limbs cold and the fear crept into the edges of my consciousness. Not after waking up in the adolescent psych ward at McLean Hospital. Not after telling Shannon I'd never speak to her again.

Matt was a lot of things but he wasn't a pushover, and he tolerated my unrelenting hatred of every psychiatrist in Boston. He tolerated it, but he never let me stop the search.

Rhonda Brissett wasn't a pushover either, and she told me under no uncertain terms that I was finished with sex. And drinking. And pills. And cutting. All of it, it was over, if I had any interest in counting another birthday.

I did, I really did.

She let me run away but only because she believed I couldn't recover in Boston. It was the land of bad decisions, bad memories, bad people. That first year in Hawaii, when I discovered the taste of true loneliness and homesickness, we had phone sessions every other day.

But then, when the second year rolled around, I found fire.

Maybe the fire found me. I still wasn't sure, but Rhonda and I cut our calls to twice a week.

That fire, I *understood* it, and it was wild to think this way, but the fire understood me, too. I found new patterns in the geologic record, quiet signals in the volcanic noise, and I feared nothing about those explosive mountains because I recognized their fury. For the first time in my entire life, I was smart and accepted and *good* at something, and I wasn't suffocating with the sense that I was a used-up piece of trash anymore.

By the time I graduated from the University of Hawaii at Manoa—a full year early because I couldn't get enough of my studies and I couldn't go home—Rhonda and I were down to once a week. I was still on the sex-drugs-danger-to-myself timeout, but that didn't figure into my daily life. Men didn't register on my radar. Neither did women, despite my roommate's repeated suggestions that I give her a whirl. When the occasion called for it, I sipped a beer but rarely finished one. There was, of course, some Portuguese moon-shine, but that was a once-in-a-lifetime experience.

And *everything* didn't hurt anymore. Plenty of things hurt often enough to notice, but it wasn't everything and it wasn't always, and that was an eternity away from having my stomach pumped and my veins patched.

It was three years ago when Rhonda started nudging me toward relationships, and she revisited that topic when we spoke in late December, after Angus's death. It was the first time we'd connected in eleven months, and she reminded me that I'd survived and I'd keep surviving. Oh, and I needed to get back to work on the whole 'interacting with humans' thing. I wasn't good at relationships. I wasn't good with people—some called me *prickly*, others preferred *bitch*—and I was only able to get away with that because I was fucking great with volcanoes.

But I didn't always want to get away with it. I'd regretted leaving places without saying proper goodbyes, and moving on to new adventures without committing to staying in touch. I'd worked with a dozen field study and laboratory teams, lived in six cities, and finished one and started another doctorate degree—geology and geophysics, and atmospheric, oceanic, and planetary physics, if you must know—and I could only count my friends on one hand. None of them knew about sleeping pills or paring knives or Shannon abandoning me in a psychiatric hospital for a month. And even those friends teetered closer toward acquaintances than individuals willing to bring me chicken soup when I was sick or celebrate my lobster-boat marriage.

I didn't know how to do relationships. I didn't even know how to start the conversation, and for that, I came off as aloof, disinterested, pretentious. But the one thing I did know was how to be destructive. I knew how to burn not just bridges but boats, villages, and churches. Burn it all down before it burned me too.

"Knock, knock."

My gaze whipped to the door, but it was still shut. Thank God. I needed a few more minutes before dealing with my I-dare-you-to-marry-me husband. I really did run headfirst into catastrophes.

"Erin?" he called. "You've been in there for a bit, darlin'. Everything okay?"

I held up my hand and stared at my water-pruned finger-tips. Maybe I'd lost track of how long I was taking for this timeout.

"Yeah, great," I said. "I was pretty dirty. Taking some time to get clean, you know?"

"I'd apologize for that, but I wouldn't mean it so I'm not going to." His laugh rumbled from the other side of the door, and it sent a curl of warmth through me. "Want some help?"

"Ummm." I stared at my toes and the tile and all the water that I was wasting. "Not really."

There was a pronounced *thunk* against the door, and I imagined it was his forehead dropping there. He wanted me to say yes, to invite him in and wow him with sensational shower sex.

I didn't come equipped with that feature.

"Take your time, darlin'," he called. "I'm not going anywhere."

Eventually, the water ran cool and I found my way off the shower floor. I scrubbed my hair and skin, maybe a little harder than necessary. When I stepped out, the wide bath-room mirror caught everything. The red welts from my scrubbing, the fingertip-sized shadows along my ribs and backside that would darken to bruises, the love marks on my breasts and belly. My hands skimmed down, lightly touching each one. It was as if I didn't know whether they hurt until I poked them.

They didn't. *None* of this hurt.

I finger-combed my hair and changed into the t-shirt and undies I'd snagged on my way into the bathroom. Bright sunshine was peeking through the curtains in the bedroom and it shot warm, glowy fingers of light to Nick's bare abs. He was leaning back against the headboard, the sheets bunched around his waist. Naked underneath, of course.

He offered me a lazy smile while he rubbed a hand down his chest. I leaned against the wall, watching as that hand followed the dark trail of hair beneath the sheets. Slow and unashamed, he stroked himself. No taboo to be found. I tugged my lips between my teeth, a silly attempt at concealing my smile.

"Clean?" he asked.

I didn't have an answer ready, not when a single word was packed with filthy suggestions. Instead I shrugged, and dropped more of my weight onto the wall. The top of my foot was skating over my calf. His eyes followed my foot while he stroked, a little faster now, as if the slide of my skin could turn him on.

Nick held out his free hand to me. "Come back to me," he whispered. I pushed off the wall. "Be here with me, Skip. I need you."

I took his hand, and he yanked me to the bed.

"Want you," he whispered into my hair. "Want that pussy."

"That word is *awful*," I said, cringing. "Say something better."

"Bite your tongue, wife," he said. He brought my ring finger to his lips, kissing it as if he could force me to acknowledge that our vows were authentic. That they were more than a dark-of-night dare. "And now I want you to explain to me what's wrong with pussy."

His hand slipped under my shirt and moved down my belly with all the leisure in the world, and his knuckles brushed back and forth over my panties. I didn't like that word either. *Panties*. Ick. It sounded delicate and precious and *girly*. And it wasn't that I abhorred girly things or took issue with *being a girl*, but I did hate the stereotypical nature of it all.

Pussies and panties and the rest of the socially ingrained shade machine that stomped all over the strength and power of women. It was amusing how much of the universe was on board with regulating and governing all over women without recognizing that we *all* came from pussies. It was good enough to give you life, but not good enough for a little dignity, right?

The goddamn patriarchy. Fucking obnoxious.

But here was the problem with all that: I wasn't upset about panties or pussies right now. It was moments like this one that made me wish I wasn't aware of the inner workings of my every thought and reaction. At least not *this* much. If I was blissfully ignorant, I wouldn't know that I was winding myself up with this self-righteous rant because then I could gather my indignation and breathe through the tightness in my chest.

It was easier to argue and lash out than it was to admit that I was afraid. Afraid that he was a solid wall of muscle, and could hold me down without trouble. Afraid that he'd be different this time. Afraid that I'd read him wrong and he wasn't a kind man. Afraid that I was new to relationship sex (also, relationships), and doing it all wrong. Afraid that I wanted this, and I wanted to enjoy it.

Afraid that I liked him. Maybe a lot. Maybe more than I could manage.

I was scared and that wasn't an emotion I willfully accepted. I'd spent years kicking fear's ass and purging it from my life, and I didn't give a single fuck if that meant I'd pushed everyone and everything far enough away that I never had to risk feeling anything.

And within the span of a single night, a necklace brought me to my knees, my sister blew a hole through my confidence, I'd revealed the worst of myself to a stranger, and then I married him. Fear was everywhere.

"You're going to give yourself a headache if you keep thinking that hard," he murmured. He tucked me into his side and ran his thumb down the center of my forehead, smoothing the tension bunched there. "Now I'm the curious one. What's wrong with pussy?"

I shrugged, and my shoulder bumped against his hard chest. "I don't like the sound of it. If you're going to talk about my dewy petals—"

"Oh, stop right there, darlin'," he interrupted. "*Dewy petals*?"

"Yep," I said, peeking up at him with a teasing smile. I softened a bit every time he called me *darlin'*. There was nothing to be afraid of when I was someone's darlin'. "Petals sounds so much better than pussy. Whenever I hear pussy, I think of warm pudding. That's not sexy. Have you ever met warm, sexy pudding? I haven't. I want to be a flower instead."

Nick's arm curled around my shoulder and pressed me flat against his chest. "I want to study your brain," he said, laughing. "You're accessing regions the rest of us don't even know about."

His fingers were drawing circles on the small of my back

and his cheek was on my head and his heart was beating against mine and my breath caught as I felt everything *faster faster faster*. I was trembling from the inside out. It started under my breastbone before engulfing my stomach, and it was about to take over my entire body. It had all the makings of an anxiety attack but instead of breaking out into a cold, clammy sweat, I melted against Nick.

This wasn't panic…it was anticipation. I wanted to be here with Nick. I had to reach far back to get my hands around that sensation, and in doing so, I recognized that I'd never *chosen* to be close to someone in this way. Not the right kind of choices, not really. Only Nick. This was different, and completely overwhelming.

"Wouldn't that involve cracking my skull open?" I asked, struggling against the quiver in my voice.

Nick's head bobbed against mine. "Nah, we don't need to do that. Technology, it's advanced a bit," he said. "Now tell me about the other words you don't like."

"Twat is awful. Pure awful," I said. "It's a rather shabby term. It's not particularly dirty but it also doesn't carry any reverence. My dewy petals"—he snickered at that—"deserve more respect than twat. When most Americans say twat, it sounds like they're choking on a chicken nugget. It sounds better with certain accents, but that's not the word for me. Twat is in the same category as snatch, as far as I'm concerned. At least cunt is revered."

His hand moved down my back, slipping under my undies to caress the skin there. "You're saying you prefer cunt?"

"Shannon hates that word," I murmured. "But you probably know that."

"Don't do that," he said. "I've never told Shannon that my grandmother believed, right up to the day she died, that my mother was trying to have her deported. I've never agreed to steal a lobster boat with Shannon, and I definitely haven't married her either."

He ran his nose along my neck with a needy growl. Fuck, I liked that sound. It screwed with my feminism to admit this, but I liked reducing him to his basest instincts. I liked him hungry for me, and desperate to kiss and bite and growl and fuck. Or maybe that was exactly how feminism was supposed to go.

"Can we go back?" I asked. "What were we talking about before the pussies?"

"Me wanting you," Nick said. "I always want you."

"How can you say that? You met me last night, and—"

There. I'm doing it again. Burning everything down before it begins.

I nodded to myself and blinked up at the ceiling before grabbing another condom from the drawer.

"Come here," I said, pulling Nick on top of me. I ran my palm over the tattoo on his bicep. It was a circular maze, one larger than my entire hand, with spear points that seemed to form a compass. It was just like the compass on my wrist, but layered with mythology and ancient history. "What's this all about? I really hope I didn't marry one of those faux-tribal tattoo guys. That would be terrible."

"Terrible?" he repeated, laughing.

"Completely terrible," I said. I held up the condom, glancing at it as if to say, *Put this on now before I talk myself out of it for entirely irrational reasons*. "The only thing worse would be Chinese characters on your ankle that translate to something entirely different than you think."

He rolled the condom on while I wiggled out of my shirt and undies. "It's the Mayan calendar," he said. His thumb was passing over my nipple, and I really wanted his mouth there. "I got it after my grandmother died."

"You were really close to her," I said. "Could you maybe, um"—I jerked my chin in the direction of his thumb—"uh, use your mouth instead?"

"I'd be happy to," he responded with a sharp nod, and then turned his attention to licking my nipple. That was surprisingly simple, and I was only halfway to bursting into embarrassed flames. "You can ask for anything at all, lovely."

"Mmm, okay," I mumbled. Still halfway to self-immolation.

"What's on the back of your shoulder?"

"*Alis volat propriis,*" I said. "She flies with her own wings."

"Mmmm, that you do."

He levered up on one arm, and smiled down at me as he pressed against my center. This cock of his was an exaggeration. It was the kind of appendage guys pretended they had, and they made sure everyone heard all about it, too.

"I still want you, you know. All these weird things you've said? They just make me like you even more," he continued. His grin said that he knew all about the living legend he had in his pants. "Not the nipple licking thing. That wasn't weird, but the rest of it, the dewy petals and the twats."

I brought my hands to his hips, tugging him closer. "There are tornadoes in my head sometimes," I said, my words growing progressively sharper as he pushed inside me.

"I know," he said as his lips met mine. "But your storms, they don't scare me."

MATT AND LAUREN'S wedding was nothing like my own. They had all the trappings of tradition that Nick and I'd skipped last night. Pretty dress, suit and tie, flowers, rings.

We had a lobsterman named Bartlett.

I couldn't decide if the moonstruck urgency of it all made us silly, or that much more serious. As I watched Lauren floating down the petal-strewn aisle on her father's arm with a photographer tucking and rolling around her to get the best shots, I knew she'd have every second of this day documented. Did that make this iteration better or more meaningful, or was it just planned better?

Not that it mattered. Our marriage was a whim, pure and simple, and it would end. At the next Walsh wedding—I was betting on Patrick and the apprentice with all the hair—Nick and I would share a drink and laugh about the wild night when we got married. It would be better that way. I didn't know how to care for a houseplant, let alone another human being, and I'd built my life to those specifications. Love, it wasn't something I could do.

"This is horrible," Riley said, turning away when the officiant started with "Dearly beloved..."

I swung my arm around his shoulders in support. "I know, kid," I whispered. "It'll be over soon."

Nick glanced over his shoulder from the row ahead. He shot a concerned frown at Riley, but I shook my head.

"He's fine," I mouthed. I circled my finger, gesturing for him to turn around.

He didn't.

Nick's gaze pawed over my dark blue dress, stopping first at the v-neck and then raking down the bodice. He stared at my legs, exposed at the knee, significantly longer than necessary.

"I want under that skirt," he mouthed.

"Turn around," I whispered, swatting him with the wedding program. He obeyed my request this time, but not without sending a longing gaze to my breasts. It wasn't gratuitous, and I wasn't objectified. If anything, I was treasured, and that was powerful for me.

The ceremony concluded with a kiss that was too intimate for this audience, and it had Riley dropping his head between his legs. I couldn't tell whether he was nauseous, dizzy, or just avoiding this exceptional display of affection, and I went on patting his back.

"It's over," I said after Matt and Lauren made their way up the aisle.

"I need a scotch on the motherfucking rocks," Riley said, wrenching his tie loose as he stood. He didn't wait for me to protest, and I didn't offer. I knew he wasn't going to hear it right now.

It was odd seeing Riley hung up on anything, let alone Matt's new wife. Growing up, he took a lot of hits from Angus, and then he took even more after stepping in to protect me. But through it all, Riley never allowed any of it to bother him. He wasn't haunted by it the way Sam was, and he didn't need to bury it under a mountain of self-inflicted pain like me. He drew in his sketchbook and smoked a lot of weed in the attic, and those were his coping mechanisms.

A hand settled on my back, and I found Nick at my side. "Come on, lovely," he said. "I meant what I said about getting under that skirt."

He led me around the backup of guests showering the happy couple with well wishes, and through a side entrance to the inn. His long legs gobbled up the stairs, and then he had me pinned to my door. His lips ghosted over my neck as his fingers ran up and under my dress to land on my backside.

"Where's your purse?" he asked, his gaze swiveling between my empty hands. "Where's your stuff?"

I reached into the side of my bra and produced my key. "I don't have fancy party purses. All the important stuff's in here," I said, cupping my breasts.

"I'm gonna say this right now: I love you. You're going to tell me I'm ridiculous, but I don't care because you just pulled stuff out of your tits. You're incredible," Nick said as he grabbed the keycard.

"You're right," I said, "you *are* ridiculous."

We were inside within a heartbeat, and he backed me up against the wall.

"They're going to be looking for us," I murmured against Nick's mouth while he slipped out of his suit coat.

"Let them," he said, dropping to his knees in front of me. True to his word, he dove right under my skirt.

My panties were off. My leg was over Nick's shoulder. I had one hand in his hair, one hand flat against the wall for some semblance of balance. But then his tongue stopped doing that crazy-amazing thing that made my toes curl.

He stopped, pressed the softest kiss in the world to my clit, and said, "You are so fucking beautiful right here."

Oh, Jesus. That one hit me hard, and it hit a spot I didn't understand. "Take me," I said, gasping as I pushed his head away, "to the bed. I want you now."

Nick stood, his hands on my backside as he lifted me up. "Yeah?" he asked.

I sighed against his neck, smiling. He was always checking in, asking if I was okay. He'd taken all of my caution and sexual awkwardness, and made it part of our normal. Someday, when he wasn't squeezing my ass, I was going to let that sink all the way in. "Yes," I said, "and take your pants off, too."

My husband, he didn't need to be asked twice. Within an eye blink, I was flat on my back with my skirt around my waist, and within another blink, Nick was pushing inside me. We cried out in unison, a noisy mash up of groans and sighs and swears meant to express that this—this insane, not-gonna-last thing we were doing here—was too amazing for regular words.

I grabbed his tie, yanking him close to me. "What makes this so good?" I asked. "Is it because we're married, or because you're just that incredible in bed?"

"Yes," he said, smiling down at me.

"Don't be a logical asshole while you're fucking me," I said, laughing.

Nick slowed, retreating until I was empty. "Would you rather I stop?" he asked.

"No," I cried. "I'm not done with you yet, and no teasing about stopping."

"It only seems fair," Nick said. His hand moved to the

back of my neck, his fingers tangling in my hair, and he leaned down to kiss me. "And if you giggle again while my dick's inside you, I can't be held responsible for this ending quickly."

I laughed. I couldn't help it. "I'm sorry," I cried as Nick growled into my neck. "You didn't judge me for coming too quick this morning, so I won't judge you. It'll be our little secret."

"One of many," he murmured as he thrust into me again. "But let's just see if I can fuck the giggles right out of you, lovely."

Oh yeah. He did exactly that.

"HOW LONG UNTIL I can get you back here?" Nick asked, meeting my eyes in the bathroom mirror. I was fixing my smudged mascara; he was attempting to blow dry the wrinkles from his shirt and tie. My hair was a mess and a bright flush still lingered on my cheeks, neck, and chest. We both looked thoroughly fucked.

"Listen, dude. You have to pretend we're nothing more than acquaintances and stay on your own damn side of this reception."

"Fuck," he said. "I hate that. You're the smart one in this marriage. Come up with something better."

I spared him a glance. "That's your option. I have a long, messy history of fucking up other people's nice things, and I'm not doing that tonight. Neither are you, for that matter, and we need to watch out for Riley," I said. "Oh, I almost forgot. One of Lauren's brothers is supposed to be keeping me in line, so—"

"The fuck he is," Nick snapped. "Which one? I'll sedate him for the night."

I ran a brush through my hair and smiled at him in the mirror. "It's okay. I can shake him. He's not especially dedicated to the cause."

I ran my hand over Nick's shoulders, plucking off a strand of red hair that was clinging to his shirt. It gave me a moment to study the long lines of his body, and admire him in a suit. This worked for him, but I also knew he'd look good in anything. Almost as good as he looked in nothing at all.

"You know, I could stand here watching you think dirty thoughts about me all night," he said, catching my eye in the mirror. "Please, continue."

I couldn't help myself. "What do you wear at the hospital?" I asked. In my head, I had him dressed up in scrubs like my own little Spanish Ken doll.

"Come back to the city with me tomorrow night," he said, "and you can find out for yourself."

No, that wasn't one of our options. The end of our weekend wasn't among the things I wanted to think about right now. Pivoting, I ran my hand down Nick's back. "Let's go be strangers."

We maintained a civil distance for the remainder of the evening, always averting our eyes before a glance turned into a gaze. I got to know Patrick's apprentice, Andy, over sweet vermouth, and she was a treasure. She had all the right cool and quirky to go with Patrick's dark and grumpy, as impossible as it seemed.

Nick was on the other side of the tent with Riley, and everything about their posture said they were talking sports. When men were standing together, angled at forty-five degrees with one hand on the waist while the other hand cut sharp, definitive signs in the air, the topic was college or professional sports. If there was any doubt, their expressions gave the rest away. Their faces morphed as if they were offering incontrovertible fact only for their opponent to volley back the argumentative equivalent of a stale cracker.

I didn't want to interrupt that. Not when I could observe from a distance and invent new ways to be completely irresponsible with my husband.

While I waited for the right time to steal Nick away, I discovered that Lauren's brother Wes and I knew all the same expat hideouts in Italy, and that he was only on board with this babysitting mission to keep his sister happy. He was primarily concerned with whether he'd get time with his fuck buddy while on leave this weekend. Andy asked *one question* about the buddy, and Wes answered with the most detailed history of every time they'd been together, right down to longing stares across a briefing room. He wasn't heartsick so much as hung up on this guy.

That was a shabby situation, but after telling his forever-long story, Wes got a text and hightailed it out of the beach-side reception tent. Andy left for a walk along the shore, and I blew out the don't-screw-up-the-wedding breath I'd been holding all night.

Seven

NICK

ERIN'S FINGERS were in my hair and her mouth on my neck, and my hips were jerking up, desperate for her heat but also painfully aware that we were on a patio chair, with waves crashing only a few yards away. Translation: the wrong place to fuck my wife.

"You," I said, my lips on her jaw. "*You* did this to me. You're a witch, darlin'. Wicked, wicked, wicked witch."

"What are you talking about?" Erin murmured. She shivered, but it had nothing to do with my technique. The night was heavy with fog, and the damp air had her skin pebbled with goose bumps. Where were the goddamn beds when I needed them? "You're the one who had to stop halfway down the path. *You* couldn't make it to the cottage, not me. This is about endurance, not witchcraft."

My hands landed on her ass and I yanked her down, hard enough to feel her wetness through my trousers. "You're the one who took your panties off, dropped them in my lap, and then proceeded to do shots with Andy for half a damn hour," I said. "You did this."

"I had *one* shot, and you're the one who forgot to grab

condoms from your room when you got dressed for the wedding," she said, gesturing down the path connecting the cottage to the inn's main building. "Perhaps that was your subconscious telling you to stop having sex with me."

That was it. That was fucking *it*.

I reached between us, fighting with my belt and zipper and nearly mutilating myself in a feverish attempt at getting my cock free. "Or my subconscious doesn't like the idea of fucking my wife with a condom," I said.

"Yeah?" she asked, taking me between her folds and shuttling over me before allowing me to slip inside.

I caught her nipple between my fingers and tugged hard enough for her to know that I wasn't playing. "It's like I've been trying to fuck every one of those damn things off," I said.

"Have you made peace with God yet? I'm not sure you should be pulling and praying until you've atoned," she said.

"Why do I always walk in on this shit?"

Groaning, I turned my head just enough to catch a glimpse of Riley. But it wasn't just Riley. Nope, that would've been too easy.

"Shit," Erin whispered as Shannon and Lauren's brother Will stared at us. My hand was on her breast, and that was what they *could* see. I was straight up groping her in front of her brother, her sister, and a guy who could snap me in half with one hand, and we had a game of Just the Tip going on under her skirt.

"Could you not wait until you got inside?" Riley yelled.

"I dare you to tell them that we're married," Erin whispered. "That would add some spice to this conversation. Maybe even some legitimacy."

"It doesn't lack for spice, darlin'," I said.

"This fucking night...I'm tellin' you," Riley said. There was blood all over his shirt, and his nose appeared newly broken. "I just want to go to sleep but no, I get punched in the goddamn face and swallow a pint of my own fucking blood, and I don't even get to stay on the couch!" He glared back at Shannon and Will, shaking his head.

"Why isn't he in your cottage?" Erin asked under her breath. "And what happened to him? Can we not leave him alone for five minutes?"

I cut a glance at her. "Why don't you ask him that?" I challenged. "Then you can explain to Shannon and Captain America where your panties went."

"Captain America?" she whispered while Riley glowered at Shannon and Will. "You come up with that on your own?"

I shook my head. "Riley."

"Ah," she said knowingly. Riley was the Jedi Master of nicknames. "Maybe you can ask them if they have any condoms."

Will and Shannon were barely clothed. She was wrapped in a short, thin robe that kept catching the wind and flying up, exposing her thighs. He was wearing boxer briefs and a scowl. "We're too late for that," I said. "They've used them all. All the condoms on the Cape."

Riley shifted to face us, equally furious as he was with his older sister. "You really want Matt to blow a gasket on his wedding night? Really? Because that's what would happen if he saw this. I can't even go there with you two. Can't. Even."

"There's no reason to tell Matt," Erin said easily.

"Don't tell Matt? Are fuckin' kidding me, E? You're here one day and you're starting shit like this?" Riley yelled, pointing at me. "No, no. *No one* is telling Matt a fucking thing about any of this." He gestured to both his sisters. "We're all pretending none of this happened. We're pretending there's no attention-whoring or hate-fucking going on right now."

"Am I the attention whore or the hate fucker?" Erin whispered.

I held up my hand, trying to walk back some of Riley's frustration. "I think you might be exaggerating the situation, buddy," I said. "Really, we're just having some drinks and hanging out."

"You might be a smart guy, Nick," Riley said, "but right now, you have no idea what you're talking about. And you —" He pointed at Erin. "If you don't want shit storms everywhere you go, don't stir them up."

"Riley," Erin said, and his gaze snapped to her. "I got this."

"You fucking owe me," Riley called as he walked past me and Erin, his head shaking and his hands fisted at his sides. "All of you fucking owe me."

Riley disappeared down the path, and Shannon studied us a beat longer before returning to her cottage with Will in tow.

"That was your fault," Erin said as she choked out an uncomfortable laugh.

"No way," I said. "All on you. You take your panties off, you kiss my neck, your fault."

She wiggled her shoulders, definitely not taking responsibility for anything, and nodded in Riley's direction. "We should wander that way," she said. "He's a big boy, but he'll sleep on the beach if we let him."

"Okay, sure, we can follow him," I started, "but we're not going on a humanitarian mission tonight. We're putting him to bed, getting condoms, and then going back to your room and hanging the Do Not Disturb sign."

"Me? On a humanitarian mission? Unlikely." Erin pointed to herself, and that drew my attention to her breasts. She brought her fingers to my chin, tipping my eyes upward. "That was almost gratuitous, Doctor Acevedo, and I liked it. You can do it again later. After you've refilled your condom supply."

"Understood. Off you go," I said, lifting her from my lap. I tucked myself into my trousers as I gained my footing, and followed as she headed in Riley's direction.

We found him at the far end of the path, his head hanging low and his fingers on his temples.

"What the hell is going on?" I asked. "You have my room key. Why aren't you in there?"

He laced his fingers together at the nape of his neck and blew out an aggravated breath. "I left the key in the goddamn room, and," he said, tipping his head toward me and Erin, "I didn't want to bang on the door get an eyeful of this."

"What happened to you?" Erin asked, gesturing to his face while I dug through my wallet for the other room key.

Riley laughed humorlessly. "I can't even begin to explain it," he said. "No, wait. It's not that complex. I walked in while Captain America was *conspiring* with the Black Widow, and since Batman isn't one of the Avengers, I got tossed out on my ass. Or face, or whatever."

She nudged me, glimpsing to Riley. "Go make sure he's okay."

"I thought this wasn't a humanitarian mission, Skip," I murmured.

She didn't answer, only looking up at me with her lips pursed in a tiny pout. It wasn't intended as manipulative, but more than that, it wasn't intended as a gesture of concern, either. I didn't think she realized how much she cared, and if she did, she didn't want anyone else to know about it.

"Goddamn it. We're goin' to the cottage, RISD," I said, pointing at him. "I need some decent light to check out your face, and you—" I turned back to Erin. "—are shivering." I shrugged out of my suit coat and draped it over her shoulders. Leaning close, I whispered, "I can see your nipples through that dress. Stay covered, or we're not making it back to the room after this."

"And I can see your dick through those pants," she replied.

I pressed my thumb to her lips. "You will have to fight me," I said. "You might leave, but I'm not letting go of you. If that's what you want, you'll have to fight me."

Eight

ERIN

NICK and I existed in a sphere that knew no time. Sleeping, eating, none of it mattered. Who needed rest when we could talk about science or music, or indulge in the wild need we had for each other? It was an unending surge of fight-or-flight, one gut-fluttering peak after another, and instead of escaping a saber-toothed tiger, we were blind to the eventuality that our weekend would end.

"I want to know about you and Shannon," he said, drawing circles on my belly.

"We don't talk anymore," I whisper-sighed. The technical term for this condition was *sated*. I was most wonderfully sated, and my body hummed with the contentment of being used in the best ways. Everything was loose and warm, and it made the words fall from my lips with ease. "It's complicated."

"Try me," he said.

I started to disagree, but then I realized I wanted nothing more than to drop my weapons and walk away from this fight. A small, petty part of me laughed at that, reminding me that *of course* I'd be the one to capitulate first. I might've been the stalwart here, but Shannon was the brute strength. She did everything I couldn't, and she did it better.

"I send her rocks," I said, as if that made a lick of sense. "I found the first one along the Chile-Argentina border when I was watching deformation trends at Copahue. That's a stratovolcano with a lake-filled crater, and it sprang to life about one million years ago. In the past decade, it's seen some action. Pyroclastic rock ejections, constant fumarolic activity, chilled liquid sulfur fragments, a lake that drained and then subsequently refilled. As you can see, I had my hands full."

He met my eyes, nodding as if he understood that I couldn't simply say 'a big volcano in South America' and not because I was an unapologetic geology geek. I needed the cushion of these technical words to wade into the ones that were far less objective. He pulled the blanket up, and tucked it tight around us.

"Anyway, I was hiking around the cone one morning. I wasn't looking for anything, just trying to get a feel for the pulse of it," I said. "I found a stream, one that seemed to originate from Copahue's glacial peaks. There was some rough quartz in there. I didn't really think about it when I sent it to her, it just felt like something I needed to do. Shannon used to tell me this story, about Mom bringing a little rock collection here with her when she emigrated from Ireland. That leaving home was scary, and those pieces of earth were all she needed to find her way back. When I found that quartz, it made sense to me."

"Did Shannon respond?"

"I didn't make it very easy," I said, running my fingers through the dark patch of hair on his chest. I loved that he was fuzzy, and not bald and glossy like a string bean. "No note. No return address. Sure, she could've beaten my email address out of Matt, but what would she have said? 'Hey, did you mail me a rock?'"

Nick laughed at that, and slipped his fingers through my hair. "But you continued sending them?"

"When I discovered something interesting, yeah," I said, but then, with my fingers tracing the hard lines of his chest, thought better of it. "I mean, interesting to people who don't look at rocks all day. The sparkly and shiny things, mostly. I didn't keep a schedule or go looking for something to ship back to Boston. I let the earth show me something worth sharing."

"Did it help?" Nick asked.

"Every time I wrote that address on a shipping label," I said, my cheek pressed up against Nick's shoulder, "it was like I was reminding myself that I could go home at any time."

"But..." he started, his forehead wrinkling in confusion, "you can. Right? Your family, I've known them a few years now, and while I don't know what happened with you and your sister, I do know that you're welcome home anytime. This weekend isn't the exception, lovely."

Nick's hand moved from the small of my back to my hip. He squeezed, punctuating his point.

God, look at us.

We were naked, tangled together, running on mere minutes of sleep as we fought to consummate the shit out of our fledgling marriage, and even managing to knock out some deep conversations about sibling-on-sibling violence. We deserved a medal for our efforts.

"Long story short," I said, dropping kisses on his neck between words. "I went to live with Shannon when I was sixteen."

Nick's lips brushed over my temple and he murmured, "Continue."

I opened my mouth but the words didn't come out. This wasn't a story I was accustomed to telling. It was steeped in years of hurt, resentment, and the omnipresent hint that I should've dealt with my abuse the same way my sister did.

Meet my therapist, she'd said. *It will help.*

Come to the gym with me. It will help.

Focus on school. It will help.

Talk to me. I want to help.

"I told you," I said with a sigh. "I was the kind of girl who reeked of vulnerability and chronically bad choices. I was like a special blend of catnip, the kind designed for deviants and people with flexible morals. I didn't know any of that at the time. God, I didn't know *anything* at the time, but I definitely thought I did. And if you know my sister, you're probably aware that she prefers to be the one who knows everything. Clearly, you don't need my assistance to spell disaster. We had some disasters. That's what happened."

Nick laughed, and I felt curls of his warm breath on my neck.

"I'm on your side, Skip, but I don't buy that you can't sort this out. Talk to Shannon in the morning," he said.

"Matt specifically requested that we keep our issues out of his wedding weekend," I said, and that earned me a skeptical gaze from him. "That's how I ended up with a Navy SEAL babysitter, remember?"

The festivities were coming to a close, and no one would give a damn if I stole some time with my sister. But even if I did reach out, I wasn't the fixer in this relationship. I didn't know how to tear down the wall we'd erected between us—even if I wanted to—and I didn't have the words to make any of this right.

"I never pegged you to take the easy way out," Nick said.

"It's not easy," I said. "That I can promise you."

"But it's a way out," he said, and I nodded. "That's not going to work for me."

His cock was hard on my leg. It was an affliction he couldn't seem to shake, and that gave me a flush of pride. I didn't think I'd taken credit for a man's arousal before Nick. I reached for him, and grinned as he moaned into my hair.

"What's not going to work for you?" I asked, stroking him slowly.

He closed his eyes and breathed deeply. For a second, I thought he was going let me run this show, but then his palm was pressed between my breasts and I was on my back.

"This isn't over," he said. "You can leave but it's not over, lovely."

There was a furious scramble to kick the blankets away, grab a condom, surrender to each other. My hands were balled around the sheets as he drove into me, like that fabric was the only thing keeping me from floating off into space. Maybe it was.

"Say it, Erin," he growled, his fingertips digging into my hips. It stung with the promise of a bruise to come.

I'd asked him not to make it hurt. Pleaded, really, and he'd agreed. But this wasn't the hurt I'd long associated with sex. It was a hug that made your bones creak, a kiss that left your lips swollen, an ache in your chest that was only the product of your heart wanting to tunnel its way out because it belonged to another.

But I knew who I was, and I knew that the spot inside me created specifically for the purpose of loving and being loved was gone. Amputated, like a limb damaged beyond repair in the bloodiest of battles. In its place was a thick stump of scar tissue that had no business feeling anything at all, but that didn't stop the phantom pains.

"Not over," I said. I reached for him, wanting my hands on his body and not these starched sheets because even though I knew who I was and I knew I'd never be the woman Nick deserved, that didn't mean I couldn't *pretend* to be that woman.

Even if only for a few more hours.

Nine

NICK

"YOU COULD STAY," I said, my lips on Erin's back. She had a tattoo there, that stray bit of Latin I couldn't stop kissing. Her body was a map written in scars. The splice in her eyebrow, hidden by a platinum ring. The uneven gashes on her legs and back. The fine crinkle on her cheek. The lines on her inner thighs, the ones on her wrist. I kissed every scar I could, and then I kissed them again. "You could come back to Boston, and we could—"

"I can't, Nick," she said, her voice heavy with remorse. She wasn't running because this was edging past her comfort zone. It was our reality. "You could come to Iceland. I'm sure Iceland needs doctors."

The theory was great but the practice wasn't an option. Getting into this fellowship had been impossible, and staying in it was brutal, but walking away with five months to go was ludicrous. I was nearly finished with the requirements for gaining another board certification, and all of this was nine thousand percent more complicated than the vows we exchanged only twenty-four hours ago. But I didn't feel an ounce of regret. Maybe I should've, or maybe that was a reminder the vows *were* easy and everything we did after could be as easy—or difficult—as we made it.

"The hospital owns my ass right now. My schedule opens up in late November," I said. "I can treat kids in Iceland then, or at least spend some time with you."

Her head bobbed. "I didn't think I'd like you this much when I married you."

"That's not true," I replied. I squeezed her ass for emphasis. "You knew everything that needed knowing."

"Maybe," she conceded. "I mean, Matt has been telling me your secrets for years."

"That's good of him," I said through a yawn.

We'd been up all night. Nothing could stop me from wanting to kiss, talk, lose myself in her, and she was right there with me. I knew exactly what it looked like when Erin wasn't ready or didn't want something, but I hadn't seen those expressions in a good twenty-four hours. She was just as hungry as I was, and equally aware that we didn't have a comfortable solution to the distance between our lives.

Those solutions only existed in the idyllic world where all families were capable of dissolving years-long grudges with a quick heart-to-heart, and pesky issues like board certification requirements and Icelandic research posts were waved away with a magic wand. Our hands were tied, and nothing that transpired here could change any of that.

And I hated it. I wasn't prepared to see her go, and I couldn't get my head around what would come after that. Erin was facing months of intensive study at Oxford and fieldwork in Iceland, and I powering through the final hurdles of my training. Nothing about that was primed for a healthy, happy long distance relationship.

"You know what we should do this morning? Get your whole family around the table for a talk, pour some champagne or maybe something stronger, I don't know."

"Stronger," she said, laughing. "Much stronger."

"See? We can do this, we can solve problems," I said. "So we go straight for the Irish whiskey, announce that we got married—"

"On a lobster boat," she interrupted.

A noise rumbled in my throat, a sound that expressed my disinterest without forming the words. "Details," I chided. "Like I was saying, wife, we tell them that we got married, you and Shannon apologize to each other and decide to join ball-busting forces, and then I keep you forever. Good plan, right?"

Her body rocked with quiet laughter, and all of those vibrations went straight to my cock. Conventional wisdom would suggest that I'd be spent by now. I was expecting my testicles to call me in for a chat and explain that I was using semen more quickly than my body could produce it, but I was also expecting my penis to barge into that meeting and say, "That's just too fucking bad, guys. You're gonna need to work some overtime."

"It's an awesome plan, husband," she said, reaching back to pat my bare ass. "But it's not right to make this about us when it's Matt and Lauren's weekend."

"Maybe it's Nick and Erin's weekend," I muttered, a little grouchy now.

"It's that too," she said, earning me another pat. "I'm not saying no because I don't want to, Nick. I'm saying no because what I want and what makes sense are two different things."

I thought about this while I kissed the words inked on

her shoulder. She flew with her own wings, and I had to let her. She'd come back to me in due time, and she'd come home, too.

"My grandmother liked to say that instincts were the soul's road map, and that if you followed them, you'd find your way."

That earned me a skeptical glance over her shoulder. "Oh, we're gonna need to embroider that on a pillow."

I barked out a laugh but I was dead serious. "Spare the pillow and promise me it's not going to be another seven years before you get back here."

Erin twisted in my arms and brought one hand to the nape of my neck, the other to my chest. "It won't be seven years," she said. "Not even close."

That gave me a drowsy sort of peace, and I held her close as I dropped off to sleep. She was gone when I woke up hours later. Even before opening my eyes, I sensed her absence. I reached over, grasping for some trace of her in the bed, and found a piece of hotel stationery on the pillow.

There, in simple, straightforward print was her phone number and email address, and a brief note that had me laughing out loud.

Husband –
When seventeenth and eighteenth century sailors returned home from a voyage, they often brought pineapples with them. They'd spear it onto a fence, or hang it from the front porch as a method of announcing that they were in town and ready to mingle. That's why it's known as the symbol of hospitality, but it was also proof that they'd lived to tell about their time at sea.

I'm not a sailor, I'm not especially hospitable, and despite how things turned out with us, I had no intention of mingling. I guess what I'm trying to say is that I'm happy you liked my, ahem, pineapple.

Email me, and I'll respond.

- e

PART TWO

Confessions and Cozumel

To: Erin Walsh
From: Nick Acevedo
Date: May 30
Subject: Safe travels

Wife…there is no other pineapple that I'll ever want.

———

To: Nick Acevedo
From: Erin Walsh
Date: June 1
Subject: Confession

Hey, Dr. Dallas,
Confession: I had fun with you this past weekend. You're my
most entertaining husband.

- e

———

To: Erin Walsh
From: Nick Acevedo
Date: June 2
Subject: Confession

Hi, Skip,
I have a confession for you, too. I like getting into trouble
with you. You're my most delicious wife.
Nick

*You're also my only wife.

———

To: Nick Acevedo
From: Erin Walsh
Date: June 2
Subject: Confession

My confession for today: I didn't say proper goodbyes when
I left. I'm bad at that shit. It's easier for me to say, "Catch you
later, cunt" than actual goodbyes. I'm sorry about how I left
things. It was a really good weekend.
- e

*You're my only husband. Not sure I'm qualified for any
denomination of husbands.

———

To: Erin Walsh
From: Nick Acevedo
Date: June 3

Subject: Stop talking around it

No apologies necessary.

Can we keep it that way? Can we stay entertaining husband
and delicious wife, and then find a way to get time on our
side?
Nick

*You're plenty qualified for me.

To: Nick Acevedo
From: Erin Walsh
Date: June 4
Subject: I hate moving

You're saying that like being married is an experiment.

I had lunch with my babysitter today. You know, Lauren's
brother, Wes. He works for an agency that I probably
shouldn't disclose over email. We're both fans of the pizza
here in Sorrento (it is NOT the same in all parts of Italy), and
he informed me that the apartment I've been renting for the
past few years is owned by an old-school mafia outfit. Some
real *cosa nostra* shit. Who knew? He said it's a good thing I'm
moving.

Speaking of moving, I need to complain for a minute. Here it
comes: I fucking HATE moving. I'm not sure if you're a
Harry Potter fan (if you're not, you need to either lie or
divorce me right now because I can't be married to someone

who isn't down with the lifestyle) but I need a goddamn portkey like you wouldn't believe. I don't even have that much stuff, just books, rocks, little things I've picked up in my travels. I guess do have a bunch of Moroccan pottery. Anyway, I don't enjoy consolidating it and relocating it. I stood in my apartment this morning and sincerely wished I could wave a wand to send everything into boxes and trunks.

To: Erin Walsh
From: Nick Acevedo
Date: June 4
Subject: I hate moving

So it's an experiment. You're there, I'm here, and that's not changing. Let's see how long we can do this.

I'm a kid doctor. I speak enough Hogwarts to get by.

Also—what? You rent from the mob? Who the hell are you, Erin Walsh?

To: Nick Acevedo
From: Erin Walsh
Date: June 5
Subject: Low bar…

You're fucking with all my scholarly sensibilities, dude. All of them. Let's set aside the fact that this research proposal of yours is wholly subjective and not data-dependent. At the very minimum, it's not a meaningful experiment without a control group.

It sounds like you've seen the movies but haven't read the books. Weak.

———

To: Erin Walsh
From: Nick Acevedo
Date: June 6
Subject: Low bar…

We have a control group. We have Matt and Lauren. Think about it, Skip. We got married the same day they did, and I know for a fact that he lost his shit when she was out of town for a couple of weeks last fall. It's as close to a control group as we'll ever get.

Downloading the books now. See? We've got this.

———

To: Nick Acevedo
From: Erin Walsh
Date: June 6
Subject: Do you even have a theory to test?

I heard alllllll about that. She was gone for three weeks and I got a long, drunk email that was 17% intelligible. It was fucking troubling. I sent Riley to make sure Matt wasn't attempting a swan dive into the bay. Were you there when they sorta-kinda-but-not-really broke up? When he ran his own little marathon in the middle of a blizzard? As Riley would say: shambles.

You think you can do better than that? Or do you think I'll be the one in shambles?

But let's get back to my scholarly sensibilities, please. What are we even studying? Which outcome are we trying to evaluate? How long it takes until we start writing unintelligible emails and jogging through snowstorms? What happened to 'do no harm'?

———

To: Erin Walsh
From: Nick Acevedo
Date: June 7
Subject: I have several theories

We're studying how long it takes for one of us to bring you home.

No betting on the outcome. It's not scholarly.

———

To: Nick Acevedo
From: Erin Walsh
Date: June 11
Subject: in other news…

I'm in Iceland now. It is not Italy. It's remarkably cold. I just ordered everything that The North Face sells.

Also, I'm still not magical. I tried to unpack by yelling some charms, and then I tried some incantations to turn on the internet at my apartment, but nothing happened. Until that's patched up, you'll only hear from me when I'm at the lab.

———

To: Erin Walsh
From: Nick Acevedo
Date: June 11
Subject: in other news…

Ah, there she is.

I thought we agreed you'd tell me about the limits before I crossed them.

*You're quite magical.

*Please tell me you're not renting from any organized crime families.

———

To: Nick Acevedo
From: Erin Walsh
Date: June 11
Subject: in other news…

Yeah, I just don't like talking about that shit but it seems that I have to be really explicit when it comes to this topic: I'm not interested in any discussion of me relative to home, Boston, my relationships with (or lack thereof) my siblings, or my parents. Call it the third rail, call it a trigger, call it whatever the fuck you want but home isn't a place that I belong, Nick.

I need to work on setting up my lab. So…catch you later, cunt.

To: Erin Walsh
From: Nick Acevedo
Date: June 12
Subject: there are other ways to do this

You're the only woman I know who comfortably integrates that word into conversation. Is that something you've picked up overseas or are you under the impression you can shock me? (you cannot)

*You have my number. You're allowed to call or text me if you want. Encouraged, even.

To: Nick Acevedo
From: Erin Walsh
Date: June 14
Subject: not really

Hey, Dr. McCuntcautious,

I have one of those old-school data plans that only provides for a certain number of texts per month, and Riley uses them all. He's fashioned himself as quite the gossip girl.

And on the topic of cunts: I acquired that word in Australia. It's an interesting place, you know. Very tectonically active. The Indo-Australian plate is moving so frequently that GPS can't recalibrate quickly enough to appropriately capture its location.

- e

*We're stopping with the asterisks now. You're giving me improper footnote twitches.

———

To: Erin Walsh
From: Nick Acevedo
Date: June 15
Subject: WHAT?

What do you mean, Australia is moving? Where's it going? (not an asterisk) Which footnote style do you prefer? Are we breaking out the Chicago Manual of Style? APA? MLA?

You make the rules here, Skip. You always have.

———

To: Nick Acevedo
From: Erin Walsh
Date: June 16

Subject: WHAT?

It's moving northward, and rotating slightly clockwise. This isn't new. Australia has recalibrated its international coordinates four times in the past fifty years, and it looks like they'll do it again soon. Maybe this year.

(not an asterisk but still structurally annoying) There are no easy footnote mechanisms in email. So if you have something to say, put it in the body of the email.

———

To: Erin Walsh
From: Nick Acevedo
Date: June 16
Subject: WHAT?

Are we talking inches here? Or miles?

In the body of the email: My wife is a nerd and I fucking love it.

Also in the body of the email: What's the status of that internet service at your apartment? I want to see your sweet face while you drop the nerdy science talk on me.

———

To: Nick Acevedo
From: Erin Walsh
Date: June 17
Subject: WHAT?

A little more than 2.5 inches per year. It adds up. From what I hear, the next GPS update will be around 1.5 kilometers.

The plates are geologically fluid. Things move, dude. You need to deal with it. You know what else is moving? The moon. It's about two inches farther away each year.

This husband of mine has quite the sense of humor. Don't you know not to poke the academics where they hurt? It makes us less interested in video chatting. Also, I keep forgetting to call about getting the internet turned on…

———

To: Erin Walsh
From: Nick Acevedo
Date: June 18
Subject: WHAT?

I'm calling the University of Texas at Austin right now and requesting a refund. I don't know how I earned a degree from the College of Natural Sciences without hearing anything about Australia moving or the moon floating away.

I'll upgrade your data plan, Skip. Let me text you. Anything, please.

———

To: Nick Acevedo
From: Erin Walsh
Date: June 21
Subject: how do you have time to text?

I recognize that this is yet another thing we've failed to address in any way, but Angus left me with more than enough blood money to fund my own data upgrades. I don't need a dime from you or anyone else. I won't, ever. But aside from the financial logistics, I never have my phone with me inside the lab or when I'm out doing fieldwork, and even if I did, I wouldn't spend all day texting. Not trying to pull a Shannon here, but I'm really fucking busy.

(also: I'm concerned that the brain surgeon in this relationship, the one trying to return his diploma, has plenty of time to text. I pray that your scrub nurses aren't taking dictation. Do they write your emails too?)

To: Erin Walsh
From: Nick Acevedo
Date: June 22
Subject: No dictation here

The nursing staff is outstanding, and they all have far better things to do than send my texts or write emails. This is all me, in the downtime between surgeries or when I'm waiting for imaging studies. Sometimes it's just when I'm wishing you were in bed with me. Like right now.

To: Nick Acevedo
From: Erin Walsh
Date: June 23
Subject: That time

It's been a little more than three weeks. Should I expect any long, drunk, semi-intelligible emails in the spirit of Matt from you?

To: Erin Walsh
From: Nick Acevedo
Date: June 24
Subject: That time

It's really cute how you fish for affection, Skip. I miss you too, and life would be significantly improved if you weren't 2400 miles away, but instead of drinking that issue, I'm studying for board certification exams.

I get that you're an independent woman and I admire the fuck out of that, but if the internet in your apartment isn't working within the next 48 hours, you'll be handing the management of that issue over to me. I need you, Skip. Make it happen.

To: Nick Acevedo
From: Erin Walsh
Date: June 24
Subject: That time

You know, you pretend that you're this chill, easy-going guy but peel back the layers and you're pushy and impatient.

You're an irritable onion.

To: Erin Walsh
From: Nick Acevedo
Date: June 25
Subject: Irritable onion?

Let's pretend for the sake of argument that irritable onion makes any sense (it doesn't). By that logic, you're a moody raspberry, both sweet and tart.

Can we get back to the issues now: WHAT THE FUCK IS GOING ON WITH THE INTERNET IN YOUR APARTMENT?

To: Nick Acevedo
From: Erin Walsh
Date: June 26
Subject: I am NOT moody

You know how no one—not a single person in all of human existence—has ever calmed down after being told to calm down? Telling someone she's moody and then busting out the caps lock and unleashing some motherfucking fury isn't the way to prove that *I'm* moody.

It will be fixed in a few days, and I seem to think this exchange proves that you're an irritable onion.

To: Erin Walsh
From: Nick Acevedo
Date: June 27
Subject: Such a moody raspberry

But I think I love it.

Eleven

ERIN

I WAS WEARING tinted lip gloss. *Motherfucking lip gloss.*

There was no clear reason why I was freaking out about seeing Nick tonight, but I absolutely was. I sawed my teeth over my upper lip and adjusted the pillows behind me again. There was no reason to worry about any of this. We were already married, for fuck's sake.

I checked my watch again, and then stared at the time on my laptop screen, as if I'd discover some major divergence between the two. I didn't. It was still a few minutes before midnight here, and if I really set my mind to it, I could've twisted myself into an emotional pretzel before our agreed-upon meeting time.

The screen pinged with an incoming video call, and I ran my hands through my hair one last time before answering. Nick's face filled the window, a smile tipping up his lips.

"Skip," he said on a sigh. His eyes crinkled and his hand went to the back of his neck as he grinned at me, and I couldn't bring order to the wave of emotions hitting me at once. He was there, close enough to touch—but not really—

and it was like going back to the tireless nights we shared on the Cape. And there were maps on his wall.

I pointed at the screen, angling my head to get a better look. "Are those old maps?" I asked.

He shook his head, laughing to himself. "The words you're looking for are 'Hello, my husband' and 'I've missed the hell out of you and your frighteningly large cock.' Try that, Erin."

"Hello, my husband. I've missed the hell out of you, and the penis that torments my dreams," I said, an angelic smile spreading across my face. "Do I see that you favor old maps?"

Nick glanced over his shoulder, at the brick wall lined with nine square frames. The movement showed off the tendons in his neck, and I found myself leaning forward as if I could drag my tongue along those cords and taste him. "I do," he said, still looking at the block of maps. "Lauren likes flea markets and vintage shops, and Connecticut is a good trip."

I was still gazing at his neck, now focused on the dark stubble covering his Adam's apple, and it took an extra second to comprehend those words. "Lauren picked those out? In Connecticut?" I asked, squeezing my legs together because I could almost feel his scruff between them.

"No, that made no sense," he said, shaking his head as he looked back to the screen. "Lauren likes flea markets, and there's a big one in Connecticut. She drove there last spring, while Matt and I biked. We met her there and had lunch, and I saw these great old maps from the Civil War."

"And then you biked back," I said.

"Yeah," he said, as if riding a bike from Boston to God-knows-where Connecticut was the most regular thing in the world.

I pointed to the maps again. "Are you a fan of the War of Northern Aggression?"

That earned me a sheepish look. "Not yet," he conceded. "But I keep telling myself that as soon as I finish this fellowship and pass another board certification and have a life that doesn't involve power-napping in on-call rooms, I'll read a book or watch a documentary on the Civil War or... anything." He cast another glance over his shoulder. "I'm preparing for my post-residency life. I'm told that hobbies are allowed."

"How much longer?"

"It's July now, so less than five months," he said.

"Stonewall Jackson was a hypochondriac," I said, and full seconds passed while Nick registered my words, then his eyes widened, understanding that I was giving him some Civil War trivia. "The Confederate general. He was always worried about something, and resorted to old wives' tale treatments like sucking on lemons for his upset stomach, dunking his head in cold water for his bad eyesight. He didn't like sitting. He thought it was unnatural for his organs to be compressed."

"Fuck, I've missed you," he said.

I nodded, not quite ready to say the words yet. I wanted to, but I was afraid that with them would come a torrent of others like *When can I see you again?* and *How are we going to make this work for months, years?* and *Do you even want to make this—whatever the fuck* this *is—work?* and *I don't understand how it's possible to feel so much, so soon, and when I stop to think about this, it's terrifying.* So I said, "Yeah, me too."

"You look good," he replied. "Really good, Skip."

And *Right now, I wish things were different.*

"So what's going on with you these days?" I asked.

Nick was thoughtful for a moment, bobbing his head as

he looked away. "I had some really good oatmeal this morning," he said. "A bowl of warm dirt would've been great after spending all night in surgery, but I think it was the little chocolate chips that made all the difference. I snagged them from the frozen yogurt bar, but the cafeteria police don't mind me." He uncapped a stainless steel water bottle and took a sip. "What do you eat for breakfast, Skip?"

"I spent four years in the Mediterranean. Espresso is the only breakfast anyone needs," I said, and the words weren't even out before he was shaking his head in disagreement.

"And that's why you're pocket-sized," he said, holding out his palm as if he'd solved the last great mystery of my existence. "For Christ's sake, Erin, have a banana."

"I don't *like* bananas."

"Okay, fine. Let me give you a list of alternatives because coffee isn't breakfast. Get a pencil."

"Oh, don't even start that shit with me," I said. "Any more paternalistic commentary from you, and I'll have to start calling you daddy."

"We do not want that," he murmured.

"No," I replied, laughing. "Not at all."

We'd talked about *everything* before, all the important things that shaded our world views and shaped our identities, but somehow this—*nothing*—was better. There was a foreign comfort in learning all of Nick's quirks and preferences, and the burgeoning love affair at his hospital, one between a gastro surgeon and her resident. Telling him about Iceland and my lab and the curious research fellows I'd inherited was an odd pleasure. I didn't talk about everyday things with anyone, not with much frequency.

"You're tired. I should let you go," Nick murmured. We'd been talking for more than three hours. "But I just don't want to. It's kind of a problem I'm having, not wanting to let you go."

I pushed my glasses to my head and rubbed my eyes. I was scheduled for a long day at the subzero lab bench in a matter of hours. "When was the last night *you* slept?"

"Remember what I said about power naps in on-call rooms?" he asked. "Yeah. That. Around two o'clock this afternoon."

"What are we *doing*?" I asked, and at the same time, Nick asked, "When can you get back here?"

We stared at each other for a moment, and then returned to talking at once.

Nick: We're running a highly scientific experiment that's currently measuring how long I can stare at your mouth before I come in my—

Me: I want to see you, I do, but between the lab and commuting between here and Oxford, I can't—

Nick: I hate asking you to do all the traveling and—

Me: You think you're making it any easier? All scruffy and sleepy and fucking adorable like—

Nick: —I know it isn't easy for you to come here, but my schedule sucks right now and I can't—

Me: I fucking miss you, and I don't even understand that emotion—

Nick: Wait. *I'm* adorable?

Me: —and it isn't entirely welcome! I never wanted to like you or miss you or any of this—

Nick: You think I'm adorable?

Me: —and maybe it was a mistake. Maybe we're inventing problems for ourselves. Maybe we shouldn't—

"Stop right there, darlin'." Nick pointed a finger at me, his serious expression snatching away my words. "We didn't make it easy on ourselves, no," he said. "But I believe you told me there's no time to live with regrets."

I rubbed my eyes, stealing a second away from his watchful gaze.

"There's gotta be a few days, a weekend, something," he continued. "This is good, and I intend to thank the Lord for your tits and stable wi-fi, but I'm greedy. I want more, and I'll sell my soul to anyone who's buying if I can see you again soon."

My fingers slipped away from my eyes, down my cheeks and over my lips. They stayed there, pressed into my skin as if I was barricading my most honest words from this conversation. But words weren't entirely necessary as I was nodding eagerly, agreeing to this plan long before it was fully formed.

"I want *you*," he said. "It's as simple—"

"And really fucking difficult," I added.

"—as that."

Nick smiled and dropped a hand to his belly, as if he could feel my words right there. But *his* words? I felt them everywhere.

———

To: Nick Acevedo
From: Erin Walsh
Date: July 12
Subject: Here's an idea

I have a week in early November, right before I'm back at Oxford for another six-week session, and I think I can swing that.

Would that work for you?

———————

To: Erin Walsh
From: Nick Acevedo
Date: July 13
Subject: Here's an idea

It depends which week. My oral boards are November 7-9.

———————

To: Nick Acevedo
From: Erin Walsh
Date: July 13
Subject: Here's an idea

Yeah, that was the exact week I had in mind.

(going outside to smash some rocks now)

———————

To: Erin Walsh
From: Nick Acevedo
Date: July 14
Subject: Here's an idea

Fuck it. I don't need another board certification.

(I know you know what you're doing with those rocks but
be careful)

To: Nick Acevedo
From: Erin Walsh
Date: July 14
Subject: Here's an idea

Yeah, overachiever much?

*I'm not letting you blow off your boards for me. That's insane. More insane than any of this already is, and I won't be the one responsible for you fucking up this fellowship. Put on your big boy undies and deal with it.

**Guess what? When you pass, you won't be able to give me shit about getting another doctorate anymore. We'll be even.

To: Erin Walsh
From: Nick Acevedo
Date: July 14
Subject: Say more about those underwear

I'll be out of surgery by 7 or 8 tonight, and then you can get on video chat and tell me all about these underwear you speak of. Maybe you can show me this process.

*That wasn't just one footnote-styled asterisk but TWO. Are you okay over there, Skip?

To: Nick Acevedo
From: Erin Walsh
Date: July 14
Subject: Maybe this?

What about immediately after your boards? I can fly in for a
weekend, and then go straight to Oxford. It'll be tight, but
it's something. Or…maybe late December? I'm not sure I can
handle any traditional Christmas at home, but maybe we
could meet somewhere? Or something? Anything?

*Did you see that? It's me, trying.

———

To: Erin Walsh
From: Nick Acevedo
Date: July 14
Subject: I saw

We can talk about it tonight, while we have that lesson on
underwear.

Twelve

I DRUMMED my fingers against my laptop, waiting, none too patiently, for Nick to answer my video call. He'd been in surgery all day, all week, all fucking month as he raced down the clock to meet the practical requirements for an additional board certification. And before that, I'd been locked up in full-day sessions at Oxford through August and September. That's how it was with us, one jam-packed day after another, and squeezing in time for video chats often required heroic efforts. The four-hour time difference between Boston and Iceland didn't help matters.

The screen blinked to life, and Nick said, "Hey, lovely. What's your news? I have some, too."

He was walking down a dark hallway in his apartment, and it wasn't until he came to a stop in the kitchen that I got a good look at him. He was wearing an unzipped hoodie and nothing underneath. I shifted my head from side to side, trying to get a better look at him.

"Erin?"

"Quiet now, pumpkin," I said. "I'm having a special moment here."

"Special moment?" he repeated. He set his laptop on the counter and crossed his arms, and that pushed the hoodie farther apart and gave me a look at his belly. A pair of blue scrubs sat low on his waist, and that fuzzy path that started at his navel and pointed downward had never looked better.

"Yeah," I murmured. "I'm gonna need this when I'm trapped on a research ship for the next two months."

His shoulders slumped as my words hit him, and that teasing smile slipped. "*What*? When?"

"We leave port after my next session at Oxford, right before the holidays. We'll be gone until the end of February," I said, blinking away from his abs. "The research fellow who was supposed to head up that expedition broke her leg last weekend. She was hiking the Laugavegur Trek, and it didn't end well. I don't have anyone else who can go. It has to be me."

He leaned back against his refrigerator, frowning. "So that long weekend in December…?"

I shook my head slowly. "I can't," I said, "and I really wish I could."

He ran his hand through his hair as his tongue passed over his lips. "I know," he said.

I hated this. I fucking hated this, and I wanted anything other than the world where Nick was anchored in Boston and I was tethered to ice sheets for the foreseeable future. I could've emailed this turn of events to him, and saved myself the anguish of watching his disappointment, but I was on the hook for this. For him.

"What's your news?" I asked.

Nick reached across the countertop—cue bare chest close-up—and presented a typewritten letter. "This is my news," he said from behind the paper. "You're the first to know, other than the hospital."

I leaned in, squinting to read the words, but half of them were out of view. "This would be easier if you put that letter through a paper shredder, pasted it back together, and then faxed it to me," I said. "In other words, I can't—"

"I'm staying in Boston," he interrupted. He held it up again, watching the screen in the top corner to make the entire document visible. "I accepted the offer from Mass General."

"Why?" I asked as I skimmed the letter. He made a vague sound and jerked a shoulder. "What made you choose MGH over Houston or Children's of Colorado?"

He'd talked through the options on several occasions when we didn't want to end our video calls, and I knew he was leaning toward Colorado, with Texas Children's as a distant second. Right? Or was I ignoring all of his arguments in favor of Boston?

"I wasn't feeling Colorado, and I like MGH," he said, nodding toward the letter in his hand. "The offer was decent, too."

Yeah, I'd noticed that. I couldn't miss that mid-six-figure salary.

"Did you think I'd…we'd be together in Boston? That I'd go back there, and *stay* there?" I asked, growing increasingly mortified. Talk about things beyond the realm of possibility.

"That wasn't the deciding factor, no," he said, waving away my suggestion. "But even before you came along and put me under your spell, I had reasons to stay. Matt and Riley and everyone else…they're family to me. Matt's like the brother I never had."

That gave me—and my expanding panic—pause. "Is this —I mean, you and me—has this been hard?"

Nick drew his fingertip down his jaw as he offered a

small shrug in response. "I don't know, maybe," he said. "I don't like withholding this from him."

"I'm sorry," I murmured.

"It's good, in a perverse way, that Riley's avoiding Matt right now, too," he said, laughing. "I'm not the only one. Matt's making it easy on us, though. I think he has a meniscal tear that he refuses to get checked. He hasn't been running much, and seems to be enjoying the hell out of newlywed life. I haven't had to lie to his face too often."

Newlywed life. The *real* newlywed life. What was that like? It definitely wasn't arguing over video chat. "I'm sorry," I repeated. "Nick, maybe it's time for us to end—"

"Nope," he interrupted before I could revisit this marriage experiment. "No, darlin'. I don't want to hear it. But you need to get real with yourself about why you won't even consider coming back here."

I sighed, shaking off the anger I'd accumulated. "My research is not in North America," I said flatly, as if there wasn't plenty of earth to study on the other side of the Atlantic.

Nick circled his hand in front of him, asking for my next reason.

I rolled my eyes. "America's political capital isn't engaged in climate change," I snapped.

"Just fuckin' go there," he said, dropping his hands to his hips. "Just admit that being in the same city as Shannon scares the shit out of you. Admit that you don't know how to make things right, and instead of figuring it out, you'd rather put an ocean between you."

A loose thread on the sleeve of my sweater was suddenly captivating, and I didn't respond.

"Admit that if I was headed to Colorado, you'd get there," he said. "You'd restructure your research schedule and convince a university to hand over some lab space, and you'd be there within a couple of months. A year, tops."

So interesting, this thread. Perhaps if I studied it long enough, I'd be able to abstain from this conversation altogether.

"Admit that Boston is dangerous," he said. "That coming home is the only thing that actually scares you."

None of the usual suspects scared me. Danger didn't scare me. It should, but it didn't, and I couldn't trace the exact origin of all that. Maybe it was the brutally abusive father; maybe it was running toward the lava flows instead of away from them. Either way, I was steeped in danger, but more than that, darkness.

I used to spend my time calculating when volcanic eruptions would obliterate human existence and send enough ash into the atmosphere to induce the next ice age. On the surface it seemed that my new explorations were less disastrous, but when all the political clutter of climate change was brushed away, I was calculating how long it would take for the remnants of the last ice age to raise sea levels and alter civilization as we knew it.

And that didn't scare me either. I didn't wallow in that black hole of uncertainty because I didn't see it as entirely uncertain. If anyone was living proof that even the most damaged creatures could recover, it was me.

But home… There was no volcano with the potential to hurt me the way that city—and everything there—could.

"You're scared," he said softly. "But you can end this."

"I'm scared," I said. "And even if it ends, I don't think I can go back to Boston. I can't stay there, Nick."

He ran his knuckles down his belly with a resolute nod. "Let me worry about that, lovely."

Thirteen

NICK

To: Erin Walsh
From: Nick Acevedo
Date: November 20
Subject: I know it's not Thanksgiving in England, but…

When was the last time you were home for the holidays? I got back to Dallas for Thanksgiving and Christmas two years ago, but I'm either working or on-call every day in December. The joys of being the newest attending, I guess.

My mother understood during my internship and residency, but she's less thrilled about it now. Then again, she has Maya and Dahlia's kids to spoil at Christmas, so not making it home isn't the biggest deal in her world.

What do you usually do this time of year? I hate the idea of you being alone. I hate it more than I already hate you being alone as it is.

To: Nick Acevedo
From: Erin Walsh
Date: November 20
Subject: I know it's not Thanksgiving in England, but...

There's always someone who insists on herding the stray
cats and hosting a non-denominational event around the
holidays. Always, and they never take no for an answer. I
say this as the person who tries to get out of the non-denominational hodgepodge events.

Back in Iceland, there's a researcher who shares lab space
with me, and he's been there for several years with his
family. He's having all the forlorn Americans over for
pseudo-Thanksgiving later this week. I'm sure there will be
someone at Oxford who does the same thing.

The Iceland guy, he's an interesting one. We talked about the
ancient Gálgahraun lava field outside of Reykjavík before I
left. It's apparently inhabited by elves. Huldufolk, to be
exact. The locals have some strong feelings about researchers
traipsing all over the elfdom. It started with me asking
whether he knew of any grocery stores that carried premade
cookie dough. I think it was his way of apologizing, maybe.

Like, no cookie dough, but we do have elves so that's
something.

It's not traditional American Thanksgiving, but I am having
dinner with Lauren's brother Wes over the weekend. He's in
the area for something James Bond-inspired, and it seems he
has a few minutes when he's not averting some international
crisis. So that's nice. It's better than elves.

To: Erin Walsh
From: Nick Acevedo
Date: November 21
Subject: Elves…

Somehow that fits perfectly with your stories about alien black diamonds, Stonewall Jackson's hypochondriasis, and the relative location of Australia.

*Were you baking cookies? What kind?

**Should I be worried about the James Bond-inspired dude taking my wife to dinner?

To: Nick Acevedo
From: Erin Walsh
Date: November 21
Subject: don't judge me but…

I don't like cookies when they're baked. I only like the dough, but I can't always find it overseas. You could say it's my white whale.

*No. He's more attracted to you than he is me.

To: Erin Walsh
From: Nick Acevedo

Date: November 22
Subject: don't judge me but...

Okay, I've been thinking about this all night.

Did you know that I wouldn't judge you for any of the other things you've shared with me in the past six months or did you think I'd find raw cookie dough consumption that revolting?

To: Nick Acevedo
From: Erin Walsh
Date: November 22
Subject: don't judge me but...

Yes.

*happy thanksgiving, husband.

I WASN'T BITTER, and I was going to keep telling myself that until I believed it.

Bitter didn't have a place in my life. I'd always had it easy, and losing what little contact I had with my wife to two months in the Arctic Circle wasn't the worst thing in the world. It was really fucking frustrating and I was still pissed about the pediatric neurosurgery board certification exam falling during the one week that our schedules spoke to each other, but I wasn't bitter.

Although if I didn't see her soon, I'd get there.

I grabbed my phone and scrolled through my alerts. It was a good distraction from the chatter around me, and Matt and Lauren's Thanksgiving celebration was low-key enough to endure phones at the table. Riley was on his phone too, but the glazed-over look in his eyes told me he wasn't focused on the content.

I was on call for the next few hours, but I'd discharged my last three patients this morning, and my service didn't take many hits on this particular holiday. Cardio, gastro, emergency medicine, they took the hits.

"Oooh, I think that's them," Lauren whispered, popping up from her chair. "Remember—we're all being nice and friendly and not weird. Got it?"

Matt refilled his red wine, shaking his head. "You say that as if you're not speaking directly to Patrick. I'm nice. I'm the nicest one here."

"Wrong. Miss Honey's the nicest one here," Riley said, invoking the nickname he'd chosen for Lauren.

Looking up from my phone, I rolled my eyes at Riley. He didn't even try to hide his obsession with her.

"You're all wrong," Andy said, taking the wine bottle from Matt. "I'm definitely the nicest one here."

That earned a hearty round of laughter. No one would mistake Andy for warm or fuzzy.

Sam appeared in the doorway, a dark-haired woman carrying a pie dish at his side. She looked familiar, but I couldn't place that familiarity.

"Hi," Lauren said as she approached them. "You must be Tiel. I'm Lauren, and I'm so happy to meet you. Come on, sit down."

I wasn't up to date on Sam's new girlfriend, or any other family developments. I'd been spending all of my free evenings with Erin, or as close as I could get to her. This distance was good. Too much time around happy couples like Matt and Lauren and Patrick and Andy only reminded me that I didn't get to spend every day with Erin, and it encouraged the bitterness to creep in.

Despite my absence, I knew it was fairly remarkable that Sam was introducing a woman to his family, since he was a card-carrying manwhore and had the one-night stand market on lock. But people grew and changed, even stubborn-minded Walshes. I was counting on it.

"So you've met Patrick and Andy," Lauren said to Tiel, gesturing down the table. "That's Matthew, he belongs to me." Matt tugged her onto his lap. "That's Riley, and Nick."

Riley was staring at the ceiling and offered little more than a nod in Tiel's direction.

"I've met you before," I said, standing to shake her hand across the table. "Where have I met you?"

"I have no idea," she said, but it sounded like *Shut the fuck up*.

I tapped my phone on the table as I nodded. "It'll come to me," I said.

"I thought you weren't with us today," Sam called to me. He was in the adjoining kitchen, pouring himself a drink.

I grabbed a dish of paella—Matt and Lauren's version of Thanksgiving—and forked up a mouthful. "Technically, I'm on call," I said. "Until midnight. Then, you know, it's time to rage. Or whatever people who have lives do these days."

"And by *rage*, you mean you'll be hanging out at the hospital?" Sam asked.

Laughing, I murmured in agreement. It was much simpler than telling him I'd be stealing video chat moments with his sister before she, the one I'd married six months ago, left for the North Pole. That, and Erin had to be the one to tell them. Yeah, I could drop that morsel right now, just nestle it in between the paella and empanadas and sit back while everyone blew it far out of proportion, and take this one for Erin. That was the quick and dirty solution. It would save me from many months of lies by omission, and her from a confrontation she obviously didn't welcome. But I wasn't playing the short game, and I didn't think Erin was either.

"Is this tapas?" Sam asked, frowning at a dish of grilled corn with cotija cheese.

"Yes," Matt said from the far end of the table. Lauren was still on his lap, and now he had one hand tucked right between her knees. Riley was still staring at the ceiling. This was either really good exposure therapy, or the worst night imaginable for him. Probably both. "With the Black Widow in New Mexico, no one reminded Tom to pick up the turkey. So, we called Toro last night and ordered everything on the menu."

"Who's Tom?" Tiel asked.

"Shannon's assistant," Sam said. "Has anyone determined whether she's actually in New Mexico?"

"We are not talking about this. She's entitled to a little space," Lauren said, holding up her hands as if she was keeping Sam and Matt in their respective corners. "Instead of dragging all that drama out like a prize pig at the county fair, why don't you two tell us how you met?"

"It certainly wasn't the way Sam usually meets women," Tiel said, and she was either really fucking hilarious or a prickly pear cactus disguised as a human lady. Not that prickly pears weren't great. My grandmother made the best prickly pear jam. I didn't even like cornbread unless I could drown it in her jam, but finding the fruit required getting past the thorns.

"We met over Labor Day weekend," Sam said. "Tiel introduced me to bluegrass, and a few other things."

The paella recaptured my attention, and I tuned out talk of Tiel's work as an adjunct professor at Berklee College of Music and Riley's newest *Dexter* theories. He'd only recently discovered Netflix. But the spicy rice triggered some neural connection, and I snapped my fingers as it came to me. "You did the seminar on the comparison of music therapy and pharmacological sedation using chloral hydrate in pediatric EEG captures," I said, thrilled that I'd finally figured out how I knew Tiel.

"What were you doing there?" she asked.

Right, prickly pear it is.

"I cut brains," I supplied. "You know, for medical purposes. I had eight first-year pediatric neuro-surgical interns with me." I paused, thinking back to that session and my attempt to implement those practices. "I don't let them sedate toddlers anymore unless they've already tried and failed non-pharma measures, and I can only think of a few cases."

She softened a bit, and said, "I'm glad it's working."

I asked, "You're at Berklee?" Tiel nodded. "What else are you working on? I have plenty of residents who need to publish, and enslaving them brings a lot of joy to my life."

"Well," she murmured, glancing around to find everyone watching her. That couldn't have been fun, especially considering she'd bared her teeth at our very own Miss Congeniality. "I've been applying some new therapeutic approaches with children on the autism spectrum. Too early to draw any correlations."

"All right," Patrick said. It sounded like he was ready to make his ruling on Sam's date. "You're obviously very intelligent. What the hell do you see in the runt?"

"Don't answer that," Andy said, shaking her head. "What he meant to say was Lauren and I go to an incredible winter farmers' market on Saturdays, and you should come with us this weekend."

I checked out of the conversation and went back to the room-temperature paella, and my not-bitterness. I decided that I resented the ice sheets. Fuckin' ice. I took no issue with her work or the fact that she wasn't the kind of scientist who made a home for herself in the bowels of a university course catalog. There was nothing hotter than imagining my girl kicking ass on a frozen tundra, and it gave her too much meaning for me to ever steal that from her.

But fuck if I didn't want to stumble into the universe where I went to bed with my wife every night.

"Erin's heading off on a research trip," Matt said, and that caught my attention.

"Yeah, I heard from her last week," Patrick added. "I don't think there's anywhere she hasn't been."

My apartment, if we're starting a list.

"Where's she headed now?" Sam asked. "Obviously, I wasn't on the short list of people she notifies about her journeys."

I scowled at him. It was the only thing I could do to keep from growling.

"Antarctica," Matt said.

Other pole, asshole.

"Wait," Andy said. "I think I know the answer to this but…are there volcanoes in Antarctica?"

Patrick shook his head. "I think it's the Arctic, Matt," he said. "Not volcanoes. Not exactly. She said she'd spent so long looking at these"—he held his arms far apart, as if he was measuring something—"I don't know what they're called, but all the layers of rock and lava, and in it she kept seeing evidence of little ice ages and periods of drought, and it got her wondering about change over time. Not just recent history, back to when people started recording daily temperatures and all, but back as far as she could find."

"Is that meteorology?" Sam asked. "Or...I'm at a disadvantage here since no one tells me anything. What is she studying now?"

"Climate change," Matt said. "I think."

"Sounds more like planetary physics," I added. I could've given a brief sermon on Erin's studies, but stopped myself right there. Not bitter *at all*.

"Whoa," Andy murmured. "And now she's going to...one of the poles?"

"You're probably right about it being the Arctic," Matt said to Patrick. "She sent me the details of her trip but I didn't read them through. I just told her it would take me a lot longer to bail her out if she got into trouble up there."

I'd never wanted to punch my best friend more.

"I'm so confused," Lauren said. "She's not in Italy anymore?"

"No, she's in Iceland now," Matt said. "But she's attached to a research institute in London."

Oxford. Not London.

"Guys, you make her seem like some wild child on the run," Andy said. "That wasn't the vibe I got when I talked to her at the wedding. I think it's time to dial down the big brother routine."

"Erin only does extremes," Matt said.

Give me a fucking break.

"Oh, spare me," Lauren murmured.

Matt looked from Andy to his wife, incredulous. "I'll dial it down when she and Shannon power wash the past. Until that happens, I'm still on hair-trigger watch. With Erin, anything can happen."

"Agreed," Patrick said, reaching for the wine again. "That shit with Shannon and Erin is sweating dynamite. Someone needs to keep an eye on her."

Patrick, too. That fucker. He was on my list.

I didn't know which part was more irritating: that I'd been hearing some version of this from them for years, or that they truly didn't understand the depth of their wrongness. I knew it was different from their seat, that they saw all the shit Erin had experienced—and instigated—as a teenager, and couldn't distinguish that from the reality of Erin now. And I was really fucking bothered that they didn't see it necessary to fix their outdated perceptions.

"Thanks for mansplaining that, bro," Lauren said, holding out her fist to Patrick for a bump. As far as I was concerned, Riley's unrequited love for her required zero explanation. She was fucking amazing. "Now let me do a little pussy-splaining while I have you here. None of you need to be on *patrol*. She's not a kid, and the whole thing is bullshit. She and Shannon will get there, but not because any of you were standing around telling her how to do it."

"Agreed," Andy said.

Riley growled and kicked me under the table before I could add my support to Lauren's comments. He shook his head at me, all too knowing, while he scratched his chest like a sleepy bear. He looked around the table and said, "I feel like doing something irresponsible tonight." He kicked me again. "Come on, Acevedo. Let's have an adventure."

"You should know," Matt started, laughing. Clearly, he wasn't still annoyed about someone suggesting that his brilliant sister required babysitting. "Riley's version of irresponsible adventure involves waking up in the bed of a truck on its way to Canada or getting his nipples pierced by a random guy in an alley."

Riley rubbed his chest, frowning. "Those hurt, man. I still have scars, physical *and* emotional."

"He's also been permanently barred from Howl At The Moon," Patrick added. "Something about getting naked and dancing on a piano."

"As if that wasn't standard fare," Riley muttered. "And if we're airing all the dirty secrets, why don't we talk about the party after Matt and Miss Honey's wedding?"

"Nope." I stared at my mostly full wine glass. "Let me stop you right there."

"Why?" Matt asked. He looked between Sam, Riley, and me. "What happened?"

Riley stared at me, smirking. I shook my head, mouthing, "Stop."

He shrugged as if to say *Stop what?*

This time, I kicked him under the table. His eyebrows shot up, prodding me to slide further into this death roll. The harder I fought to keep him quiet, the louder my secrets became.

So I raised the stakes. I watched Riley with a slightly manic smile, and then slid my gaze to Lauren. One nod in her direction, and his expression fell.

Everyone watched our standoff, and if it wasn't heavy after that chat about Erin, it was heavy now. We all trafficked in inside jokes and odd references, but it was somehow obvious to our present company that the source of our disagreement involved no humor.

Finally Riley shook off his stricken expression and laughed. "Nothing happened," he said, spooning up a bite of pumpkin pie straight from the dish. "Acevedo knows how to have a good time. Not surprising for the good doctor."

I reached over and grabbed the pie plate from him. "I will fucking end you," I hissed.

"We're fucking lucky that they're too drunk and happy to give a shit about us," he said under his breath. "Buy me a beer, and then we'll kiss and make up."

"IS IT GETTING ANY BETTER?" I asked.

Riley stretched his arms across the bar top at The Green Dragon and dropped his head. "No," he murmured.

"Do you think either of them know?" I asked. My finger traced the edge of the cardboard coaster under my beer. "Matt and Lauren, I mean."

"No," he repeated. "Why does Lauren have fucking brothers? Why couldn't she have a sister so I can be happy and stop wanting Matt to trip in front of a train?"

"Sisters wouldn't make a difference," I said. "My sisters are complete opposites of each other. No guarantees there."

Riley lifted his head and regarded me with the kind of glare historically reserved for traitors and pedophiles. "You're not funny."

"You know what else isn't funny?" I asked. "You almost inciting a brawl over dessert. That wasn't cool, man."

Riley knocked his knuckles against the bar top twice. "If you'd just tell me what went down with you and Erin, I'd stop instigating."

"Why do you need to know?" I asked, returning to the coaster.

"Consider it quid pro quo, man. I confessed all of my unrequited love for Miss Honey, and what did I get for that? I found you molesting my sister. Multiple times."

I shrugged, not sure how much I wanted to admit. "It

wasn't multiple times, and I did put your nose back together," I said. "She needed a breather from the festivities, so we went into town. We got a drink, walked around the harbor. That's it."

Riley tipped back his drink. "Yeah, that sounds like a nice way of telling me nothing," he said. "That's not even a tenth of the truth, is it?"

I shook my head. "Why are you entitled to a full report?" I asked. I was definitely bitter now.

Riley held out his hands, conciliatory. "Okay, okay. You don't have to say anything. I'll guess," he said.

"Please don't," I said, groaning.

"Hmmm. Let's see," Riley said. "It was the night before the wedding. It was the first time she'd been back to Massachusetts in years. That must've been a lot for her. She probably wanted to get the hell away from the inn because she knew everyone was waiting for her to fuck some shit up and—"

"I'm really fucking tired of hearing that," I interrupted. "Y'all need to give her some credit."

Riley leaned back, his arms folded on his chest as he looked me over. I'd already given too much away. "She wanted to do something crazy," he said, "and you couldn't say no to her."

"Let's talk about football," I said. "Football is a much better topic. Safer."

"Her crazy isn't my crazy, dude," Riley continued. "She likes getting lost in dark forests and climbing fucking glaciers and flirting with priests—"

"She flirts with priests?"

He jerked a shoulder. "I mean, I don't know of specific instances, but would it surprise you that much?"

"A little bit, yeah," I said. Erin lost her religion a long,

long time ago. Could anyone blame her? "I don't think she hangs out with many priests, and she's not…" I almost said she wasn't a flirt, but the truth was that she wasn't an *intentional* flirt. She didn't know how alluring she was, and she didn't use it with any strategy.

"*Salud*." The bartender placed another round in front of us, and Riley knocked his bottle against mine. "So what did Rogue dare you to do, and are you sufficiently traumatized?"

I lifted the beer bottle to my lips, drinking deeply while I watched today's college football highlights on the television at the end of the bar.

"It looks like you're significantly traumatized," Riley mused. "Well done, Rogue. Well done."

Shifting in my seat, I leaned an arm against the bar and studied him. There was a smudge of pumpkin pie on his shirt, his socks didn't match, and his fly was open. He played the part of the black sheep, the dumbass, the fuck up…but he was none of that. He was as scatterbrained as they came, and he sincerely struggled with zipping his pants, but he was a good guy, the kind I'd trust with my sisters.

If they hadn't been primarily concerned with marrying for money, mineral rights, and social status, of course.

And Riley was a motherfucking vault. He had a gift for being in the wrong place at the wrong time, and was often party to his siblings' most confidential moments, but even under the weight of alcohol, he never let those stories loose. It was everyone else who told those stories first, never Riley.

"Remember how we promised we wouldn't let you object during the ceremony?" I asked.

"Yes," he grumbled. "My worst good decision ever."

"You have to promise me that you won't repeat this," I

said. "You can get as many medical favors as you want, but you're not allowed to even hint at it. Ever."

"Shit," he huffed. "What did she get you into? Did you get a tramp stamp of a volcano? Dick piercing? Absinthe shots? Cow tipping? Goat theft?"

"That involved a lot of farm animals, man, and that made it strange." I gave him a curious look, waiting for some explanation of his fascination with livestock, but none came. Blowing out a breath, I said, "We got married."

He slammed his beer down on the bar. "You fuckin' *what*?"

"We got married," I said. "On a boat."

His miserable-yet-amused expression turned cold, his eyes incredulous. "I should take you outside and beat the snot out of you. What kind of man marries a woman on a damn boat without her family? I can't believe you, man." He huffed out a breath and shook his head, then gestured for the bartender. "Jäger! Bring me some fuckin' Jäger. I need something to quench my rage."

I held up a hand to stop the bartender from setting a shot glass in front of Riley. "No one is drinking any Jägermeister tonight. If anything, we'll drink tequila"—cue filthy memories of tequila dripping from Erin's nipples—"like men."

"Miss Honey drinks tequila," he said, and no fucking shit, he was on the verge of tears.

"Don't do that to yourself," I said. "It's damn near impossible, I know, because everything reminds me of Erin. There's an ER nurse with glasses just like Erin's, and I found myself staring at her this morning. It fucking killed me, and it was very awkward. I had to make up a lame excuse, and then pretend I was being paged."

"You actually like her?" he asked, a little incredulous. "Erin, not that nurse."

"Yes, I like her," I cried. "Of course I do."

"But she lives in Europe," he said.

"She does," I conceded.

He rolled his eyes as if I was being remarkably obtuse. "Doesn't that make marriage a bit difficult?"

"She'll come home," I said. "When she's ready, and when she figures out where home is."

We sat in silence after that, staring into our drinks and blindly watching college football highlights.

"What are you going to do about it?" he eventually asked. "Because if you're waiting for her to make the next move, you've got to know she doesn't act particularly quickly. She only reacts when she's been pushed past her breaking points."

I gave him a *what can I do?* shrug. "If I figure it out, I'll let you know."

Riley waved me off with a sour frown. "Erin is incredible with many things, but she's terrible when it comes to taking care of herself. She lets dickface guys like you take advantage of her and leave her."

"I'm not a dickface guy," I said. "I'm not taking advantage of her, and she's better at taking care of herself than you think."

Riley studied his beer bottle for a moment, intent on peeling the label off. "What am I gonna do?" he asked.

"Well," I said, clearing my throat. "Have you thought about spending less time with Matt and Lauren?"

"Why the fuck do you think I go to Rhode Island every weekend I can, and leave the office as soon as possible every evening? I don't hate my job. I'm actively trying to avoid Matt-and-Lauren moments. That's why I went to the mat with Patrick to get my own office. I couldn't share a space with Matt all damn day. Not with him and Lauren texting back and forth about how much they love and adore each other, and they're going away for romantic weekends, and they want to have a million babies."

I pointed at him with my beer bottle. "But you also spent the summer helping out at her school, man. How many classrooms did you paint for her?"

"All of them," he said, groaning. "Every single one…with primer. And three coats. I can't say no to her, Nick. She invites me to dinner, or asks for help, and a really fucked-up part of me thinks that if I do, she'll suddenly realize that she has feelings for me, too. And, no, you don't need to tell me that any of that is fucked up. I know it's fucking terrible, and I'm lower than dick cheese for wanting my brother's marriage to fall apart. And fuck…I don't know. I just feel good when I'm around her, and I think I could make her happy."

It didn't seem necessary to state the obvious—that Lauren was *very* happily married to Matt, and Matt wouldn't walk away from her without a fight to the death. So I offered the only appropriate response.

"You've gotta stop that shit," I said. "Get her out of your head, man."

"And look how well that's working for you," he said. "We're basically in the same boat, you know."

"Which boat is that?"

"The fucked-over boat," he snorted. "I'm in love with my brother's wife. You're in love with your living-three-thou-sand-miles-away wife. We're completely fucked over, and neither of us can look Matt in the eye."

"Yeah," I said, knocking my beer bottle against his. "That's the boat."

To: Erin Walsh
From: Nick Acevedo
Date: November 29
Subject: Check your mailbox

Hi, Skip.
I sent you a few things before you head out next week.
Looks like the box should arrive today or tomorrow.

When can we talk this week? I want to see you, even if I
have to rearrange my schedule.

How goes it in the climate change trenches these days?

Nick

To: Nick Acevedo
From: Erin Walsh

Date: November 29
Subject: Check your mailbox

The trenches are wet, the trenches are warm, and the trenches are not regaining much perennial ice. The trenches have also seen a small but noticeable change in the planet's gravity field as a product of redistributed water in oceans and atmospheric vapor. So the trenches are a little hectic, and a little stressful.

There are days when I wonder why I couldn't research something simple, like the origin of the croissant. It comes from Vienna, actually, and Viennese bakers crafted it to celebrate victory over the Turks. Marie Antoinette brought it to Versailles when she was married off to Louis XVI. For her, it was comfort food.

But then I remember that I really, really like volcanoes and oceans and ice sheets, and I forget all about flaky Viennese breads.

*Have I told you that I love bread? I fucking love bread. It's boring, I know, but one of the best parts of living in Europe is all the amazing bread.

**Did you think I'd forget? Happy birthday, husband.

To: Erin Walsh
From: Nick Acevedo
Date: November 30
Subject: Check your mailbox

Let's take this piece by piece.

1. Are you okay? That sounded a little severe, even for you.
2. Have you checked your mailbox?
3. If not, please do that.
4. When can I see you this week?
5. Apparently, you already know everything there is about croissants. You wouldn't be able to research that for more than 45 minutes. I'll call Le Cordon Bleu, and get the ball rolling on an honorary doctorate.

*since you've been gone, Boston has fashioned itself as quite the foodie capital. There are all manner of authentic bakeries and such here. Come visit. You might find some worthwhile bread. And your husband.

**I never doubted you, wife.

ERIN WAS SITTING on her bed, pillows on either side of her and her glasses resting atop her head. She was wearing an unbuttoned flannel with a thermal shirt beneath it, and black pants that were close-fitting and looked soft. I couldn't tell whether they were yoga pants or leggings, or what the difference was between the two to begin with, but I loved them. None of this was seductive, not in any obvious way, but that didn't matter. Erin made thick wool sweaters and fleece-lined jeans that hid her curves look sexy. Sexier than anything I'd ever seen.

She was talking about an issue she was having with

making her preliminary research findings comprehensible to philanthropists and politicians. I was listening, but also reminiscing about the texture of her clit against my tongue.

"And I'm not being a snotty scientist who thinks everyone else should just learn some planetary physics. I get it," she said, running her fingers through her hair. "It needs to be bite-sized and digestible, or it's not going to stick. No more complicated than Henry VIII dumping Catherine of Aragon to marry Anne Boleyn."

"Right," I murmured, smiling as her side-swept bangs fell across her forehead.

"Ignoring all the issues with his general inability to produce a male heir with basically anyone, anywhere," she continued, almost to herself.

She did that a lot, babbling about science or history or whatever information was in her head. She didn't say these things to show off her encyclopedic knowledge. It was a defense mechanism of sorts, a way to shield herself from revealing anything of her own until she was ready. There were days when it took longer to get through the random facts and reach Erin, but that didn't bother me. How could it? In the end, I got her, and that was all that mattered.

"And the fact he made wild changes to the English constitution mostly because he was a power-hungry manwhore with a God complex," she said. "That obviously complicates the analogy."

"You have me at a disadvantage with the random history facts, Skip, but keep talking. I'm gonna miss this. I'm gonna miss you."

She stopped, mid-thought. "Don't do that," she warned, pointing a finger at me. "We're not starting with that. We have a few more days." She threw her hands up and her gaze snapped somewhere in the distance. "The package, the one you sent. It arrived today. I grabbed it on my way in but then left everything at the door because I was covered in snow. I'll grab it now."

I was left staring at her yellow and blue pillows, wishing I could copy and paste myself into her bed. There'd never been a time in my life when I'd wanted anything or anyone this way while so much stood in my way. Even thinking back to those grueling years of internship and residency, when I was competing for procedures, surgeries, fellowships… None of it was this difficult.

It was as if we'd had this one miraculous weekend where everything was perfect—we were perfect—but then our paths diverged. Maybe the challenge wasn't in retracing our steps to get back to that weekend, but building new paths where none existed before.

Erin climbed back on the bed, tucking her feet beneath her as she pulled her computer onto her lap. "What do we have here?" she murmured, taking her Swiss Army knife to the box I'd sent.

I sat back, folding my arms over my chest as she sliced through the tape. Being aroused by a knife-wielding woman was new for me, but not unwelcome.

Erin shook out the t-shirt with a laugh. "Oh, this is special," she said, dropping the shirt and looking into the camera. "Where did you find it?"

"The guy who lives downstairs, the one in cardio-thoracic, not the gastro girl," I said. "A bunch of interns on his service started a dodgeball league, and they had those shirts made."

She held it up again, shaking her head. "'Hot enough to stop your heart,'" she read. "'Skilled enough to restart it.' I'm amazed you didn't add 'my husband is' anywhere."

"Thought about it," I said.

Erin unfolded the gray Harvard Med School hoodie next, and smiled at it before looking to me. "You know, I don't have any college stuff. I've just never thought to acquire any."

"Now you do," I said. "Keep going. There's more in there."

"All right, all right," she murmured, her arm disappearing inside the cardboard. She pulled out a small box, glancing from me to the box without opening it. "What's this?"

"Do you regret the lobster boat?" I asked. "Marrying me?"

She continued staring at the box. For a long fucking time.

"No, I don't regret that. I don't believe in regrets," she said eventually. I'd suffered five major heart attacks from her silence. "I can acknowledge that I should've handled things differently, or want to be better in the future, but wishing the past away, no matter how awful it was, is a disgrace to the moments you've lived. All that you've survived."

She wasn't talking about us or the lobster boat, though I wanted to yank her back to those topics and hear her say, *No, I'd never regret marrying you.*

"I'm coming for you," I said.

When Erin frowned, I recognized that my comment only made sense in my head, where I was aware that the feelings I'd had for this woman last summer were painfully superficial. That was lust mixed with some self-flagellating heartache, all compounded by her being beautiful, and more mysterious than any ancient artifact. But what we had now —the late night video chats and snarky emails, the challenge of finding time to share the same space again, the truths laid bare—there was nothing superficial about this. It was that awareness that sent me in search of a little piece of me by way of a Harvard hoodie, and when it was clear that wasn't nearly enough, I found something more substantial. More permanent.

"I mean, when you finish your research trip. I'm coming to Iceland. We can have a few days, a weekend, as long as you want. But know that I'm coming for you."

Erin's fingers traced the edges of the box. "Let's talk about that when I get back," she said. "It's not *no*, it's *let's take it one day at a time*. I don't even know for sure when we'll return, and I'd hate it if you were here, and I was somewhere in the Norwegian Sea. I'd have to stage a mutiny, and I'm not sure I want that on my record."

I could deal with that, and I nodded toward the box. "Open it."

Her forehead crinkled, not pleased with my barked order, but she tore into the container. There was a velvet pouch inside, a robin's egg blue one emblazoned with a Newbury Street jeweler's name, and that sent both eyebrows up.

"What's this?" she asked, loosening the ties.

I didn't answer, instead watching while she upended the pouch's contents into her palm. She pinched the ring between her thumb and forefinger, staring at the narrow strip of diamonds on platinum.

"There's probably something unwise about picking out diamonds for a geologist, but—"

"No," she interrupted, her eyes still focused on the band. "Not unwise. Not at all."

"You don't have to say that," I continued. "I just didn't want you going to the North Pole without a ring."

Her shoulders shook as she laughed. "Are you worried about the research station hook-up scene? Even if I wasn't married, and long past the hook-up phase of my life, I wouldn't be giving Arctic Sea researchers a second glance. I have to share some cramped quarters with them for two months, and I don't want them giving me the smarms."

"I wasn't worried about *that*," I said. "It hit me that my wife's been walking around without a ring, and that's a problem."

"So we're doing this," she mused, still studying the band. "We're being married now. It's real."

I took a sip from my water bottle before responding. "What've we been doing the past few months, darlin'?"

Erin rolled her eyes and held up the ring as if it could make her point for her. "Have you told your parents?"

I scratched my chin while I thought that through. "Do you want me to? I don't think I've even told them that I took the job at Mass Gen," I said. "If you want me to do that, I will, although I'd rather take you to Dallas and introduce you the right way."

Erin nodded slowly. "See what I mean? Your family doesn't know, my family doesn't know, it's just us and this little experiment."

"About that," I said, gesturing toward her. "Riley knows."

She blew out the longest, loudest sigh I'd ever heard, and then stared at me, stone-faced. "Of course he does," she said.

I started to explain, but then Erin slipped the ring onto her finger. A bolt of adrenaline spread through my body, warm and light like bubbles in my bloodstream, and I smiled. It was loose, and she moved it to her middle finger.

"I guess I'll have to grow into it," she said.

And that was our marriage, right there in a single breath. It didn't belong to tradition, and we were still trying to make it fit.

Was it strange that my wife lived on another continent, and neither of us could make moves to change that? Sure.

Was it odd that we'd been married for months, and

neither of our families knew anything about it? Definitely, but it was worth noting that our families were also odd.

Was it possible that this would go up in flames and leave us burnt and broken? Absolutely.

Was it also possible that we'd uncover the path that made this work for both of us? Yeah, and that was what made this chaos worthwhile.

Fifteen

NICK

CHRISTMAS EVE WAS BRUTAL. It started with an unpleasant call to my parents, both of whom seemed miserable for reasons of their own creation. They couldn't remember what they liked about each other but had little interest in confronting that issue, and the consequences bore themselves out in an assortment of misplaced hostilities. My mother was forever hiring and firing decorators or contractors, none of them ever up to par. My father spent all of his hours on horses, often traveling hither and yonder to find his next great beast. Dallas society and charity events were too busy, or not busy enough, or whichever private club they belonged to was being impossible again. And I lived in Boston, which I couldn't be bothered to leave for even one holiday a year.

Insert eye roll.

Going home was nothing more than an invitation for my parents to complain about each other to me, and it drove me crazy that they were unhappy together but were content to piss and moan their days away instead of changing anything. The most annoying part was that my family didn't have *real* issues. They had old, middling issues that lent themselves to passive-aggression and side-taking. When I considered that alongside Erin's family, and the abuse and neglect she endured after her mother died, I was even more annoyed.

Home hadn't been the same since my grandmother passed away during my senior year at UT-Austin. She'd never understood my mother's world of big oil money, and she didn't understand my sisters' interests in pageants and debutante balls, but we understood each other. My grandmother taught me how to care for every living thing on the ranch. I'd delivered more than a dozen foals before I was ten years old, and I knew how to suture cuts, treat scorpion stings, and diagnose common ailments before I was fifteen.

My grandmother was known locally as a healer, a medicine woman who always had a handmade salve or potion at the ready. She traveled between ranches and migrant camps, always checking on someone and bringing a balm to someone else and asking after so-and-so with the stomach pains. She delivered babies and performed rudimentary surgery, ministered to the sick and dying and shouted at ranchers to take better care of their people.

Medical school taught me nothing about bedside manner; I owed it all to my grandmother. She taught me to listen to the things people said, and the things they didn't, and she taught me to trust my judgment. I probably owed the profound sense of failure that I experienced each time I lost a patient to her as well. She didn't believe in giving up hope, even on the hopeless, and she had no problem cursing all the gods she could name anytime someone passed before their time.

She would've hated the way my Christmas Eve was going. The ER received six critical patients from a highway rollover, four young children and their parents. Two of the kids died at the scene; the parents died in surgery. I treated the other two for concussions, and kept a crew of interns with them until their grandparents arrived.

It didn't matter that I'd been living in hospitals for years now, I'd never get used to telling people that their loved ones were gone. It wasn't going to get easier for me, and though it tore me apart every time, it was better than growing immune to it all. If ever there was a day when losing patients didn't knock me in the gut, I was doing something wrong.

By the time I reached Andy and Patrick's apartment in the North End, I was drained. I wanted to tell Erin every last thing about my day, including an update on the secret affair my downstairs neighbor, the gastrointestinal surgeon, was having with one of her residents. It was like a telenovela, unfolding right before my eyes. But Erin was off the grid and I was alone.

I drifted through the evening, mindlessly talking about this spring's city marathon, sports, the weather. It was good to be with friends, and even better to have somewhere to be when the quiet interior of my apartment would be altogether too empty, but it was also difficult to keep up the cheerful ruse.

And I was still bitter. I was angry at the world for putting the perfect woman in front of me at the most imperfect time, and I was angry with myself for not finding a solution to it all. Sometimes I looked at Patrick and wondered how he was so damn lucky. The love of his life was his apprentice, a woman who worked with him all day and shared a bed with him every night. I couldn't imagine getting that much time with Erin, but that didn't shut down any of my envy.

Later that night, Shannon and I started walking home, both of us traveling in the same direction. But instead of our homes, we ended up in the saddest, loneliest bar in town. I didn't know which ghost was haunting her shadows, but she looked about as terrible as I felt. So we tucked ourselves into the bar, sipped whiskey, and listened to the greatest hits of Journey and REO Speedwagon.

Totally, completely bitter.

I glanced into my glass. It was mostly full. We hadn't been drinking heavily, but the atmosphere seemed to make every minute feel long and drowsy.

Shannon turned to me, her eyes hooded as if she was somewhere between comfortably intoxicated and asleep. "Where's Erin these days?"

I laughed into my drink, and even that sounded bitter. Of course she'd ask. I was willing to bet that Shannon had been dying to ask about Erin since Matt's wedding.

"She's not here," I said. I was being obtuse, and I didn't care. "That's all I can say for sure."

"Consider it a gift," she said, leaning toward me as she spoke. "She's too young for you anyway."

I'd been waiting for it all night. Just fucking waiting so that I could throw it right back at someone. I wanted to call them all out over their absurd attitude toward Erin, and remind them they'd committed their share of crimes, too.

"That's a fucking miserable thing to say," I murmured. "And the thing about age is that it stops mattering around the time you hit twenty-three or twenty-four. Definitely when you hit twenty-five." Fuck it. I wasn't due back at the hospital until tomorrow night, and some dreamless whiskey sleep might help. I downed the amber liquid and signaled for another. "It's also my position that Erin knows no age. The eight years between us are—" I held out my hands as if I could gather all the beautiful, brilliant pieces of Erin and scoop them up and make sense of them. "They're nothing. She's lived more lives than I have, and she knows more of the earth than I do, and—"

Shannon grabbed my wrist, a pained look on her face. "If this is where you tell me how she's captured your heart, I'll need to say goodnight and walk out the door because I cannot handle that right now."

I was ready to take her to task over the mountain of bullshit between her and Erin, and demand that she do something about it, but I also knew that crossed all of Erin's lines. She required choice and autonomy, and hated being boxed in. She was the only one who could dismantle this mess.

"That's not quite how it went down," I said, laughing. "No, but I'd like to point out that you've been operating under the assumption you know what happened with me and Erin that night, and believe me when I tell you that you're wrong."

Shannon glared at me for a long moment, making no mistake about her disdain for me right now. "Right, so you had your hand under her dress because...what? Checking for ticks? Trying to find the 'mute' button?"

I didn't understand her hostility at first, but I started to see her reaction as protectiveness. The inquiry about Erin's whereabouts, the sharp comment about her age, it was all in the vein of parental interrogation. Erin wasn't the out-of-line little sister in this scenario, and that was a small victory. I'd rather be the cradle robber than watch my wife take any more hits.

I folded my arms on the bar and leaned forward,

glancing at her when the bartender refilled our drinks. "It's not what you think," I said, shooting for a peaceful tone.

Shaking her head, she said, "I don't think I want to hear any more of this. Not tonight."

"Good," I said, tipping back my drink. "I don't want to talk about it anymore."

Sixteen

NICK

To: Erin Walsh
From: Nick Acevedo
Date: December 25
Subject: Confession

Confession: I fucking miss you. All of you. More than the words "I miss you" can even express.

I miss the obscure history and science that's way over my head, too.

I hope you're safe and warm, and I want you home soon because I will be seeing you as soon as possible.

To: Nick Acevedo
From: Erin Walsh
Date: December 27
Subject: Confession

My confession: I fucking miss you, too.

But I keep thinking that I can't give you what you want. I can't give you *anything*. Seriously. What kind of relationship is this? We're like pen pals who've seen each other naked, and you're a nice guy. The nicest. But you're stuck with me, and I'm on a goddamn ship headed for the North Pole, and I'll be there for months.

You deserve so much more than someone who can't get on the same continent as you more than once a year.

————

To: Erin Walsh
From: Nick Acevedo
Date: December 27
Subject: Confession

We're going to blame that last message on the cold. Or sea sickness. Or something relating to magnetic north and shifting poles and God knows what else.

Before you come back and tell me it's not some Arctic shit making you crazy, let me tell you this: you can't shake me off that easy. I'll buy some snowshoes, hike my ass up to the North Pole, and carry you home if I have to, but you're not done with me yet.

Answer me this: who do you think about when you touch yourself?

————

To: Nick Acevedo
From: Erin Walsh
Date: January 4
Subject: No confessions here

After the American Revolution, the colonists started drafting their own laws, there was one that showed up in the constitutions of nine of the thirteen original colonies—although I've always wondered what was wrong with the other four—and was a tenet of the common law at the time. It's known as *nemo tenetur*, which translates to *no one is obliged*. The colonists were pretty fired up about this notion.

It was a direct and proportional response to the British courts of equity that dated back to the late 1400s. Colonists took issue with the courts' inquisitorial approach. The burden of proof didn't lie with the courts, as it does now.

Come to think of it, the inquisitorial approach does have a home in this age. Yeah, it's now known as enhanced interrogation. Hmm...funny how these things come full circle.

Today, *nemo tenetur* is known as the Fifth Amendment of the Constitution and I am invoking it. There are a lot of things I'll do to myself, but self-incrimination is not one of them, thank you kindly.

To: Erin Walsh
From: Nick Acevedo
Date: January 5
Subject: It was definitely a confession

I love your nerdy history talk. The way you tell it sounds really fucking filthy, and I love it. Don't ever stop.

That was an exceptionally detailed way of telling me that yes, you definitely think about me. You should, since I think of you quite often. We've shared many showers, lovely.

To: Nick Acevedo
From: Erin Walsh
Date: January 9
Subject: It wasn't an admission of anything

I know my rights, sir, and I know that I confessed nothing.

Am I correct in assuming you spent the holidays with my family?

To: Erin Walsh
From: Nick Acevedo
Date: January 10
Subject: It was more than nothing

I was at Patrick and Andy's place for Christmas Eve. That girl can make tamales better than my grandmother, and it's sacrilege to even say that. My grandmother's probably going to climb out of her grave and haunt me now.

It's probably dangerous to ask this, but when is that ship

heading to port? I need some motivation. A date on the calendar, a month, a moon phase, anything.

———

To: Nick Acevedo
From: Erin Walsh
Date: January 21
Subject: Confession

Hey, Dr. Hot Pants,
This ship is like a big old nerd carpool. We're always dropping people off, picking people up. If we could've gone straight to the research station, we'd be there by now. Once we arrive, I'm heading off the grid. I'm not going to have reliable internet access for a few weeks. I'm trying to get a first look at some samples from a new coring site, and it's really remote.

And here's my confession: I will miss you so damn much that I hate those words. They seem totally inadequate. I'm frustrated that I can't find anything better. I missed you when I left the Cape after Matt and Lauren's wedding. But now I want to tell you what I ate for lunch and how I didn't pack any matching socks and that I had a really strange dream about dolphins. I want to know what you ate for lunch, too, and I want to hear you talk about your surgeries, and the Adventures of Gastro Girl, and everything else you're doing. I want to share my good news or bad news with you, and tell you when I'm happy and sad, and tired and stressed, and all the feelings in between.

I guess what I'm saying is that I'd roast a chicken for you. At the very least, I'd get out of bed after sex and make you a sandwich.

I don't know when I'll be able to see you. I know I say that all the time, but I'm not avoiding you. I promise I'm going to make it soon. If it isn't winter, it will be spring—and before you ask, yes, spring in the Northern Hemisphere. I might have to commandeer this ship and sail it back to Iceland myself, but I'll do it.

To: Erin Walsh
From: Nick Acevedo
Date: January 21
Subject: Confession

I'll see your confession, and raise you mine: I don't remember how I lived before you.

I was thinking about our wedding when I was out running last night. The stars always remind me of you, and I remember how much I liked you that first night. I thought I knew you back then, but I knew nothing compared to these past few months.

To: Nick Acevedo
From: Erin Walsh
Date: January 26
Subject: Arrived at the station

It's good that we can agree on liking each other, such that we made poor old Bartlett marry us on the spot.

To: Erin Walsh
From: Nick Acevedo
Date: January 26
Subject: Arrived at the station

Come on. Bartlett enjoyed the fuck out of us. We brought a whole lot of amusement to another boring night of lobster-ing. That's your gift in life, Skip. You make the most ordinary things quite extraordinary.

Stay warm up there, Skip. When I get you back, I want to see all fingers and toes intact.

Here's my confession: I can't stop thinking about you.
Nick

To: Nick Acevedo
From: Erin Walsh
Date: January 26
Subject: Arrived at the station

Me neither. It's annoying.
*but not too annoying.

To: Erin Walsh
From: Nick Acevedo
Date: February 16
Subject: Sam

Hi, Erin,
Not sure if you're in range yet, but you should touch base with Sam at some point. He's having a rough week.

Nick

*After you check in with Sam, I want a detailed report about life in your bunk. And everything else. I fucking miss you.

———

To: Erin Walsh
From: Nick Acevedo
Date: February 20
Subject: Happy birthday, lovely

To my wife on her birthday –
I'd make cookie dough for you.

Tell me you're warm and coming home soon.
Nick

To: Nick Acevedo
From: Erin Walsh
Date: February 25
Subject: Finally, finally, finally home

Hey, Strange Boy,
You had me at cookie dough.

I'm sorry it's taken so long to get back to you. There was an ice storm in Lapland, up in northern Finland, and the team was delayed in getting back to the station from the new coring site. I just saw your message about Sam, and nine thousand text messages from Riley, and a brief "everything's fine but I thought you should know" email from Matt, too.

Tell me if this is an accurate summary of the events before I yell at him for being a fool: Sam broke up with the girlfriend, got super wasted (like dumb fool wasted, not regular frat bro wasted), and ended up at your hospital.
- e

*My bunk and sleeping bag were unremarkable, though you might have made an appearance or two or ninety-four. How've I been in the shower?

**How's Gastro Girl?

To: Erin Walsh
From: Nick Acevedo
Date: February 25
Subject: SKIP!

Hello, lovely.
I'm forfeiting the asterisk/footnote debate and telling you right now that I've missed the fuck out of you. I want you, anywhere that I can get you, as soon as possible. Name the time and place, and I'll bring the extra-large penis. I'll need an entire day with your dewy petals, and now that I think of it, that's probably not enough. A week. Maybe more.

You know, I'd text you all my filthy thoughts from bed if you let me. Admit it, Skip, that would be fun.

Okay, now that we've covered that: yeah, that's the gist of things with Sam.
Nick

*I want that time and place, lovely.

**Gastro Girl isn't great. Things went sour with the resident.

To: Nick Acevedo
From: Erin Walsh
Date: February 25

Subject: demanding much?

Dude, I haven't been in my apartment in two months and my ass is still partially frozen. Give me a couple of days to sort out my life before you come at me with the grabby hands. Pretend (just for shits and giggles) that you want more than my tits.

Keep me posted if you hear anything on the Sam front, por favor.

*Stop it with the texting. I don't like texting.

To: Erin Walsh
From: Nick Acevedo
Date: February 26
Subject: Very demanding. Totally demanding.

Of course I want more than your tits! Are you fucking kidding me, Skip?

I want to hear some random historical facts, and a detailed accounting of all the things you've researched since the summer. And yeah, I want you naked and underneath me but it's not about sex. It's never been about sex, and I think you know that.

Por supuesto, mamí.

*Why don't you like texting? Isn't that your generation's thing?

To: Nick Acevedo
From: Erin Walsh
Date: February 26
Subject: Confession

Here's my confession for today: I know it's not about sex. I was being bratty when I said that, and I'm sorry.

This expedition has been exhausting and I'm behind on everything, and that's not some bullshit blow-off line. I'm overwhelmed right now, and that's not something I say to people. I avoid and I do unhealthy things. I wait until I'm so far past overwhelmed that I can't remember the origin of it all, and then I get even more unhealthy, and then I beat myself up for letting any of it happen. But I'm telling you and I need you to understand.

So...maybe you could hang tight for a bit? I know I'm asking a lot, and you probably don't want to wait for me much longer. I get it.

*It hasn't escaped my notice that we're now utilizing multiple asterisks on a regular basis. I'm not fond of this.

From: Nick Acevedo
To: Erin Walsh
Date: February 26
Subject: Confession

Erin…

I'll always wait for you. Don't you dare doubt that, Skip.

Churn that data. Write those papers. I'll be right here when you're ready for me.

*It didn't escape my notice that you trust me enough to tell me when you're overwhelmed. Keep doing that, okay?

———

THEY SAID the first year of marriage was the hardest. I believed it, even though I knew conventional wisdom was never meant for marriages with thousands of miles of distance on top like an extra serving of rainbow sprinkles. Those first-year marriage struggles were about household chores and money, where to spend the holidays and remembering to put the toilet seat down. Did it make us stronger to spend our first year hunting free moments for video chats and negotiating with the schedule gods for a few days together? Or was that just more proof that we were playing a fantastical game with no real consequences?

But it didn't feel like a game. That was the least confusing part. It felt like I'd left a chunk of myself with Nick, and while I could steal it away from him, I'd never get it—*me*—back in the state I gave it. Nick changed me, or maybe I changed while Nick was watching, but I was different now. I wanted things that I didn't understand, and cared for him in a way I didn't believe possible, and I wanted this to work. I didn't want to stop pretending, or whatever I was doing.

Eighteen

NICK

"YOU STILL HAVEN'T GIVEN me a date," I said, glancing at the screen before returning to my leftover lo mein. "I need to see you, Skip."

"How can I?" Erin asked, her eyebrow arched. "Your schedule has been brutal. If I wasn't so selfish, I'd feel guilty for keeping you up tonight."

"You're allowed to be as selfish as you want," I said, but I nodded while I stabbed the carton.

I *was* tired, and a little grouchy, too. I'd logged more operating room time in the past four months, since becoming an attending surgeon in December, than I imagined possible. Being the low man on the pole meant I had all the overnights, all the weekend on-calls, all the ER consults, all the clueless interns. I hadn't been running in weeks, and my diet consisted exclusively of takeout from Cambridge Street restaurants. We were surviving on emails, quick calls, and a measly bunch of brief video chats since she'd arrived back in Reykjavík last month.

"Will it always be like this for you?" she asked, a bit tentative. "Crazy hours, no time off?"

I kept stabbing at the noodles. "No, it gets better," I said. "Surgeons are notoriously cannibalistic. We want everyone to suffer on the way up just like we did, and once that's achieved, it's all good times and golf." She nodded as if this made any sense. "Private practice would be easier."

"You'd hate that," she said automatically. "I don't even know what that really entails, but if it's anything like the difference between *Grey's Anatomy* and *Private Practice*, I'm comfortable saying you'd hate it."

"That's probably accurate," I said. "But there's a new attending coming in, someone from U-Wisconsin, and we'll haze her next. She'll get all the extra coverage, and I'll step outside and figure out which season it is right now."

"Still winter in the northern hemisphere, hon," she murmured. "About three weeks until the vernal equinox."

"Thanks, darlin'," I said, but I wanted to get back to the topic at hand. "You know I like you selfish. I also like you naked. When can I have that?"

Erin turned her attention to the small spiral notebook at her elbow, the one where she recorded all of her to-dos, reminders, and notes. I used to think she was hyper-diligent, almost in the way that Shannon was Type A all the way, but I'd come to realize that Erin was the classic absentminded professor. She wrote it all down to remember what to do, and what she'd done.

"What's on deck for fieldwork?" I asked. She didn't have to be at Oxford for several months; I had those dates marked on the calendar hanging in my kitchen.

She bobbed her head from side to side as she flipped through her notebook. "I need to get over to Greenland," she said. "Maybe June, and then a few more times after that. There's a lot going on there, but at least it's close by."

"Okay," I said, thinking through my surgical and on-call

schedule for the month. "Okay, that leaves March, and then April and May. Right?"

Erin blew out a heavy breath. She was still catching up on work after being in the Arctic for the past two months, and she had a lot of balls in the air right now. "Yeah," she said. She shook her water bottle. "Hang on, I need a refill."

She unfolded her legs from beneath her and went to climb off her bed when I said, "Whoa, whoa, whoa. What is *this*?"

I'd been looking at her black long-sleeved thermal shirt with the Harvard Med hoodie I'd sent her a few months ago on top—the one she wore *all* the time—and foolishly assumed she was wearing jeans or yoga pants, too. But the smooth, bare skin that filled my screen proved otherwise.

"You've been sitting there in your little pink skivvies this whole time?" I asked. Erin pushed her glasses up her nose, smiling though she tried to fight it. "If you're not wearing any pants, darlin', you'd best announce that up front."

Erin cocked her head to the side. "Oh? And why is that?"

I set the lo mein and my laptop beside me on the sofa and pushed to my feet. "So I can join you," I said, shoving my flannel pajama bottoms to the ground. That left me in a Longhorns t-shirt and boxers. Thinking better of it, I yanked the shirt over my head. Superfluous.

"Good Lord," she muttered, staring at my chest.

"Yeah?" I ran my hand over my abs. "How about you take that shirt off, darlin'."

"No, Nick," she warned, holding up a hand. It was the same hand with her wedding ring on the wrong fucking finger, and I growled at that reminder. "I can't do this."

She sounded like I was asking her to jump out of an airplane without a parachute. Abandoning the lo mein, I carried my laptop into the bedroom.

"Where are you going?" Erin asked. "Seriously, Nick. I *can't* do this. You know how awkward I am when it comes to sex, and I can't—"

"Awkward?" I asked, leaning back against the pillows. "You are anything *but* awkward, darlin'."

She tossed her head back and covered her eyes. "I'm so awkward," she said, groaning. "I'm not comfortable with sex or saying dirty things or—or—any of this. I can't."

"If that's the case, then we have very different recollections of having sex with you," I said. I had the computer propped up beside me, and in a strange, digital-society kind of way, it felt like she was in bed with me.

"Oh *no*," she said heavily. "You can't do that. No sleepy eyes and rumpled faces. Put that filthy smirk away, sir. You can't do that."

"Do what?" I asked, pillowing my head on my bicep. Her lips parted and I could almost feel her sigh on my skin.

"*That*." Erin gestured to me, her hand outstretched as if me, lying in bed shirtless, explained it all. "You are unreal, and I'm a hot, hot mess. Just admit it."

Frowning, I scratched my belly while I considered Erin's comment. She was a hot mess if hot messes were gut-churningly gorgeous. Then I heard her sigh. It wasn't her usual exasperation either, it was the breathy type of sigh that rang with longing. Glancing back to the screen, I found her gazing at my torso.

"I love that you're fuzzy," she whispered, as if she was sharing a secret with my abs. Her teeth sank into her bottom lip, and it only made me want to taste her more.

"Yeah?" I asked, dragging my fingers through my chest hair. Later, when my cock wasn't demanding attention, I'd file this nugget away with all the other things I'd never expected to hear from Erin.

She nodded a few times too many, like she was in an eight-pack trance and couldn't shake free. "I like your hands, too."

I didn't expect that one either. "Why is that?" I asked.

She lifted a shoulder and then tugged at her sleeves, pulling the cuffs down over her hands. It was too fucking cute. I couldn't articulate why I liked that as much as I did, but it always turned me on more than any show of cleavage.

"They're strong," she said. So shy. "And your veins, they're…they're nice."

"No one's ever complimented my vascularity before," I said. That wasn't true. Phlebotomists loved me. Not relevant to the current situation.

"Oh my God!" she cried, burrowing inside the hoodie to hide from me. "See? I'm *so* awkward."

"Come back here," I said. "You're fucking adorable. Nothing awkward about you."

"I just said you have sexy *veins*," she cried from behind the sweater. "That's evidence that I'm not qualified for video chat sex…or any kind of sex."

"Then you don't have to say anything, darlin'," I said, reaching into my boxers. Relief and need combined into a steely groan when I gripped my length. "But I dare you to watch."

"Oh, I can watch," she said automatically, emerging from her hiding place.

I didn't know what it was about Erin and dares, but goddamn did they work.

"I want you here, Skip. Right here," I said. My hand was moving inside my boxers, and though the fabric kept the goods from view, Erin squeaked out a whimper when she noticed my arm flexing with the motion.

"I want to be there," she whispered, one sweatshirt-covered fist pressed to her lips. "You know how much I want you."

My head swiveled from side to side as I stroked harder. I was trying to stay in control here, but with Erin's soft voice and her fingers barely peeking out from her sleeves, and her wide, wide eyes and absolutely rapt attention, I was losing, falling fast. "I don't know, lovely," I said through a groan. I forced myself to slow down, and drew a breath into my lungs. "You have to tell me."

"This is so dirty," she said, her fist still shielding her mouth like she was afraid of what might tumble out. I was jealous of that hand, the hoodie, everything. "I remember the way you feel, and how I couldn't get my fingers all the way around you. I think about that...a lot."

"*Ohmygod*," I choked out. "Every time I touch myself, I'm thinking it's you."

"I never got to taste you. I think about that, too," she said, her tongue sliding over her top lip. She hummed, low, deep in her throat. There were goose bumps along her collarbone, and her shirt was tight enough to show off her stiffened nipples. How I was still going was a mystery.

"Take off that shirt," I barked.

Erin's forehead was pinched as her eyebrows shot up. "It's cold, and I'm—"

"Shirt *off*, woman," I repeated. The throbbing tension in my body was turning me into one greedy motherfucker tonight.

"Fine," she snapped, but it wasn't an angry snap because she *wanted* me bossing her around. It made it less complicated for her to do something uncomfortable. She continued on, muttering about me being impossible and how some deviant surveillance analysts were definitely getting their jollies from this.

I didn't answer. I went on stroking my cock, as leisurely as the clawing need inside me would allow, and waiting to see her skin. The black thermal inched up and my grip tightened to the threshold of pain.

"Ah, *fuck*," I growled as the undersides of her breasts came into view. No bra. I repeat: *no bra*.

The shirt sailed out of view, and Erin yanked the hoodie over her shoulders. Somehow that was hotter than her sitting in bed, nude save for her panties. That hoodie was shy and defiant, and sexy, too, in a *Sisters of Tri Delta Annual Charity Calendar* kind of way.

"Love those tits," I said. It was more of a grunt. I was deep in grunting territory now, and holding on to the muddy faith that she'd reciprocate, and then I'd let go. "Touch them for me, darlin'. Please."

For a second, her eyes dipped from my arm, glancing down at her bare skin. She smiled, a small, private grin that reveled in my agony. Then her teeth speared her bottom lip, and her hands skimmed up her torso to cup her breasts.

"Like this?" she asked. Her thumbs brushed over her nipples, and I wanted to slap myself for not making this happen sooner. "Or this?" She traced the rosy skin before pinching her nipples, tugging on them just enough to have her shoulders loosening. "You liked licking them, and… biting. Is that what you want now?"

An incoherent bundle of sounds burst out at once, all determined to express that, yes, I absolutely wanted to bite her nipples right now, and I definitely enjoyed it the last time I had the pleasure. Additionally, my balls were going on strike if I kept backing away from release. They weren't hanging around for this kind of abuse, and they'd be sure to get back at me with some premature ejaculation in the future.

"Say something," she whispered, jutting her chin toward the forearm lost to my boxers.

I thought about kicking off my shorts and angling the screen lower. But me and Erin, we didn't get to this point because of sex, and sex wasn't why we *needed* to be together. Sex was the benefit that came along with meeting the coolest, quirkiest, smartest, hottest woman in the world, and marrying her the same night. That weekend was brief, but more intimate than anything I'd imagined a marriage could be. I'd looked into her eyes and kissed her lips while I moved in her, and I liked it that way.

So I wasn't exchanging intimate for explicit tonight. Time was on our side, and we'd find plenty of it for adventure, kink, and explicit when we didn't have an entire ocean between us.

"If I was there," I said in a rough voice, "I'd get my hand in those pretty panties. Do that for me, lovely."

Erin paused, her chin cocked to the side, and then her hand moved down her tummy and beneath the pink fabric. Her shoulders were bunched tight again, and while she was working hard at maintaining the impassive exterior, she was breathing quickly. She was hungry for this. Hesitant, too.

A still, silent moment passed and I started to believe I'd pushed her too far, but then I caught the slight bend of her elbow. Through a cock-sick haze, I studied her, realizing she wasn't nearly as still as I'd thought. Just incredibly subtle.

"When'd you get so wicked, Skip?" I asked. "Don't even let me watch."

"Gotta keep some mystery in the marriage," she whispered, sighs and moans punching through each of her words. "That imagination of yours has worked well enough in the shower."

"The only mystery is how long you're going to make me wait," I said. "It's not possible to jerk my cock any harder. Not fucking possible."

"If you were here," she started, "would you come on my belly? Put it all over me?"

I murmured in agreement, nodding as my entire body tensed. That was it. That was what I needed from her. "All over you," I said, gasping as a million pinpricks covered my body. Erin cried out, her brows pinched and her lips falling open, and heat swept over me.

My pager sounded, and a beat later, my phone started ringing. It was an auto-tuned symphony to herald long-overdue orgasms, and it felt like the requisite explosion scene in every modern action film. I dropped my head back, sinking into the pillow while my shoulders shook with each powerful spurt.

Ragged breaths. Wet, rapidly cooling puddle stretching from belly button to breast bone. All the happy hormones. Soul-deep desire to sleep for days. Even greater desire to sleep with *this woman*.

"How was that?" I asked.

I reached in the direction of the dueling noisemakers, fumbling for my devices while I smiled at Erin. She was swaddled in the sweatshirt now, the sides held close to her chest and her knees tucked up, under the waistband. Her eyes softened when she was sated, and I wanted to give her that every day. It wasn't the conquest of pleasing my wife that I was chasing, it was the possibility of that peaceful glow, where her troubles weighed less and the world was gentler and nothing mattered but us.

A smile pulled at her lips and she blinked. "It was good,"

she said. "I'm still completely awkward, but it was good. Surprisingly so."

"Give it up, Skip. You're not awkward." I glanced at the readouts, and then turned them to the camera. "Duty calls," I said, still panting. "But let me promise you this: I'll be there this month, lovely."

Nineteen

NICK

A NONSTOP FLIGHT from Boston to Reykjavík clocked in around six hours. Of those six hours, I spent only seven minutes without Erin on my mind. I wondered whether she preferred aisle or window, and if she was an anxious traveler. She couldn't be, not after years chasing volcanoes around the planet. Once, over a late night video chat, I'd asked her to tell me about the places she'd been and everything she'd seen. She'd flipped through her dog-eared passport, offering up stories to accompany each stamp. Portugal, Japan, Indonesia, Norway, Mexico. This world, she knew all of its corners and crevices.

I debated the likelihood that Erin would want to *do things* this weekend. Yes, I desperately wanted to enjoy some normal coupledom with her, but my only desire was to put my hands all over her naked body and remind her to whom she belonged. Coupledom could wait until my next visit…or whenever we'd be able to find a more grounded existence.

Then I pictured her in an endless combination of leggings and long-sleeve shirts, and imagined stripping her out of them. At one point, I had to press my iPad to my lap to avoid public indecency charges. To snap my attention off the creamy skin I'd find when rolling those stretchy leggings down, I puzzled through the conversation I wanted to have about Doctors Without Borders.

At her ceaseless urging, I'd applied to the medical relief organization that worked primarily in conflict-ravaged regions. They were willing to accommodate my schedule at the hospital, and that was a blessing, considering that I was only able to commit for two eight week tours. It helped that before specializing in neuro, I'd completed surgical rotations in neonatal and obstetric surgery, as experience in both were desperately needed.

This time, I'd be the one going off the grid for months. I was looking forward to the experience, but not the separation. I was a wuss when it came to separation, and I'd only survived these past months because I was too exhausted to make sense of it all. My tolerance for distance wasn't the same as Erin's, and while I respected that Boston wasn't the warmest, friendliest place for her, I couldn't do this much longer if our contact was limited to email and video chat.

I wanted more, and I couldn't gather the right words to express that to Erin. It was tricky with her, knowing when to broach subjects like home and family. To her, both were on par with a swimming pool full of snakes supervised by evil clown lifeguards. Okay, maybe not *that* terrible but certainly not her favorite things.

Erin believed there wasn't a home for her there, and there were moments when it sounded as though she didn't believe she deserved one either. Regardless of where the research took her or how many doctorate degrees she wanted to collect, I'd find a way to give her a home. And I wasn't talking about Boston, or even her siblings. Home had nothing to do with place. It was a sense of belonging that Erin had never known.

I didn't have a clear vision of our future, or how we'd get there. I only knew that my compass pointed toward Erin, and bringing her home—wherever that was for us—was the endpoint.

"I HAD ALL THESE IDEAS," Erin murmured between frantic kisses while we hug-walked up the stairs to her apartment, "about how we'd—"

"Fuck ideas," I said, slamming her against the stairwell. One hand was on her ass, squeezing like I was trying to mark her, and the other up her shirt and under her bra. This was only marginally more discreet than the hand job she gave me to *near* completion in the cab from the airport. "Please, woman. You're brilliant but don't think right now."

Her palm slapped over my lips but I shook my head in protest. She wasn't going to keep me from tasting her. Her hand was a fine alternative to her mouth. "One more flight," she said through a laugh. "I'll race you up there."

She took off running, but my little lovely's legs were short and I caught her around the waist before she hit the first stair. "Here's the only idea we need: I'm not letting go of you until I get on that airplane Sunday night. How's that work for you?"

I slapped her ass for a bit of emphasis, and she tried to return the favor but only succeeded in yanking the tail of my shirt from my jeans. "When did you turn into such a beast?" she asked.

"When I spent months away from my wife," I said, glancing up and down the hallway when I reached the land-

ing. I didn't know where I was going. There wasn't enough
oxygen headed toward my brain, and I required an entire
minute to remember her apartment number. Then I stomped
in that direction, and pressed her against the door. That it
didn't magically open was annoying. Everything was
annoying right now, everything that got in the way of me
and my woman.

Still annoyed, I set Erin on her feet. I ran my hands up
her calves, between her thighs, and over her breasts. I was
on a mission.

"We're still outside, husband," she murmured into my
neck. Her fingers were under my shirt and on my skin, and I
couldn't stop growling. I didn't have any intelligible sounds,
and I was too damn close to buckling under her touch.

"I know," I said, palming her ass. "I'm looking for your
keys." Erin held them up with a devious grin, and why we
were still standing out here in the goddamn daylight was a
mystery to me. "*Inside*. Get your ass inside, woman."

She turned to unlock the door, and that was *it*. Coats off,
jeans unbuttoned, scarves and bags falling all around us. The
door was barely shut when I tugged her shirt over her head
and threw it into her apartment like it'd insulted me. We
hopped around, leaning on each other as we shook out of
our clothes and kicked off shoes. She flung her bra aside,
and I hooked a finger around her panties, dragging her
toward me.

It would've been a smooth move if I hadn't tripped over
my own pants in the process. We both went down, hitting
the pile of lumpy outerwear.

"Why is it so fucking difficult to fuck my wife?" I yelled,
kicking off the jeans that'd ruined my attempts at getting her
in bed without a disaster. I rolled, pulling Erin under me as
she laughed.

She brushed my hair off my forehead. "Hi," she replied, and her smile was bright and familiar, and it struck me how much I'd missed her. It was the way you missed the sun of summer in the dead of winter, when it didn't seem like you'd ever know warmth again. I snagged her bottom lip between my teeth. "Show me that beastly husband of mine."

"I hope you're not planning to climb any glaciers next week, because you won't be walking right when I'm done with you," I said, reaching back to grab the protection I'd stowed in my pocket. I was prepared this time, damn it. "Hang on, lovely. Gotta grab the condom."

"Don't worry about it," she said impatiently, dragging me back to her. "I have an IUD."

I levered up on my knees, and the movement had my cock slapping against my belly with an indelicate *thunk*. "Since when?"

Erin squinted while she wiggled out of her panties, as if she really needed to think it over before responding. "About three years ago."

"But minibar condoms!" I cried as I positioned myself between her legs. "All the minibar condoms!"

She offered a slightly apologetic frown. Only slightly. "I didn't know you."

I grabbed her left hand, the one with the wedding band on her goddamn middle finger. I moved it to her ring finger with a growl. I didn't care if it was loose. "You *married* me!"

Erin hooked her legs around my waist and jerked me down. She was small, but strong. "I did," she said, dragging her lips up my neck. "But I didn't know what would happen afterward. What if it was just a dare for you, and then it was over? I wasn't going to be on the hook with your herpes."

Groaning, I scrubbed my hand over my face. Ever the pragmatist, this wife of mine. "Holy Jesus, woman," I said under my breath. "It wasn't just a dare for me, and I don't have herpes."

"Right, so," Erin started, reaching for my erection, "no condom."

I batted her hands away. "No, darlin'," I rasped. "No matter how we play this, I'm coming in thirty seconds flat. I want to be inside you when it happens."

Her heels pressed into my backside in agreement, one sock on, one sock off. Her fingertips skimmed up her body, over the soft plane of her belly and up to her breasts in a move that was a million times more self-assured than anything I could've expected.

"Nick," she said, her lips pursed in a pout.

Her voice, her lips, her scent, her everything. It was all swarming around me and buzzing with emotional significance because we'd made it. We'd survived research trips and board certification exams and all the adult bullshit in our lives, and we were here, on the goddamn floor, hot and desperate for each other even after all this time. I couldn't move past the rush of finally—*fucking finally*—having her in my arms. Desire was heavy in my veins, condensing all of my thoughts into primitive needs and wants. I wanted to take her apart and then put her back together again so that every inch of her was stamped with my possession.

"I see you," she warned. "I see that look you're giving me. If you come on my belly, I'm going to make you lick it off."

"Erin," I growled. I couldn't decide whether I was impressed or shocked by that suggestion. And she thought she couldn't do dirty talk.

Instead of exploring that any further, I slammed into her, and everything went fuzzy. I could hear my pulse in my ears and feel her short fingernails scoring my biceps, but my cock was bare and I didn't think I could speak if I tried. My body was acting of its own volition, thrusting and gripping her hips as words fell from her tongue in a chaotic tumble of demands and pleas.

More, more, more.

Oh, God yes, like that.

Oh, oh, oh, fuck.

Please, please, please, Nick.

I love the way you fuck me.

There was none of the measured patience of our first night together, and that meant something. This woman of mine, she'd been through hell and back, and she knew enough about the place to give directions to the newcomers. But right now, with those filthy words on her lips and her body clamped tight around me, the ghosts of that history weren't haunting her. She knew she was safe with me, and that she could trust me to respect and protect her. Defile her a little, too.

"Nick," Erin whispered, reaching out to cup her hand around the back of my neck. "I want you right here."

She arched up while I drove into her. Her eyes crinkled and her lips fell open, and I pressed my thumb there. I wanted to feel her gasps and sighs, and I wanted to own the ragged breath that came with her orgasm. I wanted everything.

But Erin had other plans, and she caught my thumb between her teeth. That pressure, followed by the soothe of her tongue, sent pulsations careening down my spine. I came like a tsunami, crashing down and then winding back up for more before it was over. Wave after wave until I was certain that only my bones remained as I'd given everything else to Erin.

This wasn't one of my countless shower orgasms from recent months, or the kind from a satisfying one-night stand, or even decent dating sex. This was the class of orgasm that compelled men to profess their undying love and promise forever. And I would've said it all, every damn word of it, but I *knew* Erin. It didn't matter that she was right there with me. She needed a little more time to find comfort with the words, and when it came to time, we had plenty.

"Welcome to Iceland," Erin said, her lips a breath from my ear.

I groaned, something between aggrieved swamp monster and dying tyrannosaurus rex. I'd finished marathons and triathlons without feeling this wrecked before. "We're instating this as the official greeting. Welcome to Iceland, have some sex in the hallway."

"If you're making a habit of coming here," she started, a playful lilt in her voice, "I'll make a habit of greeting you this way."

"Yes, yes, I will be making a habit of coming," I said, all puns intended. "Yes to all of it. Just tell me when you'll have me, woman, and I'll be here."

It required all of the strength in my body to ease some of my weight off Erin and push up on my forearms. Her fair skin was dotted with fingertip-shaped welts and some light beard rash. I bent to kiss each of them.

"It's fine. They'll fade," Erin said, her fingers sliding through my hair. "Come on. Let's climb into bed."

I leaned into her touch as my eyes drifted shut. In that moment—and it *was* that one, not the one where I came like a natural disaster—the months apart and the distance disintegrated. Our relationship straddled the line between impossible and illogical, but it was too fucking right to give up.

I DIDN'T HAVE the interest or energy to take in Erin's home until later the following morning. The studio apartment was small, minimally decorated, intensely modern, and filled with books. Seemed fitting.

"Sorry," she said, noticing me looking at the bare walls. "No Civil War maps here."

I studied her, taking in the way her shoulder-length hair fanned out across the pillow and the sheets cast a silhouette over her curves, and decided there was no time like the post-orgasmic present.

"It's all good. We wouldn't want redundancy," I said.

I scratched my chin. Glanced out the window, then toward Erin's sparse kitchen and living area. There wasn't much else to the space. There was a tiny bathroom on the other side of the apartment, and I did mean *tiny*. I'd bullied my way into the shower with her last night, ignoring her insistence that it was only suitable for solo bathing. She was right about that. I couldn't bend my arms without hitting a tiled wall, and the spray was about six inches too low for me. We were stepping all over each other, and there was nothing we could do to keep the elbows from flying. I lost my footing and ended up sprawled on my ass on the cold floor when she accidentally popped me in the jaw while washing her hair.

"I've got the old maps, you've got every book ever written on just about every subject. We're good," I said. "There's nothing else we need. Sure, furniture and stuff, but we'll figure it out. Maybe Lauren can help. You give her something to look for, and she goes all foxhound, especially if you want vintage stuff."

"Really?" she murmured. "Already planning our future cohabitation? Don't I have a doctorate to finish first? Oh, and you have a couple of months of practicing medicine in the developing world, no?"

I threw back the sheets and changed position, moving down until I was resting my cheek on her tummy and smiling up at her. We'd discussed my Doctors Without Borders assignments late last night. She was thrilled about my new adventures, but with that came the recognition that we'd be contending with even more distance and time apart. No one was thrilled about that.

"I am planning for our cohabitation," I admitted. "I want to do this exact thing with you for many, many years."

Erin's eyes widened, as if I'd said something brash but not altogether shocking. A minute or two ticked by before she responded. "Riley texted me the other day," she announced. "Apparently Sam's taking a sabbatical in Maine. A rural fishing village or something of that nature."

Well. That was quite the detour.

"That's fascinating," I said carefully. Sam had been in rough shape when Riley brought him to the ER, and it was no small feat to get him stabilized. The guy had some serious issues to work out, and I wasn't convinced that a solitary expedition into the woods was the safest choice for him.

"According to Riley," Erin continued, "Sam hasn't specified when he'll return. I mean, I'm assuming he *will* return and he's not going all Henry David Thoreau on us now. It's surprising. He's always liked the great outdoors, but it's only ever been short camping trips. He's quite the fan of city life and creature comforts. I would've pegged him for the executive spa. You know, some place with a sweat lodge or private yurts."

She was right about that. Sam was definitely a high-end sweat lodge kind of guy. "Do you think it's good? That he's spending some time away?"

"It's not necessarily a bad thing," she said. "Getting away…it puts a lot of things in perspective."

I kissed the skin beneath her belly button. I loved that she was strong and fit, but also soft in certain places. It was a reminder that beneath all the stoicism were sensitive spots and womanly curves.

"What did it put in perspective for you?" I asked.

Erin's shoulders wiggled as if she was struggling to land on a response, and then she blew out a breath. "It turns down the noise," she said. "It lets you hear your own thoughts, and then fix the ones that don't sound the way you want them to. It makes you see the lies you were feeding yourself, and the angel-faced devils you trusted. It forces you to prioritize, and that helps you decide what can stay and what must go."

My eyes dropped to her torso. Each of her words was a secret passageway to other stories, longer ones with context and meaning, but I didn't know how to unlock them yet.

"Some people have to leave to find their way home again," Erin continued. "I'm one of them. I went away because it was the healthiest, safest option for me, but there are many reasons why I've stayed away. They're not about grudges or revenge. They're only about needing to find my way home, and no one else can do that for me." She pinned me with a pointed stare. "Not even you, husband."

I nodded, accepting that I didn't get to barge into her world and dictate how she mended her fences. Barging and dictating weren't things Erin Walsh appreciated.

"I can't find your way home, you're right about that," I said. "But you don't have to find it alone, either. I think you've been on your own for so long that you forget you can lean on someone, and you don't have to do everything by yourself."

"Oh Lord," she murmured. "Add that to your pillow embroidery list, honey."

I thought about her words for a minute. She was deflecting, but that was okay. This stuff was intense, and she was the one carrying most of the weight. So then I raked my scruffy chin over her belly until she was screaming with laughter and twisting away from me.

"Get your ass back here," I called.

"You're gonna have to catch me first," she cried.

I wrapped my arm around her thighs and dragged her back to the center of the bed. I pinned her down and teased every ticklish point on her body. There were many. She went right on yelping and giggling while tears streamed down her cheeks. I didn't know whether it was the wiggling or the laughter or the simple pleasure of touching her naked body, but I was absurdly aroused and I wanted her to know that. Straddling her waist, I brought her hand to my cock.

"Caught you," I said.

Erin shook her head as she stroked me. "Oh no," she said. "I caught you."

Twenty

ERIN

IT WASN'T EFFORTLESS, this long distance marriage thing, but we were making it work in our own bubble-gum-and-duct-tape way. Every five or six weeks, Nick flew to Iceland and we spent incredible, over-too-quick weekends together that invariably included minor injuries in co-showering. Even if I did wind up with a black eye from one particularly catastrophic body wash incident—yeah, Nick lost all of his chill over that one—I couldn't get enough of our temporary little reality.

I shopped for soft new bed sheets and picked up his favorite beer whenever I saw it in the local grocery. I drew complex countdowns to our next time together in my notebook and gleaned an obscene amount of joy from marking each day off. I locked myself in the lab on the days when his surgical schedule prevented us from video chatting, and plowed through work at a pace my advisors at Oxford couldn't believe. I explained that I was motivated to report on my findings, and while that was true, I was also starved for time with my husband.

After Nick's first handful of visits, we found time to leave my apartment and see Reykjavík. We explored the restaurant scene—Iceland was much more than salted fish, by the way —and leveraged the endless sunlight of summer in the Arctic to check in with the area's population of elves. We did not find any, but Nick did get a midnight blowjob on a glacier to celebrate our first year of marriage. We were all about seizing those once-in-a-lifetime moments.

Nick always came bearing goodies from the States. First it was cookie dough, and I've been parceling it out in spoonfuls ever since. After that, he brought four UT-Austin t-shirts. They were straight from his personal stock, and smelled exactly like him. If I ever showed up to one of our video chats wearing his shirts, I could be certain that chat would end with the t-shirt off. But it was still awkward. I hadn't outgrown that yet.

Later, Nick came armed with news that Sam had returned to Boston after his months-long sabbatical in Maine, and he'd also reconciled with his girlfriend, Tiel. Crisis averted.

But then Shannon was "struggling," and when pressed for details, Nick turned that one around on me and recommended that I inquire personally. No, of course I didn't do that.

Nick would say I was inventing ways out of a conversation with Shannon. He was right about that, but not all the way. For years after leaving home, avoiding Shannon—and everyone else—had been my superpower, and I wore it like a merit badge. It served me well. It allowed me to engage to the degree that was comfortable for me. It gave me the space to work through all—um, most?—of my issues. But it also wore the ties between me and my siblings down to threads, and my muscles didn't remember how to reach out anymore.

I wanted to, even if I was known to argue otherwise. I

wanted to make sure she was all right, and I wanted to stop fighting. I wanted to be able to say *yes* when Nick pushed me to visit Boston. I wanted to confide in her about Nick, and I wanted her to promise that I was capable of giving him even a fraction of the love he gave me. I needed to know that it was possible, that the abuse we'd endured as children hadn't ruined me forever, and she was the only one who could tell me that.

The problem was that I was certain Shannon wanted nothing to do with me. In all these years, she'd never attempted to contact me. She didn't even want to make eye contact with me at Matt and Lauren's wedding. Yes, I'd said the worst things my silly teenage mind could conjure to her, and then slammed every real and metaphorical door in her face years ago. But those things had never stopped her before, and I couldn't interpret her silence as anything other than apathy.

So, I did the only thing that made sense. I sent her some rocks. I scoured my collections for a rough amethyst geode and some obsidian that I'd found here in Iceland. My business card, the one Oxford had printed up with a spiffy logo and eight different ways to contact me, might've fallen into the box, too.

Amethyst and obsidian weren't the same as a phone call, but they were the best I could offer.

The issues weren't exclusive to Shannon and Sam. Most recently, Riley was still in love with Lauren, and he was making more off-hand remarks about his affections than fully advisable in mixed company. Nick had chuckled while he recounted a Friday dinner at Patrick and Andy's apartment—she'd taken up the tradition of hosting a Shabbat supper for my lapsed Catholic siblings, and that was spectacularly amusing—where Riley asked Lauren when she'd be leaving Matt for him. No one read Riley's question with any degree of seriousness, and Lauren laughed it off as if it was another case of him busting Matt's balls.

My siblings, they were good people. Some of the best people, actually. But sometimes, even the best people didn't notice what was right in front of them.

———

To: Erin Walsh
From: Nick Acevedo
Date: November 4
Subject: Don't kill me

Hi, Skip,
I was at Patrick and Andy's place for dinner last night, and Shannon was there. I hadn't seen her recently, and I don't know how to explain it other than to say she seemed off. Really, really off. Even worse than she was over the summer.

Call her. Email her. Send her another rock. Anything. It's been too long.

Nick
*Tell me the research is going well and you see a break in the horizon.

**You've been sensational in the shower recently. Have I been meeting your expectations?

———

To: Nick Acevedo

From: Erin Walsh
Date: November 5
Subject: Long horizon

Hey, Dr. Good Hair,
I got an email from Matt on the exact same topic two
hours ago.

Riley's texted me about Shannon a few times, too. She'd been
seeing Will—Lauren's brother, the one in the underwear,
after the wedding—and it's his theory that things ended.
Badly. Riley also said it ended *months* ago, and she's taking it
really hard. I texted my babysitter, Wes, but he said Will's
been "down range" for a mission and doesn't have any other
information.

I'm not sure what you'd like me to say to Shannon, or how
you'd like me to explain my knowledge of all these issues.
We know that we talk about each other all the time, but
there's a difference between carrying on back room conversations about your siblings and then telling the sibling in
question that you've heard their tales of woe from multiple
sources.

I'm also not sure that I can say anything of substance or
comfort. She obviously didn't interpret the rocks I sent last
month as an opening, and I have to respect her wishes.

Further, I've never really experienced a breakup, and the last
thing I said to my sister was that she ruined my life and I
hoped she died, so calling her up to say "Hey, sorry it didn't
work out with that guy" is probably a whole lot of salt in the
wound.

Before you tell me that salt creates an antibacterial environment and is actually beneficial for healing, let me clarify that I'm referring to the discomfort one experiences when salting a wound. If Shannon's in a bad place right now, I'll only make that place worse.

I'm not saying never...I'm just saying not right now.

*Research is on track. Maybe even ahead of schedule, and that's good. Dumping a terabyte of data into position papers is pretty fun, and I should have many new findings soon. If things work out, I might be able to take an entire week later this month, right around Thanksgiving... How's that? Maybe I could fly to Boston? Maybe we even see my family. Like, you know, together. Me, you, us. Is that crazy? It's crazy. It's completely crazy.

**You've been outstanding. Exceptional, even. And tireless.

To: Erin Walsh
From: Nick Acevedo
Date: November 6
Subject: not that long

Skip...
Yes. Come here. Stay with me. It's not crazy, not at all. We'll do whatever you want, lovely.

Also, we need to chat this week, because I need to know how you find a terabyte of data "fun" and I want to see your face while I say dirty things to you.

*You're damn right I'm tireless.

**You're like Jason Bourne the way you evade.

———————

To: Nick Acevedo
From: Erin Walsh
Date: November 6
Subject: long enough

Okay. That's what we'll do. Video chat me when you get home and we can look at schedules. I'll let you say dirty things while I book my flights.

*If you haven't noticed, I'm having trouble getting rid of you. That's my confession for today.

**I might be a little infatuated.

***A lot. So much. I don't really know what to do with it.

———————

To: Erin Walsh
From: Nick Acevedo
Date: November 7
Subject: tired and so worth it

For the first time in my life, I sent an intern to get me coffee. I've decided that I'm okay being that doctor if it means I get to hear your filthy fantasies while you touch yourself.

To: Nick Acevedo
From: Erin Walsh
Date: November 7
Subject: tired and so worth it

Are you okay being that doctor who finds someone to cover
his Friday surgeries and fly to Iceland?

To: Erin Walsh
From: Nick Acevedo
Date: November 8
Subject: you have to ask?

The answer to that is always yes but I thought you were tied
up with that big data download. That's the only reason I
wasn't planning to fly there in the first place.

To: Erin Walsh
From: Nick Acevedo
Date: November 8
Subject: never mind

Forget that I asked. I know how to get your attention.

I'm on the Friday night flight. I suggest you rest up and get
plenty of protein. You'll need it.

NICK'S FINGERS were tracing my spine, and I knew he was still in that dreamy place where his body was loose and languid. I liked him there, and I liked being responsible for it too.

"Can we talk about what we're going to say?" I asked. "To my siblings. When we see them for the holiday."

Most people saw me as flighty and chaotic, and in a few ways, I was. But at the same time, I couldn't walk into high stakes situations without a detailed plan. Going back to Boston for the holiday and telling my family that we got married—surprise!—was the highest stakes.

"We say something along the lines of 'y'all owe us some wedding gifts'," he said, yawning.

"I can see Patrick now," I said, laughing. My oldest brother was nothing if not predictably grumpy. "He'll just stare at us, frowning, for twenty minutes."

"Sam will want to know why we didn't tell him," Nick said. "He has the worst fear of missing out."

"And you know what's sad about that?" I asked. Nick shook his head. "He usually *is* the last to know."

"Poor guy," Nick murmured.

"He'll survive," I said. "Riley needs some advance warning. He's at his best when he knows what to expect."

"I'll take him out for a beer before you fly in," Nick said. "It'll give him a chance to unload some of his unrequited love issues."

"Lauren will scream," I continued. "She can get away with that kind of reaction."

"Will that be before or after Matt dives across the table to beat my ass?"

I nestled my cheek against Nick's chest, not at all

comfortable with that idea. "He wouldn't do that," I said, but I wasn't convinced.

"Probably not," he said, and sounded about as certain as I was. "Sometimes he forgets that you're not seventeen anymore, and...he's not going to be happy that we waited to tell him. He probably deserves to hear it from us directly."

Let's just make those stakes a little bit higher.

"Right, good, yeah," I babbled to myself. I started tapping my index finger on Nick's clavicle. "So we should do that. We'll go to Matt's place early, and have a little discussion with him. Or maybe I should talk to him first."

Nick's fingers glided down my back and curled around my ass. "Not a chance," he said. "I've been running or biking with Matt at least once a month since we got married, and despite my every fucking desire to the contrary, I haven't mentioned it to him yet. I'm either a sociopath or operating with a shit-ton of willpower, but I know you'd hate it if I discussed *our* relationship without you there. I'd never do that to you."

"Believe me," I said, tapping a bit faster now. "I'm not interested in delivering that news to my brother alone. At the same time, I'm not interested in witnessing a brawl."

"We'll go together," Nick said. "He'll appreciate some time to talk it over without everyone else around, but you have to know he'll have questions."

"Of course," I said. Now all of my fingers were drumming his chest. "And we'll be prepared. We'll give him a short version of the night before his wedding, and leave out all mention of video chat sex and christening the floor of my apartment. What else could he want to know?"

Nick layered his hand over mine, putting an end to my tapping. "When he asks about our long distance arrangement, when shall we tell him it's ending?"

That right there? That was how you painted yourself into a corner.

"What should we say, lovely?" Nick asked.

Oh, he knew what he was doing and he was trying to be sweet as a motherfucking cherry pie about it, too.

"We'll explain that I have another twelve to eighteen months of research and analysis before I'm finished with my work at Oxford," I said.

"And when you're finished?" he asked. "What happens after that?"

"I don't know what happens after that, Nick," I said with a sigh. God, if only I could give him the answers he wanted. But that was where all of this was messier than I could comprehend. "I can't really think about any of that until I get through all of this. It's the same way that I couldn't listen to Christmas music until after my fall semester finals were finished in college."

"What are some of the possibilities?" he asked.

"I'm not sure, but I can't promise that going back home to Boston is an option," I said. "Let's not forget that I *like* field-work. I don't want to be closed up in a windowless lab all day, and I'm not meant to be a professor."

Nick murmured in agreement. "That's fine," he said. "When you're finished at Oxford, you decide where we're going. That's what we'll do."

I started tapping again. "That's not fair to you," I said. "I don't want this to be all about me. I don't want you leaving Mass Gen because I find a research position in, I don't know, Madagascar."

"But we can't keep doing this, darlin'," he said quietly. "You need to finish your research here, and then we figure out where *we* are going."

"No, Nick," I protested. I sat up, wanting to have this

discussion face-to-face instead of face-to-beautifully-carved-pecs. "You can't throw away your training and fellowships and board certifications because I end up in Madagascar. That's absurd, and I'm not letting you do that. You're too talented to give it all up to follow me around."

He pushed up from the mattress and settled against the headboard, his arms crossed over his chest. "Would you rather we continue living on different continents, wife?"

I leaned over, reaching for the glass of water on the table beside the bed. It bought me a moment to deal with the defensiveness that sprang to life every time someone suggested that I make my way back to Boston. When it was empty, I slammed the glass down. The water didn't help.

Then I pushed my hair away from my face, out of my eyes. It was getting too long, and I hated long hair. It didn't look right on me, and it started looking dreadfully flat when it was even a millimeter past my shoulders. Since I'd been spending all of my free time with Nick—either he was in my bed, on my computer screen, or blowing up my email inbox —I'd neglected my hair. Now it was long and flat and horrible.

"I see what you're doing over there," he murmured, pointing at me. "You have that mad pout going, and you're shaking your head like you're winning a hot little argument with yourself."

Fuck. I wanted to yell at him more than anything. I wanted to push him the hell away and remind him that I needed wide-open spaces and adventures and choice. Too many people had taken my choice away from me at too many turns, and I was protective of it now. Territorial even. I stared at him, letting all that frustration boil right at the surface.

But then he lifted his shoulders with a lopsided grin,

sweet as that motherfucking cherry pie again, and I burst out laughing. "How do you do this to me?" I asked, my words tangling and drowning in my giggles. "How are you always taking the wind out of my pissed-off sails?"

"It's a gift," Nick said. He wrapped me in his arms and eased me down on to the bed. "Much like my abnormally thick cock."

He ran his hand up my leg and between my thighs, and stroked me there. I blinked, realizing that he'd touched my scars and I wasn't drowning in panic. I wasn't screaming for him to stop. Pressing my palm to my mouth, I scrolled back through all the times we'd been together and sure enough, this wasn't the first time. He'd never asked but I was certain he knew they were self-inflicted. He wasn't disgusted, he didn't treat me like a fragile little psycho who shouldn't be trusted around sharp objects, and he didn't drop any well-intentioned-but-totally-painful suggestions that I get professional help because I obviously needed it.

Nope, he didn't do any of that. He loved me the way I was, and he let me love him in my scraggly way.

"I hate this, too," I said, and that had Nick looking up at me, concerned. Of course he was concerned. I was telling him I hated something while he kissed my thighs and rubbed my clit. No one could ever tell me I wasn't awkward as all hell. "I hate being apart from you. I don't want us living on different continents."

"But Boston isn't an option yet," he said.

I shook my head. "For now, no."

He hooked his arm under my knee as he nodded. Cock— the abnormally thick one—in hand, he pushed into me, and we groaned "Oh fuck" simultaneously.

"I can live with that," Nick said as he drove into me. "For now."

Twenty-One

Nick: Hey. Fucker.

Riley: Is that what we're calling me now?

Nick: Just got home from biking with Matt. Funny conversation we had this morning.

Nick: He wants to know why he should keep a SHOTGUN handy around me

Riley: Yeah…

Nick: And…?

Nick: What the hell did you say to him?

Riley: He would never actually suspect anything. He thinks I'm just riding your ass.

Riley: Honestly, he's fine. He doesn't listen to half of what I say.

Nick: WHAT DID YOU SAY

Riley: Nothing

Riley: He just mentioned that Erin was flying in for the holiday

Riley: Which was news to me

Riley: Perhaps you two could loop me in, you know? It's

easier to keep a lid on the shit when it's not flying at me blind. I don't appreciate getting my news from Matt.

Nick: …and?

Riley: And I offered some humorous commentary along the lines of him keeping an eye on you

Nick: Oh. Awesome. Thanks for that.

Riley: I was joking!

Nick: Yeah, well, he took it seriously enough to ask if there was something he needed to know

Nick: And it was five in the fucking morning so no, I didn't handle that one well at all

Riley: Sorry man. My bad.

Riley: For what it's worth, he always assumes the best.

Riley: It's really fucking annoying

Nick: Are you all good?

Riley: You mean, am I still in love with my brother's wife? Because yeah. I am.

Riley: Nothing new on that front. Same shit, different day.

Nick: You need to get laid. Get under someone and get over her.

Riley: Tried. Failed.

Nick: …failed? Do you need a urology referral?

Riley: Shut the fuck up

Riley: It was a good time for all involved until I called her Lauren.

Riley: And not, like, over dinner. On the precipice of a rather pivotal moment.

Nick: Don't tell me you called her Lauren during

Riley: Fuck yes during

Nick: Shit

Nick: Dude…

Riley: Yeah, you really don't have to explain to me how fucked up that is. I get it.

Nick: What did she do?
Riley: Asked if I called her Lauren, then asked if I knew her name
Riley: I did not.
Riley: I'd been calling her Lauren in my head since I met her
Riley: Then she took my phone and deleted her number
Riley: All I knew was that if I looked at her from the right side, she looked enough like Miss Honey
Nick: STOP WITH THE CALIFORNIA GIRLS
Riley: I know. I know.
Riley: But then I see a little blonde, and my penis starts plotting
Nick: Does it help? Finding girls that look like her?
Riley: Oh, fuck no.
Nick: Then stop trying to find a Lauren stand-in
Riley: All these things you say, they make easy words but not so easy practice.

To: Nick Acevedo
From: Erin Walsh
Date: November 23
Subject: check the weather…

There's a winter storm headed straight for me. Snow, ice, winds, storm surge. Flying out tomorrow night isn't looking good.

To: Erin Walsh
From: Nick Acevedo

Date: November 23
Subject: check the weather…

We're not going to assume the worst just yet…but see if you can get out on an earlier flight.

To: Nick Acevedo
From: Erin Walsh
Date: November 23
Subject: check the weather…

I'm going to the airport. I'm small enough to be a stowaway.

To: Erin Walsh
From: Nick Acevedo
Date: November 23
Subject: Do not get arrested

No sneaking onto airplanes, wife. I want you back here, but not because an Air Marshall found you in a cargo hold and you're being repatriated. You're tough, but not the kind of tough required for federal prison.

"GODDAMN   CUNTSUCKING   BULLSHIT BLIZZARD," she yelled. I had to hold my phone away from my ear.

"Slow down, Skip," I said. I was jogging downstairs, on

my way to meet my first-year residents in the emergency room to weigh in on a new case. "What's going on?"

"My motherfucking flight's been cancelled," she said. There was a sniffle, too, one that sounded like she'd been crying.

"It's fine," I said, attempting some calm in this conversation. "You can get another flight."

"The airport's been closed," she said. "There are no other flights."

"Okay, okay, what about…" I came to a stop at the ground floor and leaned against the stairwell wall as I searched my mind for alternatives. I had nothing, just a mental montage of the *Mission: Impossible* and *Taken* movies. None of that was going to work in this situation, and I was no Liam Neeson.

"Nick," she said, her voice soft and sad. "I'm not coming."

My head dropped back and bumped the cinderblock wall as I sighed. This wasn't just a weekend with Erin. This was the weekend when everything was going to change for us, and now…fuck. It was fucked. "The storm will pass," I said, desperate now as I felt it slipping away like sand through my fingers. "The airport will reopen. What about later in the week?"

"They're saying everything will be shut down until Friday morning. Even if I was able to get the first flight out *and* it was going directly to Boston, I'd be turning right back around. I was going to give you an early birthday blowjob, too."

My pager vibrated on my hip. "I'm so sorry, Skip. I have to get to the ER," I said, choking down my frustration. We couldn't lose this weekend. Not when she had a jam-packed calendar this winter, and I was leaving for Kenya in February, and even the most liberal reading of our schedules had us on different continents straight through the summer.

"Go back to your apartment. I don't care how many mountains and glaciers you've climbed, I don't want you out in the middle of a blizzard. I'll call you tonight."

"This one isn't even my fault," she murmured, and there would never be a time when the vulnerability in her voice wouldn't cut right through me. "The one time I was ready to go home, and I get an extratropical cyclone thrown at me."

"This changes nothing. You're still ready." My pager buzzed again. "I'm sorry, darlin'. My residents need me," I said, groaning. "If I leave them alone long, they interpret it as permission to perform procedures without me, and that's not good for anyone."

"Okay," she said. "But this storm? If I believed in anything, I'd tell you it's a sign that this was a terrible idea. That I shouldn't go home, that we shouldn't tell them that we're together, that everything I touch turns terrible."

"Stop. That's bullshit. Go home, lovely. Stay warm, and we'll talk later," I said. "And don't tell me you don't believe in anything. You believe in *everything*, and that's only one of the reasons I love you."

I hung up before Erin could argue with me, and sprinted toward the emergency room. I wasn't going to listen to her telling me that I was wrong, that I didn't understand how she couldn't be loved, but I couldn't bear to hear her say it back either.

Twenty-Two
ERIN

To: Erin Walsh
From: Samuel Walsh
Date: December 3
Subject: Looking ahead

Hey, Erin,
I want to talk to you about two things, both of which are top secret.

First – Tiel and I are getting married Christmas Eve. We're having a party at our place, and the wedding is going to be a surprise. You have to be here. Tell me you can make it.

Second – I want to take Tiel somewhere totally unexpected for our honeymoon. It's my wedding gift to her but I'm not going to tell her until after the event. What do you recommend, world traveler?

Let me know.
Sam

To: Nick Acevedo
From: Erin Walsh
Date: December 3
Subject: Spousal privilege

I'm telling you this because you're my husband, but you are
NOT allowed to tell anyone else. Got it?

Sam and Tiel are getting surprise-married on Christmas Eve.
He wants me to come home. I think I can make that work,
but their surprise wedding can't be about us.

*Now that I think about it, I'm sure Riley knows. He can
know that I know, but he can't know that you know, not
until I tell him that you know.

To: Erin Walsh
From: Nick Acevedo
Date: December 4
Subject: Spousal privilege

I want you back here, Skip. That's all that matters to me.

I can't believe I'm asking this, but… You did tell Sam that
you were coming for the wedding, right? Your reflex answer
to these things is usually no.

*Do I have any other spousal privileges?

**I noticed that you referenced a legal provision without giving me a constitutional law history lesson. Are you feeling all right? Did you get enough sleep and plenty of espresso for breakfast?

To: Nick Acevedo
From: Erin Walsh
Date: December 4
Subject: Spousal privilege

Actually, I told him I was busy. I'll let him know I'm coming later. It's fine.

Allow me to be clear: This is Sam and Tiel's wedding. We're not having any big conversations with anyone about anything. They're pulling off this huge surprise wedding thing and it's not right to make it about us. They've been through so much together, and now they're getting married, and I'm happy for them. They deserve for this to be all about them.

I'm bummed, but we'll find another time. We always do.

*You have the privilege of taking your shirt off before you hop on our video chat tonight.

**There isn't enough espresso in Iceland for me. Never will be.

To: Erin Walsh
From: Nick Acevedo
Date: December 4
Subject: Spousal privilege

Skip,
I'll chat you bare-ass naked if you want. Not sure why it's taken this long for us to get that out on the table.

I can agree that it's Sam and Tiel's day, but I won't hide anything. If I want to grab your ass in front of your brothers, I will and you'll like it. Spousal privilege.

Going out to buy an espresso machine now,
Your ever-patient and faithfully nude husband

*Just heard from Matt that Shannon and Will are living together. Whichever rock you sent worked a shit-ton of magic.

Riley: What are you doing tonight?

Riley: I need to get out of here

Riley: These assholes are driving me crazy

Nick: What now?

Riley: Sam and Matt are intent on "helping" me

Nick: Intervention?

Riley: Something like that

Riley: I took over one of Sam's big projects when he was in his Mountain Man phase, and I'm wrapping it up soon but the client is really fucking annoying. Like, nine paint color changes annoying. Like, five emergency meetings to discuss doorknobs annoying.

Riley: Now Sam and Matt have climbed up my asshole to "coach" me

Riley: Real talk: I really like this shit and they ARE helpful but fuck me, I've had dinner with all of them four times this week

Nick: So that's four dinners with Lauren

Riley: Yes sir

Riley: I think I'm having a nervous breakdown

Nick: You're not. You're going to get through.

Riley: Doubts. I have doubts.

Nick: I'm covering the ER for a couple of hours but I could go for a beer later

Riley: Outstanding

Riley: I hear Rogue is coming in for Sam and Tiel's highly secretive event. She's told me that she's told you, and we're now allowed to acknowledge that we all know about it.

Nick: Why do you call her that?

Riley: X-Men, dude.

Nick: I'm having trouble remembering that character but it feels like another slam on her. It pisses me off. Stop.

Riley: It's not.

Nick: It sounds like it is.

Riley: Ok, well...it's not.

Nick: It seems like you guys beat up on her a lot. I fucking hate it. Y'all need to stop that shit.

Riley: Rogue is a mutant. She absorbs everything around her. Memories, strength, other superpowers. She feels every-thing, all the time. It's involuntary. She can't not do it. She can't control it either, and sometimes people get hurt. She sees it as a curse and she runs away from home.

Nick: Continue

Riley: Her powers are conducted by touch. She can't allow anyone get close to her. She's always alone.

Nick: ...and?

Riley: And it takes her years to get control of her powers, and even then, she's still guarded. She grows up as a villain but in the end, she finds her way to the X-Men. They become her family, and she uses her powers to heal them.

Nick: Whoa. Fuck.

Nick: How do you come up with these nicknames?

Riley: It's a gift.

Nick: Right, well this convo has been pretty fucking real for me. When are we drinking?

Riley: How about The Green Dragon, around 8

Nick: Do you think they'll have the Cowboys game on?

Riley: Goddamn it, Nicholas.

Riley: The Dragon is over 360 years old. Paul Revere and John Hancock drank there. It's the alehouse of revolutionaries, son.

Nick: Ok. Sorry?

Riley: When you're drinking at The Dragon, you're a motherfucking Patriot.

Nick: Remember the Alamo

Riley: If Sam Adams had been at the Alamo, that shit would've been over in 3 days

Nick: ¡Viva la revolución!

Riley: Just stop. That's a different revolution, dude.

Nick: You're buying the beer.

Erin: Guess who's on American soil?

Nick: SKIP!

Nick: If I didn't have a tethered spinal cord to repair today, I'd be introducing you to my bedroom right now

Nick: Or the kitchen countertops. Or the hallway floor.

Nick: Really, I'd take any solid surface

Erin: Um, yeah. I'd be down for that.

Erin: Hey…is Gastro Girl around? I want to meet her

Nick: I'm not sure

Nick: I don't really want to share you this weekend

Erin: I just want to put a face to the name.

Nick: I'll see what I can find out

Erin: And guess who just got the "don't cause a riot at the wedding" lecture from Riley?

Nick: That fucking guy

Erin: What's the half-life on teenage transgressions?

Erin: I mean, U-238 is 4.5 billion years, and I can't be much longer than that…right?

Nick: Did you just compare yourself to uranium?

Erin: No

Erin: I compared all the shit I did when I was 17 to uranium

Nick: Stop it

Nick: I'm going to have some words with Riley

Erin: Why

Nick: Why? Because you're not a misbehaving kid. You don't deserve this shit from him, or anyone else

Erin: Let's not talk about this. We're on the same continent and I don't want to spend it talking about my brother.

Erin: Also: I can handle Riley.

Nick: I'm going to be in surgery for about 6 hours and I need to monitor this girl for a few hours before I leave. I'll see you tonight, lovely.

Erin: Lauren is taking me shopping. I'll be pretty when you see me tonight

Nick: You're always pretty, wife.

MY GAZE SWEPT over the crowd gathered in the old fire engine bay. Hundreds of strands of little white lights criss-crossed the high ceiling, and a band was playing a song I'd heard but couldn't name. There were Christmas-styled fir trees along the walls, and sparkly white branches bunched in urns around the cavernous space.

But none of that mattered. Not even a bit.

Then I spotted Erin across the room. She was wearing a

cute black dress with sleeves that stopped at her elbows and a swingy skirt, and I was almost convinced that my heart was lodged in my throat. She folded her arms over her torso as she looked around. It only took a moment for her to notice me, and when she did, the serious line of her lips broke into a big, bright smile.

My heart, the one that was in my throat? It was slamming against tissue and bone now, clawing its way out of me and back to its true owner. I stood there, one hand in my pocket and the other on my jaw to keep it from hanging open, and I smiled back at her.

Erin's stare raked over my suit, nodding in what I could only interpret as appreciation. I could see the sparkle in her eyes from all the way over here, and it was enough to get my cock's attention.

I moved toward her, blind to the noisy crowd around me. It was like parting the Red Sea while running through a wall of defensemen for the longest touchdown pass. I wasn't Moses, or New England Patriot Julian Edelman for that matter, but as I came close enough to touch my wife, I understood the triumph they felt.

"You," she whispered. "Follow me."

She turned on her heel, and I gasped. Actually fucking gasped. I stayed rooted in place, staring at her stockings and the thin black seam running up the back of her legs. It was sexy in a subtle way, and when I recovered from that flash of arousal, I sped up to catch her. I didn't care where she was leading me because I was following, and then I was tracing that seam all the way up.

Erin ducked through doorways and down dark hallways, and the click of her heels had me hypnotized. I ignored the catering staff as they bustled by, and the bartenders who were shouting at each other as they hauled cases of wine up from the basement, and followed her deeper into the old firehouse that Sam and Tiel—and Riley—called home.

"I think we're alone now," she whispered. She leaned against the door, her arms folded behind her back and that devious grin lighting her face.

A weighty beat passed between us, just like that moment in a thumping song before the bass line dropped. I pushed her against the wall and slammed my lips down on hers. "Oh, fuck," I said, sighing as I tasted her. "It's been too long, Skip."

"Thirty-seven days," she said. "Felt like forever." Her hands were on me, pressing into my shoulder blades, nails scratching my neck, fingers yanking at my belt and zipper. "I want you more than anything right now. Is that terrible?"

"Why the fuck would that be terrible?" I asked. I kissed her again, hard enough to earn a surprised squeak, and once more, softly. Then I fell to my knees to explore those stockings, running my palms up her calves as I groaned. She deserved beautiful lingerie and delicate things, if for no other reason than for me to dirty them all up.

"We're at Sam's wedding, to start," she said. "And anyone could walk in here."

"Quiet, woman. No reasoning with me now." Erin ran her fingers through my hair, laughing. When her nails reached the nape of my neck, I dropped my forehead to her belly with a growl. "You're not emotionally connected to these, are you?" I asked, tracing the seam of her stockings up, between her legs. "Don't answer. Doesn't matter. I'm buying you new ones."

"What? Why are you—*ohhhh*!" She folded her hands over her face when I ripped the stockings. "I can't believe you did that."

Panties pushed aside. Leg hooked around my waist.

Cock out and hungry. "Believe it," I said, leaning forward to take her lips. "Hold on to me, lovely. Don't let go."

I waited until Erin's arms were around my neck to slide into her, and I watched her reactions wash over her face. Bite the bottom lip, squeeze the eyes shut, drop the head forward, part the lips and whisper "Fuck" over and *over* until it resembled a sacred prayer, the kind reserved for the most faithful of the believers. I was nearly coming from that prayer on her tongue alone.

"You're destroying me with your little whispers. Stop it," I ordered, digging my fingertips into her thighs as I drove into her. "I'm going to come all over you—"

"Do it," she panted. "I dare you."

It seemed the dares worked well on me, too. That, and Erin's lips on the tender spot beneath my ear and the sharp point of her heels on my ass. My entire existence melted into a single pulsation that wound around my bones and vital organs before snapping every one of my nerves. I came with a full-body spasm that crushed her against the wall. There was a sound, too, a noise somewhere between medieval battle cry and aggressive mewl, and it probably went on for longer than I realized.

"Are you all right, my husband?" she asked, stroking my hair. She wasn't there yet, and I was going to see to her needs as soon as I could breathe, move, and speak simultaneously. "You've been muttering to yourself for a couple of minutes."

"Oh, my wife," I said, sighing when my thumb slid over her clit. She was slippery, a mix of her wetness and my orgasm. "I love feeling me all over you."

Erin's hands balled around my suit coat as I traced her clit. She gasped, humming in encouragement when I quickened the pace. "You're so dirty," she said. "These things you say, you're filthy."

"Like you wouldn't believe," I agreed.

She started to respond, but her clit gave an unmistakable throb, stealing her words. Her forehead wrinkled and her lips pushed out a sharp sigh as the orgasm rolled through her, and it would've been the perfect opportunity to watch her come if the door hadn't opened.

"If you run out of room for all the recyclables, you can set them in—"

I pulled out and yanked Erin's skirt down, holding it in place as if that could cancel out the fact that my trousers were hanging open and she was still quaking with release.

"Stay right there, guys," Riley called to the people behind him. He touched his fingertips to his temples, whimpering as if this scene was causing him actual pain. "Twice in a week," he murmured to himself. "Must be a new record for me."

"How does he do this?" Erin asked. "Every time, too."

"It doesn't matter because it's not happening again. I'm gonna kill him now," I said against her temple. "Say goodbye."

"Put your dick away, doctor," Riley said. "I have enough problems tonight." He pointed at Erin, and the cherry red blush on her cheeks. "Didn't I tell you to behave?"

"That's enough of that shit," I said. "Do *not* fucking lecture her."

"It's fine, it's fine," Erin said. "Sorry about this, Riley."

"I hate everyone," he grumbled, shaking his head as he turned to leave. "And weddings. I really hate weddings."

Twenty-Four

"THIS IS the most entertaining wedding I've ever seen," I said, nudging Nick as I spoke. I felt him nodding in agreement. Of course he agreed. Sam was wearing a red velvet tuxedo that looked vintage, but I knew he didn't go for used clothing. The likely scenario was that Sam had spent an ungodly amount of money on a designer tux that only looked vintage.

"How many weddings have you been to, Skip?"

We were watching the ceremony from the back fringe of the crowd, far enough out of the way that we could comment on the events without being disruptive.

"Just Matt and Lauren's." Aware that my tights were torn at the crotch and my panties were damp, I added, "And ours."

Nick glanced down at me, smiling. "This guy," Nick said, tipping his chin toward the officiant. He was colorful in dress and character, and that was putting it mildly. "Top hat, feather boa, sunglasses at night. He might give Bartlett a run for his money."

"Not a chance," I said as Sam promised to always chase

Tiel's rogue olives. "Three cheers for the inside-joke-themed marriage vows. Didn't think that would fly, but these two are making it work."

"That's their thing," he said. "They make things work, even when it's difficult."

"What's our thing?" I asked.

He laughed, and draped his arm over my shoulders as he kissed my hair. "We make things work when they're really fucking impossible."

The ceremony concluded with a lengthy kiss, and then the band kicked off a happy, folksy tune that had Tiel wiggling in Sam's arms. They were visibly, palpably in love, and I couldn't help but smile for them. They moved through the crowd, accepting congratulations and agreeing that they'd pulled off an incredible surprise. Nick and I probably seemed oddly blasé about it all, as we'd long known about the secret purpose of this holiday soiree.

The happy couple made their way toward me and Nick, and though I expected a morsel of curiosity—even a small one—at our apparent familiarity, Sam and Tiel had other things on their minds. It made me want to draw my fingers over the edge of Nick's belt, or maybe dip them into the space between his shirt and trousers. Just to see what would happen.

Sam scooped me up in a hug, bringing me clear off my feet. "You're here," he cried. "I'm so glad you could make it. Thank you for this, thank you so much. I needed all of you guys here tonight." He set me down and clapped his hand against my back before turning back to his wife. "Tiel, this is Erin."

She brushed a strand of dark hair over her ear and smiled at me. There was a touch of sympathy in her smile, and it was clear that she'd heard all about me. Not that I could blame Sam, or whoever had read her in on the dirty details. It didn't matter how far I ran, or how long I stayed away, because I'd never shake free from that shit. No fresh starts, not for me, not for anyone.

"Tiel, it's wonderful to meet you," I said, swallowing an exasperated sigh and reaching deep to find an authentic smile. This lady seemed like a whole lot of fun, my brother loved her, and it didn't matter whether she knew about my time in the psych ward, or me fucking my thirty-two-year-old English teacher when I was in high school. Didn't matter. Not a bit. Not at all. *Not at all.* "Thank you for inviting me."

"Of course we invited you," she replied, snort-laughing and not even trying to cover it up. I admired that. "I wish we had some time to grab coffee or something, but we leave for our honeymoon"—she glanced at Sam—"destination unknown, tomorrow afternoon."

"It's all good," I said. "I'm meeting up with a friend while I'm in town. I'm sure I'll be back, we'll get that coffee then."

And that friend *happens to be standing right next to me.*

"Even the good doctor made it out for an evening," Sam said, clapping Nick on the back as they exchanged a man-hug. "We haven't seen much of you lately."

"I've been busy," Nick said coolly. He brought his hand to his hip, positioning it there as if he was proving a point. His elbow bumped my upper arm, and it stayed there, pressing into my skin and asserting something that Sam didn't choose to see.

Sam blinked expectantly, waiting for more information, but Nick offered none. I turned my attention downward, hoping I could school my expression if I was staring at my shoes.

"Right, right," Sam said, nodding. "Well, it's good to see

you." His stare pinged between us, happy and ignorant. "Both of you."

"Do you think anyone's noticed?" Nick's gaze swept over the crowd after Sam and Tiel moved on to greet other guests. I knew what he was feeling. He wanted someone—*anyone*—to notice that we were standing here, too close for casual acquaintances, too close for polite company, even too close for friends.

"Are you hoping that they will?" I asked.

"Fuck yes, I am," he said.

"They're not concerned with us," I said, laughing. "Shannon's only looking at Will, Sam's preoccupied with being married, Riley's busy entertaining himself with that kilt, Matt's a little drunk and trying to be covert about grabbing Lauren's boobs, and Patrick's staring at Andy's ass. It's funny, though, because everyone was so worried that I was going to be a twatwaffle. Unless I'm running around naked or sucking whiskey off the bartender's Adam's apple, they're not noticing."

"Mmhmm," he murmured. He was still studying the crowd. It was like he was hoping he'd catch someone's eye and force them to put the pieces together of his hand and its position on my waist. "What about sucking whiskey off me? Would that warrant a reaction?"

"No guarantees," I said, patting his chest.

"That's disappointing," he said. "Want to try it anyway?"

"I don't drink whiskey," I said. "Bad things happen."

Nick stared at me, his light hazel eyes twinkling with a shiny new challenge. "You've never drunk whiskey with me," he said. "Maybe really good things will happen this time, like us getting drunk and telling your family we're married and they can all fuck off if they have a problem with it."

"*You* could get away with that. *I* could not," I said, a laugh thick in my voice.

It wasn't funny, not exactly, but it was amusing to see this through Nick's eyes. He was laboring under the assumption that my siblings noticed everything, always, and that wasn't the whole truth. People—all people, not only my siblings—noticed outliers and anomalies, and not normal behavior. For once in my life, I was situated in the perfectly normal seats.

"You're everyone's favorite guy. You fly right under the radar. You'd have to fuck me up against a wall for anyone to notice. That is, you'd have to fuck me up against a wall *again*."

"You're testing my patience, Skip," he said. His fingers moved lower, past the rise of my hip bone to the tender spot below. He pressed there, and I gasped. It was an *eyes rolling to the back of your head, weak in the knees, feel it every-freaking-where* kind of tender spot. "If you want a wall, there are several at my apartment."

I smothered a laugh in his suit coat. "We have to make it through the toasts," I said. "Then we can christen your apartment."

"That's fuckin' right," he murmured, pulling his phone from his breast pocket. "We have a few days before you're heading back over the pond, so we're christening everything. Walls, floors, tables, everything. There's a bookshelf I'd like you to meet."

"Hate to be the boring one here, but could we christen a bed?" I asked. "Maybe a sofa? I'm a whore for soft surfaces."

"All of the above." Nick tapped at his phone, frowning at a text on his screen and then plucking his pager from his back pocket. It was hard to believe those things still existed. "I'm going to check in," he murmured. "I'm sure everything's fine, but I'd rather touch base now than get a page in the middle of the night." He looked up at me, a feral grin stretched across his face. "Because I have plans for the middle of the night."

"Hurry along," I said, patting his backside. "I'll be right here, or—" I pointed to the cake table. "Over there. I'm thinking I need a cake pop."

"You say that," he said, his voice full of faux disapproval, "but what you mean is you need *seven* cake pops."

"Explain to me how there's a problem with any of this," I said.

Nick kissed my forehead and stepped away, glancing back at me with a smile as he headed toward the interior of the firehouse. I grabbed my cake pops—only three, thank you kindly—and watched as Sam climbed onto the platform housing the band. He grabbed the microphone and held his hand out to Tiel. With a bit of shy reluctance, she joined him.

"Tonight we celebrate my wife," Sam said, smiling at her, "the most incredible woman in my world. Tiel, you are my sanctuary, my soul, my Sunshine."

He leaned down, kissing her deeply. It was good to see him this happy after everything he'd been through, and I was happy to see that he and Tiel found their way back to each other, too.

"But I want to raise a glass to a few others who made this possible, who delivered me to this point, whether they know it or not. To the elder statesmen," he said, holding up his champagne glass and gesturing toward Matt and Patrick. "To the keepers of all the best secrets." He nodded to Riley. "And to the wanderers who know when to wander home, and…the cornerstones, the ones who hold us together."

I followed his gaze to Shannon, and found her standing beside Will. Her arm was around his waist and his hand was on her shoulder. She was wearing a white sequined top, the kind you only found in high-end shops with thick carpeting and chandeliers. I'd bet that she was mortified that she showed up to a wedding—albeit a surprise one—wearing white. It didn't matter that the bride was dressed in peacock blue and probably didn't know or didn't care about that sort of nuptial etiquette.

"Without all of you," Sam continued, pointing to each of us with his glass, "I wouldn't be here. Cheers."

I didn't have a drink but I didn't want to skip out on Sam's one and only wedding toast, so I mimed along with the crowd. Pinching my make-believe champagne flute between my fingers, I continued watching Shannon. She was always a busybody in the best ways possible, looking after everyone else and making work for herself to avoid confronting any of the unpleasant shit in her world, but tonight she looked calm. *Settled.* She wasn't micromanaging the caterers or stomping around, annoyed that the bar was fresh out of bleu cheese-stuffed olives or something inconsequential like that. She was settled in all the right ways.

My heart leapt for my sister, and I smiled through the tears filling my eyes. Then I found her staring back at me. Her lips were folded in a severe line, and I couldn't decide whether she was shocked to see me or sorry she'd looked in this direction. It didn't matter. We were staring at each other now, me with a smile that seemed to start in my belly and spread out from there, her with a look of disbelief, and there was no turning back.

Will's hold on her shoulder tightened, and he turned her toward him by a few degrees. He was like a grizzly bear, big and ferocious, and wildly protective. If only we'd known that getting all of us together on Cape Cod for Matt and Lauren's wedding was going to be the catalyst for changing everything. That she found Will, and I found Nick when all the chaos seemed too much to handle was some kind of serendipity.

I nodded, and I prayed that tiny offering was enough to express all the things I wanted her to know. That time had been good for me, and distance, too. That I understood the choices she'd made, and I didn't blame her anymore. That I hoped she understood my choices. That someday I'd have more than a negligible head bob, and I'd find the words.

"Hey," Nick said, his hand low on my back and his gaze pinging between Shannon and me. "Go talk to her. Do it, Skip."

Shannon's eyebrow quirked up and her lips twisted into a smile that seemed to say *Are you kidding me right now?* when she caught sight of Nick.

"Talk to her," he repeated.

Will's lips were moving, and Shannon was shaking her head. I imagined she was saying, "I have nothing to say to her" and I blinked back tears.

I wasn't going to cry in the middle of this amazing party, and I wasn't going to ruin it by forcing the most painful, ill-timed conversation in the world. Things we had to discuss, they weren't small issues. I didn't ruin her favorite sweater and she didn't break my iPad. No, not even close.

Was there an appropriate venue to talk through the time when the teenage version of you seduced your sister's boyfriend? Or what about the time when she came home to find that same twenty-seven–year-old boyfriend nailing you on her bed, and she told you to stop being a sad little cliché while she had him arrested for statutory rape? And then there was the time when you popped some pills and slit your wrist, and then your sister refused to bring you home after a month in the psychiatric hospital because she didn't believe you wouldn't do it again? How about the time when you accused her of letting your father abuse you so he'd stop abusing her, and then suggested no one would ever want someone as cold, miserable, and used-up as her?

It wasn't as though a simple "Sorry about all that shit" would cut it.

"Skip," Nick said, the hand on my back pushing me forward. I took a step, but it wasn't willingly.

The band kicked off a new song, and I threw my hands in the air, bouncing with the tune. "Come on. Let's dance."

I dragged him away, needing some freedom from Shannon's watchful gaze. I wasn't foreclosing the possibility of apologizing to her. I just couldn't find the entry point.

"I have to know why," he said, pulling me into his arms. "Explain to me why you didn't want to take that very obvious opening from Shannon, and I won't push you on it again this weekend."

I pressed my forehead to his chest, hoping I could hide here for the rest of the night. The month. The year. Finally, after blowing out all the sighs in the world, I said, "When Mount St. Helens erupted, it sterilized everything in its path. The blast flattened an entire seven-mile radius. There were mudslides, and the largest debris avalanche in recorded history. Hardly anything survived that eruption."

"Please tell me there's an upshot to this story," Nick murmured.

"When you look at volcanic ash under a microscope," I continued, "it's sharp and it's loaded with soil-enhancing nutrients. That ash doesn't just settle, it slices into the soil and forces it to recover. The process is known as plant succession, and it occurs in stages. First, there are lichen, and then wildflowers. Later, saplings and wild grasses. It takes time for an environment to come back from devastation."

"But it comes back," he said. It was somewhere between statement and question.

"It comes back," I confirmed. "It took a year, but the elk returned to Mount St. Helens. It took another seven years for the mountain goats. Some environments take longer than others, but they all come back. Naples recovered from Vesuvius and now it has San Marzano tomatoes. The soil of the north island of New Zealand is a direct result of its volcanic history, and every one of Krakatau's explosions have resulted in major species regeneration. It always comes back."

"When you're ready for that," he said, "I'll be here."

I knew he would. I didn't think it was possible for Nick to ever *not* be there.

"Tell me about your day," I said as we swayed with the music. "You sounded frazzled earlier."

He dropped his chin on the top of my head, sighing. "Any measurable quantity of snow or ice on the ground, and there are concussions, cracked skulls, and brain bleeds as far as the eye can see."

"Ooh," I murmured. "No bueno."

"None," he agreed. "I'm telling you right now, Skip, we're putting helmets on our kids when they go sledding or ice skating. They might have some social issues, but it's better than having traumatic brain injury issues."

My hands moved to his chest, and I pushed him back a bit to catch his eyes. "Our *kids*?"

"Yeah," Nick said, nodding as if he hadn't taken our sorta-kinda marriage and accelerated it many years into the future. "My kids getting concussions from skating without a helmet would be like the dentist's kids getting cavities from not brushing their teeth. Not an option."

"Our...*kids*," I repeated. I waved my hands at my body,

trying and failing to indicate that I wasn't prepared for that. Did he not realize that we didn't have a plan for getting through next month, let alone the next year? We were barely holding on to each other right now, and adding children —*plural*—to that equation was crazier than getting married on a lobster boat only to spend two years on opposite sides of an ocean. "You want me to sustain and nurture human baby children? Did you forget that I can barely take care of myself, Nick?"

Shaking his head, he tugged me back into his arms. "You're so much better than you think you are."

"No, that's where you're wrong," I yelled into his chest. "I know exactly who I am and where my fault lines are most unstable, and I know for a fucking fact that I'm not supposed to be anyone's mother. I'm the fun, cool, crazy aunt. The one who can tell stories about seeing every continent and going on unadvisable adventures. I'm not the settle-down mom who cuts the crust off sandwiches, or remembers to put helmets on the kids."

"That's fine because I'll be putting the helmets on the kids. They'll just have to learn how to live with the crusts," he replied. "You just need to bring yourself home to me, and then we'll sort out the rest."

"But I'm not even sure I should be anyone's wife," I whisper-cried. *I am not throwing a tantrum at my brother's wedding. I am not throwing a tantrum at my brother's wedding.* "This is all make-believe with us, and I'm not even doing a passable job at pretend-marriage."

"Oh, would you stop with that?" he asked, edging back to hold up his hands and point an unimpressed frown in my direction. "I know the trouble here is that you actually believe the shit you're spouting right now. Somewhere along the way, you got it in your head—the same head that told you that you could be a badass scientist, explore the fucking world on your own, and earn two doctorates before turning thirty—that you weren't allowed the good things in life. You're free to wring the marrow from every minute so long as that doesn't include having a family, a place to call home, a husband who worships the damn ground you walk on."

I crossed my arms over my torso, incensed but unable to zero in on a single point to refute.

We stood there, our gazes winging between each other and the polished cement floor. The band ended one song and then started another, something folksy and steeped in love's ideals.

"Do Matt and Lauren know you're not going back to their loft tonight?" he asked. His words snapped with tension, the Texas drawl heavier than ever.

"Yeah, I told Lauren not to worry about me tonight, and she said she'd handle it," I replied softly. "They're leaving for that trip to the mountains tomorrow afternoon, with Patrick and Andy, so we're good. She invited me to come along, but seemed to understand when I declined."

I wasn't adding that I had the definite sense that Lauren knew something was up, or that she promised to keep my brothers out of my hair this weekend.

"So let's go, lovely," Nick said, grabbing me around the waist and sweeping me off my feet as he moved toward the door. "You're coming home with me. *Now*."

Twenty-Five

ERIN

To: Erin Walsh
From: Shannon Walsh
Date: January 25
Subject: Hello

Erin,

I trust that this message finds you well. Lauren shared your email address with me. I hope that you don't mind.

Will and I are getting married this weekend, and though we aren't announcing this to anyone, I wanted to tell you. It's not a formal event, just the courthouse and a weekend in Montauk.

I know you're very busy with your research and fieldwork, and I'd never want to interrupt that. I'm not asking you to come home. You were just here, so I certainly wouldn't expect you to return. I just needed you to know.

I hope you're okay, and I want you know I'm always here if
you need anything.
Shannon

I STARED at that message for days. *Days.*

If one of Iceland's elves had appeared in my Reykjavík
apartment and personally invited me to go tobogganing
under the Aurora Borealis, I'd have been less surprised than
to find a message from Shannon in my inbox this week.

"What do I even say?" I asked Nick. My video chat app
was open on one side of my screen, and the email on the
other. I reread Shannon's note. Again.

He was in his kitchen, a small space dominated by
exposed brick and stainless steel appliances, and it was late.
I'd long since abandoned my practice of starting my day in
the lab before dawn in favor of midnight talks with Nick. At
first it seemed decadent, sleeping in and then arriving after
the team of research fellows I worked with, but I'd learned to
use my time more efficiently. Less falling down every
random hypothesis hole that I encountered, more checklists
and skipped lunches. It worked out well, as we managed to
eat dinner together—as *together* as any two people separated
by an ocean could get with the help of modern technology—
most nights.

Peeling the lid from a glass container, he shrugged. "Start
with 'congratulations,'" he suggested.

"And *then* what?"

Nick closed the microwave and punched in a few
numbers before turning to face me. "You're capable of
writing an email, Erin. You've written me hundreds. Maybe
thousands."

"Yeah, that's easy," I said, raking my fingers through my hair. "This...this is more complicated than that. This is *Shannon*, and for some indecipherable reason, she felt it necessary to tell me—"

"How do you not see this, Skip?" he asked, throwing his hands up. "She's reaching out. She's opening the door and all you have to do is step through and fucking end this."

I reread the email. Again. The words stopped meaning anything somewhere around the thirtieth read, and now they were landmines, each one blowing up with different memories. In my head, it sounded like a montage of Shannon the lawyer, Shannon in her bathrobe with the Navy SEAL brother of Lauren's, Shannon holding me tight when the nightmares were too much, Shannon pleading with me to see a counselor. It was moments, strung together with a fine thread of anger that didn't make sense but I couldn't release.

"Darlin', I'm not saying these things to be hard on you," he said, pointing at me through the screen with a spoon. "But that pouty little girl face, the one you're doing right now? Doesn't work on me. You're gonna respond to her, and you're doing it before the weekend."

I picked up the book I'd been reading earlier, one focused on the impact of flooding and the role of aqueducts in ancient Roman civilizations, and thumbed through the pages. My eyes moved over a page, but I didn't see any of the words. "Please don't imply that there's anything manipulative or sexually charged about *being* a little girl," I said, still staring at the page.

I heard metal clanging against glass, but I was engrossed in the page I hadn't read. I didn't look at the screen.

"Erin," Nick said, that one word a resolute request for my

attention. "Erin, I'm sorry. I shouldn't have said that, and you *know* I didn't mean it."

I nodded, my head jerking and my eyes unfocused as I turned another page. Perhaps it was all this talk of Shannon that had my triggers turned up to ultra-sensitive. But that same old petty part of my mind was still cackling away, suggesting that Shannon had stilettos-and-spin-class'd away all the ugliness she'd endured at Angus's hand.

But I wasn't as strong as Shannon.

"Hey," Nick said. I set the book down and glanced up at him. "Get out of your head."

There were tears in my eyes now, and I blinked rapidly to clear them before meeting his gaze. I sniffled and smiled, shaking my head as if to say, *No, I'm fine and I'm not going to lose my shit tonight.*

"What are you eating?" I asked, eager for a topic that didn't involve my sister or my father.

He held up the dish for my viewing. "Lauren made beef stew," he said. "I might've allowed her to believe that I'm one of those guys who only has mustard, old take-out, and beer in my fridge, and she always sends me home with leftovers. She and Matt don't cook too often, but when they do, it's really good."

"How are Lauren and Matt?"

"They're doing well," he said. "His knee is still fucked up but he thinks it will magically heal, she's excited about some new second grade teachers she's trying to hire for next year, and Riley's still miserable."

I pinched the compass pendant at my neck between my fingers, murmuring in acknowledgement. "Do they have any idea?" I asked.

"About what?" he asked after swallowing a spoonful of

stew. "At any given moment, every one of your siblings is sheltering seven different secrets."

"Seven seems like a low number," I said, mostly to myself. "There's no single reason for it. I mean, we were raised by a despot who found sport in brutally shaming us for any hint of weakness or whichever random thing he wanted to exploit"—like young girls—"and we covered all that shit up. No one outside of our home knew, and if they did, they looked the other way. None of that leads to heart-to-heart chats or open dialogues about feelings and emotions. Not when the goal is not getting your ass tossed down a flight of stairs."

"Really glad I pulled the plug on that bastard," Nick murmured around his spoon.

"It was a lot like the French Revolution. We were the angry revolutionaries plotting the overthrow of the tone-deaf tyrant. We even have our own version of the Bastille that we've stormed and reclaimed. But a side effect of winning a war is that you're not quite sure how to feel about any of it, or anything at all. That's why we keep some secrets, and only come out with them when they're old and moldy," I said, but while those words were forming on my lips, Nick's comment was sinking in. "Wait. *Wait*. You...you were there? With Angus? When he had the stroke?"

He nodded, and set his spoon down. "Yeah, I took him off life support," he said. "And I was there at the end, too. I signed the death certificate."

"Did he suffer?" I asked.

Nick squinted at me for a moment. "What do you want to hear?"

I ran my fingers through my hair. "I don't know," I admitted, feeling a bit snarly. "The last time I saw him, it was after I'd decided he'd molested me one time too many. I got a baseball bat and went into his room in the middle of the night, and I don't remember many of the pertinent details of that exchange, but I do remember Riley telling me that Angus would die a miserable death all on his own, and I shouldn't waste any energy on advancing that."

Nick didn't say anything, but I could see the muscles in his jaw ticking.

"So I'd like to know whether Riley was right," I continued. I was past snarky, and veering into straight up glib. "I want to know whether I was right to stop short of cracking his perverted fucking head open."

He looked down, his lips folded while he shook his head. "He suffered an ischemic stroke—"

"I'm aware of that," I snapped.

There was no reason to take out any of my bottomless Angus rage on Nick, especially not when he was offering up the details about Angus's last moments. When Matt contacted me with the news, I'd thrown some clothes and my computer in a bag, and hopped the next flight to the Canary Islands. El Hierro was the least explored of the Canaries, and its massive shield volcano offered zero internet access and all of the distraction I needed. I didn't want to know anything about Angus then, and I wasn't certain that I wanted to know now but I did want to stop wondering about it. It was the monster under the bed, the one I could either wish away or look in the eye.

"We weren't able to intervene or reverse the stroke in any way, and it appeared his brain had been deprived of oxygen for a significant period of time. He later experienced seizures, and increased intracranial pressure. We treated that by removing part of his skull while repairing a blown blood vessel. Two days later he failed all brain function and reflex criteria," Nick said. "He was brain dead. He couldn't feel anything when he was taken off life support. Your family said goodbye, and his heart stopped about twelve hours later. No further interventions were attempted."

I tapped my fingertips against my lips, silently absorbing this. Angus threw me out of the house after the incident with the baseball bat, but he made sure to get in some parting shots about me being a dumb whore like my mother. I didn't have a good response at the time, and I was still amassing them now, even after his death. But hearing about his final moments, it was like sunlight shining through a thick carpet of clouds. The simple reminder that Angus was gone, really fucking gone, was enough to push out the memories of everything he'd done to me and Shannon.

And I didn't need those venomous comebacks anymore.

"As a surgeon, I hate the idea of a patient suffering in death," he started, dragging his thumb along his jaw. "But as your husband, I hate that I can't say he got back any of the pain he'd caused you."

Tears filled my eyes but I squeezed them shut, not wanting to shed a single one. I smiled, shaking my head. "No, it's okay, Nick. You said everything I need," I said. "All right, moving on. What's the appropriate gift for eloping in the Hamptons?"

To: Shannon Walsh
From: Erin Walsh
Date: January 29
Subject: Hello

Shannon,

Congratulations to you and Will. You both deserve every happiness.

- e

To: Erin Walsh
From: Shannon Halsted
Date: February 3
Subject: Hello

Erin,
Thank you. It was exactly what we wanted.

It's good to hear from you.
Shannon

To: Shannon Halsted
From: Erin Walsh
Date: February 5
Subject: Hello

You've already changed your name?

To: Erin Walsh
From: Shannon Halsted
Date: February 6
Subject: Hello

Erin,
My husband was rather impatient on that front. He's cute, so
he gets away with it.

I hope your research is going well.
Shannon

———

To: Shannon Halsted
From: Erin Walsh
Date: February 6
Subject: Hello

Sounds like a bossy little shit.
Good for you. You really deserve to be happy.

———

To: Erin Walsh
From: Shannon Halsted
Date: February 7
Subject: Hello

You do too.

———

To: Erin Walsh
From: Shannon Halsted
Date: February 10
Subject: Hello

Erin,

We received the vase today, and it's gorgeous. Where is it from? We couldn't interpret the inscription on the bottom.

Thank you.

Shannon and Will

To: Shannon Halsted
From: Erin Walsh
Date: February 13
Subject: Hello

You're welcome.

It's from Marrakesh. I always pick up bowls and vases whenever I'm there. I found that one about five years ago. I hope it goes with your things.

To: Erin Walsh
From: Shannon Halsted
Date: February 13
Subject: Hello

It's perfect. It goes with our things beautifully.

Someday, I hope you'll tell me about Marrakesh and your other travels.

Twenty-Six

NICK

I BLINKED REPEATEDLY, trying to keep my eyes open. I'd spent more than twenty hours in surgery today, and it was February, which meant there were forty-five minutes of sunlight each day. I was crashing fast, but determined to get some screen time with Erin before I headed out to Kenya for two months. Part of me still couldn't believe I was going, and another part of me—one that seemed to grow with each day—wanted to call it all off. Functioning without video chatting several times each week seemed impossible, and that didn't even account for our daily email exchanges.

"I got roped into a conversation tonight," Erin said. She pulled her knees up to her chest and leaned back against the wall. It was always strange seeing her in the grad student flats at Oxford, the old, shadowy space such a contrast to her bright, book-filled apartment in Iceland. She only stayed at Oxford; she lived in Iceland. "Socializing is the worst, and there's nothing I can do to avoid it. I can roll with the science talk, and the political stuff, too. But then someone will ask where I'm from, and it invariably leads to asking if my family is still there. It's always, 'Is it just you? Any siblings?

Are your parents still in Boston? Do you get back there often?' I never have the words for any of that, but this"—she held up her hand, the one with the wedding ring on her middle finger—"generates some questions of its own."

"Was that the topic?" I asked, jerking my chin toward the hand still suspended in front of her face. It wasn't her fault but I *hated* that she didn't wear it on the proper finger, and I was too tired to wipe the resulting scowl from my face.

"Sort of," Erin said. "The hazards of marriage while pursuing a field-research-driven doctorate."

"That sounds light and cheery," I said.

She tugged her sleeves down, over her hands, and shrugged. "Everyone thought it was amazing that I was here, doing my thing, and you were heading to Africa, doing your thing. Consensus was that we are quite enlightened."

I had to laugh at that. I'd been expecting something more hostile and judgmental, but leave it to the academics to bring it back around to the research. "Is that Oxford-speak for sexually frustrated?"

"Probably not," she said. "They don't know how it is. Being married to you changes things."

I barked out another laugh. "Oh yeah?"

"Yeah," she said emphatically. "I went years without sex before you. I focused on my research and I traveled, and things were good. I was good. I didn't want anything else, and now…" She shook her head as if she couldn't believe what she was about to say. "And now, I want…everything. I don't know what *everything* is, but I want it."

I dragged my hand down over my face. It was a shoddy attempt at hiding my broad grin. I could've pressed for specifics, or reminded her that she had to take a stab at resolving her issues with Shannon. I didn't. That wasn't how I wanted to spend the time we had remaining.

"You look delirious," she said. "I should let you go."

"I'll tell you when it's time to go, woman," I said around a yawn. "What do you have going on this week? I want to hear everything. All the details."

Her lips quirked into an indulgent smile. "I need to see a guy about some data sets," she said. "They've been giving me some trouble."

"I'm a guy," I said, pointing at my chest. "I can help you with data sets. I know all about data sets."

Erin shook her head. "I love you, but the kind of number-crunching I need isn't in your wheelhouse."

I stared at her for a beat. I expected her to laugh or toss out a sharp comment to rebuke those words, but neither came. When I couldn't take it anymore, I said, "You love me?"

She gathered her hair in her hands and then released it, letting the auburn strands fall against her neck and shoulders. "Yeah," she said, her eyebrow arched as if she was challenging me to refuse her affection. Wasn't that what she expected? For every one of the people tasked with caring for her to trample over the tender heart hidden beneath the hard, spiky shell? "I guess I do."

I didn't fall in love with Erin Walsh at first sight. I'd thought I did—oh, I *really* thought I did—but I was wrong about that. I fell in love with her the way seasons slide into each other, one day at a time until you couldn't believe how much had changed when you weren't looking. It was her obscure historical facts, her dares, her unyielding desire to photograph the high-water marks on every seawall and dock she encountered. I fell in love with her smiles and her scars, and that she fought through both and still found a way to share them with me. I fell in love with the sides of herself that she freely offered, and that she let me in when she was in the business of shutting others out. And now, I was falling in love with her all over again because she'd found a way to get here, to the place where she could present her affection in the most *take it or leave it* manner possible.

"I guess I love you too," I said, giving her a teasing smile. "But promise me this: the next time you say it, you're not nearly as far away."

Riley: Hey dude. You want to get some food tonight? Sam and Tiel are doing the couple thing and I don't want to be around that shit anyway

Nick: My service is slammed and I'm in surgery until 6. Probably not walking out of here until 8 or 9

Riley: Works for me

Nick: Where do single guys go in this city on Valentine's Day?

Riley: Dude, you're not even a little bit single

Nick: Shut up. You know what I mean

Riley: So it hasn't been a great week for you guys

Nick: She's back at Oxford now, which basically means she's in seminars for 12 hours a day and then tied up with discussion groups or some other bullshit events at night

Nick: I trust her but I still imagine her at some British pub with a bunch of science guys trying to get a piece of her

Nick: It's not even sexual. I just know she doesn't like being around a ton of people, especially not after being with them all day, and putting up with pub talk is going to drive her crazy

Riley: Yeah, it's the kind of place that has oxblood leather sofas and low ceilings and fireplaces built from Stonehenge's scraps

Nick: Thanks for the imagery

Riley: And elbow patches. The guys definitely have elbow patches. Maybe tweed caps, too. And they drink porter ales.

Nick: This is off the fucking rails now

Riley: How long has it been since you've seen her?

Nick: Sam and Tiel's wedding

Riley: What's with you guys and weddings?

Riley: When I get married, there will be a strict No Shenanigans policy

Riley: On the invitations it will say "no hookups allowed"

Riley: There's going to be a big sign at the reception, too. "No Shenanies"

Nick: And when will that blessed event be occurring?

Riley: Nevermind those details.

Riley: Why don't you just fly to England if you want to see her?

Nick: I can't. She doesn't have any free time while she's at Oxford and I'm in the operating room all week before I take off for Kenya. It sucks but there's nothing either of us can do about it.

Riley: Wait a minute. I thought you were going to Ghana.

Nick: Initially it was Ghana, but DWB closed up shop there. Now it's Kenya.

Riley: Are you going to see her when you're overseas?

Nick: Fuck. No.

Nick: We've tried to make it work but it doesn't. She's presenting at an international climate change summit in Buenos Aires when my time in Kenya ends. Immediately after that, she's on a research expedition in Greenland.

Riley: Would it be insufficient to say "adulting is hard"?

Nick: There's just no way, and it fucking sucks. This has to get easier at some point

Riley: You sound like you're on the verge of a nervous breakdown

Nick: First of all, that's an antiquated term. Don't say that.

Nick: But second, yes. I overestimated my ability to deal with the long distance shit

Riley: I'm going to say that you might've also underestimated Erin's ability to deal with the long distance shit, such that she's been doing it for the better part of a decade

Riley: She's basically the Home Run Derby of long distance, and you're the farm team

Nick: We're not talking about that right now, dude.

Riley: Let's drive down to PVD and get burgers at Harry's.

Nick: Is that the place with the bbq pulled pork on the cheeseburgers?

Riley: Yes. You need that in your life.

Riley: And plenty of that thick-ass beer you like.

Nick: How long is it to Providence again?

Riley: 57 minutes but I can get you there in 42 because I know the back roads

Nick: That was oddly specific…

Riley: It's distracting you

Riley: You buy the burgers and beer and I promise to stop talking about your impending nervous breakdown

Nick: Fine but only because I really want some bbq and beer before leaving the States for two months

---

To: Nick Acevedo
From: Erin Walsh
Date: February 20

Subject: awwww

I've never gotten flowers on my birthday before.

Thank you.

To: Erin Walsh
From: Nick Acevedo
Date: February 20
Subject: awwww

You're most welcome. Happy birthday, lovely.

To: Erin Walsh
From: Nick Acevedo
Date: February 23
Subject: Itinerary

Hey, Skip.
My travel info and emergency numbers are attached.

If anything happens, you're my contact person. I hope that's
okay. I talked to my mother this morning, and she's still
distraught that I'm going to Africa. She offered a lot of
uncomfortable and socially unacceptable commentary on
that topic. If I'm trampled under an elephant, you'll be the
first to know, and I apologize in advance for the crazy things
my mother will say.

I'm told the internet access is limited and usually reserved for communicating with the central operation unit but email me anyway. Tell me everything you're doing, everywhere you're going, all the asses you're kicking.

I will miss you more than anything.
Nick

———

To: Nick Acevedo
From: Erin Walsh
Date: February 24
Subject: Of course I'm your person!

First: You're going to be awesome. You're going to be the best borderless doctor ever and I'm so freaking proud of you for doing this. I've been telling everyone about my husband, the surgeon who's going to Kenya. Thankfully, I hang with people who care about things like conflict-region healthcare, otherwise they'd be pretty tired of hearing about my Mexican Medicine Man.

Second: Getting off the grid is hard at first. It feels weird, but it will pass. Somewhat. It will be harder coming back to city life, actually. Everything will seem louder, faster, and bigger.

Third: I'm currently beating my schedule to death and bargaining with every grad student who wants some time in the field in Greenland. I don't know if it will work, but I'm trying.

Fourth: Please be careful. You have to come back to me. Watch out for those elephants, and also Ebola.

Fifth: You already know that I'll miss you, and that I hate those words because they are inadequate. I'll load up your inbox with every random thought that crosses my mind, and maybe even my thoughts on the papers I'm peer-reviewing right now. Spoiler alert: the Anthropocene is a big downer.

To: Erin Walsh
From: Nick Acevedo
Date: February 27
Subject: Watching out for elephants

Hey, Skip,
I made it to Nairobi, and I'll be heading out to the site later today. So far, so good.

Miss you, lovely. Don't get into trouble while I'm away.
Nick

To: Nick Acevedo
From: Erin Walsh
Date: February 28
Subject: trouble?

What is this trouble you speak of? I'm not familiar with such a thing, and I'm most certain that I never have nor ever will find myself in any of it.

Did that give you a good laugh? You're welcome.

I'll be fine. I'm running ice depth and salinity simulations all week, and then churning data after that. No trouble to be found.

Please be careful. You know, I'm laughing as I type this. Not in a funny-amusing way, but in a funny-not-funny-at-all way. For years, people have been telling me to be careful. Matt likes to joke that he's got money set aside for the eventuality that he'll be bailing me out of a Third World jail, or that I'll lose all of my fingers and toes in a close brush with lava. I always thought it was an overbearing, patronizing thing to say, as if he didn't trust me to survive on my own. Maybe that was part of it because I didn't always indicate that I could survive on my own (another funny-not-at-all-funny laugh), but it was probably more about caring so much that he actively worried about me.

I didn't think I knew how to care about people, and if I could, it wasn't enough that thoughts of them would interrupt my day. But here I am, researching Kenya and Honduras—I'm already prepared for your next DWB trip—and I'm really fucking worried. Apparently I'm capable of a whole fuck-ton of caring for others.

I hope you're happy, husband. You've done all of this to me.

———

To: Erin Walsh
From: Nick Acevedo
Date: March 7

Subject: yes, trouble

I am happy. It's good that you're seeing what I've known all along.

I'm not going to tell you not to worry. You've earned the right, wife.

Twenty-Seven

To: Erin Walsh
From: Shannon Halsted
Date: March 9
Subject: Hello

Erin,
Thank you again for the vase. We're moving into a new house soon, and it will be perfect in the kitchen.

We found out this morning that I'm pregnant. That's crazy, right? I'm not ready for that. There's no way I can be a mother. I don't know what I'm going to do. Will's already calling it Froggie. Him and his fucking Navy SEAL humor.

Shit. It's probably bad to call a baby "it." See? I'm not ready for this.

I'm sorry, I didn't mean to unload all of this on you. I wanted you to be the first to know.

Shannon

To: Shannon Halsted
From: Erin Walsh
Date: March 11
Subject: Hello

It's not crazy. That baby will be very, very loved.

Congratulations.

To: Erin Walsh
From: Shannon Halsted
Date: March 12
Subject: Hello

Thank you for being so kind, but I'm sorry about my message earlier this week. I was overwhelmed with this and I word-vomited all over you. I'm sorry.

To: Shannon Halsted
From: Erin Walsh
Date: March 15
Subject: Hello

There's no reason to apologize. Thank you for sharing your news with me.

To: Erin Walsh
From: Shannon Halsted
Date: March 16
Subject: Hello

I meant what I said about wanting you to be the first to
know. Some things will never change.

I DIDN'T KNOW how to respond to Shannon's last
message, and I didn't. It stayed at the top of my inbox, half
taunt, half evidence that she didn't completely hate me.
Every few days, I drafted a new message, and then promptly
deleted it. Sometimes I requested that she elaborate, as I
didn't know which things fell under the never-changing
umbrella. Other times I asked about her pregnancy or Will or
our siblings, or spilled all the beans on me and Nick.

It went on like this for weeks. Whenever my mind
wandered away from my research or I was flailing in Nick's
absence, I was struck by the urge to reconnect with her.
Instead, I reread all of her messages, mining them for hidden
meaning. This was my way of treading lightly, and not
fucking things up for either of us.

Or, that was what I was telling myself.

Shannon's emails were the exact things I'd beat to death
with Nick. He'd listen to my fears and shoot each of them
down. He'd remind me of something I'd done that he saw as
monumental, and hold it up alongside *an email* from *my
sister*, and push me to admit that I was stirring up tornadoes
where there was no wind.

Being separated from Nick was difficult. I hadn't expected that. We'd always gone through fits and spurts of togetherness, and I figured we'd go through this one with no trouble. In the back of my mind, I'd assumed I'd simply get down to business and power through a hefty chunk of work because I wouldn't be making time for video chats or email exchanges.

That wasn't the case. Yeah, I worked a ton, but I also dedicated a remarkable amount of time to missing Nick. We were able to talk every few weeks, but it was brief, and only scratched the surface of his journeys and my studies. We couldn't discuss random historical events or debate the new theory floating around the planetary physics community, and I realized how desperately I needed those conversations to build my bond with him. Without them, I was disconnected and painfully lonely.

Perhaps it was that Nick was the one off the grid this time around, and now I was on the receiving end of the prolonged silence. It was a bitter taste of my own medicine, and one that had me struggling with this multi-continental marriage situation. None of this was getting any easier, and it wouldn't get better until something changed.

Nick's time in Kenya wrapped up as I headed off to Argentina for an international summit on climate change, followed by a lengthy research expedition across Greenland. We joked that the closest we'd come to seeing each other would be when our flights crossed over the Atlantic when he left Africa for Boston and I left Iceland for South America. It was our dark, *reality was a real bitch* humor, but that was when the velocity of our distance hit me the hardest. I wanted to see him more than anything, but the summit was a big deal for me, and this—along with a couple other symposia and conferences in coming months—would set the course for my postdoctoral work. I knew that Nick wanted to see me too, but it wasn't as if we could continue having circular conversations about life after Oxford. I had to do this, and I had to start making sense of my options.

This was the first juncture when anyone else had ever figured into my decision-making. Before Nick, I'd allowed whimsy to set the sails. Hawaii, the Mediterranean, Iceland...none of that was planned. It all happened organically, and I trusted that I'd find the places and pursuits that were right for me without strategy.

And all of that was great, but my whimsy wasn't in charge anymore.

Although he'd suggested otherwise, Nick wanted me to move back to Boston. He liked it there, and he liked my siblings, too. He'd found a family with them, and that was really fucking ironic considering my sentiments were quite the opposite. It all sounded charming in a *made for TV and not even close to my actual life* kind of way, but the next steps weren't clear to me. Maybe it was the packed calendar of research, position papers, and presentations ahead of me that tunneled my sights, or maybe I needed a metaphorical kick in the ass.

Or...maybe I wasn't designed for this. Maybe the best I could give Nick was a stolen weekend every other month. There'd been a time when I didn't believe I was capable of caring for another person, and love had been an entirely separate, even more unlikely syndrome. I knew better now, and I knew that I could both care for and love Nick.

But I still doubted that I could do enough of either.

Twenty-Eight

NICK

LIVING and practicing medicine in a Kenyan refugee camp for two months changed a guy, but not in the ways I'd expected. When I got back to Boston, I knew I'd be even more pissed off about the state of managed care in the United States. I knew I'd also experience the same frustration with the systemic inequities in access that I'd felt when helping my grandmother treat ranch hands and migrants. I didn't anticipate getting a whole helluva lot better at diagnosing without the aid of imaging studies and blood work panels, or performing surgery with the fewest instruments possible. But most of all, I didn't expect to resent the distance between me and Erin quite as much as I did now.

It wasn't what I'd been hoping for, and it was possible that made me the world's biggest asshole. The truth was, I thought I'd spend some time in Africa and come to understand her preference for the untethered life. Sure, I caught a bit of the traveling bug and I was looking forward to my next Doctors Without Borders stint in Honduras this summer, but coming face-to-face with the suffering and death there only served as a reminder that life was fragile and fleeting.

We thought we had time, that the minutes and months stretched on into our future without end, but that was the fallacy of youth, wasn't it? Believing that life went on, until faced with the cold truth that it didn't. It ended—we *all* ended—and surrendering a single moment was an affront to the death and disease I worked to prevent every day. I'd believed Erin when she said that time wasn't to be wasted, but now it was a mission statement. The need to make our relationship work whipped at me in hurried, impatient lashes. I didn't care whether I had to push her past her comfort zone, and I didn't care what I had to give up.

Returning to Boston was an otherworldly experience. Erin was right, everything did seem louder, faster, and bigger, and with that strange new perspective came a sudden comprehension of her disdain for texting. It canceled out some of the separation forced by distance, but that rapid-fire form of communication never allowed thoughts and emotions to develop or digest. It took longer, and we didn't get any instant gratification out of waiting hours and days for a response. Whether she knew it or not, Erin's preference for email forced us to say more, and say it with greater precision.

My hospital-issued pager, the one I'd been overjoyed to receive at the start of my intern years, now earned my most hostile glares. My colleagues were pleasantly vindictive in that they happily picked up my patients and assorted duties while I was overseas, and then happily dumped all of theirs on me during the two months between my sabbaticals. My schedule was loaded with surgeries, on-calls, and ER cover-age, and I was basically living at the hospital. Free moments were spent showering, power-napping, or eating lukewarm cafeteria oatmeal. There were invitations to dinners and housewarmings and happy hours, but my nonstop routine didn't allow for much of that. I missed spending time with Matt and Lauren, Andy and Patrick, Sam and Tiel, and Riley.

That I was willing to do all of this again when I got back from Honduras was a mark of my obvious psychosis. I'd lost my damn mind, and I was almost certain that Erin Walsh was to blame.

It was a gift that she was pawing around Greenland's glaciers and then tied up with lab work and intensive sessions at Oxford. We exchanged middle of the night calls and stray emails, but it was chaotic and we never fell into a rhythm. The fault belonged to no one as this was the state of our lives right now. But I still resented the fuck out of that distance. If she was here, in Boston, at least we'd sleep together. Or if I was in Iceland, or wherever her research took her.

During the one week where I wasn't jogging between operating rooms all day and night, we'd made plans to video chat, but she picked up a nasty cold and slept through our scheduled time. Later that week, I had to watch her coughing and wheezing from thousands of miles away. It was then that I truly understood why doctors couldn't treat family members. I'd grown up caring for the extended ranch family, and I'd assumed I possessed enough objectivity to remain clinical. I didn't, at least not as it pertained to my wife. I almost hopped on a flight right then, and flew all the way to England, even if only to comfort her.

We tried (and tried and tried) and failed to find a few days when we could get away, but it was a losing endeavor. The two months between Kenya and Honduras were watertight, and presented hardly any opportunities. On top of wrapping up major elements of her research, Erin was also attending several gatherings on climate change, and presenting her preliminary findings at a few. She couldn't miss those events, and I didn't want to ask her to do that either. It was the delicate balance between needing to spend time with her and respecting her work, and I didn't want to be the kind of guy who dismissed her career because I wanted her in my bed.

During our most recent calendar-scouring conversation, Erin had closed her notebook with a frustrated slam and said, "It's just a bad time for us."

It *was* a bad time for us, but I struggled to identify a time that hadn't been some shade of bad. We'd spent two years chasing moments, and we were no closer to anything more than moments. Our lives were separate and distinct, only sliding together at heavily orchestrated junctures, and my ability to continue this experiment was crumbling at the base. I was finished with separate and distinct.

I wanted our circumstances to be different, and it didn't matter what we had to do to make that happen. It only mattered that we were both willing to do it.

As these tumultuous weeks continued on and I prepared for my time in Honduras, I was ready to set aside my phone and pager again. I didn't think I'd find the answers to any of this in Central America, but unplugging had a way of narrowing my focus to the things that mattered most.

Twenty-Nine

ERIN

To: Nick Acevedo
From: Erin Walsh
Date: July 6
Subject: It's true what they say about Iceland/Greenland

I can now say, with absolute certainty, that Iceland is nice and Greenland is full of ice.

Not as much ice as it used to have, but still mainly icy. That's a good thing.

I've discovered that Greenland's terrain is not designed to sustain agricultural efforts. There's a historic erosion issue, although before all that, there was *green land*. About 2.5 million years ago, it was quite green, almost like the Alaskan tundra. I've been playing around with the meteoric beryllium-9 and beryllium-10 from soil samples. That is, the soil underneath the ice sheet.

Please tell me that you've made it to Honduras and you're settling in. Miss you.

———————

To: Nick Acevedo
From: Erin Walsh
Date: July 15
Subject: too many fishes

Hey…I hope everything is going well. I'm sure you're just busy and I know that Central America doesn't have the best internet service. I've left you a few voicemails, too. Nothing important, just wanted to say hi.

In other news, I've determined that I'm not cut out for the traditional North Atlantic diet of fish, fish, and fish. I don't care whether it's dried, smoked, boiled, pickled, or any other preparation. I've had enough fish. It's kind of like my first semester of college, when the only thing I ate for four months straight was cereal bars. I can't even look at those things anymore without gagging. Apply that logic over to fish, and you'll understand why I'm eager to get back to Oxford and their shepherd's pies next month. At least they know how to make mashed potatoes.

Let me know that you're all right, love. I miss you.

———————

To: Nick Acevedo
From: Erin Walsh
Date: July 21

Subject: everything okay?

Nick,
I haven't heard from you since before you left for Honduras.
I don't want to call the emergency numbers you gave me
because I respect the term "emergency" enough to know
better, but I'm getting anxious. I have a friend working in El
Salvador, and I'm THIS CLOSE to asking him to go looking
for you.

You also have about 18 voicemails from me. Sorry about
that.

- e

To: Erin Walsh
From: Nick Acevedo
Date: July 25
Subject: all good

Hey, Skip,
I'm here in Tegucigalpa. I'm fine. I'm settled. Internet service
sucks. Cell service is no better. I have my hands full. I've
been in surgery around the clock since I arrived.

Miss you. I'm sorry I had you worried.

Nick

To: Nick Acevedo
From: Erin Walsh
Date: July 26
Subject: top of the world

Okay, good. I'll stop calling everyone I know in South and
Central America now.

Listen. I'm heading up to Peary Land next week, on the far
north side of the island. The air is too thin up there to
produce snow, so I'm not expecting great wi-fi conditions.
Getting there, doing the work, and then getting back will
take about three weeks.

I hope you're okay. I'm trying not to read too much into your
last message, but you didn't sound like yourself. If you're
able to talk before I leave for the north, even for a few
minutes, please call. I have my phone on, and I'll make time.
I'll walk right out of the cold lab for you.

We need to look at our schedules again because it's been too
long, love. Imagining you in bed with me isn't sufficient.
Please tell me I'm at least adequate in the shower.

To: Erin Walsh
From: Nick Acevedo
Date: August 13
Subject: top of the world

Hey, Skip.
Sorry, I didn't get this until now.

Tegucigalpa is not at all like the Dadaab refugee settlement. It's all trauma surgery. All I'm doing, all day, is trying to put people back together and failing. It's only been a few weeks and I've lost track of all the patients who've died on my table.

This world, it's really fucking terrible sometimes. I think about you out there, exploring Greenland, or speaking in Mumbai and Buenos Aires, and I worry about you. I know you can handle yourself, and I trust you to do that, but I still worry. You're all by yourself, and I can't protect you from a fucking thing and I hate that.

You're right, it has been too long. We need to find a time, and I want more than a couple of days. I want months, Erin. Years if you'll give them to me.

Nick

To: Nick Acevedo
From: Erin Walsh
Date: August 24
Subject: back to civilization

Hey…
I'm back in Nuuk, on the southwestern side of Greenland. I'll be here a few days before I head to Oxford.

I'm sorry that it's been difficult in Tegucigalpa. I know how much it weighs on you when you can't save them all. I wish I could be there for you.

What about that week after you finish in Honduras? Can we meet up somewhere? I can jam through some projects and make that work.

I hope things are a little easier, or at least less overwhelming. Call me anytime, love.

To: Erin Walsh
From: Nick Acevedo
Date: September 1
Subject: make it work

Can you meet me in Mexico?

*You never responded to my request for more than a couple of days, Skip.

To: Nick Acevedo
From: Erin Walsh
Date: September 2
Subject: doing the best I can

Yeah, I can meet you in Mexico although a little more specificity would be helpful in scheduling my travel. I know my way around Popocatépetl, Colima, and El Chichón, but I'm fairly certain you're not planning a volcano-inspired getaway. Correct me if I'm wrong.

As for months and years…you know that I'm attached to

this program for several months. It's not what you want to hear, but it's not changing. You knew this going in, and I'm sorry that it seems unending right now. I am truly sorry. If that isn't enough, then I think we need to have a different conversation. Please hear me when I say that I don't want a different conversation. I want us to work through the rest of this, and sort it out on the other side. We make things work when they're impossible, remember?

Please stay safe. I miss you, and I can't wait to see you soon, love.

Thirty

NICK

IT WAS hurricane season in the Yucatán, and we went there anyway.

Erin and I found a handful of days after my time in Honduras when she could sneak away from Oxford, and we agreed to spend them on the Mexican island of Cozumel. There were storms brewing on the Atlantic and Pacific sides of Mexico, and they'd either fizzle out over the oceans or slam straight into us.

Cruise ships frequented this peninsula and the surrounding isles, but none were to be seen now; they were taking cover. The island was bracing for impact, but optimistic. The resorts were empty but still open, residents still in their homes. No one was evacuating, but they were boarding up storefronts and lining sandbags around every foundation. Surf watches were posted, and those who approached the beaches were warned to do so at their own peril.

Clouds were hanging low overhead, and moving quickly. The winds whipped off the water and sent gusts of humid air over the mostly undeveloped land. The waves were choppy, and the beaches were littered with the remnants of last night's high tide. Driftwood, seaweed, and shells all covered the shoreline. In some places, odd ocean relics peeked out of the sand and tide. Plastic water bottles, broken surfboards, mate-less flip-flops, sun-bleached tennis balls. It seemed like the sea and the skies were moving into place for a tandem purge, and we were getting front row seats.

My work in the Honduran city of Tegucigalpa had been gut-wrenching. The violence and disease was unending, and I'd lost more patients than I saved. And those who survived, they'd never be the same. My respect for the nurses and doctors who dedicated their *lives*—not just a couple of months when their prestigious hospital granted them sabbaticals—to healthcare in conflict-stricken regions doubled, tripled, quadrupled. I didn't know how they did it.

I found myself even more desperate to make a life with Erin. These moments, they really were slipping by while we waited for circumstances and long-overdue reconciliations and all the other bullshit we put between us to fall into some perfect cosmic alignment. I was finished with the distance. Just fucking *finished*. I'd seen too many families ravaged and aching with the loss of their loved ones, and I couldn't comprehend why we were living apart by choice. It was fucking ludicrous. Now, after everything I'd experienced this year, our marriage resembled a flippant, selfish version of love. We were defined by our ability to exist without each other, an ability I'd long ago challenged and championed. I was wrong about that. Marriage wasn't an experiment.

There were too many things I should've done differently, she should've done differently, we both should've done it differently. *Better*. Our future couldn't be the same as our past, and I was prepared to tell her that.

So those storms, they seemed fitting.

I couldn't believe it when I saw her walk through the gate and straight toward me. It was like a dream, one I'd been having for months, except this dream had me wrapped up in a tight embrace.

"You're supposed to hug me back," she yelled into my chest. "This is going to get real awkward if you don't do something soon. People are going to think I'm accosting you."

I shook my head, snapping out of my disbelief, and shucked her backpack before scooping her off the ground. I was hit with the scent of rosewater and transported back in time to those deceptively simple nights on Cape Cod, when this was new and we were blind to the barriers.

"Skip," I said, sighing into her hair. I wanted to put it all out on the table now, tell her everything, and then make a plan. But I was also a man, one who'd been separated from his wife for longer than was acceptable. "If I don't get you naked in the next ten minutes, I might die."

"Let's not start our island getaway with public indecency," she said, her lips on my neck. "It would be rather unfortunate if we had to spend this time in the local jail, you know."

"Once again, my genius wife has it all figured out." I set her down and nodded in the direction of the sliding glass doors that led out of the airport. I'd arrived last night, and I knew she'd traveled light, with everything stowed in her backpack. I collected it from the ground, and slung it over my shoulder. "This way."

We walked through the terminal, our hands linked and our shoulders brushing, and everything about it was right. None of the unease for her well-being that had chased me while in Honduras lingered here, and as my thumb swirled over her hand, I knew she was safe. Yet another reason we needed to stop living on separate continents—I worried about her too much, and I didn't care whether that was a primitive, paternalistic urge.

"Hey," she murmured, squeezing my hand. I glanced down at her, first with the contemplative frown I'd adopted as we made our way through the terminal and out to the taxi stand, and then with a smile. Her eyebrows arched at that manic switch-up. "I can hear you thinking. Stop it, it's too damn loud."

I stared at her, struggling through a smile-frown spasm as I attempted to corral my competing desires. I wanted to take her to bed and keep her there for days. I wanted to tell her every heartbreaking story I'd acquired in Kenya and Honduras because I knew she'd be able to order them in a way that helped me understand. I also wanted to rage at her, and demand that she come home with me, or take me back to Europe with her.

Instead of doing any of that, I shoved my fingers through her hair and kissed her hard. She tasted like mint gum and that special, spicy flavor all her own. Horns honked and passengers buzzed around us, and I realized that this was what I should've done when I saw her in the terminal. I should've shut down all the noise in my head and kissed my woman until she went weak in my arms because waiting wasn't the answer for us. It was never our answer.

"Oh, okay," Erin murmured when I broke away from her. She ran her fingertips over her lips and pressed a hand to her chest. "Okay. Let's see about finding some privacy. Maybe a bed, but I'm not fussy. I'll take a broom closet if that's the best we can do."

I dipped down, brushing my lips over hers again. "I love you," I whispered.

She smiled, and she slipped her fingers under my t-shirt,

between my shorts and skin. "I love you, too," she replied. "See? I waited to say it until we weren't so far apart. It wasn't easy."

"Good girl," I said, kissing the corner of her mouth. "Now promise me that we're never going to be separated for that long again."

Her forehead crinkled, and she grimaced as if I'd said something unpleasant. Sighing, she stepped away and into the open door of the waiting taxi. I followed her, and yanked her close to me on the bench seat. I gave the driver the name of our quaint accommodations, a collection of beachfront casitas on the quiet side of the island, before turning back to Erin. "It's been months, and—"

"I *know* how long it's been," Erin interrupted.

"Turn down the defensive shields, darlin'," I said, squeezing her thigh. "I'm not arguing with you. I'm just telling you that it's been months, and I can't do that again."

She floundered at that, shaking her head as if I was forcing an impossible choice upon her. "I don't know what you want me to say about that," she replied. "You know the parameters of my work. I can't make you any promises right now, and that's nothing new."

It wasn't those months that I was worried about. It was all the months after that.

"Nick," she said, tucking her head against my chest and making me absolutely melt. "Please, let's enjoy this time. We can talk about everything else when we get back to the real world. We're on this beautiful island and we have these days, and there isn't a minute to waste. You're right, it *has* been too long. But now, I want to be with you, and I don't want to argue." She glanced up and kissed my chin. "*Please, love.*"

How could I say no to that?

I couldn't.

Instead, I shoved aside all of my desperate need to keep her. I forced myself to ignore the storms churning and strengthening around us, a not-so-subtle reminder that we'd either make it out in one piece, or not at all.

THE WINDS WERE HOWLING on our last night in Cozumel, and the surf was slamming against the shore with enough fury to rain droplets of salt water down over the roof of our casita. I leaned against the balcony railing, watching the palm trees whipping with the gusts. It was exactly as it looked on news coverage of extreme weather, with the skies green-gray and the streets empty.

A two-headed hurricane was set to pass over this island late tomorrow night, and we were getting out just in time. We'd enjoyed three amazing—if not windy—days together, and I was reminded of all the things I loved about Erin. The conversation was great, the sex was even better, and her presence put my universe back in perspective. She allowed me to sermonize about issues of disease, poverty, and access to medical care, and how it seemed so much easier when it was me and my grandmother back on the ranch. She took all of my anguish over the lives I hadn't been able to save without slathering me in meaningless platitudes. Then, she suggested that my grandmother would've been pleased to hear about my travels, even the agonizing parts, and she would've been proud.

This woman and her old soul, she was just too much.

Despite all of that, I was in a terrible mood. I hadn't been able to shrug it off while we'd traded books and newspapers in bed this morning, and it dogged me while we'd wandered through the shuttered town and shared tacos from the last open restaurant this afternoon. It was the kind of mood that had a taste, sharp and acidic, and it was in me now.

There was no one source, but all the inevitabilities coming down on me at once. My harsh journey in Central America was ending and I'd be back to work within forty-eight hours. That meant this holiday of ours was over tomorrow, and I didn't know when I'd see Erin again. We'd only discussed our travels and experiences in the time we'd been apart, and other random topics while the one—*the only one*—on my mind went unaddressed.

But we both knew. It was in the air, lingering between us, even if we'd never mentioned it. We were *two years* into this marriage and were no closer to a life that wasn't built on emails, video chats, and a fuck-ton of frequent flyer miles. I adored this woman, and I had absolutely no regrets when it came to her, but my tank was on empty. Something had to change for us.

Erin was feeling it, too. She didn't say anything when she took my hand and led me inside, away from the balcony and the far outer bands of the hurricane, onto the bed. She tugged me on top of her, brought me between her legs, and wrapped her arms around me like she was trying to leave permanent marks on my tissue and bones. Like she needed to claim a part of me. And wasn't that the same reason I'd slammed into her over and over again last night? Why I fucked every last drop of me into her, and left teeth marks on her thighs and little bruises on her hips? Why I wanted to do it all over again now?

She made me fucking wild to keep her. Just *wild*.

"Say something," she murmured.

"I want everyone to know you're mine," I said, thrusting into her hard enough to earn a deep moan. Part of me wondered whether this was normal, whether I'd always be this desperate to possess her. The other part of me believed I could live hundreds of years with Erin and never get enough.

"What else do you want?" she asked, her fingers sliding into my hair and fisting around the strands. My eyes watered when she pulled, and I fucked her harder, pressing my teeth to her breast. "Give it to me. All of it. Everything you've been holding back, I want it all."

"My wife sleeps in my bed, and nowhere else," I growled. She hummed into my skin, and some stray wisps of her hair brushed over my chest. I loved this and I loved her, but I was also fucking furious that I couldn't wake up this way every single day. "I want to put a baby in you—"

"Oh, fuck. Oh, *oh my God*," Erin cried. She arched up, and that position all but forced her breast into my mouth. It wasn't clear whether she was reacting to my words or my cock's handiwork, and I didn't care because I wasn't finished with either.

"And then I'm gonna want another baby," I said as my lips met her nipple. Her short nails sank into my shoulders when my teeth pulled at her. "And a third, if I can keep you in one place long enough to get the job done. Maybe more."

"*Ohholyfuck*," she panted. I gripped the backs of her legs, angling her body to take me deeper, deep enough that she'd remember me there for days after we parted. "Don't stop, Nick. Don't stop."

I didn't know whether she wanted me to keep talking about the babies we were going to make or keep fucking her like I hated her, and I went with a little of both.

"You're coming home with me, once and for all," I snarled. The headboard was snapping against the wall now, and I was vaguely aware of the plaster cracking. Small bits of it were breaking off and falling to the ground, tinkling as they hit the terracotta tile floor. "There's no fucking argument about it, Erin. You're mine, and you belong with me."

A damp gust blew the patio door open with a bang, but it didn't stop me. I was overheated and blind with hot, angry need. Erin was humming and murmuring as I drove into her, eyes closed and lips parted. There was a bright flush climbing up her chest and neck, and I dipped down to taste her there.

"We're fixing that ring, and your name, too," I continued. I was on a fucking roll, and I wasn't stopping until all the desires I'd locked away were out in the open. "I'm changing that last name of yours, lovely. No wife of mine walks around with a maiden name and a wedding band on the wrong finger. You just don't understand who you belong to, do you?"

"Make me understand, love," Erin whispered into my neck. Her fingers were digging into my back and sides, and her nails were scoring my skin. Those small bites of pain were the only things keeping me from blowing apart right there.

"You belong to me," I said, each word groaned into the sweet slope of her breast. Outside, the winds were screeching around our tiny casita and shaking the walls. Inside, we were creating a storm of our own. "Just tell me you're mine."

And that was when she came, all incoherent cries and sharp wails, and she brought me along with her. Wrapped in each other's arms, we shook and panted and kissed like we'd never get another moment together.

But she never said the words I wanted to hear.

I SHOULD'VE BEEN able to shake my awful mood after sex like that, but I couldn't and I let that mood take over when we snagged seats at the airport bar before Erin's flight early the next morning. The airport was nearly empty, and it was clear we were among the last to take the storm's threat seriously enough to leave.

"I meant what I said last night," I announced, interrupting her musings about the rise of catastrophic hurricanes in recent years.

"You said *a lot* of things last night." She grinned, offering me chance to qualify my possessive demands. But I wasn't walking any of it back, not today, not tomorrow, not any day.

"I want everyone to know," I continued. "We've been waiting for a perfect moment to appear, and we need to stop waiting."

"Oh," she said, frowning. "Okay…"

"Don't you want to tell your family?"

"Yes," she replied with all the defensiveness a single syllable could contain.

"We could send them an email," I suggested, gesturing to her phone. "You're quite proficient at that."

"Yeah, sure," she snapped. "I don't think you really want that, but go right ahead."

"If we put it off much longer, we'll never tell them," I said. "At this point, the method doesn't matter."

Erin tapped her fingertip against her lips before responding. "Why don't you tell me what does matter?"

"What the fuck are we doing?" I asked. "Why are we even here?"

She leveled a cool glare in my direction. "I didn't think I needed to remind you that I rearranged everything just to spend this time with you. I did that because I wanted to be here. With *you*. I don't know what you think I'm attempting to do, Nick, but I'm not blowing you off."

"I know, I know," I said. I was being a fucking asshole. Time to rein it in. "I want to know what to expect, and when I can see you again. That's all."

That was not all.

"I'm busy the next few months," Erin said, pulling a few strands of hair between her fingers. "I'm trying to get onto a panel during a climate summit in Geneva after the new year, and then there's a renewable energy conference in Munich in February. There are some people trying to capture the energy generated from everyday tectonic shifts—not the shifts that cause eruptions or earthquakes, but the small stuff—much like wind or solar power. It's really cool, but it sold out about ten minutes after the event went live and—"

"Are you ever coming home?" I interrupted. I wasn't doing too well at reining it in.

"What?" she asked. "What do you mean? I think we can find some weekends in—"

"No," I interrupted. This wasn't the conversation for an airport bar. This had all the makings of an at-home argument that started somewhere innocuous, like the living room, but quickly moved to the kitchen where cabinets could be opened and closed, and dish towels repeatedly folded and replaced on the countertop. From there it would move to the bedroom where the bed could serve as the physical representation of the disagreement, and sides could be taken. Also, sex was great for ending these things, and beds were mighty helpful when it came to throwing my woman down and solving some shit.

"No, I'm not talking about weekends," I said. "I need to wake up in the same place for a few months, and I need more than weekends from you."

Erin started to say something, then stopped. She looked everywhere but me. Her drink, the news crew that had arrived from Los Angeles, the jungle-edged runway.

"I'm realizing now that I can't give you all the things that you want," she said.

"You don't care what I want," I said. "You've never cared about what I want, Erin."

Her eyes widened as she nodded, staring at her hands. "This isn't the first time I've been called a self-centered bitch," she murmured. "Probably won't be the last."

"That isn't what I said." I shook my head and looked away while I drew in a breath. That was exactly what I'd said. I was frustrated. With myself, with her, with everything. "You already know what happens next, after you're done in Iceland, don't you? You're gonna find a new overseas research venture, and you're going to hide behind that for a couple more years. You have no intention of coming home. Right?"

"It's complicated, Nick," she said with a sigh.

"It's not, actually," I replied. "You don't want to deal with Shannon and the rest of your family. I get it, Skip, I really do. They don't always make it easy on you, and they're hung up on the shit you did three lifetimes ago, but you don't make it easy on them, either. You show up for moments, and nothing more. You don't talk to them unless they talk to you first. But they're *my* family just as much as they're yours, and I don't want my wife to be a secret, a spire in the distance, one that I can see but never, ever reach."

"Nick, my work and my family are two separate issues," she said. "And quick reminder—my work is all about field research. I can't just hang out in Boston, measuring how quickly the Back Bay is sinking and tracking the sunny day floods in Rowes Wharf."

"I've never asked you to give up your research, but we both know you'll have your choice of projects when you're finished at Oxford. You won't have to be stuck on expeditions for months at a time, or living in airports and train stations. You can come home and be with me, and—"

"Maybe I like fieldwork," she snapped. "Have you considered that?"

"Have you considered that I know you about as well as you know yourself?" I asked. "You were miserable last winter. Don't lie to both of us and say you liked that trip to the Arctic Circle."

She rolled her eyes. "It's not all good times and glam," she said, "but neither is medicine. You constantly complain about managed care and hospital politics, but I'm not over here suggesting that you give it up, am I? No, and that's because I know you love being a surgeon and I'd never want to take that from you."

"I'm not taking a fucking thing from you," I cried. "I want you to have a place. I want *us* to have a place."

"As long as it's Boston," she said under her breath.

"I'm not gonna lie and say I don't want that, but I want you more," I replied. "If you told me that you wanted to research the Alaskan ice sheets, or Mount Tambora, or fucking *anything*, Skip, and you wanted me to come along, I'd be there. Why won't you do the same for me? Don't stop traveling and researching, but when you come home, come home to *me*."

"It's simple for you," she said. "My siblings don't look at you and see every shitty thing you've ever done. They don't hide the breakables when you're around, or warn you not to cause a scene. The home you want isn't a place that belongs to me, not anymore."

I stared at her for a sharp, painful moment. "Whatever

happened to not wasting time because life was too short? Whatever happened to living without regrets? Where is the woman I married, the one who wanted to steal a lobster boat and beat the shit out of every minute because these years are so fucking inadequate? Where the fuck is she because this"—I gestured to her—"is not that woman. This is you letting your father's ghost and the fear of a rough conversation with Shannon win, and the woman I married is better than that. She'd tell her siblings to get the fuck over themselves and catch up because she's really smart and successful, and she doesn't have time for any of their bull-shit opinions."

"This marriage isn't real," she said softly.

"When the fuck did that start mattering to us?" I snapped. "You're not weak, Skip. Stop taking that way out."

"Then I'll keep my self-preservation to myself," she said.

"I'm not attacking your self-preservation, and I think you know that. I'm attacking your willingness to do things that scare you, and reminding you that you don't have to be scared alone," I said. "You can end this. You're the only one who can."

"I'm neither Harry Potter nor Frodo Baggins," she murmured.

"That's good," I said. "Deflect. Blow it off."

"I'm not blowing anything off," she said. "You've just listed all of my flaws, and I need some levity right now because it feels like all I ever hear is what I do wrong. Maybe I *am* deflecting, but that's what I need to take care of myself. I'm not ignoring anything you said, Nick. I'm just trying to survive it."

"I don't know much longer I can do this," I admitted. "I can't wait for you if there's no end in sight."

Her lips flattened into a grim line as she nodded. "We

probably should've straightened that out on the lobster boat, huh?"

"You're not even budging an inch, darlin'," I said. "Do you notice that? Or are you being intentionally obstinate?"

She gave me an oblique glance and then finished her beer. Before she could respond—I could see her cooking up something good and snappy—the loudspeaker blared with flight announcements. First in Spanish, then English.

Erin pointed to the ceiling. "That's me." She hopped off her stool and shrugged on her backpack. "I guess…" she started, her thumbs hooked around the straps and eyes cast down. "I guess this is goodbye, Nick."

Goodbye. She'd never said that before, never once, and now I heard it like a door slamming shut.

I tossed some cash on the bar and followed her through the terminal. We were silent and apart, no longer seizing every moment of togetherness. We reached the gate before I could cut through my outrage and figure out how to fix this before Erin spent the next eighteen hours flying back to England.

"Come here," I said, tugging at the hem of her shirt. "Don't go like this."

"Maybe…maybe there will be a time for us," she said as she stepped into my arms. "Maybe we'll get a second chance, and we'll be able to do this all over again."

"Erin, don't," I pleaded, my lips on her hair.

"Maybe we'll do it right," she said, looking up at me with a sad smile. "Maybe then I'll be better. You never know. I could change, and…be everything you want."

"*Erin,*" I said, trying to pack all the agony I was feeling into that one word.

"Don't," she whispered, shaking her head against my chest. "Don't try to take it back. It's okay that you meant it, and it's okay that it hurts. But I've never been able to give you all that you want, and all that you deserve. I shouldn't pretend that I can."

She turned, and walked to her gate without a backward glance.

PART THREE

Little Mermaid and

Lightning

I SCOWLED at the group texts from Lauren for a long moment before shoving my phone in my pocket and returning to my surgical notes. I got through two charts before pulling it out and rereading it again.

Lauren: It's time!!!!!
Lauren: Baby Froggie is coming! Shannon and Will are headed to the hospital now!
Lauren: They don't want anyone coming by yet or hanging around in the waiting room (shocker) but my mom's there and will let us know when Froggie arrives

"Um, Doctor Acevedo," one of my residents started. I called this one EMA, Even More Annoying. I hadn't stopped to learn this rotation's names. In my head, they were Really Annoying, More Annoying, Even More Annoying, Weird Hair, and Super Annoying. "Do you need someone to scrub in for that—"

"No I'll tell you when I need you go away right now," I said, all the words flying out in a single breath.

I grabbed the hospital phone and called over to Brigham and Women's while I stared at Lauren's texts. Shannon was delivering there, and I wanted to see who was on duty tonight. I had privileges at that facility, and knew many of the residents and attending physicians. Once I got through to the nurse managing the labor and delivery floor, and I asked about staffing and let her know that Shannon was a friend. That heads-up served all interests, as I wanted the best for Shannon but also knew she required a room far away from other laboring mothers. I was betting that she'd invite everyone in earshot to suck her dick at least once before this baby arrived.

When I was finished, I resumed scowling at my phone, and toggled to Erin's contact information. It was Monday afternoon in Boston, which meant it was early evening in Iceland. Odds were good that she was still in the lab. If she wasn't heading home to meet me for a video chat, time was known to fade away for her, and she'd work straight through the night without noticing. I closed my address book app, and opened an internet browser.

Not that I knew anything for sure, as we'd barely communicated since parting in Cozumel.

She'd texted from Charles de Gaulle to share that she'd landed and was enjoying some Parisian breads before her connecting flight to Heathrow, and that felt normal. Like we hadn't unraveled the past two years of us in an island airport terminal because I'd lost my fucking mind.

So it was no surprise that after confirming that she'd arrived in London and then Oxford, the texts stopped. I knew she was tied up with research and our schedules were out of whack with me back at the hospital, but it had been five weeks without an email or call, video chat or text.

Erin's silence was like a slow, painful suffocation. The

oxygen was sliding out of my lungs and there was nothing I could do to stop it. At first, I struggled against it, flailing and fighting and shooting off ten emails in a single day. But then I found myself sinking deep, deep, deep as I surrendered to the reality that I was without air, without Erin. I was cold and alone, and I'd done this to myself.

She only shut down and shut out as a means of protection. She wasn't doing this to hurt me—or Shannon or anyone else she'd muted—because the one thing that mattered most was her free will. Her choice, her autonomy. Robbing her of that only guaranteed that she'd take cover in a quiet, separate place. And that was what I'd done. I'd pushed her to the point of ultimatum, and those were never choices. So I waited, emailing every day, even if only to say "I'm sorry and I love you."

There was no spectacular spin-out on my part, no epic alcohol consumption or destructive behavior. All of that required gathering a certain level of energy, and I didn't have it. I was tired and heartsick, and the worst part was that I knew she could lose herself in enough research and travel to forget all about me. I fucking hated it, but it was true.

My life shrank down to three small priorities: work, sleep, and running. That, plus the occasional visit from Riley, was all I could manage. He'd been making a habit of showing up at my apartment with a six-pack of beer to watch Monday Night Football recently, and that qualified as my only non-professional interaction with humans most weeks. He kept the discussion localized to football, and I appreciated the hell out of him for it.

Getting back to the hospital wasn't as jarring this time around, or maybe I was too numb to notice. All of this translated into a grouchy demeanor that had the residents gossiping about Africa and Central America "changing" me.

To them, I was a cautionary tale, proof that the best surgeons shouldn't sully their skills on lost Third World causes.

Unfortunately, my problems were of the First World variety.

When I wasn't working, I was out hitting the pavement and reteaching my body how to run farther than the distance between operating rooms. The exercise was good for me, and it came with the added benefit of clearing my head. I could focus on the road, my breathing, my pace, and get away from all the things I should've said in that airport terminal. So I ran my soles thin, and for once, I was thankful that Boston wasn't loaded with memories of Erin.

I slept with my laptop beside me, powered up and dialed in to the video chat app we favored on the off chance Erin wanted to talk. She was most reflective in the middle of the night. Most honest with herself, too. But it was ridiculous. She wasn't reaching out. If there was one thing I knew about Erin, it was that she didn't feel entitled to taking the first step.

"Fuck it," I mumbled to myself, thumbing my phone to life. "Just fuckin' fuck it all." I tapped Erin's contact information, initiated the call, and pressed the phone to my ear, all while grousing about her penchant for only checking her phone a few times each day. "If she doesn't fuckin' answer, I'm goin' to Iceland and pickin' her up my-fuckin'-self."

"What's that Doctor Acevedo?" one of my residents called. He'd been lurking around all day, just waiting to scrub in or get his hands on a procedure, and now he was listening to me talk to myself.

Still ringing.

"Why aren't you in the ER?" I snapped. I'd been doing that with some frequency, yelling at residents. Interns, too. I feared the nursing staff enough to know better.

Still ringing.

"You didn't send me to the ER," he replied.

Still ringing.

"Go there anyway," I said.

Still—

"Hey," Erin answered. It was the bashful kind of *hey* that said *Yeah, I have been ignoring your calls and emails but please don't forget that you like me a whole lot*. It also could've been *Yeah, we broke up in an airport but you won't stop emailing me and this is getting weird* but I was rooting for the former.

"Hey," I said. I was stunned that she'd answered, and didn't have my response ready yet.

"Not to end this conversation before it starts, but...I'm kinda busy," she said.

Of course you are. "With?" I asked, hoping that she'd fill the silence with news of her research and data analysis problems so that I could figure out how the hell to get her back here before Shannon's baby was old enough to drive and vote.

She hummed for a second, and I imagined that crooked smile-scowl that she made when she was thinking about her work. "Lab stuff," she said.

There was a punch of dismissiveness in those words, and it was clear I wasn't getting an update on the chemical composition of the soil beneath Greenland's ice today. I cleared my throat and stepped into an empty patient room to avoid the roving pack of residents that seemed to sense I was engaged in a highly personal conversation, and chose this minute to hover even closer.

"Shannon's having the baby tonight," I said, shutting the door behind me. "Come home."

"Who's asking?" she snapped.

That right there, it brought the first true smile to my face in weeks. I loved Feisty Erin.

"Because I'm comfortable stating that I'm neither pivotal in the childbirth proceedings nor am I useful," she continued. "I know all about things that explode, but not as it pertains to amniotic sacs, or vaginas. Hell, me showing up would probably make the experience worse for her, and that would only add another crime to my tab. If anything, it will make this all about me and Shannon, and not Shannon and Will and Froggie. I don't want to force an awkward scene. Don't you think she has enough to worry about right now?"

"And I'm comfortable stating that vaginas do not explode during childbirth," I said. I laughed at that, and it didn't feel like a brittle spasm anymore. It felt good.

"But if Patrick's asking," she started, "it's because he thinks he's going to reenact the Christmas Truce of 1914, and that is ludicrous—"

"I love when you force obscure bits of history to fit your arguments," I murmured, smiling like a lunatic.

"And this isn't the trenches of Saint-Yves," she said, carrying on as if I hadn't spoken. "If Matt's asking, please tell him that he's been formally relieved of his official role as Walsh Family Arbitrator."

"But he really likes it," I said. The biggest smile possible. "Don't rob him of that joy."

"I know Sam isn't asking because he sent me an email two hours ago," she said. I could picture her in the stark white Reykjavík apartment—I still had her schedule on my kitchen calendar, and knew she'd returned from Greenland late last week—ticking off her siblings on her fingers. "Sam and Tiel, they're having a boy, by the way."

Another laugh, and that brought my total for the day up to two. Tiel was four months along, and Sam was the text-book definition of an anxious father-to-be. He texted me with no fewer than ninety-seven questions about pregnancy and babies each day. "Trust me," I said. "I've heard and I believe he's buying the Green Monster at Fenway Park so he can have it painted with that news, too."

"It's not Riley. He texts me whenever he has something worth sharing," Erin continued. "So, tell me: who's asking?"

Several things were unbelievably positive about this. First, she'd taken my call. Erin was the queen of ignoring calls from people she didn't want to talk to—her brothers, namely—and then immediately emailing or texting back to find out what they wanted. She could've done that but didn't. On top of that, she was *talking to me*. Real, hyperbolic babble that only this woman could pull off with a semblance of sense. And finally, she *wanted* to come home. She wanted this request and she had to stage some opposition in the process, but she wanted it.

All this time, I'd thought it would be me. I thought I'd be the one to convince her to end the war with Shannon and allow her siblings back into her life, but I was wrong.

Shannon was bringing Erin home, and she was the only one who could.

"Your husband," I said. "Your husband is asking because nine years is nine too many."

"Nick, you're—" she protested.

"I'm not having it, lovely," I interrupted. "It's time for this to end, and it ends here. There's a flight out of Reykjavík tonight, and it still has some available seats. Get your ass in one of them. I'm heading into surgery soon, but I'll see you in the morning."

Thirty-Two

ERIN

I SHOULD'VE TURNED off my phone and hunkered down with my data sets after that call with Nick ended.

I didn't.

Instead, it went something like this. Turned off the phone, then immediately turned it back on. Glared at the phone for all that it represented. Stared into my closet for five minutes, repeating over and over "I have nothing to wear to a birth." Read through all the emails popping up like prairie dogs from Matt, Sam, and Patrick. Muttered to myself about them needing to coordinate their messages to me because they were announcing the same damn fact and asking the same damn questions. Threw some clothes on my bed, and then threw them back in the closet because fuck this, I wasn't going anywhere. Read through texts from Riley, and told him to corral his boys because they were giving me the inbox sweats. Muttered about the state of the world, and how people used to communicate with each other and now they banged out a string of characters like the monkeys with the old-school Macs. Grabbed my backpack and shoved some clothes in there without concern for what I was shoving. Read Nick's most recent emails, the ones that insisted he was sorry about the things he'd said in Cozumel and he wanted to talk again. Muttered about how I cried over him every fucking day, so fuck talking because those things still hurt. Polished off the cookie dough I'd whipped up last week because it was the only thing I was eating these days. Muttered about wanting to talk to him more than anything. Shoved my laptop in the backpack. Debated which books to bring. Threw the books across the room because fuck this again. Booked a flight to Boston. Puked up the cookie dough. Sat on the bathroom floor, crying. Changed out of the vomit-stained clothes. Washed my face and applied some makeup, but then washed that off, too, because fuck this. Shuffled through my rocks, and stuck a few in my bag. Reapplied the makeup because it wasn't for Nick, it was for me. Stared at my passport for an eternity. Yelled at myself for thinking I was going to Boston, and then yelled at myself for thinking I wasn't going.

Slammed the door shut. Headed to the airport. Doubted everything, twice. Yelled "Fuck all the doubts" out loud in the terminal, and earned several suspicious stares. Marched down the jetway and didn't look back.

There were many reasons why I got on that late-night flight to Boston. Emails and texts from my brothers. The call from Nick. Missing Nick like I couldn't believe. Feeling more alone and empty than I had in years. A shaky belief that I'd go crazy if I spent another minute in my lab. A shakier belief that I'd already gone there, and that was why I was rambling to myself.

But there was another reason, one that stood far apart from the rest.

The world only handed out a select number of fresh starts in life, and being born was the freshest. I didn't want this baby to inherit any of the baggage that had pushed me and Shannon apart. This kid didn't deserve our shit.

When I arrived in Boston, Nick was waiting on the other side of Customs, feet anchored a shoulder's width apart, arms folded over his chest, expression stony. He was wearing blue scrubs, a fleece jacket emblazoned with the Massachusetts General logo, and running shoes. A full beard was part of the package now.

He was a *Grey's Anatomy* fantasy in the flesh.

But still, it hurt to see him. Everything inside me lurched forward, wanting to reach for him. Just as quickly, it all slammed back down. It was as if my organs were sliding together to form a shield around my heart because they knew it couldn't withstand any more bruises.

Even if we'd laughed about Sam's brand of expectant father exuberance.

Even if he'd said he loved my random history.

Even if he'd called me *lovely* again.

It was just like old times, but it wasn't.

I stopped in front of him and tucked my thumbs under my backpack straps. "You came," I said, and that was definitely the lamest thing I could've said. Six hours in the air, and the best I could manage was this. Lame. Pitiful. Pathetic. And it wasn't like I did anything else on that flight. Books, laptop, all stayed shut while I stared at the ring on my middle finger and wondered what the hell I was going to do when I got to Boston. With Nick, with Shannon, with my whole fucking life.

"Of course I came," he said. I was moving closer to him, he was moving closer to me, and everything around us faded away. The multilingual loudspeaker, the people streaming by, the roar of buses and taxis just outside, it all faded into the background. My pulse was whirring in my ears and my body was melting toward his, and my heart—the one hidden behind all the other organs—couldn't remember the bruises he'd left. It couldn't remember anything but loving him more than any one person should be able to love another.

"And you have a beard." Ugh. Fuck. Now *that* was the lamest thing I could've said.

He ran his knuckles along his jaw. It made a soft rustling sound, one that landed right between my legs with an aching *whomp*. "I've been a little distracted," he said.

I didn't stop to think about what I was doing when I reached out and dragged my fingers through his dark beard. I did it, and I didn't care that it went against all breakup protocol.

"Me too," I murmured. He leaned into my hand, his eyes closing as he sighed. "The distractions, not the beard. I don't have a beard, obviously." I snagged my bottom lip between my teeth before it could quiver. I didn't know whether I was repressing a hysterical laugh or a relieved sob, and after the misery of these weeks without him, both were equally possible. "Are you heading to the hospital now, or—"

"No, I'm not letting you out of my sight."

His hand darted out and curled into the front of my waistband, dragging me flat against him. I let out a startled squeak when he took my face in his palms and slammed his lips down on mine. For a beat, I was really fucking angry. He had no right to tell me he couldn't do this anymore, and then —weeks and miles later—kiss me like he loved me. He couldn't have it both ways. But then his hands were cradling my skull and his teeth were nipping my bottom lip and he was sighing like he'd found his serenity, and my anger bowed down to the affection I'd never be able to deny. I stopped caring about everything else, at least for this moment, and I ran my hands over the strong planes of his back, savoring him.

It was a rare pleasure, seeing him in scrubs. It was a taste of his everyday life that I'd been missing, one that reminded me of all the other everyday things we didn't share. That was all it took to bring me back down and remind me that he'd drawn his lines in the sand, even if he was sorry for them, and I still lived on the other side of those lines.

"Stop, Nick," I murmured against his lips. "Please."

"You're not walking away from me again," he said as he kissed my jaw and cheeks. "That was the last time, and I don't care what it takes, but—"

I pressed my palms to his chest, more insistent now. "Nick," I breathed. "The baby. I'm here to see the baby."

His fingers raked through my hair before fisting around the strands. "Then that's what we'll do, lovely," he said. "But you're not leaving until we straighten this out."

His hazel eyes met mine, and he raised a brow, as if he was challenging me to argue with him. What he didn't seem to understand was that I was all out of fight. I'd fought with myself since leaving him in Cozumel, and I'd fought with my entire universe. He'd held the ugliest parts of me up for viewing, and then demanded that I do better.

Didn't he see that I was trying? That I was *here*?

"That's fine," I said. I tried to touch my fingers to my lips without drawing his attention there. Failed. "I'm pretty sure my sister's going to tell me to get the fuck away from her baby. And you know, now that I think about it, the last time I was on the T, they still accepted tokens. They were phasing them out, but there was still a slot. I don't think there's a slot anymore, and I don't know where I'm going. Also, I don't think I brought anything other than t-shirts. There might have been earmuffs. I don't know. It was a blur. I'm probably going to need to buy some jeans or something. So, yeah. A chaperone would be nice."

Nick laughed to himself, and he shoved his hand in my back pocket. "Ah, Skip," he said, squeezing my ass. "I've missed running into those storms of yours."

IT WAS EARLY, and the late November morning was like apple pie, all golden and bright and hearty. The city felt different today, a thick-armed embrace rather than the icy prison I'd remembered. Nick felt different, too. He didn't say anything while he drove through Boston, toward the Long-wood neighborhood that housed many of the city's hospitals and medical research facilities. Maybe that was the differ-ence, that he wasn't speaking.

He's not the only one who can talk.

Eyes closed, I flattened my hand to my chest, pressing the hard lines of my compass into my skin. If only the right direction was as simple as north, south, east, or west.

I got myself here, and I can get myself through this.

"How is she?" I asked. "Shannon."

Nick dragged his fingers over his beard again—I was *not* complaining—as he thought. "She's good," he said. His words were soft and measured, as if he was trying to calm an attack dog. "She delivered around two this morning."

"And Froggie?" I asked. That my voice didn't wobble over those two words was a small gift.

He pulled into an underground garage and flashed a badge at the parking attendant manning the gate. "She's doing well," he said, pulling into a spot reserved for visiting surgeons.

"Do you know if anyone else is here?" I asked, pointing upward, meaning the hospital. "My brothers?"

"They aren't here yet," he said. "Visiting hours don't start until nine, and Shannon and Will asked that everyone wait until then."

"But it's only seven thirty," I said, gesturing to the dashboard clock.

"Yeah, it's a good thing you're with me," he said, holding up the badge that'd gained him access to the garage. He released his seatbelt and leaned on the center console, watching me. "Are you ready? We can wait. We can grab some breakfast, and come back later." He glanced at my body, frowning. "When was the last time you ate? You're wasting away, Skip."

I shook my head, brushing that last comment aside. I wasn't regaling him with tales of cookie dough, or vomit. "We're not waiting," I said, tracing the compass through my shirt. I reached for the door handle, either to exit the vehicle or puke all over myself again. Maybe both. "We're here. We're doing this."

He tapped his fist on the steering wheel with a nod, and opened his door. A thick stench of exhaust and stale water filled the garage, and the antiseptic smell of the hospital was only slightly better. The elevator was much too big and quiet for me and Nick, and he was much too calm, leaning against the wall with his arms crossed. I tapped my boot against the floor. Toe, then heel. Toe, heel, toe, heel.

"Calm down, darlin'," he said.

"I'm calm," I snapped as the doors opened. "Completely fucking calm."

"Ah," he murmured, his hand settling on the small of my back. He steered me down the hall, and stopped outside a closed door. "So we're lying to ourselves today. Good to know."

"Is this her?" I asked, studying the room number as if it would reveal something essential.

He nodded and edged me forward with a firm shove. "I'll be out here."

"You're not coming with me?" I said, panicked.

"This isn't about me," he said, shaking his head slowly. "I thought I could drag you back here and force this conversation. You, me, and everyone in Cozumel knows how that ended."

He scowled at the floor for a moment, then propped his hands on his hips. Another time, when my stomach wasn't performing back-handsprings in my throat, I'd enjoy the hell out of that bossy doctor pose.

"This isn't about me," he repeated.

Nick stepped away, leaving me staring at the door. It was just a door, pressed wood and plate glass, and yet it was the threshold between then and now. It was the barrier I'd erected to keep me safe, but it'd long outlived its purpose. I couldn't exist around the door anymore, and I couldn't pretend it wasn't sheltering all the awful remnants of my childhood. This division allowed me to hold years of abuse and self-inflicted agony close, and push away the one man who tried to love me in spite of it.

So I shoved the door wide open because fuck all of that.

Shannon was sitting up on the bed, a tiny little bundle of baby in her arms. She stared at me, stunned at first but then curious, like she was trying to figure out who could've brought me here. I lifted my hands up and let them fall back to my sides, hoping that was enough of an explanation.

Her hair was tied in a neat ponytail and she was wearing a purple and white cardigan over a camisole, and there was no way either one were hospital-issued. Only my sister would give birth and then immediately change back into her own clothes. I wouldn't be surprised if she'd brought her own sheets and blankets, too.

Will was leaning close to them both, his thick arm around Shannon's shoulders and his fingers stroking the baby's cheek. He was infatuated with them both, and it shone from him like the flashing neon lights of Vegas. He caught my eye, and his smile dimmed before he turned back to Shannon. "I'm so proud of you, peanut."

He pressed a kiss to Froggie's forehead, and then Shannon's, and whispered something in her ear. She nodded, still staring at me. I couldn't determine whether it was "Yeah, throw her out on her fool ass" or "Yeah, she can stay but put security on standby."

Will stepped away from the bed, eyeing me with a bit of skepticism. He paused in front of me, his gaze narrowed and his lips pursed as if he was searching for the right words, but then he glanced back to Shannon and Froggie. Something passed between them, and Will's shoulders relaxed by small degrees. The door whispered shut behind him as he left, and with him went all the words I'd planned to say. Entire monologues of apology and congratulations evaporated on my tongue. I couldn't utter a single sound, and we couldn't look away from each other. A blurry silence grew between us, burst only by the baby's gurgles and hums.

"She's beautiful," I finally said. It'd never been so difficult to form two words in my life. "Look at that hair."

Shannon smiled down at the baby. "Just like her father," she murmured. "Arrived in the middle of the night. Snuck right out. And blonde." She looked up from the baby, and beckoned me to her side. "Come see her."

She was asking me to step closer to the gurney, but a soft,

needy part of me was drawn to them both. Right then, it was clear as day that I'd let years and years build up between us like thick calcium deposits that required a chisel and hammer to dislodge. I'd done that, just like everyone had said. Nick, Patrick, Matt. Even Sam and Riley, in their own peculiar ways. They'd all said it, and they were right. I'd missed so much, and I'd miss even more if I didn't end this now.

I dropped my bag and coat, and stepped out of my boots, and though it was still possible that she'd have her husband throw me out of this hospital, I wedged beside my sister on the bed.

"Is it okay that I'm here?" I asked. An unbidden whimper caught in my throat as I dropped my head beside hers on the pillow.

"*Of course* it's all right," she cried. "Why wouldn't it be?"

She reached for me with her free hand and squeezed my forearm. Tears were glistening in her eyes, eyes that were a mirror image of mine, and I fell the fuck apart. I was bawling, shivering and sobbing on her shoulder as a flood of half-formed words spilled out. There was a mess of "I'm sorry" and "I fucked up" and lots of nonsensical babble between my blubbering and hiccupping. Shannon was crying, too, and between us, the baby's pale hair was soaked.

"Stop it," she snapped, her words too watery to keep the sharp edge she preferred. "Enough with the fucking apologies."

"What is wrong with you? Why can't you take a goddamn apology?" I asked. "I'm here, and I came as soon as I heard you were in labor, and I'm trying to do the right thing."

Shannon ran the back of her hand over her cheeks and blinked through her tears. "How many apologies am I supposed to accept? I've been sitting here for ten minutes now, telling you it's okay and it's fine, and you're still saying it."

"I'm sorry," I said. I wiped a stray drop that had landed on the baby's forehead. "Oh, fuck. Now I'm apologizing for apologizing. Just sit there and listen without legislating everything I say."

"All right, all right," Shannon muttered.

She pulled me closer, and I wrapped my arm around her and Froggie. We started crying all over again. At one point, Will walked in, stared at us for a beat, and then made a beeline for the door. We stayed there, our heads bowed together while the tears fell. There was nothing more to say today, not right now, not with a beautiful blonde baby snuggled between us.

"I was hoping you'd come," Shannon whispered. "Thank you. I know your work is very busy, and I—I appreciate it."

When it didn't seem that there was a tear left in my body, I sniffled and replied, "Of course I'm here. You're not allowed to have a baby without me. Actually, I'm kinda pissed that you didn't wait a couple more hours until I got here. Couldn't you have crossed your legs or something?"

She swatted my shoulder. "That's not how it works," she said. "When you're five days past your due date and your water breaks while you're waiting in line for your chocolate croissant at Tatte, I'll be over here, reminding *you* to cross *your* legs."

"The simple answer to that question was *no*," I said. "Have you picked out a name yet?"

"Abigael Judith," she said, her voice thick. "For Mom, and Will's mother, Judy. She stayed with me in the delivery room, and she helped me through it. I love Will, but I couldn't have done this without Judy." She laughed, smiling down at the sleeping baby. "Is that okay with you? That we're thinking of naming her Abigael?"

There was a rusty old confrontational part of me that wanted to ask why it would be a problem, or remind her that I didn't know our mother at all so I couldn't possibly object. I didn't own that name, and I barely owned any memories of the woman.

Once again—fuck that.

"It's perfect," I said. I reached to the bedside table, grabbing a handful of tissues to mop up the rivers we'd cried. "But don't call her AJ, okay?"

"Maybe Abby, but never AJ," Shannon breathed. "Mom hated nicknames. She didn't believe in naming us one thing but calling us something else."

"I didn't know that," I whispered as my finger stroked Abigael's cheek. I'd always heard people saying they wanted to gobble up little babies, and I'd never understood it until meeting this particular baby. I did, I wanted to gobble her right up. "She's so lucky. You're going to be the best mama."

"Because I've already fucked up everything with you?" she asked, a dry laugh in her voice.

In a sense, I'd been her first baby, one she'd never asked to mother. It hadn't been her job to save me, but she did it anyway and I'd thrown it all back at her.

"No," I said, drawing my finger over the baby's precious nose. I couldn't stop touching her even though exhaustion was gathering behind my eyes and the emotional impact of this morning was creeping into my bones and muscles. "You didn't fuck up anything. You did the best you could."

Shannon tapped my hand, her attention on my wedding ring. Still on my middle finger, still a bit too loose for the spot where it belonged. The simple solution was getting it resized, of course, but I hadn't considered that until now.

That was a common problem among academics. We made everything a little too complicated, and then thought too damn hard about it all.

"Will you tell me more about this?" she asked.

"I married him," I said. Those words rushed out in a gasp, and I'd had no idea how much I'd needed to share this with her. I'd considered it before, when I'd stared at her emails and imagined a flowing exchange between us, but it felt like I was saying the most real and true thing in the world now. I wanted to tell everyone, just as Nick had wanted for the past two years. "I married Nick."

Shannon laughed as she traced the diamonds on my band. "Good for you," she said. "You deserve him."

The baby shifted, kicking her legs out of the purple sail-boat-printed swaddling wrap—definitely not hospital-issued —until her feet were free. "I don't know anything about child development, but that seemed really advanced," I said, running my fingers along the sole of her foot. "And these toes! They're the cutest, tiniest things I've ever seen in my entire life."

"I know, I know," Shannon repeated, incredulous. "I can't believe she's here." We watched as she stretched and wiggled, laughing as her expressions morphed from grumpy to alert to sleepy to peaceful. Shannon traced the lines on Froggie's forehead as the baby reverted back to grumpy. "That's her father, right there. She's so much of him."

"What did you mean," I started carefully, "when you said I deserved Nick?"

I was expecting the worst. Some oblique slam about him being a self-centered devil child or vapid manwhore, and me being the patron saint of shameful behavior. By that logic, we were a match made in hell.

"I meant that he's one of the best guys I know," she said.

"Really?" I asked.

"Absolutely," she said, shifting the baby to her shoulder. "The first thing I thought when I met him was that he had the biggest heart. He came around when we were a mess, and he didn't mind any of that. It was like he recognized that we were all a little bit insane, a little bit fucked up, and for some unexplainable reason, he wanted to be part of it." She paused, frowning as she stared at the blankets over our legs. "My second thought was that I wanted to bite his ass."

Suddenly flustered by her admission and more than a little possessive, I asked, "Have you thought that recently, *Mrs. Halsted*?"

"Have you seen his ass, *Mrs. Acevedo*? I've watched grown women—and men—cry in the street as he walked by," she replied. "I might be married, but I am *not* blind."

"Well, Shannon," I started, "I'll have you know that I have seen his ass. And you know what? I've bitten it, too."

And as those words fell from my lips, Shannon's mother-in-law, Judy, strolled in with a pair of nurses.

"Well, I hope it was a good one," Judy said. "All asses are not created equal."

Shannon laughed as she gestured to me. "Judy, this is my sister, Erin."

"Of course," she cried, tossing her hands up in the air like she was seeing an old friend again. "We met at Matt and Lolo's wedding. When did you get in, sweet cheeks?"

I untangled myself from Shannon and the baby, and moved to the edge of the bed. "This morning," I said. "I caught the red-eye out of Reykjavík."

"And you're staying for the holiday," Judy continued. All statement, no question.

"You should stick around," Shannon said. Her tone was casual, and the accompanying shrug confirmed it. She was giving me the option. "We're not doing anything fancy, just dinner at the house."

I hummed as I ran my fingers over my face and through my hair. "Let me think about it," I said. Bending down, I pulled on my boots and grabbed my things. I reached into my backpack, feeling around for the rock I'd selected for the baby. Too many damn compartments in this bag. "I brought something for her. It's in here somewhere."

"You can give it to her when you visit later this week," Shannon said. "We don't have to figure it all out this morning."

At that, the baby released a rippling cry, and Judy and the nurses converged around the bed.

"Oh, this little girl is hungry," Judy cooed.

One nurse was stacking pillows at Shannon's elbow, and the other was pulling my sister's breast from her camisole. It didn't matter how much shit we'd worked through, I wasn't ready to watch this.

"I'm gonna go," I said, pointing to the door as Froggie's cries intensified. "We'll talk. Later, or…whatever."

Shannon said something, but I couldn't determine whether she was speaking to me or Froggie or the cadre of women helping her, and I didn't stop to clarify. I marched out of the room without a backward glance, stopping only when a pair of hands closed around my shoulders.

"Skip, hey, slow down," Nick murmured, setting my backpack on the ground. "Are you all right?"

I stared at my hands while I blew out a breath. I was wrung out, physically and mentally exhausted from this conversation, but I'd survived. It wasn't the screaming match I'd expected, and now that it was over, I couldn't remember why I'd expected that to begin with. "Yeah," I said, bringing my fingertips to my forehead. There was a headache blooming there, the kind borne of sleep-deprivation and sobbing. "It was good."

"That's a fucking relief," Will said from beside Nick.

"Are you sure you're okay?" Nick asked. "You were in there for a long time, and you've been crying, darlin'."

The lights were too bright, the sounds too sharp, and the hospital scents too oppressive. A jerky nod was the only response I could offer.

"Come home with me," he said, running his knuckles down my back. He reached for my wrist and moved the diamond band to my ring finger. It was still loose, but not falling off. He leaned closer, his breath passing over my cheekbone as he spoke. "I thought I made my position on this ring, and several other things, clear in Cozumel."

"You said an awful lot in Cozumel." I stepped back and crossed my arms over my torso, scowling. "You can't have it both ways. You can't love me while I'm here and then resent me while I'm gone. Until you get that fact straight, none of those things are up for discussion."

Nick edged back and mirrored my stance. "Erin. Darlin'. You're saying meaningful words and I'm really trying to listen, but all I can think about is getting you home," he said. "We have a lot of issues to discuss. I'm not disputing that. But I'm not going to be able to do that until after I've—"

"Oh, for fuck's sake. The foreplay can wait," Will yelled. "Come on. Your brothers and the girls are all here, and they're going to redecorate the waiting room if we don't give them an update soon."

Before I could object, Will herded us down the hall and through a set of doors armed with a specialized security system that Nick explained was meant to prevent kidnapping. Will grumbled about it being "really fucking inadequate."

Then the sliding glass door whooshed shut behind us, and we found the entire Walsh tribe. Everyone fell silent, and they were all watching us. Their gazes moved as a synchronized unit, starting with Will, quickly bouncing to me, then Nick and back to me again, only to linger on the hand he had resting between my shoulder blades.

"Okay, I'll ask what we're all thinking," Matt said after the longest stare-off in human history. "Where did Erin come from and why did she come with *you*, Nick?"

"Should I tell them that you always come when you're with me?" he whispered into my hair.

"Oh, that's delightful," I murmured. Sweet, cherubic Jesus, this might've been a terrible plan. I spared Nick a glance that said *You're amusing no one*. He offered a lopsided smile in response, and dug his thumb into the knots in my neck. "Please, Matt, continue. Talk about me as if I'm not here. It's wonderful to see you as well."

Matt approached us, glancing back and forth between me and Nick. I shoved my hand—the one with the sparkly wedding ring—in my pocket. I'd been through the emotional meat grinder today, and needed some baby steps here.

"Someone explain to me what the fuck is going on," Matt said, and that was all the invitation this group required to talk at once.

Riley: Rip the bandage, doc. Put it all out there.

Matt: There's something to *put out there*?

Sam: I emailed you last night. You could've responded, and said you were coming home.

Patrick: I don't like any of this.

Matt: When did you get here, Erin? *How* did you get here? Why didn't you tell me? Why didn't anyone tell me? And why the fuck are you wearing a Harvard Medical School hoodie? Is anyone else seeing this?

Tiel: Okay, so I'm the only one who has no idea what's going on?

Lauren: We're going to leave this poor girl alone. She's traveled very far to be here, and we're not grilling her now.

Sam: No one's grilling her. We just want to know why Acevedo's got his hands all over her.

Patrick: I really don't like this.

Andy: Guys, it's *Nick*. He's good people.

Nick: Thanks, Andy.

Patrick: I'm not comfortable with any of this.

Lauren: Can we turn down the overprotective big brother thing? It's weird and creepy and not necessary.

Will: Not your call to make, Lo.

Andy: I tried to tell you that they were hanging out at Sam and Tiel's wedding, but nobody wanted to listen to me.

Tiel: I listened to you, and I agreed.

Lauren: Me too.

Patrick: I don't remember any of that.

Matt: No one told me a fucking thing!

Sam: Does Shannon know about this? Did you *talk* to Shannon?

Lauren: Oh my God, she's already seen Froggie! Damn it, Erin, I was on your side. *I* was supposed to get the first baby snuggles!

Sam: You *did* talk to Shannon. It's interesting how the building isn't on fire.

Nick: Shut the fuck up, Sam.

Matt: Does no one notice that he's still touching her? Is anyone else really fucking confused right now?

Riley: Isn't this fun?

"That's enough." Will wedged between Matt and Nick, and dropped his hands on their shoulders with a meaningful squeeze while everyone else continued discussing us.

"You've gotten that out of your systems, and now you're done," he said. "No one is doing a goddamn thing to disturb my wife or baby today, especially not you two." He turned his gaze to Matt. "I believe you know that I'd seize any opportunity to drop you. Don't give me one."

"We're not talking about any of this right now," Lauren said, yanking Matt away. "A baby was born, and we're not yelling and fighting this morning." She turned to me, but kept her palm flat on Matt's chest as if he couldn't manage without the physical reminder to stay put. "You're coming to Thanksgiving, right? What am I saying? Of course you're coming, you're here."

She looked to me for confirmation, and I found myself nodding. "Yeah, okay."

Matt edged forward and pointed at me and Nick. "Both of you? Together? Both of you will be there, together? Because this is a thing that's happening, even though no one told me?"

"Look, Walsh," Nick started, holding out his hand toward Matt. "We were waiting to tell you until Erin could get back here, and we could talk to you in person. Together."

Lauren positively beamed at this while the rest of my family murmured and chattered away. They'd be talking up these five minutes for the next month, if not longer.

"This wasn't how we wanted to tell you, Matt," I said. "But—yeah. We'll be coming together."

"Soon, I hope," Nick said under his breath.

Matt stared at us for a long moment, his expression chilly. "I don't know what I think—"

"You think this is fantastic," Lauren interrupted. "You're happy for them both, and you're not going to say anything that you'll regret later because he's your best friend and she's your sister. You're happy for them, Matthew, and no one is required to justify their decisions to you." She delivered several sharp pats to his chest. "Now that we've handled this development, someone needs to bring me to that baby."

Nick shifted, pressing his lips against my temple while kneading my shoulders. "When I go home with you for the holiday," he started, "who am I, darlin'?"

"You're my husband," I said, rubbing my eyes.

"Yeah?" he asked.

"Maybe," I said around a yawn. I couldn't remember the last time I'd slept. Even if it was yesterday, I felt like I'd be out for days if I closed my eyes. "You have to get your shit together and stop hating me for doing things at my own pace."

"Can I buy you breakfast and promise that I don't now, nor have I ever hated you?" he asked. "There's a place near my apartment that serves an assortment of breakfast breads. Cinnamon rolls, sticky buns, banana bread, morning glory muffins, croissants, scones. All in a basket with butter and jam. Espresso, too."

"*Yes*," I said resolutely. "You could be trying to sell me on France's revanchist foreign policy toward Germany following the annexation of Alsace-Lorraine as the primary driver of Europe's polarization in the years leading up to the First World War, and I would still listen if that basket was involved."

Thirty-Three

NICK

WE DIDN'T MAKE it to the bakery. Erin fell asleep before we exited the hospital's parking garage, and she stayed asleep while I drove us through the city to my Beacon Hill neighborhood. She barely stirred as I carried her into my apartment and tucked her into my bed. For a moment, I stood there, watching the breaths move through her chest.

Then I stripped down and snuggled in beside her. My skin hummed when it connected with hers, warming through and feeling alive for the first time in weeks.

We slept all day, waking only when raindrops started pelting my windows. It was dark outside, the type of disorientating wintertime dark that could be early morning or evening. I sat up, blinking, upside down in this day.

"It's weird, right?" Erin asked. Creases lined her face and her eyes were still red and puffy. "Sleeping together, I mean. Without the sex."

"Why is that weird?" I asked. "Our relationship isn't based on sex. It's just one of the perks."

Her lips pursed in a small pout and she nodded before kicking off the blankets. She pushed up from the mattress and headed into the bathroom, the door clicking shut behind her. It gave me a moment to check my phone and pager. I'd been lucky to have the day off and even luckier that I hadn't been called in.

The bathroom door opened, and Erin leaned against the jamb, pointing to my devices. She was only wearing a t-shirt and panties, the most perfect combination ever, and I grinned at her pale, freckled legs. "Do you need to go?"

"Nope," I said, showing her the blank screens. "The city must know that my wife is home, and I need to stay right here all night."

"So that's it?" she asked, crossing her arms. "Everything's fine, all's forgotten? I mean, a whole bunch of your demands were met today. You've gotta be happy about that."

She was too far away. I needed her here for this, with me, as close as we could get. "Come over here, darlin'," I said, reaching for her. "Don't keep yourself away from me. I want to hold you and appreciate you, and say all the things I won't put in emails."

She pushed off from the door, marching toward her backpack in the corner. She riffled through it, pulling things out and shoving them back in until she found a pair of yoga pants. Facing the wall, she stepped into them and said, "Today has been overwhelming."

"That's an understatement if I've ever heard one," I said.

Erin laughed, and turned to face me. "I've worked really hard to feel good about myself," she said. She brought her palm to her chest and patted her clavicle. "I went away because I needed room to breathe and distance to feel safe, and most of the time now, I do. I stayed away because I didn't know how to fix any of the things I broke, and I'm better at keeping people at a distance than letting them in."

"You let me in," I said.

"That's because you let me babble about philosophical geology," she said. She dragged her fingers through her hair, gathering the strands into a bun and then letting them fall. "I shut you out. Since Cozumel, I've shut you out. I read all of your emails, but I didn't respond to any of them. I never know how to fix things, Nick."

I shook my head and reached for her again. She edged closer, one step at a time until she was standing between my knees. "There's nothing you can't fix, Skip," I said, placing my hands on her hips. "Just look at all the things you've done in the past twenty-four hours."

Her fingers passed over my beard. If I was looking for proof that the world worked in mysterious ways, I'd point to this beard. It was a product of my post-Cozumel depression, but every time Erin looked at it, all I could see were her fuck-drunk eyes.

"I could break them all over again," she said. "I could shut you out, too."

"I won't let you," I said. "You think you live dangerously? You squeeze the life out of every minute? Then do something really dangerous. Stop running away from things that scare you. Let your family love you. Let *me* love you."

"You don't even know what scares me," she snapped. She was hurt, and I'd been the one to hurt her. Now she wanted nothing more than to yank out her emotions like the vestigial organs they were, toss them at me, and gird herself against any further heartache.

"Then tell me," I said, gripping her waist. "Give it all to me."

Erin looked away, shaking her head as if she'd already determined that I couldn't handle her. But then she sucked in a breath and balled her fists in my t-shirt. "I can't erase my history," she said. "I will always be the girl who was abused, who cut herself, who tried to kill herself, who had sex with more men than she can remember because she needed to feel wanted, even if it was awful and degrading. Who fucked up everything. You can't erase that either."

My jaw tightened as I blinked up at her. The strength and control that it required to absorb those words without recoiling in rage was significant. "I am in love with your scars," I said, bringing her wrist to my lips. "I hate that you have them. I hate that you endured a single second of that. But you fought like hell and you survived."

Her palm moved to my cheek, and I leaned into her touch. Minutes passed where I toggled between believing she was finding the words to tell me it was over and asking whether there was enough room in my apartment for all of her books. For the record, we'd need another apartment exclusively for her books.

Eventually she said, "I have to finish my work in Iceland, and the program at Oxford. I have to do that, Nick."

"I know," I said, easing up her shirt to kiss her belly.

"I need to think," she whispered, "about what comes after that."

"Stay," I said, pointing to the floor between us. "Stay for the holiday, with me, with all of us, and then decide what you want. I dare you."

Thirty-Four

ERIN

NICK'S BEDROOM was glorious in the morning. This wasn't my first stay here, but it was the first time that I paused long enough to take it all in. In this rare circumstance, I appreciated the effects of jet lag that had me awake long before him. It had also given me time to ponder his request that I stay with him. Somehow, those words weren't quite so complex anymore.

The perfect amount of sunlight streamed in from the east. It was just enough to brighten and warm the room, but never so much that it was blinding. I was convinced that the bed was actually a linen-covered marshmallow. And it all came with a sexy doctor who didn't see a reason to wear pajamas.

"What's on your mind, lovely?" he asked, his voice thick with sleep. "You've been humming to yourself and tapping out Morse code on my arm for an hour."

He kissed the delicate spot beneath my ear, and I squirmed as his beard tickled my skin.

"You don't want to know," I said through my giggles.

That stopped all the ticklish kisses. "Of course I do," he

said, levering up so that I was caged beneath him. "Talk to me, Skip. Tell me anything, everything."

"All right, you asked for it," I murmured. I dropped my gaze to his chest, raking my fingers over his skin. "I was thinking that the last time I had Thanksgiving with Shannon, I spent the subsequent forty-eight hours vomiting."

"Yeah," he said, wincing. "I think I've heard about that. You don't have to worry, though. Andy cooks, and she's very precise. Before Andy came around, Shannon had the entire meal catered. No incidents of food-borne illness, darlin', and even if there was, I'm qualified to handle that."

I hooked my ankles around his waist and pulled him down. There was something delicious about his body pressing mine into the mattress. "What I'm hearing you say is that I'm definitely going to this shindig."

"You know what I love about your family?" he asked, avoiding the hell out of my question. "Anytime the whole group is together, but especially around the holidays, they have the best time ever. Every single holiday is the new best holiday ever. Last year, it was at Matt and Lauren's loft, but Andy wanted to brine the turkey ahead of time, and that left Matt and Patrick jogging from the garage with a fifty-five gallon tub. Important note here, the tub was uncovered. They argued the entire way, and the turkey almost went flying when Matt tripped. And there was a trail of turkey water all down the hallway. The year before, we had paella at the loft, and Tiel brought an incredible pumpkin pie."

The sun was sliding in through the far window, and the light seemed to brighten Nick's light hazel eyes. "What I'm hearing you say now is that you're only there for the food," I said.

He dismissed my comment with a disinterested murmur, and continued on with his story. "It was kind of strained, with Tiel. But she's the type of person who needs to get comfortable with new folks before she can loosen up."

"And what should I learn from all that?" I asked, pinching his ass. "I'm inventing reasons to avoid my food-loving family? They're only enemies in my mind? If I stopped imagining disasters, I'd enjoy things more?"

"Yes, yes, and yes," he said, shooting each of my concerns out of the sky. He pinched my ass in return. "And I want them to know you're mine."

I reached between us, stroking his cock until he moaned my name. "Haven't we already accomplished that?" I asked.

"Somewhat," he said, thrusting into my hand. "We laid the foundation. Now we're building the house."

"Quick, embroider that on a pillow," I said, laughing. His hips were moving faster now, his cock shuttling between my fingers with unrestrained need. "When you're finished with the handicrafts, do you think you could throw my legs over your shoulders and fuck me?"

"Are you using me for orgasmic courage?" he asked, sliding his hand between my thighs.

He growled when he found me wet, and pushed his fingers inside me. My hands gripped the pillows at my head, and I tossed them toward the floor. One landed on Nick's back, and he stopped moving to give me an unimpressed stare. "Your aim, Skip. It needs work."

"Back to that orgasmic courage," I said. I batted his hand away and brought him to my entrance. Fingers were nice, cocks were better. "If I say yes, will you have a problem with that?"

"No," he said, laughing as he filled me. "That's what husbands are for."

"If that's the case, what are wives for?" I asked.

Nick was quiet for a moment, offering nothing more than

growls and groans as he moved in me. "The same," he said, his lips pressed to my neck. "But also blowjobs."

Before Nick, I'd never experienced an orgasm during sex. I didn't think I could. I didn't think I wanted to, either. My introduction to sex wasn't a kind one, and after that, the mere thought of intercourse skated a fine line between tolerable and torturous. But then I'd spent a weekend on the far edge of Cape Cod with Nick, and a switch flipped. No one had ever touched me the way he did, like he wanted to wreck me but be gentle while he did it. A little voice kept saying "This moment, this man? They're safe. This time won't be like any of the ones before," and I believed it.

And now, with my ankles on his shoulders and his hands kneading my breasts as he drove into me, I still believed. I could feel good and wanted in the right ways. I could have sex without feeling all of my broken and scarred places. I could love him, and I could deserve his love in return.

RILEY WAS at the door of Shannon's beachfront home north of the city when we arrived, and he regarded us with more *this is going to be good* amusement than strictly necessary.

"Shut up," I snapped, shrugging out of my coat.

"I didn't say anything," he replied.

I rolled my eyes. "You said plenty."

"Would you stop bothering my wife?" Nick asked, edging between us. "Who's here? What's going on?"

"That's a great question," Riley said. He stroked his chin. "Shannon's not allowed in the kitchen. She's good with this, but that's not stopping her from lurking. Also, we're not allowed to mention that she's still eating for two. Sam's grumbling about turkey. He'd prefer a salmon-and-asparagus type of Thanksgiving, but he's smart enough to know when he's outnumbered. Speaking of menu complaints, Andy will stab you in the heart if you have a problem with what she's cooking. Apparently, we all had plenty of time to weigh in before this afternoon, and bitching isn't permitted."

I rolled my hand in front of me. "Continue," I said.

"Patrick's playing sous chef, and he's enjoying the hell out of that. Not sure about power exchange dynamics there, but it's fun to watch."

"I don't want to know what Patrick and Andy do in their bedroom," Nick said.

Riley turned to him, smirking. "It's interesting that you went there," he said. "Will is yelling at everyone who tries to get within five feet of Froggie without adequately disinfecting themselves first. He's already threatened to cancel dinner and throw everyone out. Twice."

"Her name is Abby," I said. "Let's call her that."

"Tiel is napping," Riley continued. "Judy's been fussing all over her, and pissing Lauren off with comments about needing more grandchildren. Judy's decided she's stepping in as grandma for Sam and Tiel's kid. She's either the nicest lady in the world, or the master of passive-aggressive moves."

"Are you doing okay?" Nick asked. "With all of…*that*?"

"Thanks for the reminder that my life is in shambles," Riley muttered. "Helpful. Really fucking helpful."

"Your life isn't in shambles," I said.

"It's not in *complete* shambles," Riley said. "Matt just got back from a bike ride along the coast, and—"

"Wait," Nick interrupted. "He went for a ride? He didn't mention that to me."

Riley waved between me and Nick. "That's the price of doing business with the Little Mermaid here. Did you really expect him to call you up, two days after he found out about your new pastime? Please. You're smarter than that."

"Do *not* use that nickname on me," I said.

"Oh God," Nick said, clutching his chest. "I love it. You're the Riot Grrrl version of the Little Mermaid. You're the Third Wave feminist Little Mermaid who told the prince to go fuck himself, and then went on to turn the underwater community into conservation activists, aren't you?"

"So you've seen the film," I said. "What's your nickname around here? Hmm?"

"Kristoff," Riley said, snapping his fingers and jabbing a finger at Nick. "I've been thinking about this for a long time, dude, and I'm feeling it now. You're Kristoff."

"Who the hell is Kristoff?" I asked, and at the same time, Nick said, "Jesus, no. Not *Frozen*. I'd rather be Hawkeye than anyone from *Frozen*."

"What's your problem with *Frozen*?" Riley asked. "It's a delightful movie. I listen to the soundtrack at the gym. You're obviously an Anna guy, but have you seen that dress Elsa wears in her ice palace? Talk about a smoke show."

"So you've seen that film, too," I said, blinking up at Nick.

"We've had a conversation about you and blondes, bro," he said. "Unhealthy. Needs to stop."

"Speaking of Miss Honey," Riley said ruefully, "she and the Commodore are in the laundry room. They're pretending to play with the puppies, but they're eating pie."

"And what are you doing?" I asked. "Other than loitering around the front door."

"I left my phone in my coat pocket. I was coming out here to get it because I want to stream the game while I'm working the bar," he said, gesturing to the highball glass in his hand. "I'm mixing up some kilt-lifters and watching football. Liquor and sports are keeping me distracted and desensitized."

Judy came around the corner, a burp cloth slung over her shoulder and five different styles of pacifier in her hands. "Oh, hello," she called. "The chef tells me we're eating soon. Go on in and get settled." She lifted the pacifiers when a baby's wail sounded from upstairs. "Shannon's getting Abby dressed now, and we're trying these out to see if we can find a nipple she likes."

"I've found two," Nick said under his breath. That earned him an elbow to the belly.

"Wow," Riley murmured after Judy headed toward the staircase. "I had no idea Kristoff would be such a pervert. Think about keeping that under wraps for the next hour or two, okay?"

WE WERE GATHERED in the dining room, seated around Shannon's antique table with a beautiful meal, all by Andy's hand, laid before us. My siblings were busy passing platters and bowls, loading up their plates while Will listed all of Abby's achievements to date. He was particularly proud of her ability to grip his finger and open *and* close her eyes in his presence, and anyone who suggested that those behaviors weren't extraordinary could go fuck themselves.

"Erin, honey, it is such a joy to have you here. You have to tell us about Iceland. Bill and I haven't been there yet. It's on our list for next year, and we need some recommendations. But I'm dying to know," Judy said, smiling at me as she patted her fingertips on the table like the sweetest, most eager mom of all moms, ever. "How long have you two been seeing each other?"

Nick squeezed my thigh, and I noticed the corners of his lips tipping up. "Why don't you take that one, darlin'?" he suggested.

There was an unusual sensation bubbling up inside me. It felt something like happiness, all fizzy and light and forcing me to smile.

And with that, everything stopped. Dishes and wine glasses were set down, serving spoons dropped into bowls, and all eyes locked on me and Nick. This was one of those defining moments. The kind where several paths presented themselves. Many were acceptable, some were convenient, but only one was *right*. They'd all lead to other, new paths, and most of them would block the way from ever wandering back and attempting a different route.

Basically, there was no going back.

"Or I can do it," Nick said, glancing at me with his eyebrow arched in question. "It's your—"

"We got married the night before Matt's wedding," I said, cutting him off. "We're married, me and Nick."

Riley yanked the cork from a wine bottle, and the *pop* seemed to echo around us. Then, the rumbling started. At first it was all *huh* and *hmm*, but then it graduated to "What did she say?" and "Wait, what?" Nick kept his hand on my leg, his thumb drawing little circles on my inner thigh.

Riley passed the bottle to Lauren's father, the Commodore, and rubbed his palms together vigorously. "Great, we're going there," he said.

"Now that wasn't what I expected to hear," Judy murmured, her eyes as wide as could be.

"Wait, so—" Sam stopped, gesturing at Nick and me as he processed. "Could you run all that by us one more time?"

"And you knew?" Andy swiveled toward Riley, and it took all that long, dark hair of hers an extra few seconds to follow.

"Of course he knew," Matt yelled, tossing his hands in the air like we were discussing heresy and high crimes. "He has dirt on everyone."

"That's an unsettling prospect," Patrick said, his eyebrows pinched together. It was clear that he still didn't like any of this, but that was his way. He took the longest to come around.

"Pick your battles, boys," Will warned. "And while you do that, please remember that you do *not* govern your sisters' lives."

"Why aren't you saying anything?" Matt asked Shannon. "Why are you quiet? You're the one who's supposed to freak out right now."

Shannon rolled her eyes at Matt before glancing to me. She was wearing leggings and a long sweater, and while it was definitely casual for her, I never would've guessed that she gave birth days ago based on that look. "She told me the other day," she said, her tone dismissive. Almost flippant. Bad Bitch Shannon was the *best* Shannon. "And we've been emailing since last January."

"Emailing. Since. January," Sam yelled, bewildered. "Why am I always the last to know these things?"

"You girls certainly like eloping," the Commodore said, glancing between Shannon and me.

"I don't even know what to say about all of this," Patrick murmured, rubbing his forehead.

"You don't have to say anything, Patrick," I said, reaching for a dish of mashed potatoes. I dropped a scoopful on my plate, and then another. Nick's brows winged up at that. "Don't judge me."

"I'm not judging you at all," he said. "I love your affection for carbs."

"What is it with you guys? You're supposed to be happy for her, and accept that she's capable enough to make smart decisions," Lauren cried. "And before you forget, we like Nick. We should be thrilled that she's keeping it local. If we're lucky, we'll get to see her more often now."

"Lolo, the baby is sleeping. Quiet down," Judy said. "You'll understand the value of sleep when you have a child of your own."

"Thanks for that, Judy." Lauren rolled her eyes and muttered something under her breath as she reached for her wine glass. She drained it, then passed it to Sam for a refill.

"Listen, people," Shannon said, wagging her finger at the table. "Froggie's going to wake up any minute and I'm starving. You go right on hollering at each other, but I'm going to eat."

"Thank you," Tiel murmured.

"Then I'm eating too," Riley said. "Someone pass me a drumstick."

"I'm warning you right now, RISD," Shannon said. "If you drop that drumstick on my new rug, I'll beat you with it."

"It's good that we're still irrationally violent," I said. "That keeps things fun."

"She lives in Europe, and you live here," Patrick said to Nick. He flipped open his cuffs and set to rolling his sleeves up to his elbows. "And you're...*married*. How does that work? How does any of this work?"

"You're right, we do live on separate continents right now," Nick said evenly. "It's not ideal, and the past two years haven't been easy. But there will never be a distance too far or a wait too long for Erin."

I was blushing, but not a delicate, rosy kind of blush. It

was the bright, flaming kind of blush, the one that was easily mistaken for a dangerously high fever.

"My grandmother, she was something of a mystic," Nick continued. "She used to say that some people fell in love as easy as a leaf fell from a tree, and only when they were ready to fall." He reached for his wine, drained the glass, and returned it to the table. "Others crashed as hard as lightning bolts. Neither was better or worse, but the lightning bolts? It was never simple for them. It was chaos and electricity, unpredictability and fire, and the fall was hard, but it was worth it." He turned back to me, his hand firm on my thigh. "We're the lightning, Skip."

"And the crash was worth it," I whispered. He leaned to me, and kissed the corner of my mouth.

From across the table, Judy pressed her napkin to her chest and sighed. "Aww," she said. "You two are precious."

"Oh, shit," Matt murmured. "You're serious about this. This is a real thing."

"Goddamn it, Matthew," Riley shouted, dropping the drumstick to his plate. "Catch the fuck up, would you?"

"Are we good now?" I asked, dipping my fork into the mashed potatoes. "Any other questions?"

Sam started to speak but Shannon held up her hand for silence. "We're good," she said. "Congratulations, you two. Someone who isn't pregnant or breastfeeding should pop some champagne."

"Would this be the wrong time to mention that we're engaged?" Andy asked.

"What!" Lauren screamed, slapping the tabletop.

"Lolo, the baby is *sleeping*," Judy said with all the exasperation a sweetheart like her could muster.

Patrick nodded, and held up Andy's arm as if she was a prizefighter claiming another victory. "It's true," he said.

"I'll get the champagne." Will pushed back from the table and clapped his hand over Patrick's shoulder. "Took you long enough."

LAUREN HAD me cornered in the living room after dessert, and she was working hard at getting me on board with tomorrow's spa day and shopping plans. "Please come with us," she said, gesturing to Tiel and Andy. Riley was sprawled out on the opposite end of the L-shaped sofa with his baseball cap pulled down over his face. He was alternately moaning about eating too much and requesting more pie.

"I don't think I've ever had a pedicure," I said. My feet lived in steel-toed boots.

She shook her head as if my comment didn't compute. "I'm sorry, honey, it sounded like you said you've never had a pedicure."

"So shiny and pretty," Tiel murmured, gazing at the rock on Andy's finger.

"Um, I haven't had one," I said, bracing myself for the impact of Lauren's reaction. "Not a lot of spas on the glaciers and lava fields, you know?"

"Well, you're definitely coming with us now," she said. "You're not leaving right away, are you?"

I shook my head. In my haste to get back to the States, I hadn't purchased a return ticket. I was due in Reykjavík soon, but it wasn't like I was departing tomorrow.

"Good, good. We have to plan her baby shower," Lauren said, pointing to Tiel. "And now we have another wedding, and a bridal shower, too." She wrapped her arm around Andy's shoulders and squeezed. "Oh! And we need to have a party for you and Nick, of course. How amazing is all this?" She leaned forward and spoke in Riley's direction. "You're the only single one left now, RISD. Time to step up the game."

He pushed back his cap and edged up on an elbow, staring at her for a long beat. "Yeah, about that," he said, almost to himself. "I need another drink."

"Okay, so we're on for pedicures, lunch, and party planning," Lauren said while Riley shuffled into the kitchen. "Right?"

Tiel glanced over at me with a sympathetic grin. "The first time I heard about the pedicure outings, I said a few sassy things that I didn't really mean because it felt a little"— she gestured toward Lauren and Andy—"suffocating. But it's not like that. *They're* not like that."

I appreciated this girl. We shared similar definitions of *suffocating,* and we were both prickly as hell. "Okay," I said. "What do I need to know about pedicures?"

"I always go for black polish," Andy said, extending her hand to show off the shade.

I passed my thumb over her glossy nails. "And no one gives you any shit for being a dark-hearted Goth girl?" I asked.

"Being given shit doesn't require me to accept it," she said.

I liked this one, too. I liked them all, and that was really surprising. Friends, they weren't something I did. "When is my brother going to marry you?" I asked.

Andy shoved a chunk of hair over her shoulder and shrugged. "As soon as Minerva McGonagall is available to officiate."

Oh, yes. I really liked this one. She was bold and witty, and I aspired to give as few fucks as she did.

"Can I rub your belly?" Andy asked Tiel. "Now that Frog-gie's here, I'm in belly-rubbing withdrawal."

"You have so much baby fever, you're gonna get a rash," Lauren said.

"I can enjoy babies and weddings without pining for my own," Andy replied. A warm grin spread across her face when Tiel placed Andy's hand over her small bump. "Erin, are you staying around through the holidays? Or will you be coming back later next month?"

Riley poked his head in from the kitchen. "Tell me you're staying, Rogue. I can't wrangle these assholes alone anymore."

I wanted to say yes. That was my first instinct, and the one I wanted to follow.

But...*fuck*. All of this had happened so quickly. What did I want here? What the actual fuck did I want?

Taking care of myself was, by definition, self-centered. But it was also really fucking necessary.

My therapist used to tell me that, someday, I'd realize that I'd survived. That I'd walked through the fire and come out stronger. The desire to hurt myself, to let go of this world entirely, it would be gone much in the way that we forgot what it was like learning to walk. We just knew that we did learn, and everything before was a blur.

And right now, with my sister-in-law's hopeful eyes twinkling and my ass firmly planted on a sofa in Shannon's house, I felt the blur. I couldn't call up those memories. I couldn't reach that desire to feel one form of pain so that another form would abate.

I knew that I ran away because I needed it, but now the need was gone.

And that realization sent a mouthful of white wine down the wrong pipe.

I was up, waving off the concern of my sisters-in-law, and heading for a private space where I could cough and sputter and freak out over not freaking out in peace. I knew there were puppies in this house. If I could find them, I could scratch their heads for an hour or two, and then reassemble the world as I knew it.

I stormed through the first floor, searching this old, winding home for the chocolate labs. I looked in closets and bathrooms, around corners and behind doors, and finally stumbled into the laundry room at the far end of the home. Instead of finding two pups, happy for my attention, I found Shannon and Matt's father-in-law, the Commodore. He was learning over the countertop, fork in hand, while the dogs sat silent at his feet.

"You can stay," he said, stabbing his fork in the direction of the door. "But only if you tell my wife you ate the apple-cranberry pie."

It was a folksy, paternal thing to say, and a startled laugh caught in my throat. No one had ever said folksy, paternal things to me.

"All of it?" I asked. "I ate the *entire* pie?"

"Every crumb," he said. "You're tiny but I can tell from lookin' at you that you're something mighty."

Tears prickled at my eyes, and I stared at the floor, blinking, to keep my composure. It was like I'd waited all my life to find good, decent men, and now I couldn't turn around without one trying to feed me.

"Okay," I said, glancing up to find him smiling at me. My stomach chose that moment to growl and gurgle.

"There's a squash pie back in there," he said, gesturing toward the kitchen. "I've been saving it for breakfast, but I'll share it with you."

I shook my head. I couldn't rob this man of his breakfast.

"No, I'm fine," I said, shaking my head as my stomach rumbled in disagreement.

"I'll get another fork," he said, setting his down and exiting to the kitchen. He quickly returned, offering me a napkin and fork without a word, and we dug into the butternut squash pie.

"Thank you," I said, nodding toward the dish. "I mean, you could've kicked me out—"

"Why aren't you out there with the kids?" he asked. He pointed to the stool tucked into the countertop, indicating for me to sit.

"Overwhelmed," I said, and that earned me a concerned glance from the Commodore.

"Family can do that," he said. "Something you want to get off your chest?"

I stared at the hunk of pie on my fork, scowling. "I appreciate that, but I've spent years processing things on my own, and I'm fine. I can handle it," I said.

"I don't doubt that in the least," he said as he tapped the ceramic dish with his fork. "But being able to handle it doesn't mean you *have* to handle it."

"I'm still working my way through that concept," I said.

"And where is Doctor Acevedo?"

I folded my arms on the cool marble countertop and shook my head. "I don't know. Around here somewhere. It's a big house."

"I'd bet he wants to know where you are," the Commodore said.

"You're right," I said. "But I'm sure he knows I can't go far unless I'm leaving by sea, and it's nine degrees outside."

"Don't tell me this is cold for an Icelander like you," he said, chuckling.

I shrugged in response. I still preferred Mediterranean winters.

"Wesley tells me you've spent some time together in Italy," the Commodore continued, referring Will and Lauren's brother. "He's fond of you."

Wes and I hung out whenever we were in the same area at the same time, which hadn't been recently. We'd caught up with each other once before I moved to Iceland, and then again when I was at Oxford.

Me and Wes, we knew the highs and lows of expat life. The States weren't *home* to us anymore, and our families... well, they were complicated. Me because I was learning how to mend fences and him because he believed his father to be a brutal homophobe.

I wasn't sure how the man in front of me, the one spooning whipped cream onto every single bite of pie, was that kind of monster.

"He's a good guy," I said. "Knows his ways around Europe."

"He is a good man, and a good sailor," the Commodore agreed.

"Do you tell him that?"

He focused on scraping the butternut squash from the piecrust, and didn't meet my eyes. "I do, but your question indicates I could do it more often." He tapped his fork against the dish again and looked up at me. "We miss him. It would be good to see more of him."

"Coming home can be hard," I said. "When you've been gone...it's hard to figure out where you belong after all that time away. It's hard to take it all in, when...when there's so much, so quick."

"I used to think that, too," he said, "while I was deployed. It was difficult coming home, even when I wanted to be there. Being away changes you, and you can't explain all those changes to your family. I always thought Judy and the kids struggled with me coming home, too. Finding a place in the rhythm of their lives."

He reached for another pie, and tore off the tinfoil covering. I'd wondered why we'd stocked this event with more than a dozen pies, but I was starting to understand it now.

"Now that my boys have been deployed, and my daughter chooses to make her life in Boston," he said, "I know that coming home is a lot easier than I thought. It doesn't matter where they've been, what they've seen or what they've done. I only want to see my kids, and there are no other expectations. Nothing they do, nothing that they *are*, nothing changes that."

"Hey."

We looked up, startled, and found Shannon on the door-way. "Froggie just nursed again, and now I'm starving. Any apple-cranberry pie left?"

The Commodore swung a stern glance in my direction.

"I ate it," I said. "All."

Shannon raised an eyebrow at the Commodore. "Judy is worried about your cholesterol," she said.

"And that's why I'm sticking to cholesterol-free scotch." He lifted his glass as proof, but didn't set the fork—loaded with chocolate crème pie—down.

Shannon pointed at me while keeping her gaze trained on the Commodore. "She only likes cranberries in sauce form."

"Is there no honor among thieves?" he grumbled, and Shannon shook her head. "Sit down, sweetheart. What can I get you?"

She settled on the stool beside me, yawning as she re-tied

her ponytail. "There's cheesecake in the fridge. Go grab that, and I won't say anything about the missing pies."

"Roger that," the Commodore murmured, and he darted from the room. He was gone and back within a blink, and I didn't know how any human could move that quickly while also being dead silent. He set the plate in front of Shannon, and dropped a kiss on the crown of her head. "I'll be listening for Froggie. You eat."

Then, in a gesture I'd never known I wanted from him or any man, he squeezed my shoulders and kissed my head, too. "Don't forget what I said. You're mighty."

I gazed at my hands while a throb of emotion stuck in my throat.

"He's stealthy like that," Shannon said. "Acts all tough and stern. Basically threatens to kill Matt every time he sees him. Then he turns into a big, sweet teddy bear."

"Jesus," I said, clearing my throat.

"Yeah," Shannon said, laughing. "Let's take these snacks upstairs. We can dress up the baby and take pictures of her."

"Oh, yeah," I said, pressing the foil remnants over the pie. "We're definitely doing that."

Thirty-Five

NICK

THERE WAS a heated discussion of college football, team rivalries, and the Bowl Championship Series ranking methodology underway after dinner. We were still seated around the table, now with coffee, whiskey, and pies. Judy and Shannon were upstairs with the baby and the Commodore was walking the dogs. The women were in the next room over with Riley, planning an outing for tomorrow.

Will had salt shakers and spoons lined up in front of him, each representing a different college conference, and Sam was leaning over, wagging a finger as he argued the SEC's dominance. Patrick was fixing his whiskey with a dash of coffee, and randomly interjecting thoughts like "Boise is completely underrated" and "I like North Carolina State this year" and "What happened to Stanford's offense?" He was drunk, but more than that, off in his own thoughts.

It all would've made for a typical Walsh gathering if not for Matt glaring at me from across the table. His jaw was locked hard enough to grind his molars to dust and his arms were banded over his chest.

"I see what you're saying," Will replied, pushing a spoon

toward Sam. "But I don't see anyone shutting down Alabama."

"Clemson," Sam said, pushing the spoon back in protest. "I'm telling you, it's Clemson."

"Are you *fucking* kidding me?" Matt yelled, throwing his hands up only to slam them on the table. "Are you fucking *kidding* me?"

Patrick shook his head, confused. "What's your problem with Clemson?" he asked.

Matt ignored him, instead staring straight at me. "You married *my sister* and didn't tell me," he roared. "For years. For fucking *years*!"

Will pointed at Sam and Patrick. "The Boise State game should be starting soon," he said. "Let's check that out." He glanced at Matt. "If you're going to kick his ass, do it outside. Don't trouble my wife with your issues either."

Once we were alone, I reached out and topped off his glass with an extra finger of whiskey. Did the same to mine. "We should've told you sooner," I said.

"You're damn right you should've told me sooner," he said, lifting the drink but putting it down before sipping. "I thought you were my fucking friend. I thought you were my *best* friend, like a brother."

"I know," I conceded. "I wanted to tell you. Erin did, too."

"But you didn't," he cried. "You fucking didn't, and you should have."

I scowled at the amber liquid in my glass for a moment. "I didn't think it was going to take this long to bring her home," I said.

He regarded me with a smug smile. "So you're familiar with my sister's stubborn side," he replied.

"Very familiar," I said. "Listen, Walsh. I was wrong, and I hated keeping this to myself. But I had to respect my wife's wishes. She didn't want to steal anything from Sam and Tiel's special day by putting the spotlight on us, and she didn't want to take anything away from you and Lauren either. You were the one who commissioned a *babysitter* for her. Y'all treat her like she's a punk-ass teenager. That shit needs to stop."

He turned his gaze to the table, eyes wide as he shook his head. "We don't know her anymore, Nick."

"I do. I know her," I said.

I was prepared for him to chuck an empty pie dish at my head, or lunge across the table and beat the snot out of me. But he didn't. His shoulders sagged as he blew out a breath. He reached for his glass, swirling the liquid before bringing it to his lips.

"She stopped emailing me," Matt said. He tapped his fist against the tabletop for a moment while he looked out the window. It was dark outside, save for the moon's glow illuminating the ocean below. "After the wedding, she stopped emailing me." He glanced back at me, his eyebrow arched. "That is, my wedding *and* yours." He drained his glass and gestured for me to do the same. "I didn't notice at first, but then I realized I wasn't hearing about her expeditions anymore. She only offered the details if I asked for them, and I thought I'd pushed her too far by asking her to return for the wedding. I thought she wanted some space." He laughed as he reached for the whiskey and refilled our glasses. "It turns out that she was saving her words for you."

I leaned back in my chair and drew my knuckles down my jaw. Matt was my family just as much as Erin, and I didn't want to lose him.

"Are we all right?" I asked.

"Is she back?" he asked. "Is she coming home now? For good?"

"I don't know," I admitted. "I don't know where we'll end up when she finishes her work at Oxford. But I know she's not gone for good."

Matt knocked his drink against mine, and then raised it up in salute. "We're all right."

"WHAT ARE we doing out here again?" Matt asked, leaning against the wall with his phone in hand.

In the past hour, we'd emptied the whiskey, shared a pie, and—with some help from Sam and Will—offered Patrick all the marriage advice we had between us. Now we were a few steps outside the nursery, listening while Shannon and Erin stood at the changing table, arguing.

About baby clothes.

"I honestly don't know," I said, glancing inside. "But you heard Riley. He said Erin was talking with the girls, and then something happened. I just want to make sure she's okay."

And by *something happened*, I meant that she walked out of a conversation about pedicures like she had hounds on her heels. According to Riley, she'd spent some time in the bathroom, then shared a cheesecake with the Commodore in the butler's pantry, and that was where she'd also bumped into Shannon. From there, they'd headed to the nursery.

"Okay, I get it. You've convinced me that you're not a cradle-robbing dickwaffle." Matt pointed down the hallway. "I'm gonna go find my wife."

"You do that," I said, leaning closer to hear their conversation.

"Shannon, no," Erin said impatiently. "She's not wearing that. It's too fucking pink, and lacy. She shouldn't look like a Victorian-era tea party."

"It's gorgeous," Shannon replied.

"Oh my God, why do you do this? It doesn't matter whether it's gorgeous because she's going to be so uncomfortable."

"It's not a goddamn corset," Shannon said.

"Might as well be," Erin muttered.

"Fine," Shannon said, throwing her hands up. "Let's put it on her, take pictures, and then change her into something else."

"That's ridiculous," Erin said. "You shouldn't stuff her into these poufy dresses and delicate things. She needs to be able to move around."

"She's an infant, Erin. She's not swinging from any monkey bars just yet," Shannon said. "Come on, help me get this on her."

"Abby doesn't look happy about this decision," Erin said, shifting the baby into a sitting position. "It's not too late to put on that cute little white sleeper, the one with the frog on the bum."

"But those are pajamas," Shannon said, bringing the dress over the baby's head. "We don't wear pajamas all day."

"No, that's exactly what you do when you're a baby," Erin argued. "The greatest part of being a baby is that you're allowed to wear pajamas all the time and look adorable doing it."

"I'm putting this damn dress on her," Shannon snapped. "Stop bitching about it and help me."

Laughing at that, I stepped into the nursery to find Erin cradling the baby in her arms. She hit me with a bright smile and beckoned me closer.

"Isn't this a splendid tablecloth that we've dressed Abby in?" she asked, completely facetious.

"I'm not getting in the middle of your debate." Holding

out my hands, I said, "Let me see this little one. I haven't had a turn yet."

Erin placed Abby in my arms and then rejoined Shannon. They leaned against the changing table, their arms crossed and their heads tipped just a bit to the left, and it was as if they'd never been apart.

"Holy shit. Look at that," Erin murmured. She pointed to me, and I glanced down at Abby, confused. "I am having some very intense feelings at this moment."

Shannon nodded, saying, "I know, right? She loves it when Will takes off his shirt and cuddles her on his chest. You do realize that I'm going to be pregnant again within three months, don't you?"

"Whatever you do, don't take off your shirt," Erin said, stabbing a finger at me.

I loosened the buttons at my collar. "Are you sure about that? Skin-to-skin contact is outstanding for helping newborns regulate their body temperature."

"And ovulating on command," Shannon murmured.

"Shannon, take the baby," Erin said. "I need to talk to my husband."

"If I wasn't going to bring her back to my room and feed her now, I'd remind you that this is Froggie's nursery and no one kicks her out. We also have several other bedrooms, another family room on the fourth floor, and numerous walk-in closets," Shannon said as she settled the baby on her shoulder. "But we'll let it go this time."

Erin's gaze was fixed on mine, and though I'd expected to find her flustered and overwhelmed, she was calm. When the nursery door clicked shut behind Shannon and we were alone, I prowled toward Erin, gripping her hips and pinning her against the wall. "What's on your mind, lovely?"

"There's an old church, on an island off the Basque coast

of Spain. They call it Gaztelugatxe, 'the stairs above the sea,'" she said, tracing the buttons down my shirt. "It was built in the tenth or eleventh century, and since then it's been attacked, burned, sacked. It's seen the Crusades, the Black Death, the Inquisition. It's been beat to shit, but it's always rebuilt."

"That's good," I said, nipping her jaw. "Can't let the bastards keep you down, right?"

"It's an island, but it's connected to the mainland by a narrow stone path," she said. "It looks like a long, thin wall that rose from the ocean floor to keep the island from drifting away, and even though wind and waves should've eroded it down by now, it's still standing. When you reach the church, you look out over everything—the hike from the mainland, the miles of sea and sky, the rocky shore—and it all seems improbable. Like none of it should have survived so much, and yet it has." She dragged her fingers through my hair and pulled me away from kissing her neck. "We shouldn't have survived, but we did."

"I told you we would," I said. "Love, and get your heart broken, and say fuck it, and love again and then again. Right? Isn't that it, Skip?"

"Yes, but…" Her voice trailed off, and she frowned at my chest. "But I don't think I can do the heartbreak thing again."

"Fuck no," I said, groaning. "That was awful."

She pouted, and it took all of my strength not to bite her lower lip. Then I thought better of that strength and bit her lip anyway.

"The next six months are going to be weird," she declared, her lips on my cheek. "I figure I can shuffle around my lab time. Between that, sessions at Oxford, and some of the conferences I'm attending, I can stay here while I'm working on my dissertation. I can stay with you."

I pulled back. I was certain I hadn't heard her correctly. All I could do was blink and breathe.

"And then, after my program is finished," she continued, seemingly unaware that she'd robbed me of words, "we need to find a place. Together, that is. We'll need more room for books, love. I'm sure we can find something in the same area so you're close to the hospital. Shannon said she'd be happy to help us—"

"You've already engaged Shannon's assistance," I sputtered.

"Is that okay?" she asked, her brows knitting together in concern. "She knows the market, and—"

I kissed her. Hard. A squeak sounded in the back of her throat and her head knocked against the wall and my thumbs were pressing into her cheekbones because she was staying. She was fucking *staying*.

"It's perfect," I breathed, my words spoken directly to her lips. "What about your research?"

She hummed, nodding. "There'll be research," she said. "Conferences, too. But we'll make it work for us, Nick. I think—I think I know what I want now. I think I get it."

My lips mapped her jaw, her cheeks, her eyelids. "What do you want, lovely?"

Her hands were on my shoulders, and a smile was tugging at the corner of her mouth. "I don't want to wait for our life to start," she said. "We've already—*I've already*—let so much time pass, but that ends here. We have this time, this totally inadequate time, and I want all of yours. I want birthdays and anniversaries and holidays, but I want the full moons and high tides, too."

"You can have them," I said. I couldn't look away from those green green green eyes if I tried.

"We should explore the world," she said. "That rural

medicine program? The one in New Zealand? We should do that. We should get up and go and experience all of these things together because why the fuck not?"

"I'll take six months, a year, whatever," I said. "We can go to Madagascar, or wherever you want. I'll follow you anywhere."

"And I'll follow you." She tucked her hair behind her ears, taking a breath. "We should explore everything that we have right here, too. This family of ours, they're loud and nosy and opinionated, and none of that's about to change. But there are babies and weddings, and pedicures and farmers' markets, and those are adventures I don't want to miss. Not anymore."

"What changed for you?" I asked.

"I realized tonight that I don't need to stay away," she said. She squinted off into the distance, as if she didn't comprehend it herself. "And home, it's not a place. Not for me. It's people. It's you." She met my eyes and offered a shrug that told me she was as surprised about this as anyone. "Of course, all of this presumes that you want me and—"

"I want," I said, rocking against her. "I want, but I have some requests." I brought her fingers to my mouth, dragging the middle one between my lips. I caught the wedding band between my teeth and moved it to the proper finger. "This needs to be fixed immediately."

"Can I do it tomorrow?" she asked, a defiant smirk already in place. "Between lunch, pedicures, and baby shower planning? Or are we troubling the local goldsmith this evening?"

I wrapped my hands around her ass and lifted her up, growling the entire way. "Tomorrow will be fine," I said.

"While we're there," she started, reaching for my left

hand and kissing my fourth finger, "we'll get one for you, too."

"And come Monday, we get to work on dropping that maiden name, darlin'. I know it's old-fashioned but that doesn't make me want it any less. You can keep your maiden name professionally, but when you come home to me, you're mine. All mine." I kissed her, slow and soft this time. "After we do all that, we're finding a few days for a trip to Dallas. Understood?"

"All of it, Nick. But first," she said, her words rushing out in a heavy breath, "we have to find Bartlett. And this time, we're bringing a marriage license with us."

epilogue

ERIN

SIX MONTHS *later*

I HELD my hands out in the optimal spell-casting stance, and said, "Pack!"

"That's not going to work, darlin'," Nick said from behind me. "How the hell did you accumulate so many books?"

I gave the waist-high piles covering the floor of my Reykjavík apartment an unimpressed grimace. I loved my collection of books but hated packing it up for another move.

"I mean, isn't everyone reading ebooks these days?" Nick asked. The squeal of the tape roll sounded as he assembled another shipping carton. "Just think about it. Instead of boxing up everything ever printed, you could have a tablet. All of your books, in one spot."

"That's fine for fiction," I said, just a bit petulant. "But it doesn't work for scholarly texts. I see something in one publication, and that makes me think of something else, so I need to pull out another. I like to have them open in front of me, and flip between multiple books at a time."

Nick groaned into a carton. "Good thing we went with the bigger house," he murmured.

I glanced at him over my shoulder. "You can blame it on me all you want, but you're the one who went hogwild over having a backyard," I said.

"And you, darlin', went hogwild over being able to walk to Harvard Square," he said.

Hands on his waist and his head cocked to the side, he watched as I shuffled each text into place. His platinum wedding band shone in the afternoon sunlight. It was bright reminder that he was mine in every possible way.

"It's convenient. I love that my commute is a five-minute walk," I said.

My new office, the one at the environmental protection and climate think tank where I'd be serving as their senior scientist, was small. What it lacked in square footage, it made up for in analysts who would churn those data sets for me. In my mind, that wasn't even a trade-off. I'd sit on the floor and store my things in a milk crate if it meant having a team of analysts at my disposal.

"And I love that you love it," Nick said. "Even if we'll need two rooms for your books."

I knelt, setting an armload of books into the box at Nick's feet. "That we were able to find a house that we both liked is a win," I said.

We were moving into a renovated Victorian home in Cambridge, one that Shannon had tracked down before it went on the market. It was old but modern, traditional but quirky, and completely perfect for me and Nick. It'd all happened quickly, but not without each of my brothers weighing in on the property's merits and flaws. Matt had something to say about the foundation, Sam had lobbied for a rainwater catchment system, Patrick had argued in favor of replacing the windows with newer, more efficient models, and Riley had major issues with the kitchen layout. Nick had agreed to all of it.

I was still adjusting to the well-intentioned meddling. It was good—strange and somewhat uncomfortable, but good —and I was ready to get back home. I was excited about my new job, our house, and our family. It was hard to believe that I'd avoided all of those things for years, but now I was running toward them with arms outstretched. I missed my siblings and sisters-in-law when I wasn't in town, and I'd even started texting to keep in touch with them.

Sam and Tiel's baby was almost one month old now, and I couldn't wait to meet him. Not surprisingly, Shannon and Will were pregnant again. Baby number two was scheduled to arrive in late December, although I didn't think it was possible for any child to be cuter than Abby. Patrick and Andy had yet to set a wedding date, but no one seemed concerned about the lack of progress. Matt and Lauren were thinking about moving out of their loft and buying a house to renovate for themselves, and Riley interpreted that as a sign they were going to start a family soon. He wasn't handling that turn of events well.

Once we were finished packing my apartment, Nick and I were heading to Texas. His family was hosting a party in our honor, and though he'd assured me it would be a small gathering, I was certain that the Texas version of *small* was still pretty damn big.

"I'm not going to miss this shower," Nick said from the bathroom doorway.

I abandoned the books I was sorting and pivoted to face him. "Should we give it another shot? You know, for the memories?" I peeled my t-shirt up, over my head, and tossed it in his direction. He caught it in one hand, his eyes trained on me as I reached back to unhook my bra.

"Get over here, woman." He beckoned me closer, growling as my lingerie fell to the floor. "I dare you."

THANK YOU FOR READING! *I hope you loved Nick and Erin's journey. If you're ready for more one more Walsh, Riley and Alexandra's story,* Preservation, *is now available!*

TWO LONELY HEARTS.

Just once, Alex Emmerling would like to be someone's first choice.

She's strong-willed and spunky, but she's left picking up the pieces from her ex's lies and manipulations, and daydreaming about taking a scalpel to his scrotum.

Flying under the radar is what Riley Walsh does best.

He's laid-back and loyal, but he wants the most off-limits woman in his world, and nothing will ever make that a reality.

AN ARRANGEMENT OF MUTUAL BENEFIT.

Two months, four dates.

Five, if things go well.

Five at the most.

But possibly six.

Definitely no more than six dates.

Only the appearance of a romantic relationship is required, and they expect nothing more from their time together. There will be none of those benefits involved.

. . .

ONE WILD WEEKEND.

After waking up in bed together—very naked and even more hungover—the terms and conditions of their arrangement no longer apply. Now they're faced with something riskier than exposing their fake relationship: letting go of the past and zipping up the future.

SOME THINGS HAVE to fall apart before they can be put back together.

PRESERVATION IS AVAILABLE NOW. *Turn the page for an excerpt!*

JOIN *my newsletter for new release alerts, exclusive extended epilogues and bonus scenes, and more.*

IF NEWSLETTERS AREN'T *your thing, follow me on BookBub for preorder and new release alerts.*

VISIT MY PRIVATE READER GROUP, *Kate Canterbary's Tales, for exclusive giveaways, sneak previews of upcoming releases, and book talk.*

also by kate canterbary

Vital Signs

Before Girl — Cal and Stella

The Worst Guy — Sebastian Stremmel and Sara Shapiro

The Walsh Series

Underneath It All – Matt and Lauren

The Space Between – Patrick and Andy

Necessary Restorations – Sam and Tiel

The Cornerstone – Shannon and Will

Restored — Sam and Tiel

The Spire — Erin and Nick

Preservation — Riley and Alexandra

Thresholds — The Walsh Family

Foundations — Matt and Lauren

The Santillian Triplets

The Magnolia Chronicles — Magnolia

Boss in the Bedsheets — Ash and Zelda

The Belle and the Beard — Linden and Jasper-Anne

Talbott's Cove

Fresh Catch — Owen and Cole

Hard Pressed — Jackson and Annette

Far Cry — Brooke and JJ

Rough Sketch — Gus and Neera

Benchmarks Series

Professional Development — Drew and Tara

Orientation — Jory and Max

Brothers In Arms

Missing In Action — Wes and Tom

Coastal Elite — Jordan and April

Get exclusive sneak previews of upcoming releases through Kate's newsletter and private reader group, The Canterbary Tales, on Facebook.

about kate

USA Today Bestseller Kate Canterbary writes smart, steamy contemporary romances loaded with heat, heart, and happy ever afters. Kate lives on the New England coast with her husband and daughter.

You can find Kate at www.katecanterbary.com

- facebook.com/kcanterbary
- twitter.com/kcanterbary
- instagram.com/katecanterbary
- amazon.com/Kate-Canterbary
- bookbub.com/authors/kate-canterbary
- goodreads.com/Kate_Canterbary
- pinterest.com/katecanterbary
- tiktok.com/@katecanterbary

acknowledgments

Nick and Erin have been with me for a long time, and I'm thankful to several people for helping them travel from my mind to the page. Julia, Nicole, Amanda, Robyn—I owe you all my deepest gratitude, whether it be for helping me find the through-line or offering feedback or just being a friend.

The Walshes wouldn't have come this far without the readers who love them. Thank you to the smart, sassy, pervy members of The Walshery. I hope the wait—and the mysteries—were worth it.

I'd also like to recognize the good people at Wildflour Vegan Bakery and Juice Bar in Rhode Island. The majority of this book was written to the whirl and hum of Vitamix machines and espresso grinders. They kept me loaded up on almond milk lattes and didn't mind when I scowled at my laptop for hours on end.

And, of course, my husband and daughter. Their patience with me is unmatched, and I'm incredibly fortunate to have them both. I wouldn't be able to do any of this without them.

Ingram Content Group UK Ltd.
Milton Keynes UK
UKHW010717200423
420491UK00001B/116